No Secrets
Leo McNeir

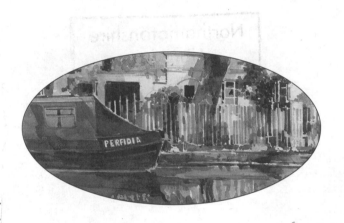

enigma
publishing

Also by Leo McNeir

Getaway with Murder (ISBN 0 9524052 6 1)

Death in Little Venice (ISBN 0 9524052 7 X)

Kiss and Tell (ISBN 0 9531742 1 2)

Devil in the Detail (ISBN 0 9524052 2 0)

and published by enigma publishing.

see the author's website: www.leomcneir.com

enigma publishing
PO Box 1901, Milton Keynes, MK19 6DN

First published 2006
Text © Leo McNeir 2006
Cover art © Alex Prowse 2005

The moral rights of the author have been asserted.

The events and characters described in *No Secrets* are entirely fictitious, and any apparent resemblance to real people, companies or occurrences is entirely coincidental.

A CIP record for this book is available from the British Library.

ISBN 0 9531742 4 7

Typesetting and cover design by *specialist* publishing services ltd, Milton Keynes/Argoed

Printed in Great Britain by Bell & Bain, Glasgow

The author

Leo McNeir is a linguist and lexicographer and has edited ten dictionaries in fifteen languages in the past decade, the standard works in their field.

No Secrets is his fifth novel, following the successful publication of *Getaway with Murder* (2000), *Death in Little Venice* (2001), *Kiss and Tell* (2003) and *Devil in the Detail* (2004).

He lives with cookery writer Cassandra McNeir and their cat, Mog, in a 300-year-old cottage in a Northamptonshire village.

They have four children between them and a narrowboat on the Grand Union Canal.

Dedication

For Stephen
and for
Les and Gloria

Friends in all weathers

Prologue

The woman got up from her desk and went out of the office with papers in her hand, walking along the short corridor to the lobby where the photocopier stood. Reaching the machine she steadied herself against its corner, pausing to take a series of slow deep breaths, waiting for the dizziness to clear. She recognised the signs, knew this vertigo had nothing to do with the new life inside her. Like almost everyone else in the office, in common with much of the population, she knew she was going down with flu.

Slowly the feeling passed. She raised her head, blinked once or twice and looked over to the window, reassured that the world was coming back into focus. Outside in the cold dark air of the wintry late afternoon lights were twinkling between the bare branches of the trees across the water. In the windows of some of the houses Christmas trees with their own lights were struggling to create a festive atmosphere in the great city that had been so ravaged by illness in recent weeks.

What a season! Ten days to go to Christmas, her last day in the office, and scarcely a friend to wish her a safe confinement or offer her a mince pie. There would be no office party, no cheap plonk – or orange juice in her case – not even a harmless peck under the lonely sprig of mistletoe dangling unheeded in the hallway.

She cocked her head on one side and listened. Only the faint hum from the copying machine disturbed the silence. Two of the other women had gone home soon after coffee time that morning, both complaining of headaches and aching limbs. She herself would have left had it not been for the need to make sure all her files were up-to-date, ready for taking over by her successor. At the end of her maternity leave – or sooner if anything went wrong, God forbid – she would return, and it would be more than embarrassing to find she had left chaos in her wake.

Snapping back to reality, she lifted the lid of the machine to copy her first page. Surprise. A single sheet of paper lay face down on the glass panel. She turned it over. Typical! But perhaps not so surprising. The boss was not used to copying his own documents. Leaving the original behind was the easiest mistake anyone could make if they were not in the habit of using the machine. Everyone was having to cover for missing colleagues, and he had had a busy day, with meetings and a steady flow of phone calls as everyone tried to clear their desks before the Christmas break.

She placed her first paper on the machine, closed the lid, pressed the button for three copies and hit the start key. While the machine whirred into action, she walked along to the office at the end of the corridor and tapped on the door. There was no reply. She pushed the door open a fraction and looked in. The single desk lamp lit the room. She crossed to the desk and dropped the letter she had found into the boss's in-tray.

Back at the copier, she finished her work and returned to the office. The dizziness swept over her again. In haste, she slotted the papers into their respective files, ticked off the last item on her jobs-to-do list and made a decision. It was time to go. She quickly switched off the copier and turned out all the lights as she grabbed her coat from the hook and opened the front door.

With no one to see her on her way, she exited the building, pulled her coat collar high against the chill and headed out into the darkness.

1

Beep.

'Hi! You've reached Beth and Paul. We're not home just now, but leave your message and we'll be right back.'

Beep.

'It's Marnie. I want to talk to you about *Sally Ann*. I'm in the office till mid-afternoon. Y'all have a nice day, hear?'

The last sentence was as close as Marnie Walker could come to a Southern-fried finger-lickin' accent. She put the phone down, smiling and shaking her head. That sister of hers! Their regular academic visits to the US of A in connection with Paul's work had really warped her brain.

Just then, a sudden movement outside caught Marnie's eye and she looked across the office towards the large window facing the courtyard. Beyond the cottages on the other side of the cobbled yard the breeze was rustling treetops visible over the slate roofs. The morning sun was breaking through the early clouds, picking out the red, yellow and gold leaves. There was almost a touch of the New England fall there in Northamptonshire that coincided with Marnie's line of thought. That year's extra rich colours had something to do with it being a long hot summer; increased sugar in the foliage that made the autumn transformation more brilliant. She had read that in the Sunday papers.

It had certainly been a long hot summer, a time filled with incident for Marnie and her immediate circle. Her lover, Ralph – or maybe she should now think of him as her *fiancé* – was insisting that Marnie should have a relaxing autumn with nothing more exciting than occasional outings on her narrowboat, *Sally Ann*, plus visits to the theatre or concerts. And then a peaceful Christmas at home. Good idea.

On an impulse Marnie stood up, went to the kitchen area at the back of the office barn – the office had been converted from one of Glebe Farm's outbuildings – and switched on the electric kettle. Anne would be back soon and would be glad to return to the aroma of fresh coffee after her walk up to the village shop in the crisp air. While the water heated, Marnie wandered over to the window to look out at the stone cottages and house that had once been a working farm dating back to the seventeenth century. Bought when virtually in ruins, Marnie was gradually converting it to a complex of three cottages, two of which were already rented by young couples from the village, adjacent to the original farmhouse that she was refurbishing to become her home. While she was surveying the scene, the sound of sawing wood reached her from somewhere inside the house.

Marnie folded her arms, standing with feet apart. She was taller than average and casually dressed for a day to be spent in the office. Thirty-something, she looked good in close-fitting jeans and a long woollen cream sweater. Her hair was dark and wavy, reaching to her shoulders, eyes brown, with a clear complexion and what Ralph described as intelligent features.

The question exercising Marnie's thoughts at that moment was centred around cottage number three which was renovated, had been occupied for a short time by a colleague and was now vacant. Should Marnie and Ralph move in for the winter? The alternative was to hang on until the spring when, with luck, steady cash-flow and good planning, the rebuilding of the main farmhouse should be completed. Her thought process was interrupted by the phone ringing.

'Walker and Co, good morning.'

'Hi, Marnie, it's me! What's with the "y'all" business?'

'Just trying to keep up with the Transatlantic theme on your answerphone.'

'Transatlantic …? Oh, right … Marnie, Paul's work takes us to Connecticut, that's New England Yankee territory. They don't "y'all" each other up there.'

'We don't "be right back" each other over here, as far as I recall.'

'Well, this is fun. Do you want to continue the discussion on language differences, or was there something else you wanted to talk about?'

'*Sally Ann*. I wanted to talk to you about my boat.'

'Pardon me?'

Pause. 'About *your* boat.'

'That's better. How many years have you been *borrowing* her, can you just remind me?'

'That's the point. I want to pay you for her.'

Silence.

'Beth? … If you're going to do a frothing-at-the-mouth-while-passing-out routine, don't bother. It's old hat.'

'Marnie, this is genuine shock, bordering on the mind-bending.'

'I'm being serious. I know I've had her for … a while, and I want to buy her from you … properly.'

'Does that involve the sordid passage of coin?'

'That sort of thing. I've been meaning to do this for some time, but things seem to have got in the way.' Marnie ignored the squawk at the other end of the line. 'I mean it.'

'Sorry, Marnie. Okay. No more jokes. Now I'm being serious. I do realise you've not had it easy, what with almost being murdered, almost being shot, getting caught up in –'

'That's fine, Beth, I do remember those things. I was there.'

'Of course. Well, this is a surprise. I'll tell Paul and he'll no doubt do some research on how much boats cost these days, and we'll get back to you with a price. That okay with you?'

'I can save you the trouble. I've been checking prices in the boat magazines and I've even phoned up some brokerage firms.'

'Great. So what's *Sally's* current value?'

'The starting point is fifteen thousand for a boat of her size.'

'Fair enough. That seems reasonable. D'you want to send us a cheque?'

'I said that's the starting point.'

Suspicion. 'Meaning?'

'Given her age, I think an offer of around … thirteen thousand would be appropriate in the circumstances.'

Another pause. 'Er … *circumstances* … mm … You mean like the fact that you repainted her topsides, put in new curtains and brass rails, refurnished her … That kind of thing? And I suppose you did get her taken into dry dock to have the hull reblacked … oh, and the engine serviced each year. And paid for the licence and insurance. Is that what you had in mind?'

'Hell, no! That's another two thousand off the price.'

'*What?*'

'Sure. I wanted the first reduction to take account of all the wear and tear she's suffered in the past couple of years. That boat's been through a lot!'

Marnie held the phone away from her ear so as not to suffer permanent hearing damage.

• • • • •

Minutes later Anne arrived back at the office barn. She walked briskly across the room and perched on the corner of her desk, breathing heavily, her cheeks and nose tinted pink. Marnie began pouring coffee.

'Have you been jogging?'

Deep breath. 'Power walking.'

'Impressive.'

'You didn't see me. Actually it was more like … power slouching, even downhill on the way back.'

Marnie carried the mugs of coffee over and put them down on the desks. Anne smiled thank-you. Almost as tall as Marnie, she was thin and pale, with urchin-cut blonde hair, sharp features and light blue eyes. She took off her blouson jacket and hung it on a hook. Like Marnie she wore jeans, topped by a navy sweatshirt. Dropping into her chair she gave Marnie an appraising look.

'You've been talking to Beth, haven't you?'

'How do you know that? You're as bad as my sister. Any witches in your family?'

'The whole tribe. Dad's changing the house name to *The Coven*. And you're trying to change the subject. You always have that amused look in your eye after you've been winding her up.'

'That's an exaggeration.'

'Who hung up first?'

Marnie stuck out her tongue.

'Did she accept your offer for *Sally Ann?*'

'Not in so many words. But she will. I teased her a bit by knocking off another two thousand … for wear and tear.'

'*Marnie!*' Mock indignation.

'I know. Anyway, the broker at Braunston said twelve to thirteen would be a fair price.' Marnie pulled a cheque book from a drawer. 'So I'll send them thirteen. It'll cheer her up.'

Outside came the sound of tyres crunching on gravel. Anne glanced up. 'Are we expecting anyone?'

'Probably just a delivery.'

Anne got up and went to the window. An elderly Ford Escort pulled up outside the farmhouse and the door swung open. Out stepped a woman in a navy blue jacket, unbuttoned to reveal a clerical grey dress surmounted by a dog collar. The vicar was calling.

Anne called over her shoulder. 'It's Angela. I'd better get another mug. She never refuses coffee. I think it's against her religion.'

Angela Hemingway tapped on the door and walked in. 'Mm ... that smells good.'

Marnie pointed to a chair. 'Good morning, vicar. What brings you to this den of unbelievers? Come to save our souls?'

'Gave up on that ages ago.'

'Threats of ever-lasting damnation are not permitted during office hours.'

'Actually, Marnie, I'm here because I've got a problem.' She accepted a mug from Anne. 'Thanks. That's great.'

'You've run out of coffee?' Marnie suggested.

'No. That just determined the timing of my visit. I'm about to be made homeless.'

Marnie sat up. 'Really? How?'

Angela took a sip. 'Delicious. It's a long story.'

'Just give us the Sunday school potted version.'

'The church is trying to economise – as usual – and the diocesan surveyor is looking at old vicarages with high running costs.'

Marnie pictured Angela's large and elegant Georgian house standing in spacious grounds.

'You've guessed, Marnie. They're putting the vicarage up for sale.'

'The market's sluggish, Angela. You could have to wait *ages* for a buyer.'

'They've accepted an offer at virtually the full asking price ... subject to survey.'

'Already? That's amazing.'

'A wealthy businessman from the City, wanting to retire to the country. They came up and had a look yesterday, he and his wife. Phoned in their offer first thing this morning. Straight cash. The diocesan office rang to let me know the couple are pressing for early completion.'

'How will that affect you? Where will you go?'

'I'll be moving to a new house in the village, one of those semis being built the other side of Martyrs Close.'

'So, problem solved. Still, I expect you'll be sad to leave the vicarage. It's a lovely place.'

'That's not the point, Marnie. The new house won't be finished till Easter or thereabouts, depending on what kind of winter we have.'

Marnie quickly grasped the point. 'You want to move in here until then.'

'Well ... I was wondering about your third cottage, though I realise you probably want to use it yourself. It's a long shot, I know, but I thought I'd check it out before looking further afield.'

'To be honest, Angela, I hadn't quite worked out my plans for number three.'

'No. And I think I may've made a mistake. I thought you'd be moving into the main house by now, but I see the builders are still in there.'

'There's quite a lot to be done before it's ready for occupation: new floorboards, replacement windows, replastering ...'

'I should've realised. I certainly wouldn't want you to have to spend another winter staying on the boat because of me, Marnie.' She shivered.

'Boats are fine in the winter as long as you have a reliable heating system, which we have. They're quite cosy.'

'Come to think of it, that's what Mr Taverner said. They're bringing their boat up from London. One of the attractions of Knightly St John is having the canal near the village.'

'Did you say Taverner?'

'They're the buyers.'

'Not … *Charles* Taverner?'

'You know them, Marnie?'

'And his wife is called Barbara? He must be getting on for about sixty and she's … forties, at a guess – auburn hair, smart dresser, vivacious?'

'That's them.'

Anne frowned. 'Do I know them, Marnie? The name isn't familiar.'

'They had a boat in Little Venice when I first took over *Sally Ann*, but they moved away. I think they bought a house on the river with its own mooring. I'm not sure where exactly, but I think Charles said he could walk to the office from home.'

Angela was nodding. 'He's taking early retirement. That's why they want to move to the country. I don't want to be uncharitable, but I got the impression they fancied the life of the country squire and his lady.'

'And a Georgian vicarage just fits the bill perfectly. Perfectly for them, that is. But it leaves you without a roof over your head.'

'Strictly speaking, Marnie, it's a problem for the diocese, not me. They have to find me suitable accommodation.'

'The diocese …' Marnie looked thoughtful. 'I suppose …'

'What?'

She shook her head. 'No. Not practical … too far.'

'What is it? I'd consider anything.'

'I was just wondering about you moving in with Randall. After all, you are an item, and he does have that beautiful big house in Brackley beside his church.'

Angela grinned. She was not outstanding in looks, but when she smiled, it lit up her face. 'Not an option, I'm afraid.'

'No, of course not. It must be a good fifteen miles away … not at all practical.'

Angela laughed. 'That's not the reason, Marnie. Randall is Rural Dean of Brackley and I'm the incumbent of Knightly St John. We can't decide to live in sin like …' Her voice petered out.

'Like Ralph and me?'

'I was going to say like a lot of people do these days. It isn't an option that's available to us, even if we wanted it.'

'But you would say that we are living in sin?'

'I didn't mean it like that. In any case, you two are in a mature settled relationship. It's not just some casual thing based on sex.'

'It wouldn't be for you and Randall either. At least, I'm making that assumption. Correct me if I'm wrong.'

'Marnie, we can't just shack up together!'

'Naturally.' Marnie grinned. 'Mr Randall Hughes and his vicar-on-the-side! I was overlooking a small detail.'

'You certainly were. And so was I, of course. Even if you didn't want to use the cottage yourselves, you and Ralph, you'd probably want it for Anne.'

'No. I'm perfectly happy in my attic.'

Anne pointed a finger towards the ceiling. She occupied the upper floor of the small barn, and had turned it into a comfortable base, with rugs, atmospheric lighting, a spacious bed and her hi-fi and video equipment. Although it only had a single slit for a window and was reached via a wall-mounted ladder, it would be the envy of any young person.

Angela drained her coffee and stood up. 'Well, I'll leave you good people to get on with earning your living. Nice to see you. Hope I haven't interrupted things too much.'

'Nice to see you, Angela. In fact –'

'Oh – sorry to cut you off, Marnie – but there were two things I meant to tell you. The first is that it isn't *Mr* Randall Hughes any more. He phoned to say he's just had his doctorate confirmed by the university. He's now *Dr* Hughes, or he will be when it's conferred.'

'Brilliant!'

'Yes, and the other thing is for you. The Taverners want a designer to replan the interior of the house. I told them we had one right on their doorstep, and they said they'd like to meet you.'

'Fine.'

'If you'd like to give me your business card, I'll pass it on.'

'Great. And you can tell them at the same time that you'll be staying in the village. The new temporary vicarage of Knightly St John will be number three Glebe Farm Cottages.'

'But, Marnie, don't you want to talk it over with Ralph?'

'No. We're fine where we are for the moment. And I think we definitely need you around to keep us on the straight and narrow.'

Angela reached the door. 'You make it sound as if I'd be coming to keep an eye on your moral welfare … trying to convert you, even.'

'Well, vicar …' Marnie smiled impishly. 'You could regard it as your … missionary position.'

Opening the door, Angela turned and wagged a finger. As she left, her laughter was most unpriestly.

2

Exactly three weeks after the discussion on Angela's housing problem, Marnie and Anne presented themselves at the vicarage to meet the new owners and discuss plans for redecoration. Anne drooled as they walked along the drive. Standing in front of the house was the smartest car she had ever seen.

'Look at that, Marnie.' Wide-eyed wonder.

'Beautiful,' Marnie agreed.

'Is it a Jaguar?'

'Certainly is.'

The object of their admiration had cherry red metallic paintwork and shiny alloy wheels, with cream leather upholstery and discreet inserts in walnut. It gleamed as if it had just rolled out of the showroom.

Marnie rang the bell and glanced at Anne. 'I suggest you close your mouth now. The wind might change and you'll be stuck like that forever.'

Anne's jaws snapped shut and she grinned at Marnie. Angela opened the front door and greeted them in a low voice.

'Come in. Mr Taverner's on the phone. He's just checking with his solicitor that they've exchanged contracts.'

'Already? That was quick.'

'Very businesslike, Mr Taverner. He doesn't waste any time.'

Marnie mouthed, 'Barbara?'

Angela's voice became even quieter. 'Upstairs, looking at the bedrooms.' She rolled her eyes. 'I've been tidying the place for days.'

They became aware that the murmuring that had formed the background to their conversation had stopped. A man came out from one of the reception rooms pocketing a mobile phone. He was wearing a short coat over a charcoal grey suit, a tie in bold stripes, and he beamed as he saw the newcomers in the hall.

'Yes. *Now* I know you.' He advanced towards Marnie extending a hand. 'Little Venice, of course. Your mooring was up near the tunnel.'

'That's right ... *Sally Ann*.'

'You were working on your boat, repainting her. Am I right? Do you still have her?'

'You are and I do.'

With an apologetic wave of the hand he turned to Angela. 'Everything's in order. They exchanged contracts this morning about an hour ago.'

'Oh, good.'

'That was quick.'

'Three weeks, Marnie, from accepting our offer.'

'You're not aiming to be in by Christmas, are you?' Marnie's voice betrayed her concern. Christmas was one month away, the worst time of year for getting any kind of project started.

'No, no. Completion will take a while longer and we'd like the place to be redecorated first. I'm putting our London house on the market in the new year. If work could be completed in the spring, we'd move up then.'

Anne began making notes on her clipboard, and Charles noticed her for the first time. Marnie made the introduction.

'This is Anne, my assistant, Anne Price.'

Anne struggled with clipboard and filofax to shake hands without dropping everything.

'Hallo, Anne. Charles Taverner. All this looks very efficient.'

'Her middle name,' Marnie added.

'Were did my wife get to?'

Angela indicated. 'Mrs Taverner went upstairs. She said she wanted to look at the layout of the bedrooms.'

'Ah, yes … Barbara has plans.' A conspiratorial smile. 'She's wondering about *en suite* arrangements.' He turned to Marnie. 'There are five bedrooms, you probably know, and a large bathroom on the landing. Barbara would like to convert that to three bedrooms, each with its own *en suite* bathroom. D'you think that might be achievable?'

Before Marnie could reply, Barbara appeared at the top of the stairs. The staircase was wide and curving, well-proportioned, with a mahogany handrail and balustrading. The woman who descended it looked as if she had just stepped out of the pages of *Vogue* magazine. All eyes focused on her as she made her entrance, head held high, shoulders back, placing each foot carefully and assuredly without looking down. She wore a long woollen coat in a shade of grey that perfectly matched her fashion boots, over a calf-length dress in pale grey cashmere, belted at the waist. Immaculately styled auburn hair completed the ensemble.

Anne had to be careful not to relapse into boggling mode. She kept firm control of her jaw muscles.

With one hand lightly touching the handrail, Barbara directed her attention towards Marnie, and a smile of recognition spread across her face. Marnie could almost feel the pride and admiration with which Charles regarded his wife. The words *exquisite* and *radiant* came into her mind.

Barbara advanced and kissed Marnie warmly on both cheeks. 'It *is* you. When Angela told us you'd had a boat in London, I wondered if it was the person I remembered.' A pleasing voice with no regional accent. 'So nice to think we'll have a friend in the village.'

'So you did know each other, Mrs Taverner.'

'Oh, *do* call me Barbara … sorry, unless you'd like us to address you as Miss Hemingway … or even vicar, perhaps?'

'No. Angela's fine.'

'Well, Angela, to answer your question, we knew Marnie only slightly and that was just before we moved our boat down to Limehouse.' She looked back at Marnie. 'To call us friends might be a small exaggeration, but I know we're going to get on *really* well … pick up where we left off. I hope we'll see a lot of each other.'

'We will if Marnie handles the redecoration,' Charles chipped in.

Marnie looked inquisitively at Barbara. 'Rather more than a redecoration by the sound of it.'

Anne raised her pen above the notepad, at the ready.

'I'm *so* sorry,' Barbara exclaimed. 'I didn't mean to ignore you.'

'I'm Anne, Marnie's assistant.'

They went through the fumbling handshake routine, and Anne again succeeded in not dropping her equipment.

'And you're going to take notes, are you?' The tone veered towards patronising.

'So far I've listed the remodelling to convert the existing bedrooms and bathroom to three *en suite* facilities ... depending on service runs, of course. And I've brought the Polaroid camera to make a record of what's here at the moment.'

Barbara turned to Angela. 'Only if that's acceptable to you, of course.'

'It's fine. Anne had already cleared that with me in advance.'

'Oh ... well ... I, I can see we're in good hands.'

They began the tour of the house, Barbara outlining her plans, Charles acquiescing in her wake, explaining about the exchange of contracts and the timing of arrangements, Marnie raising technical questions.

Back in the hall, Barbara stopped suddenly. 'I'll be bringing our boat up soon. I was wondering ...' The others waited. 'There's all the summer picnic furniture on board at the moment ... and the parasol ... rather a clutter ...'

Angela got the point immediately. 'You want somewhere to store it?'

Barbara put a hand on her shoulder. 'It would be a *terrible* imposition ...'

'Could it go in the garage ... or there's the shed in the garden?'

'That's *sweet* of you. Would you really not mind?'

'It's no problem at all.'

'Oh *thank* you, Angela. That would make the journey much easier. There are one or two other bits and pieces belonging to the boat ... my spare set of keys, for example ...'

'They can go with the others on the key rack, if you like.'

'Angela, you're an angel.' Barbara laughed prettily.

Everyone moved towards the kitchen where Angela made coffee, except Anne who set about taking photographs. Marnie saw with amusement that Angela had bought ground coffee in place of her usual instant brand.

'Marnie, would you be able to liaise with specialist firms ... seeing as how you're *in situ*? I know it goes beyond interior design but, for example, I'll need the kitchen replanned and I'll be asking some companies to submit layouts and costs.'

'Sure. I take it we're not talking local D-I-Y store or flatpacks here. You won't want me to bring my own screwdriver?'

Barbara laughed. 'I was thinking of Smallbone, Poggenpohl, Clive Christian ... firms like that?'

Marnie picked up the clipboard. 'Anne would never forgive me if I didn't write the names down.'

Angela, who had always regarded the house as perfect, was bemused by the whole exercise of converting the vicarage to a modern prestige home. She realised that during the planning tour a smile had been permanently fixed on her face. Its origin was a mixture of wonder at so much creative power being displayed, allied to the energy and dynamism of the chic woman whose character was going to be stamped on the house and change it forever.

Accepting her coffee – in the best china – Barbara leaned forward to speak to Angela, looking her straight in the eye. 'I do hope you don't find this … insensitive or in any way distasteful. This is your home, after all.'

'No, I don't. It's interesting. I like hearing your ideas and Marnie's comments. I've never done this kind of thing before.'

'Didn't you plan the house as it is at present?'

'No. That was my predecessor, Randall Hughes. He did it all.'

Marnie joined in. 'Randall has a real flair for colour and texture.'

'I can see that.' Barbara walked to the kitchen door and looked into the hall. 'There's a boldness, a firmness of hand. I imagine him as a strong personality … loads of self-confidence.'

'Bang on,' Marnie agreed. 'He's quite a character.'

'And a charismatic preacher,' Angela added.

'I hope I'll have the chance to meet him.' Barbara's tone of voice suggested that her interest was not in the field of liturgical practice or church doctrine. She was about to continue when she noticed that Angela was blushing.

Anne was coming down the stairs and stopped halfway. 'I'll take a shot of the hall from here. It's a good view of the whole entrance.' On impulse she turned the camera for another picture, this time of the rear passage from the hall to the kitchen. Barbara smiled up at her from the doorway.

'This is all very exciting,' Barbara exclaimed. She ushered Anne into the kitchen where Angela presented her with coffee and offered a plate of biscuits.

'Marnie, would you know where we could get one of those signs made … a nameplate for the house? I've always wanted to live in an old rectory.'

'Actually, it's a vicarage, really.' Angela spoke quietly.

'Aren't they the same thing? I don't suppose anyone would notice the difference, do you?'

Angela was not inclined to go into an explanation of the distinction between a vicar and a rector. She spoke tentatively. 'Well … I think … strictly speaking, as it were … it isn't allowed to use a name that refers to the previous use of this house.'

Barbara seemed puzzled. 'I don't think I follow …'

Angela was clearly embarrassed. 'I meant … a name like Old Vicarage – or rectory, of course – I think that kind of name isn't allowed by the terms of the contract. I believe there's some kind of … restrictive covenant or something.'

Barbara looked over at Charles. 'Do you know anything about that, Charles?'

He reflected. 'I think I might've seen a clause of that sort in the papers somewhere.'

'Oh.' Barbara was deflated. 'I've seen lots of houses with names like that. Why shouldn't it be allowed?'

Angela shrugged. 'I don't know. I just remember hearing it being mentioned when the diocesan surveyor came to view the house and draw up the particulars. It seems to be one of the usual rules.'

The atmosphere in the kitchen had momentarily cooled. Then, just as quickly, it thawed. Barbara was smiling again, and everyone relaxed.

'Never mind. It's not a problem.'

Angela looked relieved. 'Good.'

'We'll wait a couple of months before getting the sign made. By that time everyone will've forgotten the rule and we'll be able to do our own thing. After all, what are rules for if not for breaking?'

Charles chuckled indulgently in the background. Marnie and Anne glanced hurriedly at Angela, who was blushing again.

'I see.'

'Don't spare it another thought, Angela. It will only be a sign on the wall – or on the gate – in a few months' time who's going to care what it says?'

'It's not really for me to say. It's just … part of the agreement, the contract. I thought …'

'It's not worth worrying about. Once we've bought the house and paid for it, what would the church want to do? I can't see the bishop sending round a gang of heavies to tear the sign down, can you?'

She was smiling brilliantly. Perfect white teeth and coral lipstick, beautifully cut hair that looked as if all its rich colour was natural. She laid a manicured hand on Angela's arm. A discreet and expensive perfume floated on the air.

'Don't worry. Everything will be fine.' The voice was soft and reassuring.

Angela managed a faint smile. She felt drawn in by Barbara's charisma and confidence. A saying flitted briefly into her mind … *man makes plans, God laughs*. It was a modern slant on the older version: *man proposes, God disposes*. Now, that order seemed to be reversed. She suspected there was nothing anyone would do if Barbara went ahead and called the house *The Old Rectory*. In three weeks exactly the sale would be completed. In three weeks Barbara would have her house and would turn it into a magnificent home.

Angela did not know – none of them could know – that in three weeks Barbara would be dead.

3

'Your place or mine?'

Marnie reached across the desk for her diary and flipped it open. She gripped the handset between her chin and her shoulder – with Anne tut-tutting in the background – as she turned the pages with one hand, holding a pen in the other.

'I can be flexible … not too many meetings at the moment. I thought you'd probably want to come up here so that I could talk you through the house and you could get an impression of what I'm proposing.'

'That makes sense. What about … the day after tomorrow?'

'Okay by me, Barbara.' Marnie wrote the name in the filofax.

'Does that give you enough time to complete your design?'

'I've done a draft scheme. That's as far as I can go at present, until you've seen it and had a chance to comment.'

'You've *done it*? In one week? That's *amazing*.'

'To tell you the truth, I've often had thoughts about what I'd like to do with the place. Naturally I've taken on board the points you made when we met, but they only helped me crystallise what I already felt about the house.'

'That's a date, then.'

'What time do you want to come up?'

'Say … ten-thirty?'

'It's in the diary. See you then.'

Anne waited until Marnie had ended the call and finished writing the time before she spoke.

'Marnie, you shouldn't do that.'

'What, mummy?' Marnie looked over at her friend sitting at the desk on the other side of the office.

'Ha … ha.' Anne gave her the heavy eyelids look. 'But I mean it. It's not good for you.'

'What did I do?'

'That thing with the phone under your chin and your shoulder hunched up like Quasimodo. It's bad for the top of your spine. Do it too often and you'll end up stomping around like Richard III.'

Marnie suppressed a smile. 'I'll try to remember.'

'Good.'

'Here's something else to remember: Barbara's coming up the day after tomorrow.'

Anne checked her calendar. 'Did I hear you say ten-thirty?'

'Yep.'

'Oh …' She pulled a face. 'That's a pity. I'm at college that morning. … can't be here for the meeting.'

'Never mind, there'll be other times. Have a look at the scheme design anyway and let me know what you think.'

Marnie dropped the green folder on Anne's desk and went out to discuss progress on site with the foreman of the builders.

Anne spent several minutes reading through the scheme. They had often talked about decorating the vicarage, but Anne could see how Marnie had adjusted her vision to reflect Barbara's tastes. The colours were richer, less restrained than Anne expected. She appended a few comments about details. With typical thoroughness Marnie had even specified planters for the conservatory with suggestions on plants to fill them. It had been added in Victorian times and was Anne's favourite space in the whole building. She began writing notes on its treatment and was outlining an idea for it when the phone rang.

'Walker and Co, good morning.'

'I'd like to speak to Marnie, please.'

'Is that Mrs Taverner? It's Anne. Marnie's out with the builders at the moment. Can I go and find her and get her to phone you back in a few minutes?'

'Er …'

'Or I could take a message?'

'Actually, I just wanted to change our meeting arrangements for later in the week.'

'I've got access to the diary. Can I help?'

'I was wondering if she'd mind coming here instead of me coming up to you.'

'To London? I'd better check that with her and get her to ring you.'

'Thanks. While you've got the diary there, Anne … Let me see …' There was the sound of pages turning. 'With Christmas not far off, I'm starting to get a lot of social events coming up. It'd be good if I could set aside time for regular meetings to keep the project running smoothly.'

Anne wondered why Barbara should think the project would only *run smoothly* if she had regular meetings with Marnie. Holding the cordless phone, Anne went over to Marnie's desk.

'You want to fit in another meeting?'

'Let me give you some dates.'

She reeled off a list of days and times, one each week extending into the new year up to the end of January. When she had finished, she asked Anne to repeat them back to her … *for cross-checking*. Anne had the feeling that Barbara doubted her reliability. When Barbara asked if she had written them all in the diary, Anne had to conceal her irritation.

'Yes. They're all here in Marnie's desk diary and I'll add them to the office diary on my computer as soon as I put the phone down.'

'Excellent. And you'll ask Marnie to ring me about this week's meeting?'

'I will.' Anne half expected her to want that confirmed by fax. 'I won't forget, Mrs Taverner.'

'Good. Thank you, Anne. And do call me Barbara.'

Marnie returned ten minutes later and rang Barbara to confirm she would be happy to see her in London. When she ended the call she noticed that Anne was looking thoughtful. There were no prizes for guessing why.

'I know what's bothering you, Anne. I'm sorry about it, but don't worry.'

'Mm?'

'There'll be other times, like I said. I suppose it's even worse, now that the meeting is at her place rather than up here.'

'How d'you mean?'

'You're not going to pretend you aren't *aching* to see their house in Docklands, are you? I know I am.'

'I wonder what sort of style it'll have, Marnie.'

'Oh, I think I can guess the answer to that one. In fact, I bet it can be summed up in one word … *rich*.'

Anne laughed. 'Of course. Silly me not to have worked it out. Yeah, I would like to see it … maybe some time. But that's not what was on my mind.'

Marnie crossed the floor and took Anne's face in her hands. 'Come on, spill the beans. Tell auntie Marnie what's bothering you.'

'It's the way Mrs Taverner treats me.' Anne's voice changed to pure Marlene Dietrich. 'Do call me … *Barbara* …' The first syllable of the name lasted at least half an hour.

Marnie grinned at her. 'But she likes you, Anne.'

Anne sighed. 'She treats me like I'm a kid or … some kind of inadequate. You know, Marnie, she kept asking if I'd really put the dates for her meetings with you in the diary.'

Marnie sat on the corner of Anne's desk. 'Don't worry about that. She's just rather self-absorbed … probably like that with everyone.'

'You think so?'

'Sure. It's not unusual for women as attractive as she is to be spoilt so they think if they want something it must be right, and everyone else should just accept that.'

'I don't see why they should.'

'Human nature.'

'But you're not like that, Marnie. You're attractive. People are always looking at you … and not just men. Women look at you, too.'

'Great. So now I'm becoming some kind of gay icon?'

Anne sniggered. 'I didn't mean it like that. Women look at you because of your style … your taste in clothes. Men look at you for … well, that and … all the rest. I'm digging myself into a hole here.'

'You're actually a good example of the point you're making, Anne. Someone can be … attractive – if that's the word – without it being the centre of their universe, without it making them think of nothing but themselves. If that person has interests beyond their appearance or the effect they have on others, they'll be too engrossed in those interests to dwell on themselves all the time.'

'So you and I are lucky that we have things to do that mean we don't just have to think about what colour to paint our fingernails, right?'

'Right. Apart from one small detail – we neither of us actually do paint our fingernails.'

'Fair enough. But you've got to admit, Marnie, she is very attractive. I mean, seeing the two of you together, you'd never know you weren't the same age.'

'That's very comforting ... considering she's at least twelve years older than me. Thanks. I'll be back in a minute.'

'Where are you going, Marnie?'

'To see the builders. I just want to get you a shovel.'

Marnie loved Docklands. It was one of her favourite parts of London, and she asked the cab driver to drop her off on the corner of Templars' Wharf so that she could walk round the marina and enjoy the view. She estimated there were a hundred or so craft moored in the basin, mainly river cruisers, but with a scattering of narrowboats and the odd gin palace. Not exactly the Grand Harbour at Monte Carlo on the weekend of the Monaco Grand Prix, but a jaunty spectacle testifying to the wealth of the residents.

Templars' Wharf was a mixed development. Across the water from where Marnie stood, a warehouse rose up on the river frontage, several stories high. She had seen articles about some of its apartments and lofts in magazines and could imagine the spacious open-plan interiors, with exposed steel and brickwork, Oriental carpets scattered over hardwood flooring and light pouring in from windows on both sides. Away over to her right, and filling one complete side of the wharf, Marnie could see more recent modern houses, built in the same yellow London brick as the warehouse. Despite their astronomical prices she knew they were snapped up by eager purchasers as soon as they came on the market. Marnie surmised that the home of Charles and Barbara Taverner, number seven Templars' Wharf – known as Old Temple Steps – would be one of those. She was wrong.

The numbers on that side of the marina were all in the higher range. She walked along by the warehouse, past the boats at their moorings, until she came to a row of older houses, Georgian or Regency to judge by their facades. A mystery. Who would have wanted to live in the midst of all the commercial bustle of a dock in the heyday of the Port of London? It was with a feeling of surprise mixed with satisfaction that Marnie discovered number seven. Surprise at its double-fronted grandeur, rising three storeys above her, satisfaction that the front door was exactly the shade of deep red that Marnie had chosen for the vicarage in Knightly St John.

Before her finger could touch the doorbell a metallic voice greeted her. 'Hi, Marnie. Just push the door.' A buzzer sounded. Marnie did as she was told, and the door swung smoothly open.

Standing on the black-and-white diamond tiles in the hall Marnie barely had time to wonder whether Barbara had been watching out for her – *excitement? anticipation?* – when a click-clacking of shoes overhead announced her client's arrival on the landing.

'Come on up.'

She was met with a hug and air kisses to both cheeks.

'Did you drive? I'll start believing in miracles if you tell me you found a parking place! Or did you offer your body to the security man?'

'Train and taxi. Less wearing on the nerves ... and on the body.'

Barbara laughed. 'Quite. But less fun, perhaps. On both counts. Shall we go in the kitchen? I've got coffee on the go. I *love* that jacket. Suits your colouring *perfectly*.' She led the way across the landing. 'You'll have to take me as I am, I'm afraid. I just threw on the first things I found in the wardrobe.'

Marnie smiled to herself. The *first things* were a shirt and flared trousers, both of black silk, both originating in Paris or Milan. They showed off her slim figure to advantage.

'That's okay. There are times when I just pop round to the clothes rail in Tesco's myself.'

Barbara hooted and patted Marnie playfully on the shoulder. She turned to check progress on the espresso machine before joining her.

'You said you wanted to understand my taste. D'you want the Cook's Tour of the house while the coffee's brewing?'

'Let's do it.'

Barbara led Marnie from room to room. The house looked like a colour spread from a glossy magazine, everything in discreet good taste. At least one whole herd of cows – pedigrees no doubt – had been sacrificed to provide leather for the sofas in the drawing room … *the same firm that make the leather for Charles's car* … The dining furniture was in mahogany, with silver candelabra on the table and sideboard. Marnie estimated that the entire room was original Georgian, contemporary with the house itself. Marnie noticed that none of the structure had been altered apart from the kitchen, bath and bedroom areas. The master suite was at first floor level, the same as the living rooms. The three other bedrooms on the floor above were all suites that would have graced a five-star hotel. The quarry at Carrara must have been seriously depleted to produce the marble for the bathrooms.

On the way back to the kitchen, Barbara waved a hand airily towards a closed door. 'That's Charles's study. I never go in there. More than my life's worth.'

She made a similar gesture passing another room. This time the door was half open. 'That's my den … my refuge when Charles abandons me for his meetings.' Her tone was casual. 'I'd apologise for the mess, but believe it or not, that's tidy by my usual standards.'

Marnie glanced in. Smaller than most, this room looked lived in. There were magazines on the sofa, a shawl draped over one arm, CD cases on the floor by the hi-fi. Behind the TV tower one wall was filled with vinyl albums, videos, CDs and cassette tapes. It seemed that Barbara's love of music was matched by her love of technology.

Back in the kitchen Barbara checked the coffee machine. She pointed at a monitor mounted on the wall over the stainless steel kitchen units. It contributed to the hi-tech feeling of the space. 'CCTV.'

'Ah …'

'That's how I spotted you at the door. You sounded surprised when I spoke to you through the intercom.'

'Right. You're worried about security here? Is that perhaps why you're keen to move to Knightly St John?'

'No, no. The system came with the house. Charles grew up in the country. He's always wanted to return to rural surroundings. How d'you like it, Marnie?'

'Cappuccino?'

'Fine. Me too.' She offered her guest a stool at an island unit.

'And you?' Marnie asked. 'Do you long for rural surroundings?'

Barbara shrugged. 'City girl. Bright lights …busy streets … night life, that's me.'

'Then Knightly's an inspired choice. Not a lot of people notice the casinos on their first visit. Or the Café Royal, not to mention the branch of Harvey Nicholls next to the village shop. Seriously, Barbara, you don't think you'll find it a little bit quiet for your tastes?'

Barbara poured skimmed milk into a steel jug. 'Seriously, no. Sure the village itself is … a village. But variety is the spice of life, or so they say. I told Charles we could go anywhere he wanted on one condition. Either we live near enough for me to be able to nip back to London any time I chose, or we got a flat that I could keep as a *pied-à-terre* for frequent visits.'

'So Docklands's loss is Knightly's gain.'

'Exactly. Although to be accurate, it's not quite like that. We're getting a London base anyway, a *gorgeous* little loft conversion over at Bermuda Reach. I'll put the spare key for it with the others so you can have a look. You can do the decor there as well. We'll be able to give you a *By Appointment* plaque soon!'

'Handy for the January sales?'

Barbara guided the nozzle into the jug and turned on the steam valve. 'Quite. And for Charles if he has a late board meeting or a dinner and can't be bothered to travel back.'

'I thought he was going to retire.'

'My dear, businessmen never *retire*. They just stay on as non-executive directors. It's like doing lunch with the boys and getting a cheque each month plus share bonuses every year to pay for the cruise or the safari.'

Marnie raised her voice over the rushing sound of the steam jet in the milk jug. 'Bermuda Reach is that new Docklands development further along the river, isn't it?'

Barbara called over her shoulder. 'That's right. Bit smaller than Templars' Wharf. Quite exclusive.'

Marnie gestured at their surroundings. 'I couldn't imagine anywhere more exclusive than this. And I had no idea there were residential houses in amongst the commercial buildings.'

'Oh, this wasn't a residence. These were the company's offices. That's why the building's so spacious. Bermuda Reach is mainly warehouse conversions … on a smaller scale. You interested? We're getting a penthouse but there are a few *bijoux* still available.'

'I've got enough on my hands sorting out Glebe Farm.'

'Don't you ever have the need for a place in town, Marnie?'

'Like you said, Knightly's not far away. We could always try to get a mooring in Little Venice for one of the boats if we wanted a *pied-à-terre*. We have two narrowboats between us at the moment.'

Barbara grinned. 'Wouldn't that be a *pied-à-l'eau*? I wonder if that's French for a toe in the water. No, I need a bit more space, Marnie … more creature comforts than a boat can provide. Bermuda Reach will be somewhere I can entertain friends.' A rich, warm chuckle. '*Girl friends*, of course.' She set down the coffee cups and saucers, generously large in deep blue with a gold rim. 'When you've got the spare key you can look in when you've got a moment and give me some ideas for the decor.'

'I'll look forward to it. So you'll be bringing your boat up to Knightly?'

'That's the plan.'

'In the spring when you move, presumably?'

'No, straight away.'

'Can you do that? What about lock closures ... the winter maintenance programme?'

'There's a window. From now until Christmas there's a clear run up the southern part of the Grand Union as far as Braunston tunnel. I can get her to Knightly in less than a week.'

'But I read that Islington tunnel is closed for partial relining.'

'She's not here, Marnie. I've already moved her to Little Venice. I got a slot up the side arm to Paddington basin.'

'That was a stroke of luck.'

'I had to pull a few strings, my dear.' She laughed warmly. 'I know all the people round there. It wasn't difficult. I'm used to queue-jumping ... lots of practice at all those sales at Harvey Nix!'

Marnie thought that few things failed to work out for Barbara Taverner. They sipped cappuccinos together, and Marnie pulled the scheme design for the vicarage out of her briefcase.

For the next hour the two women worked their way through Marnie's proposals, room by room, space by space. Barbara asked questions on every sketch and examined every fabric sample, checking them against Marnie's photographs and floor plans of the vicarage, making notes on a pad with a black and gold pen. Each was impressed with the other's attention to detail, and Barbara smiled with satisfaction when Marnie remarked that the pen matched her outfit. Her smile broadened when she noticed that Marnie had even included a nameplate – black oval with white lettering, mounted on the gate pillar – though she had left the wording unspecified.

'But you *know* the name, Marnie!' Barbara exclaimed joyfully. '*The Old Rectory.*'

'I'll leave you to argue that one with the bishop,' Marnie retorted, smiling. 'For now I just wanted to make sure we had the right space for it. The house has never had a number. Incidentally, why is this house called *Old Temple Steps*? Was there a temple of some sort on the site?'

'No. I think the land belonged to the Knights Templars at some time ... ages ago.' Barbara waved a hand dismissively. 'There was a way down to the river at the back here, I think. History's not my scene. It used to be called *Old Temple Stairs* for centuries. I didn't like that, thought it sounded a bit mundane. So I changed it to *Steps* ... much nicer.'

'You were allowed to change a name that was hundreds of years old, just like that?'

'Frankly, with what we'd paid for this house, I'd have felt justified in calling it ... Disneyland or Buckingham Palace ... or the Planet Tharg.' She threw her head back and laughed. 'D'you fancy another coffee?'

Marnie looked at her watch. 'I think we're nearly through.'

'Good. Then I'm going to take you to lunch. Don't argue. I know this *gorgeous* little bistro round by Saint Katharine's. The chef owns the place and he's an absolute sweetie ... Italian ... or Spanish ... whatever ... you wouldn't *believe* what he can do with a courgette. Oh, what's that ... a plan we've missed?' She pointed at the corner of a drawing sticking out from under Marnie's folder.

'Yes. It's an idea of Anne's ... for the conservatory.'

'Of Anne's?' Barbara looked doubtful. 'I thought she was the office junior. Anyway, didn't you propose …' She checked her notes. '… planters made to measure along the back wall, filled with white and pink geraniums? You said they'd keep flowering continuously for years.'

'That's right. But Anne had another idea.'

'Oh …'

'She's not the office junior. Sure, she runs the office – and very efficiently – but she's a trainee designer … works with me on every project. She's doing A levels at the local college and working part-time in the office. She's got real promise.'

'If you say so, Marnie. So what's her idea?'

Marnie pulled the paper out. It was an internal elevation produced on the drawing board and looked highly professional.

'She used one of your drawings, Marnie?'

'No, she did this herself. Look, this is what she has in mind. You see the wall here reaches up quite high. It was probably plastered in Victorian times when the conservatory was built.'

'It's beautiful. One of the reasons I wanted the house.'

'Yes, but it is very lofty.'

'So?'

'Anne thought it would benefit from distracting the eye from how tall it is inside. You see here …' There was a marking like a border running across the elevation.

'What is it? Looks peculiar.'

Marnie shifted the plan to show a more detailed drawing in the corner. 'It's a stencil across the whole wall … roughly twenty-four hundred above floor level –'

'What?'

'About eight feet up the wall.'

'Right.'

'You see how it would look. She's shown a pattern based on a grapevine, but you could have anything you wanted, if you like the concept.'

'Why a grapevine?'

'The conservatory originally contained vines according to the old drawings.'

Barbara looked puzzled. 'I didn't notice that … and I'm a stickler for detail.'

'Me too, but Anne spotted it when she was going through the plans.'

'It would make the height less obvious, you say?'

'Certainly. And it would be in keeping with the space. I think it's a great idea … but it's entirely up to you.'

'And you can buy stencils in that design?'

'No. Anne would make the stencil herself. Don't worry about it. She's very good at that sort of thing.'

Barbara pored over the plan. 'Bright girl. I like this. Let's go for it.'

'Good. I'll tell her.'

'Right. And now … let's do lunch.'

• • • • •

Marnie leaned back against the head rest and closed her eyes as the Virgin Express pulled out of Euston heading north. It had been an entertaining day, and she had achieved all her goals. Barbara's bistro too had been all she had promised. The owner – who turned out to be Portuguese – had come out of the kitchen to greet her, and treated her like royalty, with a sparkle in his eye.

Marnie smiled inwardly at Barbara's ironic description of the two of them – ladies what do lunch. She found herself wondering what Barbara did to fill her days. There was certainly no need for her to add to her husband's income. Marnie could not imagine life without a career. It had been an ever-present feature of her existence, a defining characteristic, the focus of every day. She was no workaholic, but was always glad to return to the office, the drawing board and the computer.

What made Barbara Taverner tick? She was clearly intelligent, not just strikingly good-looking, not a bimbo on the make who'd married her boss. Perhaps not everyone needed the impetus of an interesting job to give meaning to their life. Obviously not. Marnie thought she was lucky in having a job she really enjoyed. This line of thought was interrupted by a loudspeaker announcement – by a man calling himself the *train manager* – listing their destinations and advising that the buffet car was open for refreshments.

Marnie slid the project folder out of her bag and extracted some bundles of photographs. One pack was her Polaroids of the vicarage – *The Old Rectory, my dear!* – another was a new set of Polaroids taken that morning of *Old Temple Steps* as a reminder of the Taverners' furniture, their general style and taste, which was rich as she had predicted. The third pack was an envelope containing shots of their boat. That had been the surprise of the day.

Over lunch Barbara had suddenly leaned across the table. 'Marnie, there's something else I want to ask you. Our boat … we'll need a mooring for her at Knightly. Do you have any space down at Glebe Farm? You mentioned you had a waterside frontage and a docking area.'

'That's right, but we have two boats so we occupy both moorings.'

Barbara bit her lip. 'Are there any marinas nearby?'

'A few. I'll ask around. When did you say you'd be coming up?'

'In a week or two. It has to be before Christmas, as I said.'

Marnie smiled. 'Not the sort of winter cruise I imagine you and Charles having.'

'Oh, Charles won't be travelling with me. Not really his scene. This'll be a solo run.'

'*Solo … in December?*'

'Sure. Charles rarely comes on the boat these days … except for an afternoon outing or an evening meal with friends. She's *my* pride and joy.'

'I see.'

'*I see,*' Barbara mimicked. 'Oh come on, Marnie. I'd expect you of all people to have a sense of fun. You're a long time middle-aged, you know!'

'True. It's just … well …'

'It's no big deal, Marnie. You can do the locks alone, if you're properly prepared and get organised. Just takes a little longer, that's all.'

'Yes, I know. I've done that trip solo myself.'

'There you are, then.'

'But that was in summer. It's a bit different in winter weather when the locks are icy and you're standing at the tiller for hours on end, wondering if your feet are still there.'

She had patted Marnie's wrist. 'I'll manage, don't worry. I know what I'm doing.'

As if to prove her point, the next photo that slipped out of the envelope showed Barbara in slacks and waistcoat holding a trophy, standing on the roof of a boat. She had explained that she won the all-comers manoeuvring competition at the Little Venice Canalway Cavalcade two years before, the first woman champion.

And that was what was so surprising. It was hard to imagine townie shopaholic Barbara Taverner running a narrowboat. Diesel engines, lock machinery, gearbox oil, grease for the stern gland … all these were a million miles away from Knightsbridge and Oxford Street. Surely the risk of breaking a fingernail was too great. *Whoa!* Marnie reined in her thoughts. She knew she was being sexist. Why shouldn't Barbara run a boat? She, Marnie, was just as keen as Barbara on nice clothes and a smart appearance – well, almost as keen – and she enjoyed nothing better than that sense of freedom from controlling a boat on the waterways. Even so …

By way of contrast, the pack of Polaroids of the house revealed an entirely different personality. Here all was dense-pile Wilton carpet and parquet flooring, heavy curtains with swags and tie-backs, the furniture an eclectic mixture of Regency cherrywood interspersed with striking modern pieces, Victorian landscapes and contemporary abstracts. Some fine portraits of Barbara in oils, watercolour and acrylic.

One thing was clear to Marnie. There was much more to Barbara Taverner than you would imagine on first acquaintance. She wondered if Barbara's request about the boat was as impulsive as she made it seem, or whether it had been in her mind all the time.

Barbara had reached over and grabbed Marnie's hand. 'I know … why don't you do a redesign of the *boat's* interior as well? In fact, why stop at the *inside*? Why not do a new colour scheme all over? A complete revamp.'

'You want me to do your *boat?*' Marnie was incredulous.

'Why not? It'll be fun. You're a designer … you know all about boats … bingo!'

'Well, I suppose I could …'

'Of *course* you could. We could work on it together … go over your plans while we do lunches!' She chuckled.

That sound echoed in Marnie's head as the train, now clear of London, sped through the countryside of the Home Counties. Glancing out of the window Marnie caught sight of lock gates and bridges as the railway and canal shared the same route away from the capital. She saw no movement of boats, had no glimpse of people on the towpath. The strip of water seemed to shimmer in a grey mist, and she suppressed a shiver, snuggling into her jacket at the thought of the damp frosty air waiting out there to chill the bones of the unprotected.

The remaining photos of the boat revealed it to be a trad or semi-trad, with a small area at the stern for the steerer, rather than having a 'cruiser' stern like *Sally Ann* where a group of friends could stand or sit sociably together. Marnie judged it to be a fifty-footer, or thereabouts, in deep blue with brass-rimmed portholes and brass mushroom vents on the roof. All the brasswork gleamed; Barbara knew how to take care of the boat. Marnie was forming the opinion that Barbara could take care of anything.

The boat. Strange. Although they had discussed it over lunch and it had arisen several times in conversation, Marnie could not remember its name ever being mentioned. She spread the photographs out to search for clues. Here was a shot of Barbara at the tiller. Part of the name was visible, but only the first few letters – *Perf* … Marnie smiled to herself. *Perfection?* The next views were bows-on or stern shots, and the side-on picture of the award ceremony in Little Venice missed the name, which was painted on the topsides too far back to be in the frame. Just when Marnie was about to give up, she came upon a photo that seemed to be from a different series, perhaps even from a different camera, as if it had been taken by a friend. In the foreground Barbara stood in jeans and T-shirt, holding both arms in the air, a gesture of exultation. She seemed to be standing on a pontoon in a marina, but it was not Templars' Wharf. Behind her, shining in the sunlight, was *the boat*, its name emblazoned on the side for all to see: *Perfidia.*

Perfidia? Marnie made a mental note to ask Barbara the next time they met why she had chosen that name. It was a question she would never have the chance to ask. She would never see Barbara again.

• • • • •

Ralph came through to the sleeping cabin that night, rubbing a towel round the back of his head. Although in his forties, he had few grey hairs, and at six feet tall had to take care not to bump his head against the ceiling in certain places on *Thyrsis.*

He was musing that the electric power shower installed when he first bought the boat had been his wisest decision. *Thyrsis* had been sound enough structurally, but the interior had needed a complete refit, and he had tackled the work himself with the help of a friend, a retired cabinet maker. The result had been functional and well-finished, with a modern galley and saloon area, a comfortable sleeping cabin, an up-to-date shower room and a spacious well-equipped study/library at the front end.

Anne teased him that only Ralph could have a narrowboat with a *library*. As a professor of economics at Oxford University and a Fellow of the prestigious All Saints College, there were not many people who ever teased him. She had teased him about the colour scheme of *Thyrsis*, too. It was a deep sage green with the name in a muted gold. He had chosen the colours himself and was proud of what he called its *elegant restraint*. Anne reminded him that the first time Marnie saw his boat she had said it was in the colours of a Harrods carrier bag. The two women in his life … one of them only seventeen … both kept his feet firmly on the ground. They had been through so much together. What cemented his close relationship with Anne was their shared love of Marnie.

Ralph finished rubbing his hair dry and returned to the shower room. He hung the towel over the rail and went back towards the saloon, where he found Marnie deep in concentration at the table, poring over drawings and papers.

He spoke quietly, suspecting that she was unaware of his presence. 'The shower's free, darling.'

Marnie looked up, her expression distant. 'Oh … right … Is that the time?'

'You're very engrossed. What are you doing?'

'Anne had an idea about the decor in the kitchen/breakfast room at the vicarage – tying it in with the conservatory. I thought I'd just see how it might all fit together.'

'You're redesigning it?'

'Yes. Have a look.' She turned the papers so that he could see and pointed at the drawings. 'If you continue Anne's stencil design into the breakfast room, it unifies that whole part of the house.'

'Does it complicate matters?'

'It means we have to rethink the colour scheme so that it blends in with the hall. I just had a thought about how we might achieve that by going one shade lighter on the walls and using shades of blue picked out with yellow.'

'Looks charming.'

'Yes. I wanted to get it down so that I can talk it through with Anne in the morning. Did you say you've finished in the shower? Good.'

Marnie packed the papers into their folder, kissed Ralph lightly and skipped along the passageway.

He was sitting up in bed reading the draft of an article he had written for a journal when Marnie emerged from the shower in her bathrobe. She sat on the edge of the bed and began brushing her hair slowly. After a minute or two she patted it carefully at the back and yawned.

'I just wanted to make sure my hair was dry. If I come to bed with it damp, it'll look all fuzzy in the morning.'

'You'll look marvellous, as always.'

'You won't say that if I look like a stunt double for Jimi Hendrix.'

Ralph chuckled.

She stood up and slipped off the bathrobe, returning to perch naked on the bedside, still feeling her hair at the back. Ralph stretched forward and ran his fingertips slowly down her spine. Marnie arched her back with a sigh that turned into a groan like the sound of a cat purring. It was a long back, the skin smooth, warm and silky to touch. In that moment of pure pleasure Ralph realised that he had been mistaken. Installing the power shower on *Thyrsis* had *not* been the wisest decision in his life. He could think of a better one.

5

'Walker and Co, good morning.'

'Is that the great designer?'

'Er ... this is Anne ... Anne Price. Is that Mrs Tav ... er ... I mean Barbara?'

'You guessed.'

Anne's voice relaxed into a smile. 'I gather you liked the stencil idea.'

'Very much. I didn't realise you were part of the design team, Anne. It's an *inspired* idea.'

'Thank you. And you'd like to talk to Marnie?'

'Don't run away. Before you pass me over to Marnie I want to talk to you about the plans ... *your* plans.'

'We're putting them in the post today for you to see how it all fits together. We went over them first thing this morning.'

'I meant your plans for the future.'

'Oh ... Simple, really. I'm doing A levels at college in Northampton. If my grades are okay, I hope to go on to study to be a professional designer.'

'What A levels are you doing?'

'I'm doing three: art, design and technology, social studies.'

'And then on to university?'

'Probably art school ... if I can get in. I don't know where yet.'

'Well, best of luck. You deserve it and I'm sure you'll do marvellously well. I *love* your stencil idea ...'

And so it went on. Barbara phoned every day, not once but several times. *Why did Marnie think carpets were right for the dining room? Could her joiner be spared to build a window seat in the drawing room? Would it be convenient for Marnie to meet the Smallbone planner this week? Did Marnie have any experience of Gaggenau appliances? Could they find a local person to make the curtains?* And so on, and so on.

It was the same for the boat. *Could they find a dry dock where the hull could be blacked while the topsides were being painted? Would Marnie be able to arrange for the engine to be serviced as well, or should that wait till spring? Could Marnie find an engineer to inspect the gas installation? There were all these strict new regulations ...*

• • • • •

Marnie walked into the office barn, dropped her briefcase on the floor, dumped her coat on the desk, sat down and kicked her shoes off.

'Phew! What a morning. Thank God it's Friday. Three meetings and no one offered me coffee. Have you had lunch, Anne?'

'No. I came straight back from college. My last day this term. That's it until January. I've got a *mountain* of project work to do in the hols. Good-bye, Christmas! Shall we have a sandwich?'

'Great idea. I could eat a buffalo.'

'No probs. We've got one in the fridge ... as usual. Guess who was on the phone just now?'

'Princess Di … the Pope … the Queen …?'

'Yes, but not in that order.'

Marnie rolled her eyes. 'What did Barbara want to talk about this time … the vicarage or the boat?'

'Both.'

'Any problems?'

'Not really. Their solicitor's on target for completion of the contract. She wants you to go ahead and order a name plate …'

'I thought Barbara was going to wait a while.'

'That's what I reminded her. She just said it might take time to get it made.'

'And she's insisting on calling it you-know-what?'

Anne altered her voice. Her reply was bright and bubbly. '*The Old Rectory, my dear! Of course … what else?*'

Marnie laughed. 'That's good. Anything else?'

Anne consulted her notepad. 'Two things. The meeting tomorrow … she has to cancel.'

They chorused in unison. '*Something has come up.*'

'She said everything was going so well, it wouldn't be a disaster. She agrees with everything on the plans we sent.'

'Good. And we get to have a free weekend. Can't be bad …'

'There was one other thing, Marnie. She's quite concerned about the boat … making sure it's all okay. She's planning to set off next week.'

'I'll give her a ring. We've got it booked in at the boatyard near Bull's Bridge. It's on her route. She can call in for them to give it a quick once-over. She's probably just anxious to have everything going well for her solo run.'

'She said one or two things were bothering her.'

'Such as?'

'Didn't specify.'

'I'll ring her … *after* we've had that sandwich.'

Anne got up and headed for the kitchen area at the back of the office barn. 'I'll dig out the buffalo.'

• • • • •

On the following Saturday morning with less than two weeks to Christmas, Marnie and Anne arrived at Euston station. They had spent most of the train journey reading, Marnie studying the project file, Anne learning about the Bauhaus. They took the stairs to the underground taxi rank and queued for five minutes before settling back in a cab for the journey west to Little Venice.

'When's she setting off, Marnie?'

'Tomorrow morning. It'll be an easy trip for her first day. She'll probably call in at Sainsbury's at Kensal Green to stock up with supplies, then she only has to chug along to Bull's Bridge. There are no locks on that stretch, remember … she'll easily find somewhere to tie up after the junction.'

'I wonder what she'll do while they're checking *Perfidia* over in the boatyard. Will they need the boat all day?'

'Depends what they find. If everything's okay I expect they'll send her on her way some time in the afternoon. She could make it to the first lock at Cowley Peachey before it gets dark.'

'She didn't seem bothered that we hadn't found her a permanent mooring yet. Isn't that going to cause problems?'

A wry smile from Marnie. 'Not for Barbara. She's got it all worked out. *Perfidia* will stay tied up opposite our boats over Christmas and new year.'

'That's fine, but she's only allowed to leave the boat in one place for fourteen days before moving on.'

'Correct. And what happens in the first week in January?'

Anne mulled this over. Enlightenment dawned. 'Ah …'

'Precisely. BW maintenance … replacing a lock gate at Cosgrove to the south of us.'

Anne continued the story. 'Of course … and the whole flight of locks at Stoke Bruerne to the north is being drained for repairs.'

Marnie raised both palms. '*Voilà!* She'll claim she's shut into that pound and can't move until the locks are re-opened.'

'And there's a fair chance she'll be iced in, too.' Anne chuckled. 'She's a smart cookie, that one … doesn't miss a trick.'

'And there's always plan B,' Marnie added.

Anne looked thoughtful. 'Amaze me. What else could she do?'

'As a last resort … charm the BW officials. They'll be queuing up to make her a special case because she's a woman … navigating her boat single-handed in the depths of winter. They won't even realise they're eating out of her hand.'

Anne laughed and imitated The Voice. '*Thank you so much, my dear!*'

'And she'll have bought time … enough time for us to find her a mooring, with any luck.'

The partition between their compartment and the driver slid open and the cabbie called back.

'Whereabouts in Little Venice did you want, love? We're nearly there.'

'If you could drop us off near the pub on the corner by the bridge and the canal office, that'll be fine.'

'That's the bridge without traffic lights?'

'That's the one. Anywhere near there will do.'

'You got it.'

Marnie checked her watch. 'Bang on time.'

'D'you know where she's tied up, Marnie?'

'On the arm going towards Paddington Basin, she said. Oh, did I tell you … Barbara's insisting on taking us for lunch.'

'That's nice. Where are we going?'

'I think she has in mind –'

The driver called back over his shoulder again. 'Sorry, love, I think there's been an accident or something. There's a police car blocking the road off the bridge.'

'This'll do. We can walk it from here.'

Marnie paid the driver and they crossed the canal, walking briskly in the chilly air.

'Not the quietest part of London at times,' Marnie observed. 'There's the police station just up the road ... ambulances from St Mary's hospital day and night ... fire station round the corner ...'

Right on cue they heard a siren wailing in the distance. They took the path down to the canalside and strode on past the sleeping waterbuses in the pool of Little Venice where tourists queued in large numbers for pleasure trips in the months of fine weather. Today the place was deserted. Rounding the corner of the arm they saw *Perfidia* straight away. It was no surprise to find that Barbara had been given the first mooring. The side door was open and, calling hallo, Marnie led the way down into the cabin. She turned at the foot of the steps to find herself confronted by a man in a dark coat and a troubled expression. Their eyes met and locked on.

'What are you doing here?' they said simultaneously.

'Marnie Walker,' said the man.

'Chief Inspector Bruere ...'

Behind Bruere Marnie could see another man moving about in the sleeping cabin, busy opening the curtains and the windows to let in the light. Bruere took Marnie by the elbow and began guiding her back to the steps. A siren could be heard some way away. It was getting nearer.

'Mrs Walker, I've got to ask you to leave. Now.'

'What's happened?' Marnie's face was draining of colour. 'Please tell me what's going on.'

The detective followed Marnie up onto the bank where Anne was standing, rigid with apprehension. All around them men and women in uniform were hurrying towards the boat. Orders were being called out. Blue and white incident tape was being drawn across the towpath to form a barrier.

'Barbara ...' Marnie muttered softly.

'You know the owner?'

'Of course I do.'

Bruere eyed their briefcases and document folders. 'We'll need to ask you some questions, Mrs Walker, but first I have work to do.'

'And I have questions for you, Mr Bruere ... though I very much fear I know the answer.'

Bruere gave her an appraising look and turned to a small group of officers behind him.

'Grove. Take Mrs Walker and her friend ... get them a cup of coffee or something. One hour, back here.'

'Sir.'

A woman of about Marnie's age detached herself from the group and came forward. Her expression was grim. Bruere left without another word and climbed through the side doorway of *Perfidia*.

'I'm detective constable Grove ... Sue Grove.'

'Marnie Walker ... and this is Anne Price. You're not going to tell us what's happening here, are you?'

'We've got more questions than facts at the moment, Mrs Walker. Come on, let's find some coffee.'

'If you want somewhere private ...' Marnie began. Grove nodded. 'There's a boat over there ... just past the other bridge ... not far.'

'Your boat?'

'A friend's.'

'And you're authorised to go on it?'

'Yes. It belongs to my solicitor.'

Grove stared. 'You want your solicitor to be present?'

'They're on a Caribbean cruise for the next three weeks.'

The bustle around them was intensifying as they walked back along the path.

• • • • •

They kept their coats on while the heating system on *Rumpole* warmed up. Marnie made coffee, her stomach a lead weight. Anne kept herself occupied by bringing out crockery and a container of sugar. She found a jar of dried milk and rummaged in a drawer for spoons.

The detective sat at the built-in eating unit. 'What brought you here today, Mrs Walker?' Her tone was conversational, but she had a notebook open on the table.

Marnie looked up from spooning coffee into mugs. She spoke quietly and calmly. 'I'm not going to tell you a single thing until you explain what's happened.'

'That's your privilege, but if you know the owner of the boat and want to help us, it could be important.'

Marnie stared at her. 'The owner of the boat is called Barbara Taverner. She's a client of ours. We're here to discuss her project.' Marnie glanced towards their bags. 'Now tell me what's going on. Please. You're obviously not here because everything is fine. As a human being the least you can do is tell me how my client is.'

Grove looked down at her pad.

Marnie continued. 'She's ... hurt?'

The police officer raised her head. 'Mrs Walker ... Marnie ... I'm not supposed to –'

'It's all right,' Marnie interrupted. 'You just did.'

The only sound in the cabin was a sharp intake of breath from Anne, who covered her mouth with a hand. 'Oh no ... She can't ...'

Marnie reached out and held Anne to her, both looking desolate. After a few moments Marnie released Anne and bent down to reach into a cupboard.

'If you don't mind, Miss Grove, I think we need something a little stronger than Nescafé.' She pulled out a bottle of brandy and poured some into two of the mugs. 'I don't suppose you're able to join us.'

The police officer shook her head.

• • • • •

DC Grove had radioed to Bruere that they were on the narrowboat *Rumpole* and had given directions to find it. The DCI joined them in less than an hour. The cabin was now comfortably warm but there was a chill in the atmosphere that penetrated to the bone. Bruere accepted the offer of coffee and while Anne made it, he came straight to the point.

'First of all I want to clear up why you're here.'

Marnie explained about the project, the meeting and Barbara's plans for the journey up to Knightly St John. Her filofax was on the table and she passed Bruere the business card given to her by Charles Taverner. She produced their railway tickets as evidence of their journey and showed Bruere the meetings arranged with Barbara in her diary.

Bruere flicked through the pages. 'So you've been having meetings every week with Mrs Taverner?'

'Not actually. We've only had one before today. I saw her at their home in Templars' Wharf. The others were cancelled.'

'Why's that?'

'We were making good progress ... they weren't needed.'

'Then why put them in the diary?'

Marnie shrugged. 'To reserve the times, I suppose. Barbara wanted to keep the options open.'

'And the meeting last weekend?'

'She said she had something else on.'

Bruere's eyes narrowed. 'What?'

'I don't know. She didn't say.'

'And you'd just arrived when I saw you on the boat?'

'Yes. So had you by the look of it.'

'Why isn't her husband here ... if they're going on a boat journey?'

'She was going to travel alone.'

'*Alone?* Is that usual?'

'It's not uncommon. Anyway, Charles isn't such a keen boater as Barbara, and he has business to attend to.'

'I see.'

Bruere handed the business card to DC Grove. 'Give that to DS Cuthbert. Tell him to make contact. I'll be over as soon as I've finished here.'

Sue Grove went out without speaking, and Bruere paused for thought. 'So ... she was going on a trip alone ...' He murmured the words, stirring the coffee.

Marnie watched him. 'That's right. The boat was hers, really.' As an afterthought she added, 'Charles hadn't been on it for years, I believe.'

Bruere looked up sharply. 'What did you say?'

'Barbara was a keen boater ...' Marnie hesitated, realising that she had been referring to Barbara in the past tense. 'Charles came on the boat for social outings, of course, but he didn't go on long journeys.'

'Are you sure about that, Mrs Walker?' Bruere sounded doubtful.

'Yes, I'm quite sure. Barbara mentioned it when we met.'

Bruere stared at his mug of coffee.

Marnie went on. 'You sound as if you don't believe me, but I assure you –'

'What shaving cream do *you* use, Mrs Walker?'

Taken aback, Marnie felt her cheeks redden. 'Sorry?'

'And what brand of aftershave?'

• • • • •

Ralph met Marnie and Anne at the central station in Milton Keynes. He had gone in by taxi, wanting them to be greeted by a friendly face and Marnie not to have to bother with driving. He hugged them both as if they had returned from a long and arduous voyage, and it occurred to him that that was not so far from the truth.

He pointed the big four-wheel-drive out of the station car park and headed for the by-pass. Marnie sighed as she leaned against the head restraint, and Anne sat in silence behind them, gazing unseeing out of the window at the trees flashing past in the pale wintry light.

'Marnie, I'm sure you don't want to talk about it, and I'm not going to force the issue, but when you're ready ...'

'It's just so incredible ...'

'Of course.'

'You know, Ralph, I can't quite get hold of my feelings. That probably sounds crazy ... maybe even heartless ... but ...'

Ralph refrained from platitudes. He concentrated on driving.

'I feel the same, Marnie.' Anne had hardly spoken on their journey back. 'I feel sort of numb ... awful about it, because I ought to be ... crying or something ... and I'm not ...'

'We're both in a state of shock, Anne.' Marnie touched Ralph's arm. 'That's why Ralph came in to drive us home.'

'I don't suppose you've eaten anything, have you?' he asked.

Marnie shook her head. 'Didn't feel like it. Are you hungry, Anne?'

'No. My appetite's disappeared.'

'I've got some soup for you when we get home.' Ralph's tone suggested there was to be no argument about it.

'It's sweet of you, darling, but –'

'Doctor's orders,' he insisted.

'Ralph, you're a doctor of philosophy,' Marnie pointed out. 'A DPhil, not a medic.'

'Exactly. That's better than not being a doctor at all. Trust me, I'm an economist.'

A half-smile floated across Marnie's face. 'You win, doc.'

'And after that,' he continued, 'I suggest –'

'After that,' Marnie interrupted, 'I have to get in touch with Detective Chief Inspector Bartlett.'

'Why?'

'Bruere wants me to make a statement ... Anne, too. He regards us as peripheral, but still needs us to confirm in writing what we told him. It'll be part of the evidence. Bartlett will arrange it all.'

'Evidence...' Ralph muttered. 'Bartlett, eh?'

'Yes. That'll be fun. He'll be overjoyed to get the news that I'm coming to see him.'

• • • • •

'Sodding hell!' DCI Bartlett exclaimed after putting the phone down. He had just returned from Christmas shopping in Oxford with his wife. His mood had been far from seasonal good cheer when he picked up the messages on the answerphone. The fourth and final one had been from the duty sergeant at the station in Towcester, informing him that DCI Bruere of the Metropolitan Police had left a word for him. Mrs Marnie Walker of Glebe Farm, Knightly St John would be coming in on Monday morning to give a statement. That was the icing on the cake. '*Sodding hell!*'

'Language!' His wife's voice above the sound of shopping being put away in cupboards and fridge in the kitchen.

'That's all I need,' he murmured to himself. 'Marnie *bloody* Walker ... What's she up to now?'

• • • • •

The soup was shop-bought but the carton claimed it was made from organic carrots and coriander and, to anyone who noticed, it would have tasted good. They were sitting in the saloon on *Sally Ann*, and in her mind Marnie was making the comparison with the bleak activity they had seen that morning on *Perfidia*.

'Did the police actually say what they were investigating?' Ralph was at the table cutting a baguette into chunks and putting them into a basket.

Marnie put her spoon down. 'They didn't go so far as to say the words – do they ever tell you *anything*? – but it was all too obvious what was going on.'

'You mean it was obvious what had happened ... concerning Barbara. But did you get the impression they thought there might've been an accident, perhaps?'

'I don't think detective chief inspectors are called out for accidents, Ralph.'

'No. So it was ...' His voice petered out.

Marnie glanced sideways at Anne who at that moment looked up and spoke.

'I think it's what they'd call a *suspicious death*.'

It was the first time anyone had said the word *death*. It echoed in the space between them like a pebble dropped into a deep well. Marnie did not want the conversation to go that way. At times like that – and they had had more than their fair share of such times since they had been together – she felt an almost maternal urge to protect Anne from the horrors of the world. That thought prompted her to change the subject.

'Anne, this business is going to get in the papers. With Charles's position in the City, plus the fact that it concerns a woman on a boat in Little Venice, it'll be irresistible to news editors. I wouldn't be surprised if it makes the front page.'

'It'll make a change from speculating about what record will be the Christmas number one.'

'Exactly. So I think you ought to phone your parents as soon as we've finished eating and let them know you're okay. Tell them they don't have to worry about us being involved.'

'All right.'

'They might want you to go home for a few days, especially as your college term is over.'

'But, Marnie, I've got to be here to see Mr Bartlett on Monday morning ... my statement.'

'Ye-e-es …'

'And there's a load of work to catch up on in the office. With me just working part time, I've got to make sure I keep everything running smoothly. And then there's my project work for college. All my books and things are here.'

'Yeah, I suppose so.' Marnie looked enquiringly at her friend. 'Anne, are you all right?'

'Known better days. My real worry … I know this'll sound odd – unkind, even – is that I don't know how I feel about what's happened. I'm really sorry – of course I am – but I hardly knew Barbara and I can't quite get my reactions sorted out.'

'It's shock.' Ralph sounded definite. 'I think you should sleep on *Thyrsis* tonight. We can make up the bed in the dining area.'

'Oh no, I'll be fine. It's –'

'Anne. Listen, darling. Of course you're fine, but it won't do you any harm to be close to us … just for tonight.'

6

On Sunday morning Marnie was awake before six. She sat up in bed in the darkness. It was cool in the cabin, the heating system turned down to its night setting. Outside there would be a thin crust of ice on the canal. The horror of what had happened in Little Venice hit her hard for the first time. *Suspicious death* could have only one meaning. *Barbara had been murdered.* Marnie's stomach turned over.

A thousand questions raced through her head, all of them variations on a theme. *Why was Barbara dead, and who had killed her?* Marnie became aware that she was breathing quickly. She realised that the previous day she had been somehow detached from reality. Shock. Yes, that was it.

'Marnie, are you all right?'

Ralph always slept longer than Marnie, but that morning there was no trace of drowsiness in the voice beside her.

'Sorry did I disturb you? I think something must've woken me ... a bird perhaps, or an animal moving about.'

'It was Anne going out. She left a few minutes ago.'

'*Left?*'

'Yes. I think she was having trouble sleeping as well.'

Marnie leaned across Ralph and tweaked the curtain over the porthole. A light was burning in the saloon on *Sally Ann*.

'I'd better get up.'

'Me too.'

'I was wondering if I ought to contact Charles. I know the police will've spoken to him but ... as I was going to see her ...'

'He might prefer to have some time to himself.'

'Mm ... It's difficult to know what to do for the best. I hardly know them. He must be feeling absolutely *awful*.'

'Of course.'

'You know, Ralph, it's only just getting through to me that Barbara must have been murdered. It's true, isn't it?'

'There are four possibilities.'

'Four?'

His voice was quiet in the dark cabin. 'Natural causes ... accident ... suicide ... murder.'

'What about manslaughter?'

'I think it's just a variation on murder ... a kind of legal technicality. It still means someone has killed you.'

Marnie shuddered. 'Well we can probably rule out natural causes.'

'Not necessarily. You can't be sure until ... until an autopsy has been carried out.'

'Then we can surely eliminate accidental death. Bruere wouldn't have been called in for an accident, even a fatal one. He'd just arrived when we got there. I wonder how he knew ...'

'Someone must've called the police.'

'Yes. So that just leaves suicide – which is out of the question – and you-know-what.'

'Marnie, I don't think anything can be ruled out until the facts have been established.'

'Well, she didn't commit suicide.' Marnie sounded almost exasperated. 'They were just about to move and start a new phase in their life. You know that. Barbara was full of plans and ideas … for the house, for the boat …'

'Marnie, as you said yourself, we didn't know her very well. Who knows what was going on in her life?'

'I had a fair idea.'

'Did you really? Can you say that after meeting her on only two occasions?'

'Mind your eyes, Ralph. I'm going to turn on the light.' Marnie reached behind her and pressed the switch. She settled back so that her face was close to Ralph's on the pillow. 'You're probably right. But could you believe she was about to take her own life after what we've been planning with her these past few weeks?'

'No. But I am saying we don't know anything about her private life … or about her past … do we?'

Marnie gave this some thought. 'I know Charles had been married before and I think he and Barbara had been together for about ten years.'

'Was it her first marriage?'

'I don't know. The more I think about it, the more I realise how little I did know about her. But one thing I'm sure of … she definitely did not commit suicide. I've never known anyone more full of life than Barbara Taverner.'

• • • • •

They jogged the short distance between *Thyrsis* and *Sally Ann* in her docking area and leapt onto the stern deck, pulling the doors open to escape the frosty morning. On board, Anne was preparing breakfast, still wearing her fleece, though the interior was warming up. The cabin smelled of fresh coffee brewing and croissants warming in the oven. The radio was playing softly, baroque music on Classic fm … not the news on Radio 4. Downlighters in the ceiling cast a cheerful glow in the saloon. *Sally Ann* was an oasis of peace and harmony whatever was happening in the outside world.

'Good timing.' Anne smiled at them. 'Glad to see your radar's still functioning.'

Marnie kissed her on the cheek. 'You're up early. How are you?'

'I'm all right. At least I was until I turned on the radio and got the six o'clock news.'

'Barbara?'

'They were full of it … the whole story.'

'Poor Charles,' Marnie muttered.

Ralph agreed 'He'll get no peace now … at least not until they've got to the bottom of it.'

Marnie put the cafetière on the table. 'Anne, did they say anything substantial, or was it just the usual speculation?'

'DCI Bruere read out a statement.'

'Let me guess,' said Ralph. '… *ongoing enquiry … appeal for any witnesses to come forward … too soon to give any facts at this moment in time?*'

'They always like to say that,' Marnie chipped in. '… *at this moment in time.*'

Anne nodded. 'That's right. You got it almost word-perfect.'

'Did he add anything else?'

'Yes. Bruere said they were treating it as murder.'

• • • • •

Shortly after eight they received a phone call from the police. After a slow breakfast Anne had gone off through the spinney to the office barn to change and prepare herself for the day, Marnie had gone to her desk and Ralph had set off on his morning walk along the towpath. They had agreed to spend the morning clearing up matters remaining from the previous week, and Anne would buckle down to the projects that had been set by the college for the Christmas vacation. Marnie, normally so focused on her work, felt listless and unsettled, unable to cleanse her mind of the thoughts that had troubled her in the night. It was almost a relief when the phone call blew away her plans for the day.

'Marnie Walker, hallo.'

'This is Detective Sergeant Cuthbert, Metropolitan Police. I hope I'm not disturbing you.'

That will depend on what you have to say to me, was Marnie's initial thought. 'Go ahead. What can I do for you?'

'DCI Bruere has asked me to contact you in connection with the case in Little Venice. You spoke to him yesterday.'

'I hadn't forgotten.'

'I understand you agreed to give a statement at your local police station.'

'It's all arranged. I'm going there on Monday morning.'

'The chief inspector wonders if instead of that you might be able to come to see him in London. Would today be possible?'

'*Today?* What could I tell you that's so urgent? I hardly knew Barbara. And I haven't the remotest idea about anything that might've happened in Little Venice.'

'I don't know if you've heard the news, Mrs Walker, but there have been developments in the case.'

'You're treating Barbara's death as murder, yes, I heard.'

'That's correct. And there are one or two matters on which the DCI would like to talk to you. That's why he'd prefer it if you could give your statement down here.'

• • • • •

Marnie had been adamant that Ralph and Anne remain at Glebe Farm while she travelled to London, though Ralph insisted on driving her to the railway station and Anne announced that she was tagging along to *ride shotgun*. DS Cuthbert had offered to have Marnie met at Euston station by a police car, but she had declined and taken a taxi.

Bruere greeted her with a handshake. 'Good of you to come, Mrs Walker, and at such short notice.'

'That's okay. I'm happy to help … if I can. At least this time I'm neither a victim nor a suspect.'

Bruere gestured her to a chair and grinned lopsidedly. 'Yes … makes a pleasant change.'

As she sat down Marnie noticed that the woman police officer who had shown her in took a seat in the corner and pulled out a notepad.

'You came to see Mrs Taverner yesterday. That was for a business meeting?'

'Yes. I'm – perhaps I should say I *was* – doing the redecoration of their house. They planned to move to the village where I live … to the old rectory.' Marnie paused, realising that for ever afterwards she would only be able to think of the house by that name.

'So why had you come to London to see her? Would it not be more customary to meet at the house to discuss it?'

'Well … yes, normally. There were a number of reasons. Time was one factor. Barbara was going to set off to bring the boat up to our area.'

Bruere frowned. 'At this time of year?'

'There's what she described as a *window*. There are no lock closures on the southern Grand Union canal until after new year.'

'Even so … that's a tough undertaking for a woman, isn't it? All that way in the freezing cold, doing everything by herself?'

'She was a highly capable boatwoman.'

'How capable?'

'Very experienced … won prizes for boat handling … a real expert in anyone's book. And she had tremendous energy … a zest for life. She was a strong character. If anyone could do that journey single-handed, Barbara could.'

'Could you do it, Mrs Walker?'

'I've done that trip solo – a couple of years ago – though that was in the summer.'

'Do you need technical knowledge to run a boat … on a journey like that? Are there mechanical things you have to know about?'

'Plenty of women are capable of running narrowboats, Mr Bruere.'

'I don't doubt that. Presumably you'd consider Mrs Taverner one of them?'

'To be honest, I'm not sure whether Barbara was technically-minded.' Marnie reflected, conjuring up an image of Barbara's hands, those fingernails, manicured and painted, those slim tapering fingers. 'Not sure at all …'

'Perhaps there's nothing to it … switch on the engine and go … like driving a car?' Bruere prompted.

'No, there's more to it than that. You need to make sure the stern gland is kept greased after a day's travelling … and the rudder tube needs greasing at certain times. I like to check the engine oil every morning on a long journey … and it's a good idea to keep an eye on the batteries. On a narrowboat you're dependent on the mechanical systems. Sorry, I'm going on a bit.'

'No, it's interesting … informative. And do you see Mrs Taverner down in the engine room – or whatever you have on a barge – dealing with all those things? Do you see her as a kind of *grease monkey*?'

Marnie shook her head emphatically. 'No! But … I mean …'

Bruere lowered his voice. 'Neither do we. Those dainty hands didn't strike us as mechanic's hands. I couldn't imagine them holding an oily rag, can you? Barbara Taverner was no *Tugboat Annie*, was she? Even her boating clothes had designer labels.'

'I know what you mean, Mr Bruere. But where's all this leading? I thought I was supposed to be giving you a statement about yesterday.'

'You are … in a way. But you see, we're enquiring into a suspicious death –'

'You said it was a murder enquiry.'

'So it is … the murder of a woman of style and fashion. Who better to help us understand such a woman than someone like you, Mrs Walker?'

'What do you mean?'

'Don't tell me you don't see the similarities, surely … You're both smart, attractive, fashion-conscious … and you both like canal barges. It's an unusual mixture, don't you think?'

Marnie sat back in the chair. 'Well … since you put it like that … and they're called *narrowboats*, not *barges*.'

Bruere shrugged. 'They still have diesel engines and all those tubes and glands and things that have to be greased all the time. Do you get *your* hands dirty … or does someone else look after that side of things for you … a man perhaps?'

Marnie smiled reflectively. 'It's no mystery. When I do the maintenance, I put on latex gloves. But that's not a feminine foible. The mechanics who maintain my car at the garage wear them too. Dirty fingernails and ingrained engine oil aren't acceptable to anyone these days … except dyed-in-the-wool petrolheads.'

'I see you keep your fingernails fairly short, Mrs Walker.'

'It's more practical like that.' She stopped abruptly. He had a point. Barbara's nails made no concession to the mechanical demands of a narrowboat, none at all. In that moment she understood the purpose of the interview. Bruere was watching her. 'That thing you said about the aftershave … You think she was travelling with a man … presumably not with Charles …'

'You told us he hadn't made journeys on the boat for a long time, Mrs Walker.'

'That's what Barbara said to me.'

'You got on well together?'

'Yes, I'd say so.' Marnie knew where this was leading.

'You had things in common.'

'She was employing me to handle a couple of projects … we both had boats …'

'Similar styles, similar tastes, similar interests,' Bruere counted them on his fingers.

'I would've said we were rather different in many respects, but I get your point.'

'You liked her company?'

'Yes.'

'You chatted about things … other than just the projects. Did you say *projects* … in the plural?'

'She wanted me to do a refurbishment of the boat as well as the house.'

'But you didn't only talk about work. Perhaps you chatted about other things … over a cup of coffee?'

'To some extent.'

'Did she talk about her private life?'

'What do you mean?'

'I think you know what I mean, Mrs Walker.'

'Chief inspector, I had only met Barbara in person on two occasions, once in Knightly St John with her husband, once in London, alone. We were getting to know each other. She was a good client ... asked intelligent questions ... gave sensible answers. She was lively, positive, knew what she wanted. In time I think we could've become friends. But we never got that time.'

'Nevertheless –'

'She never confided in me about private matters ... certainly never told me of any other man in her life, if that's what you're getting at.'

Bruere sat back and folded his arms. 'You're sure she never dropped a hint that she might be planning to take along a ... *companion* ... *someone to help crew the boat* ... that kind of thing?'

'No.'

'All right. But I'd like you to think carefully about that. It could be important to our enquiry if you remembered *any* mention – no matter how casual – that anyone else might be travelling with her.'

'You're certain the shaving things weren't her husband's?'

'Oh, yes.'

'So Charles knows of your suspicions.'

'Nobody knows at this stage, Mrs Walker. And I must ask you to keep the matter totally confidential.'

'I've already spoken about it with Ralph, and Anne was there when you mentioned the shaving cream yesterday.'

'It must go no further.'

'They're neither of them gossips, chief inspector.'

'Good.' He suddenly changed tack. 'Tell me about boats, Mrs Walker ... narrowboats.'

'It's a big subject.'

'Do they have to have regular checks like the MOT for cars?'

'Every few years. The rules are just in the process of changing ... becoming more strict, more detailed.'

'Is Mrs Taverner's boat up-to-date? Does it comply with all the rules?'

'I'd imagine so. I've only been on board for a few seconds ... that was yesterday when I bumped into you there.'

'But you'd think her boat would be properly maintained?'

'Yes.'

'Do these rules that you mentioned relate to the engine, the hull and that sort of thing, or is there more to it?'

'They cover everything ... safety ... fire extinguishers ... ventilation ...'

'Even the plumbing?'

'*Plumbing?*' So that was it. Marnie had a flashback to her arrival on *Perfidia*, Bruere pushing her out, the other officer hurriedly opening all the windows. He had not just been concerned with letting in the light. 'You mean the gas supply?'

'How often would you check it on your boat, Mrs Walker?'

'Personally I don't touch it. They probably examine it at the boatyard when *Sally Ann* goes in for service each year. And an inspector tests the whole system when the safety certificate comes up for renewal … that's like the MOT.'

'No other time?'

'If I noticed a strong smell of gas, of course, I'd investigate.'

'Has that ever happened on your boat?'

'No.'

'Do you have local gas taps for the different appliances?'

'Yes. There's an isolator for the cooker and another for the water heater.'

'If something went wrong – an escape of gas – would you notice the smell?'

'I suppose so.'

'Would you know what to do about it?'

'I'd switch off the supply at the gas bottle.'

'Mrs Taverner would know about that sort of thing?'

'Oh, yes. I'm sure she would. Are you saying she was gassed?'

'I'm just looking into possibilities at this moment in time.'

Marnie tried not to wince. 'But you've already stated that you're treating her death as murder … so you think someone deliberately interfered with the gas system?'

'Are you aware of the pipework on your boat's gas supply, Mrs Walker?'

Marnie had to think about that. She knew roughly where the pipes ran and that there were junctions and valves of some sort at the back of the units in the galley. But it was something she took for granted, like the water running when she turned on the taps. 'Well … I know more or less where they are, but it's not the kind of thing I'd ever touch.'

'You'd regard that as something for a specialist?'

'Yes.'

'And so, presumably, would Mrs Taverner?'

'It's possible.'

'Or probable?'

'Perhaps more probable. I couldn't imagine Barbara as a plumber.'

Marnie dreamed of Barbara that night. They were both clambering over a boat – she could not tell which it was – laughing together as they tried to fix a problem that neither of them could quite identify. At one stage Marnie stopped tightening a fitting in the engine compartment with a monkey wrench and pointed at Barbara's overalls. She had put them on inside out and the label was showing – it was Versace. The sight of it sent them into fits of giggles.

All the time they worked, Barbara kept up a continuous chattering ... *Where could she find a dry dock? Perfidia's hull needed to be blacked ... the whole boat needed repainting.* Marnie was wracking her brain, trying to think of somewhere, but her mind had gone blank. *Where could Barbara get the engine serviced?* It was no good, Marnie had forgotten the names of the boatyards. Barbara was looking desperate, exasperated. She began waving her wrench, screaming ... *Where could she find an engineer to inspect the gas installation? She had to comply with all the new rules ... they were so strict ... she was worried sick by them!* Marie tried to comfort her, telling her they didn't matter to her any more ... she was dead ... the rules didn't apply if you were dead ... honestly ... no one could touch you.

It was one of those moments like in the movies. She sat up in bed, breathless, wide awake. Marnie had never believed things really happened like that; it was just a device dreamed up by some film director for dramatic effect. But she really did feel cold and clammy. Ralph moved beside her.

'What is it?' His voice was drowsy. He was struggling to wake up. 'Marnie, are you all right?'

She heard him groping on the shelf over the bed, his fingers fumbling for the light switch. There was a click, and one reading lamp came on. Marnie looked at her hands to see if they were shaking. Her upper body exposed, she could feel the cool air on her skin. Ralph pulled her down and held her close to him, tugging the duvet over her shoulders to keep her warm.

'What's the matter?'

'Can't you guess?'

'Barbara ...'

'Yes. She was crying out to me, Ralph. She wanted me to find an engineer to look at the gas system. It was really worrying her.'

He put his hand on the back of her head and drew her closer, kissing her hair. 'How awful ... but it was just a bad dream ... don't think about it.' He was drifting.

'No. But Ralph, she *was* very worried about the gas. She had mentioned it to me. I'd forgotten until then ... until I dreamt it. She'd asked me to get the system checked as part of the project.'

'Mm ...'

'I'm sure she did ...'

'Mm ...'

Ralph's only reply was a long breath that settled into a steady rhythm. Marnie listened to his breathing, trying to calm her mind. Slowly the warmth seeped through to her, and he carried her with him back to oblivion.

• • • • •

After breakfast Marnie reached her desk before eight. Anne was going to spend the first hour in the office clearing up accounts and correspondence and the rest of Monday morning working on her vacation projects.

Marnie felt troubled. Something was nagging at her mind. Every time she had an inkling of what it might be, it slipped away from her. So frustrating.

'Marnie, I'll need you to sign a couple of cheques ... Marnie?'

'What?'

'Sorry, are you concentrating on something?'

'I was miles away.'

'I know. Me too. I'm trying to get down to routine things to take my mind off Barbara. I wonder what'll happen next.'

'The police will get on with their investigation, I suppose. In a few weeks time they'll announce they've caught someone or – more likely in my opinion – the coroner will give a verdict of accidental death.'

She was to be proved wrong on both counts.

'You really think it was an accident, Marnie?'

'Judging by the little I know of what happened, I think it could be the answer. People can get gassed ... it's rare but not impossible. I can't imagine anybody wanting to ... to murder Barbara.'

'Presumably you don't have to go to the police station to give your statement, now that you've seen Mr Bruere.'

'No. I'm sure Chief Inspector Bartlett won't be heartbroken about that. Although ...'

'What is it?'

'I ought to tell someone that Barbara was worried about the gas system.'

'Oh? What made you think of that?'

'I know it was preying on her mind. You remember she had some concerns about *Perfidia* ... well, the gas was one of them. It came back to me last night ... in a dream.'

'And you think you should tell Mr Bartlett about it?' Anne sounded dubious.

'He'd love that, wouldn't he, Anne? I can hear him now ... *You're telling me the Metropolitan Police should switch their murder investigation because you've had a dream? Perhaps you'd like to read the tea-leaves first before I phone them, just to be certain ...*'

Anne nodded. 'That's what I was wondering.'

'I think if I explained about gas leaks – that Barbara thought her system might need attention – that it could have been a simple unfortunate accident despite what they've worked out – maybe they'd think again.'

She was to be proved wrong about that, too.

It was coming up to eight o'clock, and Anne turned on the radio. This had become part of their morning ritual in the eighteen months since they began working together at Glebe Farm. The start of the day. The headlines on Radio 4, then switch off and down to work.

Marnie returned to the file in front of her and was bringing her focus back to the task in hand when the headlines caught her attention. The announcer had said the words, *Little Venice*. Her head jerked up. Anne was staring at her across the room, and they waited for the item that would follow the reading of the main points of the day.

... A man has been arrested and charged with the murder of Mrs Barbara Taverner, wife of City businessman, Charles Taverner. The arrest comes just days after her body was found on their narrowboat in London's Little Venice. The police have named the man under arrest as Neil Gerard, age forty-two, a freelance journalist living in west London, described as a 'close friend' of the deceased. He was arrested late yesterday evening and is being held at Lisson Grove police station. High street trading in the run-up to Christmas has so far not been as brisk as expected ...

Anne turned off the radio. 'Neil Gerard ... ever heard of him?'

Marnie frowned. 'I don't think so ... though the name does seem vaguely ... mm, not sure.'

'A journalist.' Anne repeated.

'More to the point ... *a close friend* ... I wonder if that means what I think it does.'

Anne's eyes widened. 'You think he was a ... lover?'

'No idea. She never talked to me about anything like that ... anything personal.'

'So it was murder,' Anne said quietly.

'The police seem to think so.'

'Are you still going to tell them your idea about the gas, Marnie?'

'Dunno. If they've actually made an arrest – and charged this ... Neil Gerard ... they must have substantial evidence. I could look a real idiot if I start making wild statements about a simple accident caused by a leaky gas tap or something. The police aren't fools.'

'So you're not going to say anything about it?'

'No. I'll mind my own business for once. I've done my bit to help, and that's an end to it.'

Wrong again.

• • • • •

Anne drove up to the village shop in her red Mini – her pride and joy, a gift from Marnie and Ralph – to see if the morning newspapers carried the story of the arrest of Neil Gerard. They all seemed to follow the same line, based on the police statement. They had not had time to flesh out more details before the morning editions went to press.

None of them carried a photograph or any additional facts about the accused. They merely reported that he was waiting to appear before magistrates to be committed to trial.

• • • • •

It was a long and busy day. In the week or two before the Christmas break everyone seemed to want to clear their desk of papers, and Marnie was not surprised at the volume of mail hitting her in-tray.

All day Marnie found her thoughts returning to Barbara. What would Charles do about *The Old Rectory*? He probably would not want to live there now. What would he do with *Perfidia*? There would surely be no question of keeping Barbara's boat, the boat on which she had died. What would Charles do about their house in Templars' Wharf ... what would he do about the rest of his life ... about everything?

Dusk was drawing in by mid-afternoon – they were approaching the shortest day of the year – when Anne climbed down to the office barn from working on her college projects in the attic. Marnie closed a folder and announced that she had had enough. She reached a senior management decision; it was time for a cup of coffee. Anne had the kettle heating before you could say *six shopping days to Christmas*. When Anne put the mug down on Marnie's desk, she found her slowly turning the pages of a notebook.

'*There!*' Marnie looked up triumphant, tapping the page in the open book. 'She first mentioned it during a phone conversation. It's in my notes … *engineer – inspect gas system – worried – new regs …*'

Anne leaned over to read the note. 'Are you changing your mind about telling the police?'

'No … well, perhaps … yes … no, not really. What good would it do? It doesn't prove anything. It won't bring her back to Charles.'

'Charles,' Anne repeated. 'Poor man …'

'Yes. I've been thinking I ought to contact him. I was thinking it'd be easier to write rather than phone.'

A knock on the door brought the paperboy with the local evening daily. The press had wasted no time in digging out information on Neil Gerard, including a photo. Marnie and Anne looked down at the face of the man accused of killing Barbara. Her 'close friend' of that morning had now been promoted to her 'lover'. He was shown standing between two uniformed officers, about to go through a door, presumably at the police station. There was none of the customary effort to conceal his face, no towel or jacket draped over his head. He simply stood patiently, a look of mild concern clouding his features, as if he had just been told that his flight had been delayed by fog or that a book he had ordered was out of stock.

'He doesn't look like a murderer, does he?' Anne said quietly.

'Nor did Dr Crippen, apparently.'

'No, I don't mean like that. I meant, he doesn't seem to be part of the group there. It's as if he just happens to be in the picture … the murder and the arrest don't seem to have anything to do with him.'

'As if he was a bystander,' Marnie muttered. 'I see what you mean.'

They were just starting to read the story when Ralph came in. He had just shut down the computer in his study on *Thyrsis*. The three heads moved close together while they read the articles in the paper. Under her photograph the first gave an account of what had happened to Barbara … *the wealthy owner of the boat on which her body was found in the chic quarter of London's Little Venice*. It explained that she had *died of gas poisoning after someone had drugged her and tampered with the gas system on the luxury narrowboat, Perfidia.*

'That's their line,' Ralph observed. 'They're going to stress the wealth aspect, build up the glamour angle. The press loves a good *society murder*, especially if it goes with a touch of scandal.'

'The photo of Barbara certainly makes her look very attractive,' Marnie agreed. 'Difficult not to, of course.'

A witness staying on a nearby boat had apparently heard a heated argument on *Perfidia* the previous evening. She had heard shouting and seen a man, later identified as Neil Gerard, leave the boat with an *angry expression on his face* as he *stormed off along the towpath.* Late the next morning the witness had noticed the curtains were drawn on *Perfidia* and through the gaps she could see the lights were still on, even though it was bright and sunny. She had knocked on the hatch to see if Barbara, whom she had known in the area for some years, was *all right. Remembering the commotion of the previous evening, and becoming increasingly worried about her neighbour, the witness tried the door, found it was unlocked and went in to discover the deceased lying sprawled on the floor of the saloon. There was a strong smell of gas. With considerable presence of mind, the witness ascertained that Barbara Taverner was dead and immediately called 999.*

'So that's how it happened.' Marnie sat staring in front of her.

Ralph turned and perched on the side of the desk. 'How ... exactly?'

'What do you mean?'

'Barbara died from gas poisoning – or so it suggests in that account – so how was she killed? You can't suddenly turn a gas-tap on someone in the course of a row.'

'Perhaps he turned the gas on and she died in the night.' Anne frowned as soon as she had spoken. 'No, that doesn't work, does it?'

Marnie shook her head. 'No. She would've smelled the gas, presumably.'

Ralph pointed at the article. 'It says she was drugged.'

They read the paper again. Marnie sat back in her chair. 'Not enough detail, not enough facts.'

Anne picked up the phone as soon as it started ringing. 'Walker and Co, good evening ... Yes, she's here. Hold on, please ... Sorry? ... Oh, I don't need to ask who it is. I'll pass you over, Mr Bartlett.'

Marnie rolled her eyes and grimaced as she picked up the phone. 'Good evening. What can I do for you?'

• • • • •

It was less than half an hour before the unmarked police car arrived. It had been a frequent visitor to Glebe Farm in previous months and went straight to its customary spot outside the house. Detective Chief Inspector Bartlett and his colleague Detective Sergeant Marriner climbed out and walked across the courtyard. Marnie had joked in the past that she would be allocating an exclusive parking space for their use. It was not much of a joke. But they had not had much of a relationship. She had sometimes managed to give them the wrong impression and, although they had usually found themselves on the same side, the detectives never quite trusted her. And she knew it.

Another feature of their relationship was the coffee ritual. If they were on what Marnie regarded as a *hostile* mission they refused any refreshment. On some friendlier occasions they accepted. Marnie and Anne waited for their visitors, wondering which way the pendulum would swing. Ralph had gone back to *Thyrsis* to avoid giving the impression that they were feeling embattled.

Marnie managed a smile as the men knocked and entered. 'Hallo. Come in. Let me take your coats.'

'Good of you to see us at short notice, Mrs Walker. But then we know you work late.'

Marnie was weighed down by the heavy winter coats. 'I think you know all my routines, Mr Bartlett. I have no secrets from you.'

'Glad to hear it.'

'Take a seat.'

Anne waved from the kitchen area. 'Hi! Am I making you coffee?'

'Thank you.'

Marnie repeated the smile – two in one visit was a record – and grew bolder. 'In this season of good will, are we allowed to offer you a mince pie to go with it?'

'That would be nice. Is this a season of good will, Mrs Walker?'

'The shops have been preparing us for it since around Easter.' She checked herself. Too flippant. Bartlett had not come to ask what she wanted in her Christmas stocking.

'It's difficult to remember good will when you're investigating a murder.'

'Is that why you're here, Mr Bartlett? I thought that was Mr Bruere's responsibility down in London.'

'I'm assisting his investigation locally.'

'So how can we help you? I've given a statement to Mr Bruere … told him everything I know.'

'You're aware a man has been arrested and charged? His name is Neil Gerard. Do you know him?'

'No.'

'Have you ever heard of him?'

'No.'

'Mrs Taverner never mentioned him to you?'

'No … as I told Mr Bruere. She never spoke about any of her friends or acquaintances with me.'

'Are you sure you never heard of him?'

Marnie kept her voice calm and even. 'Positive.'

DS Marriner joined in. 'You've had your boat a few years now, haven't you?'

'The boat? Yes … a couple.'

'You're quite knowledgeable about boating matters, I expect.'

'I try to keep up with what's going on.'

'You read the boating magazines?'

'When I have the time.'

'I believe you've even featured in the odd article yourself.'

A warning bell sounded somewhere in the distance. Marnie was grateful that Anne was serving coffee and mince pies, which gave her time for thought. The police had been doing their research on her. Why? The fact that she had donated a collection of important drawings and documents to the National Canal Museum two years ago was no secret. They had been bequeathed to her, and her generosity had been reported in the press – the boating magazines and the national media – in flattering terms. Where was this leading?

As soon as they had taken their first bite of mince pie and sipped their coffees, Marriner took up the line again. 'That is correct, isn't it, Mrs Walker? I understand you became quite famous at one point.'

'I just did the right thing and the press got hold of it. They must've wanted a good news story at the time and I was in the right place to provide it.'

'You were interviewed in the press and on TV, I believe.'

'Famous for fifteen minutes, as they say. Yes, but that's in the past now. I'm back to reality.'

Bartlett again. 'Do you read all the boat magazines, Mrs Walker?'

'Like I said … when I get the time.'

'Do you read *Canal and Boating World?*'

Marnie hesitated. The name seemed unfamiliar, somehow an amalgam of the titles she usually read. 'Is it a new one?'

'You don't recognise the name?'

'Not offhand.'

Marriner reached inside his jacket and produced a magazine. He held it up so that Marnie could see the title. It was indeed *Canal and Boating World*. 'Do you keep a scrap book?'

'A what?'

'I do.' It was Anne who answered. 'I keep cuttings about things we're involved in.'

Bartlett turned towards Anne. 'Is it here?'

Anne nodded towards a low filing cabinet by her desk. 'In the files.'

'Can I see it?'

Without a word Anne knelt down and in seconds pulled out a file which she handed to Bartlett. He thumbed through the pages. Everything was neatly labelled, each section relating to a story or a series of events. It chronicled the lives of Marnie, Ralph and Anne, their village, its triumphs and tragedies. One of the earliest items was the coverage of Marnie's donation to the museum. There were photographs and articles from national, local and boating papers and magazines.

'You really were famous. Politicians would give their eye teeth for favourable comments like this. They made you out to be a national hero.'

Marnie shook her head. 'I only did –'

Bartlett interrupted, holding up the scrap book. 'You recognise this article?'

Marnie craned forward to see. There was a photo of herself standing at a microphone, making the brief speech she had given at the opening ceremony. It was one of the most commonly used images at the time. She sat back. 'Sure.'

'You know it? You've seen it before?'

'Yes.'

'You don't seem to be in any doubt about that.'

'No.'

Marriner opened *Canal and Boating World*. He stood and walked across to Marnie, handing her the magazine. There was the article, there was the photo. Marnie nodded. 'That's it.' *What's the big deal?* she wondered.

Bartlett held up Anne's scrap book. 'And there it is again.'

'So I see.'

Bartlett got up and passed Marnie the scrap book. 'Compare the two, Mrs Walker.'

The label in Anne's careful printing was *Canal and Boating World*, plus the date.

Marnie stared at the page. 'I must've forgotten this one.'

'Even though you immediately recognised the photograph?'

'There were lots like it at the time.'

'Look closer, if you would.'

Marnie saw it at once, just as Bartlett began his next question. She froze.

'Did you say you'd never heard of Neil Gerard, Mrs Walker?'

Staring up at her from the page, immediately below the picture of herself, the words stood out in clear print. *Words and photographs by Neil Gerard.*

'I …'

Anne came across the room and looked down at the article. Marnie tried to regain her composure.

'The fact that someone wrote an article about me doesn't mean I knew them. There were pieces in the *Times,* the *Guardian,* the *Telegraph,* others, but I don't know the journalists who wrote them or the people behind the cameras.'

'Of course not.'

Marnie made an effort to regulate her breathing and appear unflustered. This talk was reminding her of other occasions when the police had wrong-footed her, when she was entirely innocent of anything except lack of memory. There was a pause while they all drank from their mugs. Anne offered round the plate of mince pies. Both police officers declined. A bad sign?

'It's interesting how some people are taken up by the media, Mrs Walker. Did you enjoy being feted in the press like that?'

'It only lasted for a few days. Then it was over.'

'You're not accustomed to that kind of treatment?'

'I earn my living doing designs for decorating our clients' houses and flats. It's a backroom job … unless you're one of the TV makeover people.'

'So you're not really used to being in the public eye?'

'No.'

'It must've been quite a special experience at the time … being talked to by media people … outside the ordinary routine of your life.'

'Yes.'

'Take a look at the article again, would you please.'

'It looks like all the others,' Marnie observed, patting the scrap book.

'Almost, but not quite. Have another look.'

This was getting tedious, but Marnie did as Bartlett asked. It was only then that she understood the point he was making. And her heart sank. Without trace.

• • • • •

'I felt such a *fool.*'

Ralph had sat Marnie down in the saloon of *Sally Ann* while he and Anne prepared supper. He had poured a glass of red Bordeaux and put it in front of her. She hardly spared it a glance. Anne was busy following a recipe for a white sauce to pour over leeks that would be baked *au gratin.* Ralph continued the conversation while washing leeks under the tap.

'An interview?'

'Yes. Bartlett argued that an interview wasn't like an ordinary article. An *interview* involved someone talking to me. It meant face to face.'

'Well … that's true, I suppose, on the whole …'

'Thanks. I thought you were supposed to be on my side … on the whole.'

'*On the whole* means normally but not necessarily exclusively.'

Marnie looked glum. 'I didn't actually give any individual interviews, as far as I remember.'

'Then Ralph's right, Marnie. There were probably times when you were asked questions by several journalists at once. You couldn't know who they all were, could you?'

'And some would've taken facts out of the museum's press release,' Ralph added. 'And from your speech. An article can sometimes be written in the form of an interview to create a more direct personal style. It's just a technique that journalists use.'

'*Damn!* Why didn't I think to say that? When Bartlett's got me on the back foot, I just can't think straight.'

'You can mention it when Bartlett next contacts you for a follow-up statement … if he does.'

'Oh he'll be back all right … to arrest me as an accomplice … part of Neil Gerard's plot to …' Marnie's voice died away. 'I didn't mean to joke about it.'

'I doubt if Bartlett will be taking any more action, Marnie.'

'Then why did he try to catch me out like that?'

'So you didn't recall the name of someone who wrote an article about you two years ago … so what? It doesn't mean anything.'

'I denied even having heard of the magazine.'

'Which magazine was it?'

'*Canal and Boating World.*'

Ralph finished drying the leeks in kitchen paper and placed them in the baking dish. He paused, looking at them as if admiring their symmetry. '*Canal and Boating World?*' He said it slowly. 'No such magazine … if there is, I've never heard of it.'

'Really?' A note of hope in Marnie's voice. 'Are you sure?'

'As my American colleagues say … sure I'm sure. I don't think such a magazine exists.'

'It must've existed, Ralph. The police have got it … Anne put a cutting from it in the scrapbook … I was featured in it.'

Anne poured the sauce evenly over the leeks, put down the bowl and reached for her notepad.

8

There was a tense atmosphere in the office of Walker and Co the following morning. Marnie was staring at the screen of her computer as if trying to look into its very soul. She had been drafting a letter since she and Anne first opened up and started work. On the other side of the room Anne held the phone pressed close to her ear, an expression of impatience clouding her features. Between attempted calls she took letters from the pile of that morning's post and sorted them into batches.

'Uh!' It was a sound somewhere between a sigh and a growl. 'Doesn't anybody at BW do *any* work at all?'

'BW?' Marnie took her eyes from the screen. 'Why are you phoning British Waterways? Have we got a problem with the boats?'

'No. It's this magazine business. I'm trying to get it sorted out.'

'It's only just nine o'clock, Anne. Some people have to travel to work. You only have to stroll back through the spinney or climb down the loft ladder.'

'I suppose so, it's just that – Hallo? Oh, good, there you are. I'd like to talk to someone about your magazine, *Canal and Boating World* … yes there is, take my word for it … You may not know it, but … Well can I talk to someone who deals with publications … Yes, that's fine …'

Marnie returned to her computer leaving Anne waiting to be put through. She read what she had written so far, written and rewritten a dozen times.

Dear Charles,

I'm so sorry about Barbara. It has been such a dreadful shock and I can only barely imagine what you have been going through these past few days. Please accept my sincere condolences.

In the short time I knew Barbara I regarded her as more than a client and I believe we were becoming friends. I will miss her warmth and gaiety. She was a very special person.

You will need to reassess your plans for the future, so I'll wait to hear from you whenever you are ready and able to take decisions. I realise you will have much to occupy you at this difficult time, but if there is anything I can do to help, don't hesitate to contact me.

Take care,

Marnie

It all seemed so inadequate. But what could she say? What can anyone say to a man who has lost the most important thing in his life?

'*Yes!* I knew it had to be something like that …'

Marnie was only vaguely aware that Anne had raised her voice. She wondered about the ending of the draft letter. *Take care* seemed consoling in a way, but was it too lame? Perhaps she should change that to –

'Marnie? Did you hear?'

'Er, no … Sorry did I hear what?'

'*Canal and Boating World* … it really did exist. I've just spoken to BW's public relations department.'

Marnie looked surprised. 'But we knew it existed. We had it in our hands just yesterday evening.'

'Yes, but I've found out why we didn't remember it. You can explain to Mr Bartlett.'

'Go on.'

'They only produced five issues. It was costing too much, so they dropped it. You were in issue number four. That's where I got it for the scrapbook.'

'I don't recall buying it.'

'It came free to everyone who paid for a boat licence. That's why it was too costly. I think you should tell the police. They'd believe you then.'

'I'm glad you've solved the mystery, Sherlock, but I think I'll wait and see if the police ever get back to me on this case. You never know what we might stir up.'

'Okay.' Anne went back to sorting the post.

Marnie got up and walked across to her friend. 'It was really nice of you to find out about the magazine. Thanks, Anne.'

'Don't mention it, Watson. Have you been writing something? Do you want it to go out with today's post? I'm trying to get as much sent off as possible before everything closes down for Christmas.'

'Good thinking. I definitely want this letter to go out today. Trouble is … I'm not really happy with it.'

'Can I help?'

'You can look at it and see what you think.'

They went back to Marnie's desk and read the letter on the screen.

Anne saw the opening words. 'Oh …' She read in silence and nodded when she reached the end.

'What do you think?' Marnie asked.

'It's … I've never written anything like that. It seems fine to me.'

'Really? Reading it again, it just seems like a collection of clichés, trite sentiments and platitudes.'

'What else can you say? It's not slushy or sentimental. He'll just read it and know you're thinking about him … know we all are, even though we can't do anything to make it better.'

'That's a point.' Marnie sat down and typed. She moved the reference to condolences to the end and expanded it as the final sentence.

Ralph and Anne join me in sending our sincere condolences.

'Thanks, Marnie. That's nice.'

'It still feels inadequate.'

'Show it to Ralph. But I think you should just get it posted so that it's done. That's the main thing.'

'Yes. And I expect that'll be the last we hear of Charles, except maybe a little formal note thanking us for our good wishes.'

'And perhaps something about the funeral,' Anne added.

'I hadn't thought about that.'

'I've made a note on my list to send flowers.'

'You and your lists … where would we be without them?'

• • • • •

During the break for a sandwich lunch, Marnie consulted Ralph about Charles and they took two decisions: Marnie should send her letter of condolence without further alteration; and she should phone DCI Bartlett and briefly explain why she had had no recollection of the short-lived and now defunct British Waterways magazine.

It was late afternoon with dusk already enveloping Glebe Farm when Marnie eventually managed to speak with Bartlett. He listened patiently to her account, thanked her for phoning, and that was that. Anti-climax. Anne had set off to the village shop to post the day's letters, including the one to Charles Taverner, which Marnie had written out by hand rather than sending it typed. She was alone in the office when the call came in.

'Walker and Co, good afternoon.'

'Marnie, it's Charles. Is it convenient to speak?'

'Charles …' She struggled to keep her voice even. 'Yes, of course. How are you?' She wished she could bite her tongue off. *Stupid question!*

'Not too bad. How are you?'

'Fine. Actually, I've just sent you a letter … you know …'

'Thank you. Look, I know it's a terrible imposition, but I wonder if you could possibly do something for me.'

'Of course.'

'There's a lot to sort out here, as you can imagine. I'm going to stay at a place I know in Antigua for a week or two – you know this house in London is sold and I have to work out my arrangements. Could you … I mean, would it be asking too much to … there are things that need to be done.'

'Charles, whatever help you need, I'll do it gladly. Is it about *The Old Rectory*?'

'Yes … and the boat.'

'The boat? That could pose a few problems … access … I don't have any keys.'

A pause. 'There's the spare set. I'm pretty sure Barbara left them hanging up in the box in the kitchen at the rectory.'

'Of course … I remember. What would you like me to do?'

Marnie pulled the notepad towards her and began writing. It was only after she had finished the call and was completing her notes that she realised that Ralph had come for their usual afternoon coffee. At the same time Anne arrived, her nose and cheeks pink from the chilly air.

'If it gets any colder, I'll be putting in for a sledge and a team of huskies.' She pulled off her fleece and headed for the kitchen area, dropping a bundle of letters on the desk in passing. She stopped, sensing that something was in the air. 'Everything all right?'

'I've just taken a call from Charles. He wants us to go on with the rectory project.'

'What are his plans?' Ralph asked. 'Presumably he'll want to sell it.'

'No. He's going to move up here.'

'Alone?'

'That's what he said. Their Docklands house is already sold; he has no reason to stay on in London now that he's retiring. Apparently they have a cottage in Sussex, but

Charles doesn't want to move there … says the South-East is too built-up and overcrowded. He's thought it through and thinks Knightly will give him some peace and quiet.'

'And it was Barbara's last wish,' Ralph added.

'That too. Also, he wants me to take care of the boat.'

'He'll not be keeping that, surely.'

'No. He'll be wanting to sell it, but in the meantime he has to move it from Little Venice. It's only on a temporary mooring, and there's nowhere else for it to go. They've sold their house in Templars' Wharf and the mooring that goes with it.'

'What can we do about it?'

'Dunno. It won't be easy finding a mooring up here. We'll have to make some enquiries.'

'Braunston? Yardley? Gayton?' Ralph began listing the nearest marinas. 'Whilton? Milton Keynes?'

'We'll have to try them all. But I think they may have waiting lists.'

'I can dig out a list from a boating magazine and start ringing round, if you like,' Anne volunteered.

'Great.'

'Did Charles say anything about the funeral?' Ralph asked.

Marnie shook her head. 'There can't be a funeral. Apparently if it comes to trial, defence counsel may want to order a second autopsy, so Barbara's body can't be released until afterwards.'

'When will that be?'

'Probably several weeks from now. It shouldn't last long. The police have told Charles privately they regard it as an open-and-shut case.'

• • • • •

For the second time that day Anne spent a frustrating hour on the phone. Marnie had been right. All the marinas were full, all had waiting lists. At Braunston they offered to take the boat and put it in with their sales stock. The snag was that it would be months now before they would have a clear run up the Grand Union Canal from London. The winter lock maintenance programme would be in full swing until Easter. Whole sections of the cut would be out of action for weeks at a time.

The manager at the marina thought this was no great disadvantage from the sales point of view as the market was currently very flat.

'So does this mean Marnie's selling *Sally Ann*, or is it *Thyrsis*? We've been wondering how long you were going to be running a private fleet.'

'It's neither, actually. It's a friend's boat. We're going to do a redec and then sell it for them.'

'Okay, I'll send you a sales contract. Fill in the details and let us have it back and we'll put it on the books. We'll need a letter from the owner authorising you to handle things. And a photo once you've got it repainted. I'll make up a file for it. What's the boat called?'

'*Perfidia*.'

There was silence at the other end of the line.

'Hallo?' Anne wondered if she had been cut off. 'Are you still there?'

'*Perfidia?*'

'That's right.'

'Unusual name. Not many of those around. I don't suppose by any chance it might be …'

'Yes, it *is* actually.'

'Mm …'

'What's the matter?' Anne imagined all sorts of superstitions, like old sailors' tales of bad luck and impending doom. *A death on board … and a woman's to boot … Ah, Jim lad …* She could practically smell the rum and hear the thump of a peg leg on the deck, the squawk of Long John's parrot. 'That's not a problem, is it?'

'It could be, if you're serious about selling it.'

'We *are* serious … well, the owner is.'

'Then you'd better include repainting the name as part of your redec … and changing it at the same time.'

9

Over Christmas Marnie tried to put murder out of her mind, but thoughts of Barbara would not go away. She and Ralph went to spend the holiday at his cottage in the village of Murton near Oxford. It was a charming beamy house, quiet and secluded near the river. They hung up garlands of fir and holly, and Anne drove over to help decorate the tree with gold and silver ornaments a few days before she left to spend Christmas with her family.

It was Dolly's first visit and on arrival she occupied herself prowling from room to room, eventually settling into new favourite places.

They burnt candles and joss sticks. Logs crackled in the inglenook fireplace. In the hall the scent of hyacinths flowering in a bowl gave a portent of spring to come. They took their meals in the conservatory by candlelight looking out onto the garden where Ralph had hung lights in the trees. It was a magic atmosphere. Marnie and Ralph enjoyed having time alone together. They were happy. And yet … and yet …

On Boxing Day they went for a long walk on the towpath of the South Oxford Canal and across the fields, wrapped up against the frosty air. There was a mist over the water, and the ground crunched under their feet. Without speaking, they linked hands as they passed the spot where Ralph had asked Marnie to marry him. A year had passed since then, a time full of incident and change. Crossing the canal by a steeply-arched footbridge, they saw below them a heron standing statue-like at the water's edge. They had barely watched it for a few seconds when it sensed their proximity and flapped off languidly to land further down the bank.

Ralph put his arm round Marnie's shoulders. 'I'm glad you wanted to come to the cottage for Christmas.'

She snuggled closer. 'It seemed the perfect place … just right … more cosy than staying on the boats … a nice break.'

'You needed to distance yourself … you wanted to try not to spend Christmas with Barbara.'

Marnie stiffened. 'That's a rather graphic way of putting it.'

'But it's true, isn't it? I feel the same.'

'Well … somehow she's always in my thoughts.'

They lapsed into silence, nestling together on the bridge in the deserted landscape. When Ralph eventually spoke it was as if he was picking up on Marnie's train of thought, but his words came as a complete surprise.

'A dangerous lady.'

Marnie turned to look up into his face. 'What do you mean?'

'You must've been aware of it as well as I was.'

'Dangerous in what way? I didn't realise you knew her very well.'

'I'd met them at a number of functions. She exuded sensuality … was quite blatant about it.'

Marnie frowned. 'But that's no reason why anyone would want to kill her.'

'I didn't say that … though I'm not entirely sure you're right. Who knows what passions a woman like that might stir up?'

'Ralph, I had no idea you thought of Barbara in that way. I realise she was a very attractive woman, but as for being dangerous ...'

'Marnie, *you* are a very attractive woman. The point about *you* is, you do nothing to exploit it. You don't flirt, you don't dress provocatively. Everything you do is understated. Now think about Barbara. Every time she came into the room, she made an entrance. Every time she spoke to a man, she tried to make an impact.'

'Did she do that to you?'

'Yes.'

'You mean she was flirting ... trying to lead you on?'

'No. I think it was automatic. It's just the way she was. She wanted to be admired ... perhaps desired, even. You're not like that.'

'How do you know?'

He smiled. 'If you are, you keep it well hidden.'

'Actually, Ralph, I think it's not unhealthy to want to make the best of yourself. A little pride or self-esteem isn't a bad thing. Most women feel the need to keep their self-confidence up.'

'Only women?'

'In many ways it's still a man's world. I think men are different ... their egos work in a more confident way.'

He snorted. 'We all think we're God's gift to women?'

'Jest not. Believe me. Most women will tell you stories of how men fancy themselves.'

'And there I was thinking it was only women who were vain ... telling themselves *they're worth it*, like the adverts for shampoo, or whatever it is. You're not like that, Marnie. You're somehow more ... modest ...'

Marnie's turn to laugh. 'Perhaps I have a lot to be modest about.'

'Not true. But neither do you think about your looks all the time. That's what I meant about Barbara.'

'Ralph, there are aspects of me that you don't get to see. Women do like to keep some things private, you know.'

'Such as?'

Marnie butted him gently and they began walking arm in arm. '*Private* things.'

'You don't have Barbara's kind of vanity. I know you don't.'

'Maybe not, but I got myself sorted out about certain things when I was quite young.'

'What things?'

Marnie paused before replying. 'I wish I hadn't got entangled in this conversation. Can't we change the subject?'

'You're getting me worried. Can't you give me a clue about what you mean?'

Marnie sighed. 'It'll just sound silly.'

'I won't laugh, I promise.'

'When I was in my teens, I remember reading an article in some magazine – it might've been *Cosmo*, I'm not sure – about self-esteem. Usual thing, ten things you ought to do to get the best out of yourself, or whatever.' She made a vague gesture. 'I only remember one of the points. It was something like … get a good body and keep it that way, it's an investment that will benefit you for the rest of your life … bla-bla-bla …There.'

'A good body … and you followed that advice?'

'I was around eighteen, young and impressionable, about to go to college. I didn't want to let myself down.'

'So what did you do?'

Another sigh. 'Must I go on?'

'I'm intrigued, really.'

'I spent the whole summer holidays on a regime … cut out fats and carbohydrate … drank lots of water … did a daily workout … went swimming almost every day … Get the idea? I expect you find it all rather silly.'

'As a principal beneficiary of the programme, I can hardly complain. An investment for life, as you say. Do you think Barbara did something like that?'

'It wouldn't surprise me.'

'But in your case, Marnie, the idea was just to help develop a little self-confidence before facing the major challenge of going to college. I think Barbara had a different outlook on the world.'

'Significantly different from mine?'

'Oh yes. There was more under the surface with that lady than just gas collecting under the floor of her boat.'

10

Marnie wanted to waste no time. As soon as the New Year break ended she rang the BW office in Little Venice. A woman declared she was the only member of staff on duty; the others were either still on leave for the school holidays or had phoned in suffering from flu. The woman did not have the means of checking on the availability of moorings, but she believed there was a lengthy waiting list.

Next stop, the boatyard at Bull's Bridge, and a surprise.

'How soon can you get the boat here, Marnie?' Jock Mackenzie's voice sounded like the original Glasgow fog-horn.

'You can take her now?' Incredulity. 'How come, Jock?'

'The damn' flu. Don't you read the papers? Half the people who should've brought their boats in haven't made it. We're freezing our rocks off down here and twiddling our thumbs.'

'Tomorrow. I'll clear the decks in the office and go down to London. I'll be with you before close of business.'

• • • • •

It was the first time Marnie had set foot in the vicarage since before Christmas, since Barbara had died. Angela was attending a meeting of clergy with the Archdeacon in Northampton, so Marnie used the key that Barbara had given her.

Even though the house was still occupied and the heating had been running that morning, it felt abandoned, as if its spark had gone. Not normally one for flights of fancy, Marnie had the strange feeling that the building was in a state of shock, that she could almost hear the last echo of Barbara's laughter somewhere upstairs in an empty room. Her footsteps clattered on the tiled floor of the hall, and she crossed quickly to the kitchen, opened the cupboard and took down the spare boat key.

On the way out, Marnie paused briefly, looking at the walls, imagining the house in the new colour scheme she had been planning with Barbara. For Barbara. As was so often the case, it was the woman client who took the greater interest in the design. Marnie's creative imagination thrived on that interest, and she had thrived on Barbara's vitality. Now the design was completed, but Marnie knew the project would never be the same. Her own spark had been diminished by Barbara's death.

And how would Charles cope? How could he live here without her?

She hurriedly pulled open the front door and left.

• • • • •

The next morning, Marnie travelled down in the dark with the early commuters and took a taxi from Euston station to Little Venice. It always seemed calmer here than in most of central London, but somehow that day as the light was growing it felt positively deserted.

She was reaching into her shoulder bag for the key and so failed to notice the woman looking out at her from the next boat in line with *Perfidia* as she walked past. When Marnie stepped onto the counter – the tiny stern deck for the steerer – the woman called out. Marnie jumped in surprise and almost lost her grip on the key.

It was a loud voice. 'Can I help you?' The familiar euphemism, meaning: *what do you think you're doing?*

Greatly tempted to retort *No!* or *I doubt it*, Marnie kept her composure, took a few breaths and turned to face her interrogator.

'Good morning.'

Much as she resented having to explain herself to a stranger, Marnie knew the woman was only trying to protect the boat left here by its owners. She would have been glad of such a solicitous neighbour if *Perfidia* had belonged to her.

'I know you, don't I?' The woman frowned in concentration. 'I've seen you here before.'

'Not on *Perfidia* you haven't. I used to keep my own boat further down the cut towards the tunnel … *Sally Ann*.'

'*Sally Ann* … yes …' The woman stared. 'You went off somewhere and …'

'Marnie Walker.'

'Marnie! Yes … I knew it. I'm Belle … Belle Starkey. Most people call me Bella.'

'Well, Bella, it's nice to meet you, but I've got to take *Perfidia* here down to Jock's boatyard at Bull's Bridge.' Much against her inclination, Marnie added, 'Charles is a client of mine … I'm looking after the boat.'

Bella climbed out onto the bank. 'You've got keys?'

Marnie held them up. 'Yes. Sorry to be in such a rush, but I've got a fair way to go before sunset.'

Bella walked along the towpath and rested a hand on *Perfidia*. 'Can't say I'll be sorry to see her gone. I heard them rowing that night.'

'*You* heard …?'

'Yeah. It was me … the famous witness.'

'So you'll be called to give evidence.'

'Already been questioned several times … had to give a statement …'

'So you haven't any doubt in your mind about what happened that night.' Marnie really did not want to get into this conversation, but she felt herself being dragged in. 'You saw them.'

'Heard them. There couldn't be any mistake.'

'You heard what they were saying?'

'Part. Heard him saying it was *ridiculous* … *childish* … and her shouting at him to get out.'

Marnie felt sick at the thought of Barbara's private life being the stuff of gossip on the canalside. She hardly recognised this Barbara as the one she had grown to know and like.

'She was still yelling when she slammed the door behind him.'

Marnie felt her cheeks tingling. 'After he'd left the boat, you mean?'

Bella nodded. '*You can have all the space and time you want* … that's what she was screaming at him … what I told the police.'

'Did you see him come back later?'

'Come back?'

'Well, he must've come back to …'

'Oh yes … that's right.'

'And you saw him then.'

'Yeah. He came back after about an hour. I was in the galley washing up after supper.'

'Wasn't it late at night?'

'Not really. I said *that night*, though it was only afternoon when they had the row. But it was already getting dark … the night was drawing in, you know.'

'Yet you saw him clearly, even in the dark? It's not very light down here.'

'I know, and he was wearing dark clothes … the police kept pressing me on that … but it looked exactly like him. I can't say plainer than that.'

'You need to be absolutely certain, Bella, for something as serious as murder.'

Bella shrugged. 'I saw what I saw.'

'So was it quiet when he came back … no more rowing?'

'I didn't hear anything that time … thought they'd kissed and made up.'

Marnie had had enough of this. 'Bella, you're going to have to excuse me.'

'Fancy a cup of tea before you go?'

'Thanks, but I've really got to get underway. Another time, perhaps.'

It took Marnie no more than ten minutes to go through the boat checking her for readiness from bow to stern. *Perfidia* was a fine craft with beautiful joinery in oak and ash and expensive fittings in brass. The engine oil was up to the mark, the batteries were in good order, the stern gland was fully lubricated. Barbara had been no grease monkey, but her boat was properly maintained. Marnie was wiping her hands on a moist cleaning tissue when she felt the movement. If Bella was coming on board with more offers of tea and talk, she could think again.

'Hallo,' Marnie called out.

'Hallo?' came the reply. Not Bella. Not a woman.

Marnie moved to the galley entrance and found a young man blocking the corridor by the bathroom. He was very tall and had to stoop to avoid contact with the ceiling. He was dressed in blue with a number on the epaulettes of his jacket and the badge of the Metropolitan Police on his breast pocket.

'Good morning, officer.'

'Morning. Mind telling me what you're doing on this boat?' His tone hovered on the edge of politeness.

'I'm here with the owner's permission … in fact, at his request. I'm taking her for works to be carried out at Bull's Bridge boatyard.'

'And you are?'

'Marnie Walker.'

'Ah …'

It was the usual response Marnie received from police officers on giving her name. The constable spoke into his radio, giving a brief report on his findings. Marnie heard the reply from the station loud and clear in the confined space of the cabin. He was to bring her in to headquarters. When he finished the call the young man raised an eyebrow. Marnie nodded.

'Give me two minutes to lock up.'

• • • • •

DCI Bruere flipped open a pack of Benson & Hedges. 'And there was I thinking we'd seen the last of you on this case, Mrs Walker. But you always seem to turn up when we least expect you.' Marnie looked pointedly at the cigarettes. 'You don't approve of me smoking?'

'I gave up nearly three years ago. Smoking while questioning me might count as torture under the Geneva Convention.'

Bruere gave a small sigh. 'A convert … they're the worst.' He closed the lid and rested his elbows on the desk. 'Why were you on the boat?'

'I told your constable. Charles Taverner has asked me to deal with the house and the boat. *Perfidia* needs a safety certificate for selling … has to be thoroughly checked over – and any faulty parts replaced – before I get her inspected. The rules are very strict … and after what happened …'

'We'll have to check that out with Mr Taverner.'

'Do you doubt me?'

'Routine, Mrs Walker.'

'Doubting what I tell you is routine?'

Bruere permitted himself a momentary smile. 'I must remember to tell that to Jack Bartlett. He'll enjoy it.'

'So glad I keep you amused. But why can't you believe me? What other reason would I have for being on the boat?'

'We check everything. It's what we do in the police. You of all people should know that by now.'

'Charles is in Antigua for another week or so.'

'I knew that.'

'But you didn't know he'd asked me to move the boat.'

'No. He didn't think to tell us.'

'Did you tell him the boat couldn't be moved?'

'Do you know the old Gestapo joke – *we ask the questions* – Mrs Walker? I'm supposed to be conducting this interview.'

'Look inspector, I haven't done anything wrong. Charles asked me to deal with the boat as part of our contract. I've booked her in at a boatyard. She's due there this afternoon and I'm running late.'

'No, you're not.'

'It's a full day's cruising to get to Bull's Bridge.'

'You're not running late because you're not taking the boat. It's as simple as that.'

'I don't understand.'

'The … boat … stays … put. Which bit of that don't you understand?'

'You obviously hadn't made it clear to Charles Taverner that *Perfidia* couldn't be moved.'

'Oh yes I had. I told him quite explicitly. The boat was needed in case it had to be examined for further evidence. Now I find you trying to remove it to have the equipment altered.'

'Are you saying you think I'm deliberately trying to move the boat to conceal possible evidence? That I'm colluding with Charles to – what's the expression – to pervert the course of justice? That's a very serious matter.'

'We think so too.'

'I can't believe this, inspector. You actually suspect *me* of being involved in some kind of cover-up with Charles?'

'I didn't say that.'

'You implied it. And anyway, I thought you already had your suspect … Neil Gerard.'

Bruere stared at Marnie and, without taking his eyes off her, he opened the pack of cigarettes, took one out and lit it, all in one rapid movement. Marnie's mind was racing. What did Bruere mean?

'You can't possibly be suggesting that somehow Charles and I are involved in some plot with this Neil Gerard character to destroy evidence. That's ridiculous.'

'I'm not suggesting any such thing, Mrs Walker. I just wondered what you were doing on that boat – using keys we didn't know existed – given that Chief Inspector Bartlett has established that you did in fact know the accused …'

Marnie felt she was being pushed into a corner. 'Talking of the accused – and Mr Bartlett knows my only link with Gerard was an article he once wrote about me a couple of years ago – the woman on the next boat … your witness on the night of the murder … says she didn't actually see Gerard clearly when he was supposed to have returned later that evening.'

Bruere half turned his head to exhale smoke. 'That wasn't our only evidence, Mrs Walker. We have Gerard's fingerprints … and his alone … on the gas fittings. The same gas fittings that you were trying to get removed.'

• • • • •

Marnie spent the journey home gazing out of the train window in a state of confusion. What on earth was going on? Could the police seriously believe she was participating in a conspiracy? And why had Charles asked her to take *Perfidia* away for repairs when Bruere had specifically told him the boat had to remain untouched?

It was all a mess. *Perfidia* was still in Little Venice with no repairs carried out. Jock Mackenzie had not been best pleased when Marnie phoned to say she had to let him down – even though it was not her fault. Marnie had got up before the cockerel and wasted half a day, with the added bonus of finding herself once again on the wrong side of the police.

Exasperated and bewildered, she was back in the office at Glebe Farm in time to join Ralph and Anne for lunch. Anne was heating soup in the kitchen area and waved towards Marnie as she entered.

'Hi! You've got some messages on your desk. There's one from Mike Brent.'

Marnie pealed off her coat and flopped down at the desk. 'He's supposed to be away with flu.'

'Yeah. He sounded awful.'

Marnie picked up the phone and pressed buttons.

'British Waterways Little Venice, good afternoon.'

'Hallo. This is Marnie Walker. I have a message to ring Mike Brent.'

'Er ... I'm not sure if he's still here. Hold on.'

Two clicks.

'Marnie, hi. I believe you were trying to get hold of me.' He sounded weary and slightly breathless.

'Ah yes ... that was yesterday. How are you feeling?'

'Been better.'

'I wanted to ask you about a mooring for *Perfidia*. That's rather been overtaken by events now.'

'*Perfidia*? Why did you want a mooring for her?'

'I'm handling things for Charles Taverner ... in view of ... well, you know.'

'Of course. I didn't realise you were involved, Marnie.'

'After my visit this morning that's probably not quite the way to put it. I came down especially to get her to Jock's boatyard – Charles wants a complete check-over and redec before selling – and the police picked me up.'

'The *police*?'

'It's a long story, Mike. The point is, they won't release her at present. So I suppose I do need a mooring after all.'

'Mm ...'

'Are you okay?'

'Just thinking ... Did they say how long they wanted to keep her here?'

'Didn't give a date. I'm sorry, Mike, it's rather out of my hands for now.'

'We'll find somewhere for her ... may have to box and cox. We've got some boats out for a while, but they'll be returning soon.'

'I don't like to burden you.' She felt like saying, *You sound like hell*. 'You've got enough on your plate.'

'Don't worry ... not your fault. I'll be glad to help.'

'You must've known the Taverners from their time in Little Venice.'

'Sure. I knew them quite well. Nice couple ... lovely boat. We'll take care of her.'

'Did you say you were taking her to Jock's place?'

'Yes. That'll be another day used up.'

There was a pause. 'I could take her there if that would help.'

'To Bull's Bridge?'

'Depending on when they release her.'

'Oh no ... that would be asking too much.'

'Marnie, it would be doing me a favour. I don't want an extra boat here any longer than absolutely necessary. I'd get her down there as soon as they give the word.'

It was the best news she had had all day.

11

As the weeks went by there were regular references in the press to the *Little Venice Murder*, most of them containing salacious details about Barbara's infidelity with her lover. Marnie could hardly bear to read the reports. They trivialised Barbara's death as the result of a meaningless tiff about nothing. The only good news was that the police did not pursue any further the possibility of Marnie's involvement or her alleged acquaintance with Neil Gerard.

During that time Marnie finalised the plans for the vicarage, the contract for the sale of *The Old Rectory* was completed and Angela moved into cottage number three at Glebe Farm. Marnie and Ralph presented her with a name plaque, *The New Vicarage*, which they hung on the wall beside the front door. She could take it with her to the new house when it was finished.

Marnie wondered if Charles would ever live in the village and suspected that he would only keep the house long enough to complete his contract with her. She had little contact with him apart from the occasional brief reply to her questions on the scheme design and on matters of detail. *I leave that to your judgment,* became a standard message. Marnie took it to mean, *I don't really care …*

• • • • •

The trial began in March and lasted just a few weeks. Charles did not attend the proceedings, except when he was called to give evidence about his whereabouts at the time of the murder, his wife's state of mind and details about her boating experiences. He stated that he knew nothing of her liaison with Gerard. He had never heard of him and had never met him. Barbara had always seemed happy with their life together, and he admitted that he gave her total freedom to pursue her own interests – his role as chairman of a large City finance house making it difficult for him to take as much leisure time as he would have wished. He came close to breaking down a number of times while giving his testimony, but managed to maintain a dignified composure and seemed to gain the sympathy and respect of the jurors.

The press reports revealed that Neil Gerard and Barbara had been lovers for two years, which the accused man freely admitted. He gave his testimony in a calm, quiet voice, answering each question succinctly and without hesitation. He had met Barbara while covering the London Boat Show as a journalist and they had had a drink together in the bar. They had seen each other on all three days of the event – Barbara always bought a season ticket for the show; he was there to work – and they had agreed to get together afterwards 'for a drink some time'. He insisted that Barbara had phoned him a week or so later to suggest lunch. Their next meeting had been at his instigation. He was writing a test report on a luxury river boat on the Thames, and they agreed to spend the day together cruising the upper reaches.

Two parts of his evidence shocked the court. The first was that Gerard made no attempt to produce an alibi. He admitted that he and Barbara had had a heated argument on the afternoon of her death. He described it as a 'silly row about nothing that Barbara blew up out of all proportion'. It was as if she wanted to pick a fight. He thought the only way to calm the situation was for him to leave her to cool off. He agreed he had left the boat with Barbara shouting after him, and his defence counsel stressed that this proved the accused had left the boat while the deceased was still alive. Counsel for the prosecution did not contest this point.

Where had he gone? Instead of returning to his flat, he went to his sister's house. She had been divorced for some years and lived alone. He went to see her because she had gone down with flu and he was worried about her. The court prepared itself for her corroborative testimony. Gerard admitted that when he arrived, letting himself in with his own key so as not to disturb his sister, he found her sleeping. He stayed for the night, using the sofa in the living room as a bed. In the early hours of the morning – he could not be sure exactly when it was – she woke up coughing, and he made her a hot lemon and honey drink. She had sipped this and gone back to sleep. The next day was Saturday, and Gerard stayed for the weekend, nursing his sister as she began to improve.

When questioned about his movements he was adamant that he did not return to *Perfidia* that Friday evening. He claimed he was at his sister's house all night and knew nothing of Barbara's death until the following morning when he heard the news on the radio. Why didn't he go to the police? His evidence could have been valuable. He said that he regretted not coming forward, but was sure his account could do nothing to help. With hindsight he wished he had gone to the authorities at once.

The second shock came when his sister, Sarah Cowan, gave her account of that night's events. Did her brother come to her house? Yes. Did he stay the night? *He did.* Was she certain? *No. I was asleep, probably delirious. I had no idea about the time of his arrival.* Could he have gone out again while she was sleeping? Yes. Did she wake in the night and find him there? Did he give her a lemon and honey drink? *Yes and yes.* When was that? *I can't tell you. I felt too drowsy to know.* Did the drink contain alcohol? *I assume it did. It was an old family remedy, and we usually made it with rum.* So it would make you go to sleep? *It could have that effect, but I was feeling very weak and unwell and it wouldn't have taken much to knock me out.*

The testimony revealed Gerard to be a caring and devoted brother, but as each question was put and each answer given – without wavering or hesitation – it began to dawn on the jury that she was not giving her brother an alibi. Their stories coincided in every way, but the consistency only made Gerard's situation worse. She was so ill that he decided to stay to look after her. Therefore she could not vouch for every minute – or even hour – of his presence. Was she saying that she could not – or would not – help her brother by providing him with an alibi? *I'm answering your questions to the best of my ability.* Would it not be easy to say that her brother had stayed in the house all night? Yes. Did she believe in her own mind that he had done so? *Yes, definitely.* Then why did she not simply testify to that effect? *Because I swore on oath to tell the truth and that's what I'm doing.* Wasn't she being rather naive in this? *No. Neil didn't kill Barbara Taverner. I know he didn't. So there'll be no evidence to prove he did.*

The prosecution gave Sarah Cowan an easy ride. They had no reason to treat her as a hostile witness, and there was no one else who could corroborate her brother's story, arriving at her house in a quiet street after dark on a cold winter's evening.

When the police gave their evidence, the trap closed round Neil Gerard. Barbara had died from asphyxiation caused by inhaling gas. She had drunk an excessive amount of alcohol, taken in conjunction with sleeping pills, and had died from carbon monoxide poisoning. The source of the gas had been the butane supply on *Perfidia*. Investigation had revealed that someone had tampered with a valve under the sink unit in the galley. Fingerprints were found on the faulty valve. They belonged to Neil

Gerard. He explained that he had checked the whole system at Barbara's request. There were no other fingerprints on any part of the gas connections, even though Gerard insisted that Barbara had had others – whom he could not name – look at the pipework, because she had been concerned about it.

The case for the prosecution could not have been simpler. Neil Gerard and Barbara were lovers and had had a row that afternoon. On that same evening Barbara had been drugged with sleeping tablets while drinking alcohol and had been poisoned by gas. There was no question of her committing suicide. Gerard could not prove his whereabouts, and a witness had testified that she had seen him return much later. His fingerprints – and his alone – were to be found on the faulty gas pipes that had led to Barbara's death. The Queen's Counsel summing up for the prosecution did not use the term, *an open-and-shut case*, but several newspapers described it that way when they reported the next morning that Neil Gerard had been found guilty of murder by a unanimous verdict and had been sentenced to life imprisonment.

They also reported that when the verdict was announced after less than two hour's deliberation by the jury, Neil Gerard had slumped forward, needing to be supported by the guards in the dock, and his sister had collapsed in the gallery.

• • • • •

The tabloids ran the story for a week, with scenes of Little Venice to add local colour, and photos of Barbara pulled out of the archives showing her in glamorous dresses attending functions in the City of London, at her husband's side leaving Buckingham Palace after he received his CBE, at Wimbledon for the tennis championships, at Henley for the regatta, at various charity events, and at Royal Ascot, complete with hat.

Of Neil Gerard the papers had little to show. He had spent most of his adult life behind the scenes, behind the camera. A long-range shot of him being led away after the trial, standing in a yard at the back of the court building, waiting to board the prison van, was so grainy that he was barely recognisable.

Marnie felt drawn by sheer curiosity about the life of the friend she almost had, and as she scanned each article she marvelled at how little she had known of Barbara's world and her secret love affair with the man who had touched her own life, however fleetingly.

As suddenly as it had burst into the news, the story was dropped. The front pages were taken over by a new scandal. The star of a television soap opera admitted to a 'sex romp' with the wife of a Premiership footballer. For once Marnie was grateful to the tabloids for their voracious appetite for titillation.

By the time the question arose of an appeal in the matter of Regina versus Gerard, it was relegated to the inner pages, where brief notes recorded that the motion had been denied. There was no new evidence; the police had carried out their investigation by the book; the trial had been conducted according to the letter of the law; the conviction was safe. No appeal. A life sentence. Open and shut.

'The trouble with boating in the spring is you have to take so much gear because of the vagaries of the weather.'

As if to prove her point, Marnie stowed her bulging kit bag behind the seat on the train, squeezing it in to fill the entire space, and flopped down while Anne did the same with hers on the other side of the aisle. Both were breathing heavily. The train was half empty. It was Saturday morning, too early for shoppers making their way to the London stores, too late for those unfortunate commuters who had to work at the weekend.

'You'd think we were setting off to the Caribbean rather than just popping down to Bull's Bridge.' Anne took the seat opposite Marnie. 'Still, it'll be a nice change to be on a boat again for a real trip, even if it is just one night away.'

This was an impromptu journey. Mike Brent had phoned on Thursday; the police had notified him that *Perfidia* was no longer in quarantine, and the boat could be moved at any time. He had liaised with Jock Mackenzie at Bull's Bridge boatyard and had been told gruffly that the works could be fitted in, provided it was in his yard by Monday morning first thing.

Marnie had sent an e-mail to Charles, with whom she had had no contact for a few weeks, and he had surprised her by phoning back without delay. Could Marnie arrange for *Perfidia* to be at the yard in that time? They worked out a hasty plan of action. Ralph was going to be away, so there were no complications on the domestic front. Angela would be at the cottage – *The New Vicarage* – and would take care of Dolly.

Ralph had dropped them off at the station on his way to a two-day seminar in Oxford. So here they were, dressed in jeans and weatherproof jackets, ready for whatever the fickle climate could throw at them. As soon as the train pulled out of the station Marnie went to stand by the doors at the end of the carriage and dug out her mobile. Mike Brent picked up after the third ring.

'We're on our way, Mike … should be at the boat in about an hour or so.'

'It's good of you to do this, Marnie. I'm really sorry I couldn't keep my promise and take her to Bull's Bridge. The family's got a lot on this weekend.'

'No problem. We're looking forward to the trip. Anne's coming with me. You wouldn't believe how much kit we've brought … just in case.'

'Is she in the same place as before?'

'No. That's another reason I'll be glad to see her gone. At the moment she's down towards *Sally Ann*'s old mooring, but on the south side, Maida Avenue, near the church.'

'Whose mooring is she on?'

'You know Kay and Bruce … the Bentincks … their boat *Annabel*? They're down on the Thames, due back this weekend.'

'Don't worry, they can have their slot back. We'll have her out of there pronto. I'm sorry we couldn't have shifted her sooner.'

'Not your fault, Marnie. But it's been a nightmare. I've had *Perfidia* all over the place … Blomfield Road, Paddington Basin, Lisson Grove, Cumberland Basin … I even had her up by Camden Lock for a week.'

'You've had a lot of congestion?'

'It's been *murder* … Oh God … sorry … I didn't mean … sorry …'

'It's okay, Mike … just a turn of phrase.'

'Yeah.' He cleared his throat. 'A lot of folk got caught out by the lock closures this winter. Everything seemed to be running late, and most of the work on the southern sections only started after the new year. Well, you know that yourself.'

'Never mind, it'll all be sorted now.'

'Thanks a lot, Marnie.'

'Hey, Mike, this could be a record.'

'Go on.'

'I'm phoning from the train and I haven't yet had to tell you I'm going into a tunnel. I'd better go.'

• • • • •

Anne was studying the cruising guide, her lips moving as if she was praying silently, when Marnie got back to her seat.

'I make it around fourteen miles, with no locks. So that means roughly … three and a half hours of actual travelling time?'

'Plus time to check the boat over before we go,' Marnie added. She lowered her voice to almost a whisper. 'We'll need to make sure we can operate the heating system, but the rest of the gas has been switched off.'

'I've been thinking about that. How do we wash and do the washing up?'

'*Perfidia*'s equipped with an inverter, and there's an electric kettle on board. We can shower when we get home tomorrow.'

Anne nodded. 'Then there's the time we'll need at Kensal Green to get some provisions at the supermarket. I'm looking forward to that. It'll be fun tying up outside and wheeling our trolley out to the boat.'

'Anne, we'll be buying a pack of croissants, some bread, coffee, milk and a few things like that. This is not a cruise on the *Oriana*. Anyway, they have a grid to stop trolleys finding their way out onto the canalside and diving in for a refreshing dip.'

'It'll still make a nice change from going in the car and having to drive round to find a parking space.'

Marnie smiled. 'You're excited about going on this trip, aren't you?'

'Of course I am.'

'And it doesn't bother you that – '

'Marnie, I thought you said we weren't going to mention that.'

'Sorry.'

• • • • •

Arriving at Little Venice by taxi from Euston, the first sight that met their eyes as they approached *Perfidia*'s mooring was a police car. Marnie froze.

She unlocked the gate onto the towpath, and they walked the short distance to *Perfidia*, passing a handful of other boats on the way. A uniformed constable was standing on the path outside the boat, and Marnie expected him to turn her away, but he simply wished them good morning and moved aside to let them go aboard. Marnie left Anne with the kit bags on the bank and stepped down through the side doors into the saloon. Two men were seated at the table and stood up when Marnie entered.

'Ah, Marnie, good morning.' Charles Taverner took her hand and kissed her on both cheeks. 'You know Chief Inspector Bruere, I believe.'

Bruere restricted his greeting to shaking hands. By his standards he was moderately cordial.

'Another problem?' Marnie tried not to stress the word *another*.

'Not really. I phoned Mr Bruere to make sure it was in order to move *Perfidia*. I didn't want you to come all the way here to find the boat impounded, as happened last time. That was a misunderstanding on my part, I'm afraid.'

Marnie nodded. 'You had a lot on your mind, Charles.'

'We've finished with the boat, Mrs Walker,' Bruere confirmed.

Marnie thought that summed up Charles's point of view, too. 'So I can get her repaired at the boatyard? You've no objection?'

'None.'

'Then, do you mind if I ask why you're here?'

Bruere gave a hint of a smile. 'Nothing sinister. I arranged to meet Mr Taverner to hand over the boat in person. We've been through a lot together, and he's been very co-operative. It's the least I could do.' He turned to Charles. 'Thank you, sir. Good-bye. I'll leave you to it.'

At the sight of Bruere climbing out of the boat, Anne's eyes widened. He said something to her quietly and walked away with the constable. Marnie watched him go, reflecting on the kind of treatment reserved for a VIP, a captain of industry. Charles helped bring in the bags and suggested a cup of coffee before they departed. In the galley Marnie saw a carton of provisions on the worktop. There were two bottles of wine, one red, one white.

'I got you a few stores to save you having to bother. This evening and tomorrow lunchtime, I figured you'd prefer eating out somewhere rather than cooking for yourselves.' He pointed to an envelope on the bench. 'I'd like you to be my guests. That should cover it.'

Charles waved Marnie's protests away with a hand. 'Marnie, if we were out travelling together, you wouldn't think it unusual – even for a young woman of your generation – for me to invite you to a meal.'

'That's not the same thing, Charles.'

'No, you're right. On this occasion you're making a journey on my business. Think of it as travel and subsistence expenses rather than as a personal invitation, if you prefer it that way. I am still a client, you know.'

'You've got it all worked out … got all the answers.'

'Please accept, Marnie … and Anne. You're doing this for me, and I'd like to do something in return for you.'

During this exchange Anne retreated to the galley where she heated water and began putting the provisions away. Marnie had been wondering why Charles had really taken the trouble to come to the boat to see them off. A phone call would have sufficed to check that the police were in agreement. She was soon to find out.

Standing in the saloon, Charles spoke quietly. 'This is where they found her.'

Marnie tried to keep her voice steady. 'I know.'

'Marnie, there's something I have to ask you. Do you mind?'

'I don't know the details, Charles … only what was in the papers.'

'You'll think I'm dim, but I don't know about the technical side of boats.'

Marnie shook her head. 'No I won't. I live with one of the most intelligent men in the country – Ralph's a professor at Oxford – and he's a complete technophobe. Anne had to give him lessons in operating his mobile phone.'

A faint smile momentarily crossed Charles's face. 'What actually happened, Marnie?'

'As far as I understand, there was a leaking gas pipe back there in the galley.'

'Barbara had no idea about it? She never mentioned it to you?'

'Well actually … it wasn't exactly expressed as a specific worry … I mean, about a particular leak, but … Barbara had mentioned to me that she wanted the gas system overhauled.'

Charles looked aghast. 'Really? She suspected it was dangerous?'

'No, it wasn't quite like that. She said she wanted it checked to make sure it complied with the new boat safety regulations. I included it on the list of things to be done when the boat went in for servicing.'

'I see … So what actually happened to the gas system?'

Marnie shrugged. She wanted this conversation to end before Anne came back with the coffee. Why was he asking this? Charles knew the evidence as well as she did. He picked up on her thoughts.

'I was too distraught to take in all the technical details at the trial, Marnie.'

'Apparently Gerard tampered with the pipework … loosened something when he returned that evening.'

'Didn't his barrister say it could've worked its way loose because of vibration?'

'Yes.'

'Do you believe that, Marnie?'

'I doubt it. Boats are safe if they're properly maintained. The prosecution said the boat was smooth-running … had the latest engine mountings to reduce vibration.'

'I'm sure that's true. The boat cost enough. Does your boat vibrate, Marnie?'

'Sometimes, a little, but she's old. And you don't really notice it. Boats are very solid.'

'When I was cross-examined, the defence counsel asked if we'd ever bumped into anything … if we'd ever rammed a hard surface'

'That's always possible on the water, Charles. There are lots of things to bump into.'

'No. You never saw Barbara steering. She was top class … won prizes. She didn't make mistakes.'

'*Perfidia* could've been rammed by another boat.'

'I thought of that. There's not a mark anywhere on the hull. I checked.'

A tinkling of crockery could be heard in the galley. Anne was loading a tray.

'Where's this line of thought leading, Charles? You're not having doubts, are you?'

'No. I just wanted to be clear in my mind about everything … just wanted … closure, you know.'

Marnie touched his arm lightly. 'I understand.'

Charles moved quickly to take the tray from Anne. While they drank and ate chocolate Bath Olivers, Charles asked about their plans for the journey to Bull's Bridge. He insisted that all their expenses for travelling to London should be included with the costs of the work, otherwise he would make his own estimate and add it to the bill. He stayed only long enough to finish his cup.

When he left, Marnie stepped out with him onto the bank and walked as far as the gate to the pavement.

'I hope you can feel settled, Charles … that you'll find what you need …'

'Yes.' In that one word it sounded as if there were still doubts in his mind. 'It's just … that Gerard chap … somehow he didn't strike me as being the mechanical type. You'd need to know what you're doing to cause a leak by loosening a compression joint.'

'He was a boating journalist, Charles …'

'Mm … Not a good idea to dwell on it, is it, Marnie? I keep wondering about Barbara's last moments … what it must've been like … how she died …'

Marnie felt a sudden contraction in her throat, a difficulty breathing, and tears came into her eyes. She could barely speak.

'It would be a gentle way to go, Charles … just like falling asleep.'

Charles leaned forward and kissed Marnie on the cheek. He turned and walked away without another word and without looking back.

• • • • •

They had no difficulty manoeuvring *Perfidia* out of her mooring. They only had to push out the stern, while the bow thruster moved the front end away from the bank. It was the first time Marnie had ever used one, her first reminder of the level of equipment on Barbara's boat. The engine responded with a whisper, a far cry from the clanking of *Sally Ann*'s old Lister, and they slid quietly along the last stretch of the Regent's Canal to the pool of Little Venice, passed Browning Island where the willow tree was just coming into leaf and headed west along the Paddington Arm of the Grand Union. Marnie kept the speed down to dead slow until they left behind the last of the moored boats. Neither had spoken since the engine had come to life.

Marnie handed the tiller to Anne and rested her elbows on the hatch cover. They were standing close together on the steerer's tiny stern deck.

'What length is *Perfidia*?' Anne asked.

'Fifty-two, I think.'

'She steers nicely.'

Marnie continued gazing at the houses lining the route.

'Marnie … are you all right?'

'Mm …'

'Something's bothering you, isn't it? Was it your conversation with Mr Taverner? I kept out of the way so you could talk in private.'

'And you tinkled the cups to announce you were coming back. Thanks.'

'I feel really sorry about what's happened to him … well, to Barbara as well, of course … but he's the one who has to go on living with it all.'

'Yeah …'

'There's something else bothering you, isn't there? Not just feeling sad for Mr Taverner. Shall I shut up and leave you in peace?'

Marnie touched her friend's hand on the tiller. 'Course not. But you're partly right.'

'I knew there was something. How d'you mean *partly right*?'

'There were two things …'

'*Two things*. What are they?'

'I don't know … that's the trouble.'

'You must have *some* idea, Marnie. *Something* must've prompted you. What made you think there were two?'

Marnie stared back into her memory. 'I think the first time was when we arrived … and saw the police car.'

'It made you worried that something had happened to the boat … or *on* the boat?'

'I don't think so. It was just a vague feeling … like a question … or a doubt.'

'What was the other time?'

'I had another feeling … it was about the time we cast off from the mooring back there … when I returned on board … I'd just said good-bye to Charles … No, it's no good.' Marnie pointed ahead. 'Boat coming!'

'I see it.'

Anne pulled gently on the tiller, and *Perfidia* responded smoothly, moving a fraction to the right from mid-channel. Moments later they passed the other boat left-to-left. A man and woman were standing together at the stern, and they both nodded a greeting as they went by. At the last minute the woman glanced at *Perfidia* before turning quickly to say something to the man at the helm. Both looked back at Marnie and Anne, frowning and speaking to each other.

'What's up?' said Anne, worried. 'Is something wrong with the boat?'

'No. I was expecting this. That's the first time it's happened. It won't be the last. We've just been recognised – or rather *Perfidia* has. We're travelling on what is currently the most notorious boat on the waterways. There's hardly anyone in the country who hasn't heard of *Perfidia* since the *Little Venice Murder* made the news.'

Ten minutes later another boat passed. This time they knew the crew – the Bentincks whose mooring they had just vacated – and they waved to each other in friendly fashion. Marnie guessed the Little Venice crowd would be glad to see the back of *Perfidia*.

After they had been travelling for half an hour they cruised past Porto Bello dock and came in sight of the gasholders at Kensal Green.

'Marnie … because Mr Taverner brought us those supplies, it doesn't mean we won't be going to the supermarket, does it?'

Marnie grinned. 'You like the idea of tying up there and going to the shop.'

'Well … we could do with one or two more things …'

'Such as?'

'I've almost finished my magazine, and er … we could use a couple of KitKats to have with our coffee while we're travelling this afternoon … or tomorrow morning.'

'Urgent necessities of boating life,' Marnie agreed.

'Great.' Anne joyfully handed back the tiller and went forward along the gunwale to prepare the mooring rope for arrival.

'I hope the visit will live up to expectations,' Marnie murmured to herself.

• • • • •

It took them less than ten minutes to complete their tour of the supermarket. They tied up close to the entrance, locked *Perfidia* and went in. The problem was when they came out. A small crowd had gathered on the bank, and several people were jostling each other for position, trying to look in through the portholes and windows. One man was standing on the counter, holding on to the tiller while his wife photographed him. Marnie muttered something at him in passing and, once she had gone by, he gave her the finger behind her back. Anne wanted to strangle him, but she suspected that might not help the situation, and the best thing to do was get away as soon as they could.

Pulling the boat key from her pocket, Marnie pushed her way through the onlookers and opened the central door. Some of the people took this as a signal to surge forward and try to stick their heads in through the opening.

'Excuse me!' Marnie eased herself between the interlopers and turned to go backwards down the steps into the cabin.

Anne had less luck. Her attempt to follow Marnie on board was met with resistance and the suggestion that she should wait her turn. Becoming crowded in, Marnie drew the doors closed leaving Anne stranded outside. A movement caught her eye; framed in a porthole, she saw Marnie's hand pointing towards the stern. Without hesitating, Anne withdrew and walked quickly back towards the tiller. She reached it just as the stern doors flew open. The man, who had been posing so confidently a minute before, jumped in surprise, moved smartly backwards and stepped into air. He paused for a split second before obeying the laws of gravity and dropped straight down into the canal. The sound of his squawking was subsumed into the splash of the fall. His initial landing place left him waist-deep in water, but flapping his arms wildly about him, he staggered in a scrappy interpretation of backstroke, briefly going under before regaining his footing and emerging like Moby Dick or a merman from the deep.

The crowd surged along the bank to get a better view of the spectacle, while the man's wife screamed and all but dropped the camera in her panic to go to his aid. Spitting water and wiping his face with a slimy hand, the merman began shouting abuse at Marnie who had now come out onto the counter.

She shrugged, palms up. 'I didn't touch you.' Her face was a picture of innocence. 'You came on board uninvited, at your own risk, and I asked you to leave.'

Merman staggered and almost lost his balance again, splashing about in the murky water. 'You … you … I'll …'

Marnie leaned down. 'The first thing *you* have to do is seek medical attention. You risk getting Weil's disease, going in the water like that.' She pronounced it, *Vile's disease.*

'What on earth's that?' merman's wife asked, horrified. 'It sounds *ghastly.*'

'I suppose it's like a kind of plague,' Marnie explained calmly. 'It's carried in rat's urine.'

With a gasp, the woman looked as if she was going to pass out. Her husband became silent and still and seemed to change colour under the coating of mud and weeds that partly decorated his features. The crowd on the canalside retreated a few paces, leaving space for Anne to reach the aft mooring rope, which she promptly untied. She pushed the stern away from the bank, well clear of the aquatic man, who was now attempting to slither out onto the path. Marnie switched on the engine.

No one rushed to help merman, though the whole crowd was mesmerised by his efforts to clamber out of the water, assisted by the feeble flutterings of his wife. By now, Anne had reached the front mooring rope. Releasing it and coiling it in the bows, she pushed firmly off from the canalside, forgetting they had a bow thruster, and made her way nimbly back along the gunwale to the counter. The push had the effect of swinging the stern round again towards the man who had just failed in his latest effort to crawl out.

It was not out of compassion or altruism that Marnie called over to the spectators. She was reluctant to engage the engine and set the screw turning with a man in the water near the stern. She pointed beyond the crowd.

'Why don't you throw him the lifebelt? He can put it round his waist and you can help him climb out without getting yourselves dirty.'

After a few seconds' hesitation, one person began unhooking the lifebelt from its frame. Merman waited dejectedly in the dark and cloudy water, and Marnie began to feel sorry for him. She was consoled to see Anne kneel down to speak softly to him before he turned away to catch the lifebelt. With the crowd pulling on the rope like Volga boatmen, and the man scrambling a leg up to the bank, Marnie put *Perfidia* in gear and guided her out into mid-channel.

She spoke to Anne over the gentle humming of the engine. 'I'm glad you said something to him. He looked as if he was in need of solace.'

Anne looked back to where merman was now lying on the bank like a beached whale as his wife twittered about him, and the crowed stared. 'I wouldn't exactly say I brought him solace.'

'No? I thought I saw you speaking to him back there.'

'I simply pointed out that boarding a boat without permission and seizing the tiller counted as an act of piracy under maritime law and could have serious consequences. I didn't want him thinking he could sue us.'

'Maritime law!' Marnie smiled to herself as she accelerated away, steering the boat past the cemetery and the power station. 'You know, Anne, you're all heart ...'

Looking back one last time, she saw the windows of the supermarket packed with people enjoying the spectacle that had livened up their shopping trip.

· · · · ·

After half an hour of cruising between industrial sites Marnie gave the tiller to Anne. Since their eventful stop at the supermarket Marnie had been deep in thought.

Under Anne's command, *Perfidia* eased her way smoothly onto the aqueduct over the North Circular Road, her engine barely a murmur in contrast to the thundering of the traffic below. Anne glanced down at the rushing vehicles, most of whose drivers had no idea the canal was running above their heads, and enjoyed the feeling shared by all boaters, that they are privileged, using a secret path that sets them apart from the normal world. But Marnie seemed to take no pleasure in their exclusive highway and concentrated instead on the cruising guide that she pored over intently on the hatch cover.

As if suddenly noticing the North Circular, Marnie looked up distractedly, blinked and turned to Anne. She pointed at the cruising guide and planted her finger on the open page.

'There.'

• • • • •

The change of plan suited Anne well. She much preferred the idea of eating on *Perfidia* rather than going to a pub, though she wanted to be sure they had enough provisions on board to make a reasonable meal. Handing the tiller back to Marnie, she went below to the galley to investigate the food situation. It was some time before Anne reappeared on the counter. She brought with her two mugs of tea and two bars of KitKat and confirmed that Charles had provided 'breakfast food' of a sufficient amount to feed them that evening.

Muttering that it would do them no harm to live modestly for one night, Marnie tried the tea. 'Mm … this is *good*.'

'Lapsang Souchong,' Anne explained.

'Well, if this is the standard of Charles's breakfast, we won't be roughing it too badly.'

Anne sipped her tea in silence.

• • • • •

They reached the mooring spot without encountering any other boats, and few people noticed their passing. On the north side of the canal rolling parkland extended up into the distance, and the cruising guide revealed that it was a golf course. On the towpath side they were sheltered by woodland. This was a secluded landscape, and it was hard to believe they were in the suburbs of the capital, with central London just a bus ride away.

Marnie chose to secure *Perfidia* to trees that overhung the water from the golf course side, even though this was private land and, technically, they were trespassing. She took a chance that no one would see the boat there and ask them to move on. The alternative was to moor alongside the towpath, which they had every right to do. But Marnie was concerned about being seen by passers-by and attracting unwanted attention if the boat was recognised. If harmless shoppers could cause a nuisance outside a supermarket in broad daylight, what problems might they have in this lonely place after dark?

She was checking the forward mooring rope when Anne looked out from the cratch doors.

'Marnie, I've got an idea. D'you think it could rain in the night?'

'Doubt it. I think the forecast is dry. Why do you ask?'

'I've found a dark blue sheet in the locker. What if we draped it over the boat to cover the name? That would make us anonymous.'

They adopted Anne's idea, holding the sheet in place with flower tubs on the roof and stones found under the trees on the gunwale. When their camouflage was completed they settled down to watch the early evening news on television in the saloon, and by the time the programme had finished they looked out to discover that dusk was falling. Anne volunteered to make supper while Marnie checked the cruising guide and finalised their plans for the next day.

As Anne headed for the galley Marnie remarked that it had been nice of Charles to bring food for them.

'Oh, he didn't bring it,' Anne replied. 'He had it delivered.'

Marnie was already engrossed in calculating distances and failed to grasp the significance of the reply.

• • • • •

Anne suggested that Marnie take her shower before eating while she prepared supper. Recalling Somerset Maugham's dictum that the best way to eat in Britain – before the country became obsessed with food and celebrity chefs – was to have breakfast three times a day, Marnie was expecting something pleasant on her return.

Her first reaction was that having silver candlesticks on the table was OTT. Then she checked the table, which was covered by a cloth of white linen that contrasted well with the dark blue crockery. Marnie accepted Anne's invitation to take her seat.

'What's all this?'

'Posh breakfast à la Fortnum and Mason,' Anne announced with a flourish. 'Ahem. Sorry I didn't have time to get menus printed. We're dining – can't really call it breakfasting – on quails' eggs with smoked salmon – from Loch Fyne – gentlemen's relish on Melba toast, followed by strawberries from Andalusia and kiwi fruit. To drink, we have fresh orange juice, something sparkling that's in the fridge and ground coffee – Jamaican Blue Mountain blend – with cream. I don't think we'll need to break into the cornflakes, do you?'

Marnie laughed. 'Probably not. One thing surprises me, though. You didn't make Bucks Fizz with the orange juice and sparkling wine.'

'Actually, Marnie, I was going to do that ... until I saw what the fizz was.' Anne opened the fridge and produced a bottle of champagne. It was Veuve Clicquot '89. 'I didn't think it was right to ... dilute the orange juice.'

'Wise choice.'

• • • • •

Perfidia slipped her mooring at first light under an overcast sky. It had been a dry and quiet night; no one had detected their presence tucked into the bank by the golf course. Their breath vaporising in the chilly air, Marnie and Anne were glad of the warm clothing in their kit bags. They breakfasted on hot rolls and coffee taken at the tiller as they set off to cover the six miles or so to Bull's Bridge. With no locks ahead of them, Marnie estimated a journey time of around two hours maximum. The plan was to have Perfidia safely berthed at the boatyard while most people were enjoying their Sunday morning lie-in.

The vast city did not stir – not so much as a jogger on the towpath or an angler on the bank – while they cruised noiselessly through the suburbs. Eventually they passed under a railway bridge, and the junction with the main line of the Grand Union Canal came into view. Anne stood in the bows to watch for traffic while Marnie steered across to Jock Mackenzie's boatyard.

They were making ready to tie up alongside the boats that were moored two and three-deep at the bank when Marnie had an idea. She called Anne back to outline the plan, and Anne skipped across the other boats to go ashore. Loosening the mooring ropes of Jock's other clients, they eased them away from the wharf and slotted *Perfidia* in to the inside position where her name would be concealed behind the other craft.

Within half an hour of posting the boat's keys through the letterbox at Jock's office, Marnie and Anne were deposited by taxi at Euston station where they caught a West Coast express and headed for home.

Settling into their seats, Marnie had a sudden flash of memory.

'Anne, I was meaning to ask you ... When we were in Little Venice, Inspector Bruere said something to you when he left the boat. You were standing on the path with our bags and I'm sure I saw him speak to you when he went by. Do you remember?'

'Oh, yes ... He wanted to give me some words of encouragement for our trip.'

'Really? What did he say?'

'I think it was something along the lines of ... *sooner you than me* ...'

• • • • •

When Marnie did not go to the sleeping cabin on *Thyrsis* after her shower that night, Ralph put down his book, got out of bed and went to the stern.

'I knew I'd find you here.'

'Oh!' Marnie was standing by the doors dressed only in a thin bathrobe, looking out at the canal in the moonlight. 'Yes – as you've sometimes pointed out – I come here when I've got something on my mind. I didn't want to disturb you by ... brooding in the bed chamber.'

She spoke with a smile in her voice, but Ralph knew there was something bothering her.

'Do you want to talk about it?'

A hint of a sigh. 'There's more than one thing that concerns me, but only one that I can put into words ... and that's the strangest of all.'

'Very mysterious ...'

Marnie knew Ralph was not laughing at her. 'I had a lot on my mind so at the time I didn't pick up on the things that seemed wrong ... or at least unexpected. Then afterwards it was too late. All I had left was impressions of things not being right ... very frustrating.'

'What was the thing that you do remember ... the *strangest thing*?'

'It was Charles ... when he was asking questions about the gas system ... and he was talking about Neil Gerard. He made me wonder if he thought Gerard might not have done it.'

'Really? What did he say about him?'

'It's not what he said ... more the implied reasoning that lay behind his questions.'

'This is all very deep, Marnie.'

'I know. That's why I didn't want to come to bed fretting about it.'

'That's okay. We could've talked it over.'

'I know.' She took his hand and began leading the way back to the sleeping cabin. 'I didn't want to do that ... I had other ideas ...'

13

It had not worked out as she expected. The journey from Little Venice to the Bull's Bridge boatyard was meant to be cathartic, drawing a line under the tragedy of Barbara's death. Marnie realised that her contact with Charles would continue, though she suspected it would be of relatively short duration, until all the renovations of the vicarage were completed. Then, no doubt, the house would be sold, Charles would move away – if in fact he ever moved in – and life in Knightly St John would return to normality. In time folk memory would exist only as a vague recollection that a person who had lived briefly in the old vicarage was connected with some murder case down in London. And that would be that.

Marnie had hoped that moving *Perfidia* would be the first step in distancing herself from the whole sad episode. She would collect the boat from Jock Mackenzie, carry out the redec, transport it to Braunston and get it sold. There would be no more journeys on *Perfidia*, just perhaps the occasional sighting as it cruised past on the canal, the new owners raising a hand, a cup, a glass in her direction as they travelled on their way, probably oblivious of the boat's history and of Marnie's involvement in it.

Instead, the day after their return from London, Marnie felt jaded. These were no Monday blues. Spring was slowly settling in. It should be a season of optimism, looking forward to longer, warmer days ahead, outings on the canal, picnics and barbecues, new crops, new lambs in the fields, new challenges, the reaffirmation of life. But no. Marnie struck the desk gently with her fist.

'Is that the new signal that it's time for me to make coffee, Ô Master?'

Anne stood in the doorway, grinning. She had been studying on *Sally Ann* and now joined Marnie for their morning break.

'Heavens, is it that time already?' Marnie shook her head. 'I can't seem to settle this morning.'

'What's up? Withdrawal symptoms from the boat trip? I wish we could've carried on for a week.'

Marnie slumped forward, elbows on the desk, chin resting on her hands. 'I'd tell Charles to get someone else to deal with *Perfidia* – and the house come to that – if it wouldn't feel like I was abandoning him.'

'Are you serious? I know it's been a horrible time, but I thought we were coming to the end of it now.'

'I'm serious about how I feel … but I can't let Charles down.'

'I'll make coffee … that'll cheer you up.' Anne headed for the kitchen area at the back of the office barn. She called over her shoulder. 'And don't forget … there's a big moment coming this week. The JCB is finally leaving the site. I'm planning to put up bunting and I've booked the band of the Coldstream Guards for the grand parade up the field track.'

Marnie laughed, albeit only gently. 'I'm surprised you haven't booked the Red Arrows for a fly past.' She went over to the kitchen and put an arm round her friend's shoulders. 'Idiot!' she said affectionately. 'Thank goodness you're here … you always cheer me up, even without the coffee. Actually … you've given me an idea …'

Deadpan. 'We can't really afford the Coldstream Guards, Marnie … it was meant to be a joke.'

Marnie tousled her hair. 'Now that is disappointing, but … what about having a celebration on a more modest scale? You could spare some time from your studies for a party, couldn't you?'

'No probs. As long as it takes place between five and five-fifteen on Sunday morning, I should be able to fit it into my schedule.'

'Perfect.'

Over coffee Marnie checked the forecast for the end of the week and opted for a lunch party on Saturday, outside in the courtyard. For the next hour she was on the phone inviting friends and family, a dozen or so in total. It would be her favourite kind of gathering, an informal grouping at a long table like the lunch breaks enjoyed by grape pickers during the wine harvest. She quickly wrote out a menu. There would be quiches, baked trout, salads, bowls of vegetables, followed by cheeses and fruit, all rounded off with Marnie's personal speciality, *tiramisoufflé*.

The idea and its planning had fired her with enthusiasm, and her earlier mood had evaporated. So it was that when the phone rang shortly before lunch she was feeling restored to her customary optimism.

'Marnie, it's Charles. I just wanted to say I picked up the message you left me on the answerphone … glad you got *Perfidia* to the yard without mishap. Thank you.'

'You're welcome. Jock will ring me as soon as the works are completed. You still want me to bring her up here and make arrangements to sell?'

'I do. We can discuss details when you're ready. There's no immediate rush. Can we talk about the house?'

'Sure. Most of the rooms are completed … just the hall and stairs now to be done. Carpets and curtains are due next week. We're on schedule.'

'Brilliant. I feel I'm in safe hands with you, Marnie.'

'Let's hope so. When would you like to come and see it … after it's all finished?'

'Actually, this is rather a busy time for me … winding up with the company and all that. I was wondering if I could come up at the weekend.'

A hesitation. 'This coming weekend, you mean?'

'Saturday would suit me best. Of course, I realise this would be imposing on your free time …'

'That's all right. Charles, would you be able to have lunch with us? We're having some friends round … mainly from the village. It would be an opportunity to meet people.'

Now was the chance to say he would not be coming to live in Knightly St John after all, and Marnie expected Charles to tell her so. But he surprised her.

'If you're sure it wouldn't be an imposition …'

'Not at all. It'll be an informal relaxing occasion, I promise you.'

• • • • •

Stringing up bunting around the courtyard at seven on Saturday morning was an act of faith. They had got up at six to find ominous clouds crawling across the sky with a cool breeze. But the local weather forecast was for a fine day, so they gritted their teeth and began preparations. Marnie and Anne worked in the galley on *Sally Ann*, using the kitchen area in the office barn for final touches and setting out ready for serving. Ralph put up the tables in the courtyard and acted as general factotum and dogsbody.

Well in advance of the arrival of their guests, they were ready for Charles's visit, and just before eleven he rang on his mobile to say he was approaching the village. Marnie set off in the Discovery to meet him at the vicarage joined by Angela from cottage number three. Anne went along to take notes.

Marnie swung the car in through the gateway and immediately had to brake hard. Standing in front of the building was a small Peugeot ahead of Charles's Jaguar.

'Do you recognise that car, Angela?'

The vicar craned forward in her seat. 'Never seen it before.'

They stepped down onto the drive as Charles climbed out of his car.

'Were you expecting a visitor, Charles?'

He shook his head, frowning. 'One of your contractors, perhaps, Marnie?'

'I don't think so.' She put a hand on the Peugeot's bonnet. 'Whoever it is, they haven't been here long … the engine's warm.'

'No sign of a break-in,' Angela muttered, scanning the building. 'I do hope we haven't got squatters in. Church properties have had that sort of problem before.' She began walking towards the front door when it opened.

A woman looked out. 'Oh, there you are. I was beginning to think no one was in.'

Charles advanced on her. 'Do you mind me asking what you're doing here?'

'I've come to see you, actually.' She spoke in a calm, matter-of-fact voice. In her thirties, dressed in jeans and a sweater, she was behaving as if they were calling in on her.

Charles raised an eyebrow in Marnie's direction. Marnie gave the slightest movement of her head in reply.

'Are you going to come in?' said the woman, standing aside in the doorway.

• • • • •

There were no chairs in the house, so they stood in the drawing room in an awkward grouping. One of the French windows was ajar, and the woman pointed at it.

'That's how I came in. It wasn't locked, which is why I thought someone must be at home. You couldn't leave anything unlocked like that in London … no knowing who might get in.'

Charles was looking agitated. 'Look, before this goes any further, I want you to tell me who you are and what you're doing breaking into my house.'

'I told you … I didn't break in. I just turned the handle and –'

'All right, all right. Why are you here? What's your name?'

'I'm Sarah Cowan.' She waited as if assuming that made everything clear.

The four people confronting her scoured their memories to try and recall where they had heard the name before. It was familiar to all of them, but none could identify it immediately.

Anne spoke first. 'From the trial,' she said softly.

'Good lord!' Charles looked stunned. 'You're …'

'Neil's sister,' the woman said evenly.

'Why have you come? How did you know I'd be here? I don't understand.' Another glance towards Marnie, who looked blank.

'It wasn't difficult finding the place. It was in all the papers … you'd bought a rectory in a village in Northamptonshire. I got on to the local press and found out which one … drove up, asked for the rectory in the little shop … and here I am.'

'And why *are* you here exactly? Can you give me one good reason why I shouldn't call the police and have you arrested for house breaking?'

'I've already told you I didn't –'

'Perhaps it would be an idea if you just said what you wanted.' Marnie interrupted her. 'You must've come here for a reason.'

Sarah Cowan looked at Marnie for the first time. 'Someone who talks sense.'

'And who would like an answer,' Marnie added.

'Are you with him?'

'We're all with him. Please stop avoiding the issue. Why are you here?'

'It's simple.' She turned back to Charles. 'I want you to help me get Neil released. He's innocent.' Pointedly she added, 'You know that.'

Charles looked as if he had been struck in the face. And at that moment Marnie gave a sharp intake of breath. Anne noticed it, but the others were staring at the newcomer.

'I think you should leave … now.' Charles's voice was dry, and he seemed to speak with difficulty.

'Threaten to call the police if you like, but I don't think you'd want the publicity. I wouldn't want it either … not yet anyway.'

'I don't think this is right.' Angela joined in. 'After all Mr Taverner has been through …It would be best if you left … please.'

'I've made a special journey. I'm not leaving until I've said what I came to say.'

'You gave your evidence at your brother's trial.' Charles stood clenching and unclenching his fists. 'You had your chance to clear him then. Whatever you say now won't make any difference. It's too late.'

'I told the truth at the trial. I'm telling the truth now. Neil did not kill your wife.'

'You said you couldn't swear to that. You were asleep.'

'I was ill, passing in and out of sleep. Half the country was down with flu that week. Every time I woke up and needed something, Neil was right there. But because of the state I was in, I couldn't swear on oath that he was there. Nevertheless, I know he was with me for the whole time. I know my brother.'

This was no impassioned speech. Every word was pronounced clearly in a calm, reasoned tone. However awkward the situation, none of them hearing Sarah Cowan doubted that she believed what she was saying.

'I'm trying to put it all behind me,' Charles said quietly. 'I don't know what you expect me to do. The court has decided. The motion for an appeal was rejected. Even if I could –'

'You could give support to my campaign … in public.'

'No … no. You must see that I can't get involved. This is a matter for the authorities. If you think you have a case you should go to the police … or a solicitor … your MP …'

'I am … I'm doing all that. That's the plan. And I'm going to the press and media. I'd stand a much better chance if you were with me.'

Angela filled the gap when Charles fell silent. 'Why would Mr Taverner want to help you? What you're asking of him doesn't seem reasonable.'

'Of course it's reasonable. It's more than *reasonable*. It's what he *needs*.'

Charles recovered his voice. 'What are you talking about? *What I need* …'

'That's why I came up here. You want the real killer to be found more than anyone else … perhaps even more than Neil. My brother didn't do it. So who did? That's what you need to know.'

· · · · ·

They stood outside the front door and watched the little Peugeot move off, as if they were seeing a guest on their way after a party. For some seconds after the car turned out of the drive they stood in silence, hearing the engine note fade away.

'Well …' Charles summed up their feelings in one word.

'Very strange,' Angela murmured.

Charles moved towards his car and turned to face Marnie. 'Would you mind very much … in the circumstances … if I didn't join your other guests on this occasion? I don't think I'd be very good company.'

'Are you all right, Charles? I mean, do you feel like driving? If you wanted, you could have a break on our boat … a cup of tea, at least …'

'Thank you, Marnie, but I'm sure I'll be fine. I'll just take it gently.'

Charles kissed Marnie on the cheek and nodded to Angela and Anne before driving off. They heard the tyres crunch on the gravel and watched the elegant car pull away, its engine a soft purring from twin exhausts.

Marnie breathed out, long and slow. 'Right. Well … we've got to get back in the mood for a lunch party now. Any takers?'

They walked down the track, the three of them coming to terms with the strange encounter. Marnie was surprised to find she was holding a business card. Sarah Cowan had thrust it on her as she left. What she expected of her, Marnie had no idea.

· · · · ·

Back in the office barn with Ralph, Marnie outlined what had happened. He listened intently until she reached the end of her narration and asked a surprising question.

'Did Charles seem to believe her … that Gerard was innocent?'

'*Believe* her? You mean, does Charles think there's some doubt about the verdict?'

'Not exactly. Up until now he hasn't given any sign of thinking they've convicted the wrong person, so I don't think he's had any positive thoughts along those lines. What I mean is, did he seem to think the sister had a point after hearing what she had to say?'

'I must be thick, Ralph, but I'm not sure I understand what you're getting at. He said the court had reached its verdict after taking everything into account. That's why an appeal wasn't allowed.'

'But did his reaction give a clue to any underlying thoughts on the matter?'

Anne butted in. 'Do you mean did it occur to him that the sister might be right … as if he might have had private doubts before … and she sort of reawakened them?'

'Yes. That's what I mean.'

Marnie reflected. 'That's a bit subtle for me. He didn't, er … fly off the handle and say he refuted her idea absolutely, if that's any indication.'

'Surely that would've been a natural reaction,' Ralph suggested. 'It's what I would've said … if I thought the sister was totally out of order.'

'Ye-e-es.'

'What did you think about what she said, Marnie?'

A shrug. 'A bolt out of the blue.'

'But Marnie,' Anne interjected. 'There was something that surprised you, wasn't there? You gave a reaction when she said that Mr Taverner knew her brother was innocent.'

'Did you, Marnie?' Ralph looked puzzled.

She forced her thoughts back into her memory. 'It was one of the things that didn't seem right when we were in Little Venice …'

'You said there were two things.'

'Yes, but up there at the vicarage, Sarah brought one of them back.'

'Charles said something in Little Venice that hinted that he believed Gerard wasn't the killer?'

'No … it wasn't as straightforward as that. It's very difficult to put into words … just a kind of impression, but it struck me at the time.'

'And something the sister said brought it back?'

'When we were on *Perfidia* with Charles, he asked me about the technical side of what happened … how Barbara was killed … said he was a technophobe – rather like you, Ralph – and I took that at face value.'

'That he was as technically-minded as I am?'

'Yes.'

Ralph rolled his eyes. Anne suppressed a smile.

'So I told him in very simple terms about how someone had tampered with the gas system … how it couldn't have been damaged by impact.'

'Presumably he understood what you told him?'

Marnie suddenly changed direction. 'Ralph, tell me what you know about the technical side of boating.'

He turned towards Anne. 'Do you have a postage stamp? You can write what I know on the back of it.'

Marnie grinned. 'I'm serious. Tell me.'

'Well, I must know more than most people, after all I've got a boat and I've done a fair bit of travelling. I know about checking the oil in the engine every now and then … turning the stern gland to keep the propshaft lubricated … oh, and there's the er – what d'you call it – the tube under the tiller. I put grease in that sometimes …'

'Go on.'

Ralph shrugged. 'That's about it, really.'

'And the other systems … gas, electrics, water?'

'I know where you turn them on and off. I know about setting the switch in the position to make sure the batteries are charging … which one is for starting the engine, which for domestic use …'

'Tell me about the compression joints, Ralph.'

'The *what?*' Bewilderment.

'The compression joints … what do you do with them?'

He shook his head. 'Never heard of them.'

'Yet you run a boat, you've lots of experience of travelling on it, even managing it single-handed. Have you never encountered problems?'

'Nothing major.'

'Why not? Because you look after the boat, including the technical side.'

'Of course. I may not be mechanical, but I'm not stupid. I follow a routine to keep it running properly. Anything goes wrong, I contact an engineer. Same as for the car. Marnie, what's the point of all this?'

'When Charles asked me to explain about the gas problem, I outlined the issues in simple terms. A little later he said he couldn't imagine Gerard being the sort of person who would cause a leak … by undoing a compression joint.'

'Had you used the word before, perhaps, and he was just repeating it?'

'No, definitely not.'

'There's probably a simple explanation,' Anne suggested.

Ralph looked thoughtful. 'There could be any number … and some of them unwelcome. But one thing is certain … Charles knows more about boats than I do … and more than he's willing to admit.'

• • • • •

Everyone present at the lunch party felt as if liberated after the winter. The weather forecast proved to be accurate, and the sun was hardly obscured all afternoon. The only slight cloud came to hover from time to time over Marnie, as her thoughts dragged her back to the strange meeting at the vicarage, but she suppressed all such worries for the sake of her guests.

By the time the meal was over and the plates and dishes were ensconced in the dishwashers in the office barn and in Angela's cottage, only Roger and Marjorie Broadbent remained. They had been travelling on their boat, *Rumpole*, and had timed their journey to be passing Glebe Farm on the day of the party. Marnie and Ralph walked with them through the spinney back to the canal where *Rumpole* was moored.

'So where to now, Roger?' Marnie asked as *Rumpole* came into view at the edge of the trees.

'Up as far as Stoke Bruerne for a day or two – we're meeting friends up there, joining us from Leicester – then back to Little Venice by next weekend. A spring break, like every year.'

'Can I ask you about a legal matter?'

'No peace for the wicked … which usually includes solicitors in most people's estimation …' He laughed at his joke. His wife smiled indulgently.

'Well, I'm not consulting you professionally for myself … it's more a hypothetical question.'

'Go on, then. I'll see if I can give you a sensible answer.'

'In criminal law, what grounds would be acceptable for an appeal to be allowed to go ahead?'

'You have a case in mind? No prizes for guessing?'

'Yes.'

'In the case of Neil Gerard there'd have to be fresh evidence. The petition to appeal has already been denied … the trial was judged to be conducted by the book and the conviction regarded as safe.'

'His sister's mounting a campaign for a retrial, we believe.'

'Really. Well, you can't just keep asking for a trial until you get the verdict you want. There'd have to be something pretty amazing for an appeal to be permitted at this stage.'

'Would the support of the victim's husband be amazing enough?'

Roger stopped abruptly, his mouth open. '*What?* Are you serious, Marnie? Charles Taverner supporting a bid for an appeal? That would be amazing, I grant you, but there'd have to be good reason for it. And it would be a very unwise move on his part, in my view.'

'Gerard's sister was here this morning, Sarah Cowan. She confronted Charles and asked him point blank for his help with her appeal campaign.'

'Good God … that's *extraordinary* …What did he say?'

'Not a lot. He was as surprised as you were … as we all were.'

'There'd still have to be new evidence. Presumably something would have to convince Charles that the verdict was wrong.'

They reached the boat and stood on the bank in thoughtful silence for a few moments.

'Have you ever known anything like that happen before, Roger?'

'No, Ralph. For Charles to support an appeal campaign would be quite amazing. If I was his solicitor I'd advise him to keep well clear of anything to do with Gerard's sister and her campaign.'

'You said you thought it would be *unwise* of Charles to support Sarah Cowan. Why was that?'

'I'd have thought that was fairly clear …'

Ralph pondered. 'Yes.'

14

'Marnie, sometimes I don't believe you live in the *real world!*'

Beth had a tendency to think her main role was to provide a commentary on the life of her younger sister. And not to disguise how she felt about it.

'What do you mean?' Marnie was flabbergasted.

'What I mean is, how can you even *think* about getting involved with Charles Taverner?'

'I didn't say I was *getting involved* … just helping him with the boat. Beth, he is a client, right?'

'Client –'

'If you say *client schmient* I'll hang up.'

'I was going to say, client my – '

'Foot?'

'Something like that. Marnie, after all you've been through in the last two years, you are the *last person* who should be getting … dealing with a man whose wife has been murdered.'

Marnie sagged. 'I know, I know … It's just that I promised to handle his house and boat, and there isn't anyone else who can deal with them. I can't let him down now.'

'What does Ralph think about it all?'

'He thinks it's okay. Anyway, he's very busy with his work, planning his trip to the States. He's doing a lecture tour … his new book's coming out there … the publisher wants a launch in Washington.'

'You're trying to change the subject.'

'I'm just giving you an update. Anne's almost finished her first year exams. The last ones are next week.'

'That's early, isn't it? It's not even Easter.'

'They do them now to keep the summer term free for their projects.'

'Talking of Easter, you could use a break yourself. Why not go to America with Ralph?'

'It'll be too hectic there. Anyway, we're planning a cruise in the early summer.'

'Great! That's more like it. Caribbean or Mediterranean?'

'We're thinking of Northampton and Peterborough.'

'You old-fashioned Romantics! Ralph always knew how to show a girl a good time. But seriously.'

'I mean it. We want to take one of the boats up the Nene valley. It's supposed to be very pretty.'

'You're winding me up. You need a proper break … a *real* holiday. You should listen to me, Marnie … I'm your sister.'

'Sister *schmister!*'

Marnie was still smiling a few minutes later when the phone rang again. This time it was Jock Mackenzie reporting that *Perfidia* would be ready by the end of the week. She was now fully up to standard and complied with every regulation known to man, beast and British Waterways.

That meant she would have two items of good news for Charles, the other being that the redecoration of the vicarage was finished. They had only spoken once since the encounter with Sarah Cowan, when Charles had apologised for withdrawing from lunch. She rang his number and was leaving a message on the answerphone when he picked up the receiver. As usual he was screening calls.

'Would you and Anne be able to collect *Perfidia*, Marnie?'

'Not Anne. She's in the middle of exams. I can go down to London ... start the journey myself. Maybe Anne will join me for the next leg of the trip. We can weekend her back up here.'

'Weekend her?'

'I'll have to do it in stages ... unless you have someone else in mind who might be able to get her up to Braunston more quickly?'

'No, no. If you can take her up in your own good time, that'll be fine, Marnie.'

'Well, I'd like to get her to Berkhamsted – there are good moorings at the boatyard there – but I'll probably only manage somewhere like Hemel or Boxmoor. There are quite a few locks on that stretch.'

'You mustn't overdo things. I hadn't thought you'd have to make the trip alone ... Did you say Hemel ... Hemel Hempstead?'

'Yes. Why?'

A pause. 'It's quite a long way ...'

'Forty-odd lock miles from Bull's Bridge, I think. If I can set off on Friday – the day after tomorrow – I should manage it over the weekend.'

'Well, as I say, don't overstrain yourself.'

Marnie ended the call promising to ring Charles to let him know how the journey progressed. After putting the phone down, she sat pondering the conversation. Charles had become increasingly detached as they spoke, and by the end she knew something was bothering him.

• • • • •

Jock Mackenzie was his usual abrupt self, but when Marnie met him at the boatyard on Friday morning to take *Perfidia* he was more subdued than she had known him before. He spent half an hour showing Marnie the work they had carried out, extra ventilation panels cut into the steelwork, new piping and joints for the gas system, new isolators and switching for the electrics. Marnie offered payment, but Jock waved that aside; he would send an invoice to Charles – *one of the few people I've ever known who sends a cheque by return of post ... with a first class stamp on it!*

It seemed strange to be stowing her kitbag in the sleeping cabin and making ready to set off alone. It was a cool overcast day, but when Jock was called back to the office to take a phone call she walked through the boat opening every window to give it a good airing. Reaching the stern, she fitted the brass tiller bar and secured it in place. Her mobile began warbling as she was checking the level of diesel in the fuel tank.

'Marnie, it's Charles. Is everything all right?'

'Yes. I'm just about to leave. Jock's done a great job ... says he'll send you an invoice.'

'That's fine. Look, Marnie …' He sounded strained.

'What is it?'

'I don't know how I've had the nerve to expect you to do this by yourself … it's quite unreasonable. I've been having misgivings about it ever since we spoke.'

'Don't worry about it, Charles.'

'It hadn't occurred to me that you'd make the trip alone on the boat, and after what happened …'

'Look, it's not a problem. I'll –'

'I was wondering about coming to join you.'

'*Join me?*' Marnie frowned. What did he mean … come with her on the journey … for the weekend? Surely not.

'Or rather *meet* you. You said you'd probably get as far as Hemel Hempstead?'

'It's a realistic target.'

'You'll reach there on Sunday?'

'If everything goes well.'

'Would you mind my meeting you there? I could drive you back to Knightly.'

'Oh, that's not necessary. It's a very kind thought, but Ralph said he'd pick me up.'

'Marnie, there are things I need to discuss with you. It would give us a chance to talk.'

'I see.' She did not see, but her curiosity was aroused. 'Couldn't we do it on the phone, or arrange a meeting some time? I wouldn't want you coming all that way, making a special journey.'

'I … have a reason for being in the area anyway. It'd be no problem … really.'

Marnie could see Jock coming back across the yard from his office. She agreed to ring Charles when she had an ETA for Hemel, and they ended the call.

'Right,' Jock said brusquely, as if he had been dealing with every fool in Christendom. 'Let's see if you remember how to drive this thing.'

• • • • •

For Marnie the journey north out of London on the Grand Union Canal was a trip down memory lane. She had made that same journey solo a few summers earlier on *Sally Ann*. It had been a turning point in her life, eventually leading past Knightly St John where, suffering from heat stroke, she had first landed at the abandoned Glebe Farm. Now it was her home. On that journey her mind had been constantly invigorated by the new experiences of the lone traveller. On this one, she was continuously assailed by thoughts of Barbara Taverner … and of Charles.

Why did he want to meet her? If he was going to tell her he planned to sell the boat and house, why not just come out and say it? Marnie would understand. What else could it be? As *Perfidia* slipped quietly through the water, Marnie thought back to her meetings, once alone with Barbara, once with them together. They had seemed like a normal couple. But the more she thought about it, the more obvious it became to Marnie that whatever Charles wanted to say to her, it would concern Barbara's relationship with Neil Gerard. If that was the case, *why* should he want to speak to her about it?

The answer came to Marnie while she was negotiating a bend where visibility was obscured by overhanging branches. It made her jump and distracted her for no more than two seconds. In that time, another boat appeared from the opposite direction. They were on a collision course in a restricted space, and Marnie pulled the tiller over, narrowly missing the bows of the oncoming craft. She seized the accelerator and dragged it into reverse. *Perfidia* responded well for a boat weighing fifteen tonnes, almost slowing enough to avoid hitting the bank. But not quite. Marnie heaved on the tiller to bring the nose around, but before she could squeeze through the gap, the boat cannoned into the bank on the towpath side. The nose button, a sturdy fender of rope over a heavy rubber core, struck the steel edging firmly and the boat bounced back, a shockwave travelling down its whole length. Marnie staggered to keep her balance and with good presence of mind, pushed the accelerator to slow ahead to give sufficient steerage to bring the tail round away from the other boat.

'*Jesus!*' the steerer cried out as he passed. 'What the *hell* were you thinking of?'

The man was tapping his forehead in disbelief. Then his eyes fell on the name painted in bold lettering on the side of the boat. For a second his brow furrowed as he tried to put it in context … a name he knew. At the moment he realised what boat he was confronting, his mouth opened, and it was only the need to give full attention to steering his own vessel that caused him to turn away. Even so, he glanced back more than once as the distance between the two boats widened.

Marnie raised a hand feebly to apologise. It had been a novice's error. Now, cursing inwardly, she forced herself to concentrate. Guiding the boat towards the canalside, she pulled over and made her fast with two ropes attached to mooring stakes that she hammered into the grass. Switching off the engine, she made a tour of inspection from bow to stern, inside and out. The only casualty was a mug that had been shaken off the draining board in the galley. It had bounced into the sink and snapped off its handle. Crockery had shifted in the cupboards, but nothing else was damaged.

Ultra-conscientious now, she inspected all the water and gas pipes. Nothing had worked loose; every joint and clip was sound. Righting shampoo bottles that had fallen over in the shower room, she reflected that it would take more than a collision at four miles an hour to damage a narrowboat, especially a fine solid craft like this one.

Outside there was not the slightest mark to show that *Perfidia* had suffered a mishap. Relieved, Marnie pressed the ignition, cast off and stowed the mooring pins. Still depressed, she focused on steering the boat like the expert she was. Ahead she made out the black and white shapes of balance beams and gave all her attention to negotiating the lock. She knew she conducted the operation like a text book and it restored her self-confidence.

Watching the water swirling in the lock chamber as she waited for it to fill, she smarted at the words of the other steerer. *What the hell were you thinking of?* And then it came back to her. She remembered why her attention had lapsed. Charles wanted to speak to her face to face, and she knew now what he wanted. He was convinced that Marnie knew about Barbara's affair with Neil Gerard … and he was going to confront her to tell him the truth.

• • • • •

Marnie stopped for the evening in a quiet spot south of Harefield and after supper phoned home. She told Ralph about Charles, and he agreed with her assessment.

'But you didn't know anything about her private life, did you? You had no idea she was having an affair with Gerard.'

'Course not. I was only just getting to know her when … everything ended. We had far too much to discuss about the house and the boat.'

'Once you make that clear, I'm sure he'll drop the subject.'

'I hope so.'

Digging the number out of her filofax, Marnie next rang Anne, who was spending the weekend with her parents at Leighton Buzzard, preparing for her last exams. For a few minutes they chatted about Anne's revision, her family, her brother's new job at the car factory. Sitting on the sofa with knees tucked under her, it reminded Marnie of her own years at school, gossiping endlessly on the phone while her father made tut-tutting sounds in the background until she took the hint and hung up. The words *girl talk* floated into her mind.

When Anne asked how the journey was going, Marnie broke a vow she had made. Having persuaded herself she was not going to talk about the near-collision incident, she was lulled into a cosy frame of mind by their chatting and let it slip.

'Apart from almost *crashing* into another boat?' Anne repeated loudly.

'No need to rub it in.'

'Sorry. Anyway, I suppose there was no harm done … if you didn't actually hit it …'

'Er …'

'You did say you only *nearly* ran into it, Marnie …You didn't hit it, did you?'

'Not the other boat, no …'

'But you did hit something … the bank … a bridge … a lock gate … Marnie?'

A pause. 'The bank.'

'Hard? Any damage?'

'Yes and no.'

'In that order?'

'Yes.'

'Blimey, Marnie, you're getting to be a hazard to shipping.' Mock indignation. 'It's not safe to allow you out on your own any more.'

'What d'you mean?'

'On your last journey we had the *merman* incident, when you knocked that bloke into the canal at the supermarket –'

'That was *entirely* his own fault!' Marnie protested.

'Now you're causing near-misses with other boats.'

'*One* other boat –'

'So you admit you caused it.'

'Struth! You're as bad as my sister …'

Anne was laughing at the other end of the line. 'Whatever next, I wonder …'

After disconnecting, Anne sat on the stairs thinking what it could have been that so distracted Marnie – an experienced and safe pair of hands at the tiller – that she had had an almost disastrous lapse of concentration.

Marnie too sat thinking about the conversation and about her forthcoming talk with Charles. Anne's words were echoing in her mind … *whatever next …*

• • • • •

The locks on the next section of the canal were evenly spaced out, and *Perfidia* made steady progress. Traffic was light and Marnie was content to watch the countryside go by and enjoy the quiet of the waterway. As always on a canal journey, she felt that she had stepped aside from the preoccupations of the normal world. But on this trip she could not escape her anxieties. The meeting with Charles was looming up, and although she had little information to give him, she sensed that it would be a difficult exchange. Had she had any inkling of the impact that meeting would have on her life, she would have stopped the boat and walked away from *Perfidia* forever.

On Saturday evening she repeated her phone calls to Ralph and Anne, happy to report an uneventful cruise. Then she rang the number in Docklands. Charles picked up the phone as soon as he heard her voice and responded positively to Marnie's account of the journey.

'Good, good. So what about tomorrow … where d'you think you'll reach by about lunchtime?'

'I'm on target, so Hemel or Boxmoor should be no problem by noon.'

'Fine. Suppose I meet you at that pub by the lock … we could have an early lunch. That would give us time. What do you say?'

'That should give us time for lunch, all right. Is that what you mean?'

'I'll explain when I see you. And I'll be looking out for you round about mid-day.'

Marnie made her way to the stern doors and stood looking out at the still water in the darkness. Am I getting paranoid? She wondered if it was her imagination, or did that discussion about arrangements not quite hang together? She had the feeling they were not both talking about the same thing. What had Charles said? *That would give us time*. He meant for lunch. Of course he did. *I'll explain when I see you*. No, he didn't.

15

Late morning on Sunday, cool and overcast with a hint of drizzle in the air, and Marnie had made an early start to be sure of arriving on time. It was just as well because, by Sod's Law, every lock was set against her. Evenly spaced out on the steady climb away from Cassiobury Park, she had to tie up for each one, empty it, drive in and refill it. Time-consuming and tiring. Normally, operating the locks was one of her favourite aspects of boating, but this time with a deadline, she felt under pressure.

Going through the group of Apsley locks she perched on the balance beams, staring into the chamber. Waiting for the water level to fall and rise again, she had time to wonder about her rendez-vous. Charles was going to pump her for any hints Barbara might have given about an illicit relationship. She felt sure of that. Then something else began nagging at her mind. Charles had said *that pub at Hemel*. There were two pubs on that stretch, both famous and long established, separated by about a mile and three locks. If Charles was referring to the further pub, that would add an hour or so to the journey – yet more pressure.

But Marnie had scarcely left Boxmoor lock behind when she saw Charles walking slowly along the towpath towards her. She pulled over to the bank and he stepped aboard, complimenting Marnie on her time-keeping. They tied up near the first of the two pubs, and she spotted the cherry red metallic Jaguar gleaming in the car park.

The saloon bar was almost empty as Charles guided Marnie to a table by the window giving a view onto the canal. She sipped her customary spritzer while studying the menu. Charles drank mineral water. It was twelve noon exactly, and one couple was seated at a nearby table making a determined onslaught on generous plates of fried fish and chips.

'Have you ever noticed, Marnie ...' Charles looked at her over the top of his menu, his voice low. 'No matter how early you arrive, there's always at least one other table where people are already eating?'

Marnie smiled back. He was breaking the ice as a preamble, of course, but she thought he had a point. It was the closest he came to making conversation during the meal. With the excuse that she would be having dinner with Ralph that evening, Marnie opted for a sandwich, and Charles was content with the same choice. When she suggested they take coffee on *Perfidia*, he accepted without hesitation.

Once on board, Charles wasted no further time. 'You're a very perceptive woman, Marnie. I expect you've worked out why I wanted to meet you here.'

Marnie was spooning ground coffee into the cafetière, while Charles sat at the table in the dining area. 'I'm not sure. I guessed your ... *having a reason for being in this area* might not be strictly true. I wondered if you wanted to tell me that you'd be selling the house as well as the boat. Or perhaps you were going to ask me about Barbara ... about anything she might've said to me privately ... in relation to Neil Gerard ... *girl talk* ... All those things occurred to me.'

'Interesting ...' Charles stared out of the nearest porthole.

Marnie waited, poured hot water, fitted the top on the coffee-maker. 'Was I right?'

'Wrong on all counts, actually. I'm surprised. I thought if anyone would've worked it out, it would be you.'

Glad to have something to occupy her, Marnie assembled cups and saucers on a tray. 'You don't want to talk about the house … or Barbara?'

'Not directly. You told me the work on the house was completed. I know – or I feel fairly certain – that you'd have volunteered any information about Barbara if you'd had it.'

'Yes.' She brought the tray to the table and set out the crockery while the aroma of the coffee brewing filled the air. 'You said I was wrong on *all* counts.'

'Correct.'

'Including what I took as an excuse for a meeting … your … *having a reason for being in the area?*'

'Oh yes. And that's the point, you see.'

Marnie was puzzled. 'If that's the point, Charles, I'm not getting it.'

'Will you come with me to see Neil Gerard?'

The directness of the question stunned Marnie. '*See* him? *Me?*'

'You may have been a *new* friend, but you're important in that part of our lives. Now, looking back on these past few months, it's you I think of in connection with Barbara. She was always talking about you … spent hours going through your plans and drawings. She really had a high regard for you, Marnie, as well as liking you a lot as a person.'

Marnie sat back and took a deep breath. 'I don't know … I mean … this is so unexpected.'

'You had no idea …?'

'No idea.' An emphatic shake of the head. 'I don't really understand why you want to do this, Charles.'

'Nor do I, in some ways. It's just that … somehow when we met that woman – his sister – I had the strangest feeling she was telling the truth.'

'The *court* thought she was telling the truth,' Marnie reminded him. 'It's Gerard himself they didn't believe. That was the point.'

'But don't you see, Marnie … perhaps that's the kind of family they are … truthful … honest …'

'That's a very generous assessment.'

'Will you come with me to see him?' Charles was almost pleading.

'I … I'd have to think about it …' Embarrassed. 'It would depend on my being free. I have a lot of commitments at work … I'm not sure when I might have the time.'

'You've made time today.'

'But that's different. I had to fit this into the schedule –'

'That's not what I meant, Marnie. You have time today.' He looked out of the window, across the canal. 'Neil Gerard is just over there.'

Marnie turned her head so sharply, she cricked her neck. 'What?'

'Not literally. He's in prison not far from the canal.' Charles indicated with a gesture. 'Up there on the hill. We can be there inside five minutes.'

• • • • •

Marnie had come to Hemel in the expectation of being driven away by Charles, but had not envisaged travelling with him to a prison. With no time to collect her thoughts, she felt totally unprepared for what was awaiting her. First, she had never been inside a prison before. In fact, she could not even remember seeing one from any angle, apart from on television or in films. Accustomed to determining which meetings she attended – and being in the habit of dealing generally with civilised people – she felt apprehensive even at the idea of crossing the threshold of such a building.

It seemed so incongruous. There she sat on soft cream leather, her feet cushioned by deep-pile carpet, surrounded by polished hardwood trim, being wafted along in a silky smooth limousine, on her way to a place that housed convicted murderers, rapists, arsonists, thieves. Words like *cell*, *punishment*, *prisoner* came to her. She shuddered at the thought of – what was the term? – *slopping out*. The only comfort was being with Charles, good solid Charles.

But why was she with him? What did he want from this meeting? What did he want from her? She suspected – against all reason – that he was wanting to convince himself that Neil Gerard might be innocent. She glanced at him beside her, his hands firmly gripping the wheel. Her self-confidence was returning. She needed to reassert her judgment to bring herself back up to his level. She believed she knew what he had in mind.

'Charles, what do you expect to get out of this? Are you wondering if Gerard might persuade you he wasn't guilty?'

'Quite the reverse, actually, Marnie.' Charles turned his attention to negotiating a roundabout.

'The *reverse?*'

'You were surprised when I asked you to come here, weren't you?'

'That's understatement. It was the last thing I –'

'How d'you think Gerard's going to feel when he sees me?'

'Stunned, I should think.'

'Quite.'

'So?'

'I think he might be so shocked he might not be able to argue his innocence.'

'A surprise attack from an unexpected quarter,' Marnie muttered.

'Exactly. I'm hoping to take the wind right out of his sails – to continue your sailing metaphor – get him to admit his guilt and drop his ridiculous notion of making an appeal.'

Marnie mulled this over while Charles steered the Jaguar into a parking area. She tried to understand what he was trying to do. Unaware that she had been using a sailing term, she had to admit it was a bold move. Perhaps this was the kind of tactic that City businessmen used to surprise their rivals. She recalled phrases from the news like *boardroom coup* and *dawn raid*. Perhaps *captain of industry* was itself a naval metaphor.

Accustomed to setting her own agendas, planning her meetings in advance, Marnie felt anxious about what to expect inside the walls. Approaching the heavy doors, she felt her stomach turning over as they joined the little group of prisoners' friends and families who loitered by the entrance, avoiding eye contact with each other. When they began filing into the prison, Marnie wanted to run away as fast as she could, and she was comforted by the thought that that was something she had in common with the inmates.

• • • • •

They were seated at a small table in a room painted in a subdued shade of pale green, as if at a whist drive, waiting for a change of partners. The other visitors were at their tables, a few talking in muted voices, most sitting in silence.

Neil Gerard was led in and at first panned around the room, looking for a familiar face. When the warder ushered him to the table where Charles and Marnie were waiting, he stared at them. Charles had gained his first victory, surprise.

Gerard quickly composed himself and held out his hand, saying, rather unnecessarily, 'Neil Gerard.'

Charles shook it briefly and sat down. When Gerard offered a hand to Marnie he searched her face as if trying to place her. His grip was cool and dry, a firm handshake, but not a bonecrusher.

'Marnie,' he said quietly. 'Marnie Walker.'

Charles looked up sharply. 'You know each other?'

'We've never really met as such,' Gerard began, 'but I attended a press conference with Marnie a couple of years ago … even wrote an article about her.'

He indicated the seat and, after Marnie sat down, he followed. Despite taking the advantage he now seemed wary. Charles recovered enough to pursue the line he had prepared in advance.

'I think you know why I've come here today.'

'How should I know that? I was expecting to see my sister waiting for me.'

'It's because of her that I'm here.'

'And Marnie? I take it you are Marnie …'

'Yes, I am.'

'Why have you brought her? Do you need moral support … a second opinion … reinforcements?'

'She's here as a friend … of mine … and of Barbara. They had become close.'

'But she knows nothing of my relationship with Barbara.' He turned towards Marnie again. 'Forgive me for talking about you as if you weren't here.'

'How do you know that?' Charles seemed intrigued by Gerard's confidence.

'I do. Tell him, Marnie. It's true, isn't it? Barbara never talked to you about me.'

'That's right, she didn't.'

'Ever.'

'No.'

To Charles again. 'You said you came because of Sarah, my sister …'

'She told me she's trying to organise a campaign to get an appeal hearing.'

A wry smile. 'That's Sarah, all right. Loyal to the end.'

During this exchange Marnie took in her impressions of Neil Gerard. He was different from the photographs she had seen in the press, very clean-looking and fresh, despite the grey prison uniform. Alert and interested in the odd situation in which he found himself, he managed to appear dignified and – Marnie searched her brain for the right word – undefeated.

Charles continued. 'She could've got you off the hook with one word at the trial. It's a bit late now, when you're convicted, no one believes your story – at least no one in the judiciary – and your own sister refused to back you up. I've spoken with the police. The investigating officer told me he'd never seen a more clear-cut situation –'

Gerard nodded wearily. 'I know … *an open-and-shut case* … I've heard it all before.'

'So perhaps it's time you accepted it and let people get on with their lives. After all, when your own sister –'

'You don't believe I'm guilty.'

The sentence hung in the air between them like a banner.

'What are you talking about?' Charles was almost blustering.

'If you did – if you *really* did – you wouldn't be here now.'

'But –'

'No. Don't tell me about my sister failing to give me an alibi. She told the truth when she gave her statement to the police. Afterwards it would have been impossible to change it. She told them what happened not because she wouldn't back me up, but because she never thought – we neither of us ever thought for one instant – that I would be accused, let alone found guilty and convicted.'

'Do you honestly think –'

'I honestly think there must be some doubt in your mind, Charles. Sorry to be familiar … I've only ever thought of you by that name …'

Charles flushed and glared at Gerard, and Marnie sensed him become rigid in his seat. In the awkward silence, Marnie feared that Charles might reach across the table and hit him. Instead, he took a few deep breaths.

Neil carried on in a subdued tone. 'Look, I didn't mean to cause you offence … the situation's bad enough as it is … but the fact that you've come here … brought Marnie …' Gerard looked at her directly. 'You don't believe it either, do you?'

Marnie held his gaze, but from the corner of her eye she saw Charles look at her. 'I don't think the police are fools or that the courts make mistakes. Sure, there are miscarriages of justice, but when all the evidence is clear, I think the system works. I'm sorry if that makes me sound like a backwoods reactionary, but Bruere *isn't* incompetent … and you had every chance to defend yourself …'

'Then I don't understand what you've come for … either of you.'

Good point, Marnie thought.

Charles had by now regained his voice. 'I want you to face the facts … back down from campaigning and let us try to get our lives back. As long as you and your sister are … going on … for whatever reason, I'll never recover my peace of mind. Is that too much to ask?'

Neil paused. 'I'm glad you came. I saw you at the trial … and I'm very sorry for what happened. Whether you think I'm innocent or not does matter to me … in ways that I couldn't even try to explain … but I still think there's an inkling of doubt in your mind … and if in coming here you're looking for peace of mind … then you're looking in the wrong place.'

Charles shook his head slowly. 'I've seen your sister and I don't doubt her sincerity.

But I've taken legal advice from a top barrister … someone I've known for years … got him to review the case. He told me that an appeal seems out of the question, given the evidence and the way the trial was conducted. In his view the conviction was safe.'

'He's right. The investigation … the trial … everything was properly carried out. The only thing wrong was they accused and convicted the wrong person. The trial was perfectly fair … just wrong.'

'But you can't go on –'

'We gave our evidence when we were first questioned, Sarah and I. We didn't collude … just told the truth. It didn't occur to us the police wouldn't find anything else … or anyone else.'

'Who else might they have found?'

Gerard shrugged. 'It could've been anyone. Barbara knew a lot of people.'

'You're saying this was done by someone who knew her?'

'Yes. The police always thought it was an *inside job*.'

Charles looked shocked. ' Are you implying they might have suspected … *me?*'

'You must've been as strong a suspect as anyone else.'

'Are you *mad?* I *loved* my wife.'

'If it's any consolation, Charles, I never thought it could be you.'

'I'm supposed to take comfort from that? And what are you *talking* about? If it was an *inside job*, as you put it, who *else* could it have been?'

Gerard looked down. Marnie caught the implication at once, but it took a few seconds before Charles realised what was being said.

'Do you mean …? No … that's *ridiculous!*'

'You must've known I was not her only … that there had been other lovers …'

Charles blundered to his feet. 'I've got to go.' He turned away from the table and stumbled towards the door.

Getting up to follow him, Marnie looked down at Gerard, slowly shaking her head. He stared back with an expression not of defiance or anger, but of regret.

• • • • •

Outside in the car park Charles rested his head on his hands on the roof of the car. 'You were right, Marnie … not a good idea.'

'I didn't say that, Charles. I just said I didn't understand why you wanted to see Gerard.'

'It amounts to the same thing … a crazy idea … stupid.'

Marnie had to bite her tongue. Agreeing would not do Charles any good. He turned and leaned back against the Jaguar, looking up at the prison walls, breathing slowly and deeply. Eventually he pressed a button on the keypad, the locks clicked open and they climbed in.

• • • • •

They returned to *Perfidia* for Marnie to collect her belongings, but instead of driving her straight home, Charles surprised Marnie by accepting her offer of a drink. He asked for a cup of Earl Grey, and they took their seats in the boat's dining area.

'What are your plans, Charles?'

'You mean now or in the long run?'

'Both, probably.'

'God knows. Oh … sorry if that's offensive. I –'

'That's fine. You're the one who's going to live in a vicarage.'

He smiled at the gentle joke. 'Quite.'

'Is that still your intention?'

'Of course.' The change of tack was sudden and took Marnie completely by surprise. 'What was all that about … *other lovers?*'

'I've no idea.'

He reached across the table and took her wrist. 'Do you really mean that, Marnie? You *honestly* have no idea? Are you telling me the *truth?*'

Marnie tried to remove her hand but Charles was holding it firmly. 'I honestly had no idea. Look, Charles, we didn't have that kind of relationship. We didn't go in for … whatever you call it … *girl talk* … We were preoccupied with business matters. There was a lot of work to do and not much time.'

'Not much time? You were seeing each other every *week.*'

'What?'

'I checked her diary. She always seemed to be going off to see you. You must've had time to talk about … Wait a minute. How often did you meet, Marnie?'

'Can you please let go of my wrist, Charles. It's uncomfortable.'

'Sorry … I wasn't thinking …'

'We met just once … at Templars' Wharf.'

They both made the connection at once.

'She was seeing him, wasn't she?'

'I don't know. She wasn't seeing me.'

'Do you have your diary here, Marnie?'

'Not the office one, no.' She remembered putting in several meetings … *just to reserve the dates* … only to have Barbara cancel them shortly beforehand. Barbara was using her as cover. No wonder she spent hours studying the plans. It made up for the time she was supposed to be in meetings, advancing the projects on the house and the boat. 'Charles, it was the run-up to Christmas … there was a lot going on. It's the most sociable time of the year …'

'Sociable,' Charles repeated. 'That's one way of putting it.'

'You mustn't torture yourself. You may be doing Barbara a grave injustice.'

'No, Marnie. Whoever murdered her did her a *grave* injustice. Can you swear to me that –'

'I'm really tired of telling you, Charles. I was *not* Barbara's confidante in that way. I'm not going to say it again. But I would turn the question round. Did *you* ever have a hint of anything like that in the past … a suspicion … a doubt in your mind … a question mark?'

He began shaking his head and was about to reply when he checked himself. 'I wonder …'

'Look, Charles, it's been a difficult day for you. There's no need to drive me all the way home. I can get Anne to come and fetch me. She's at her parents' place not far away. We can go back to Knightly together. It's no problem.'

'I wouldn't dream of it.'

They eventually reached a compromise and Charles rang for a taxi, fixing a price on the phone. Standing together on the towpath, waiting after locking up the boat, neither of them felt like talking. Both had used up their reserves of emotional energy.

Charles walked a few paces along the path. 'I don't suppose I shall ever see the boat again,' he said quietly.

'I can deal with all that.'

'Will you be able to fetch her soon, Marnie? You said you were having a busy time ...'

'I'll clear a few days and complete the journey. Don't worry. I can understand that you want the whole business cleared up. You don't want it dragging on.' *Closure*, she thought.

'Thank you.' He walked on and turned to retrace his steps, looking at the name painted on the side. '*Perfidia* ...' he muttered.

'Why did you call her that?' Marnie asked, making conversation.

Charles shrugged. 'We never discussed it. I was too busy with my work to go into the details ... left all that to Barbara. My involvement was writing the cheque. Then one day Barbara went to fetch her from the boatyard ... and there was *Perfidia*. I never did ask about the name ... now I'll never know.'

'It's the title of a tune.' Marnie wanted to lighten the conversation. 'A guitar piece ... used to be very popular ...' A *haunting melody*, Marnie thought to herself.

'Yes. I believe you're right. In fact I seem to recall one of our friends suggesting the boat might've been named after it ... Barbara liked the tune ... something like that.'

When the taxi arrived, Charles kissed Marnie on the cheeks, thanked her for coming and headed towards the Jaguar in the car park without looking back. She watched him through the window, bending to open the car door.

Perfidia. She heard the melody in her brain, the voluptuous sound of electric guitars. As the taxi pulled away, she saw the name. Whoever had chosen *Perfidia* for the boat, and for whatever reason, it had turned out to be appropriate.

16

In bed that night Marnie told Ralph about the prison visit. He was annoyed that Charles had dragged Marnie into his plan. Next morning, acting on Ralph's advice, Marnie rang Roger Broadbent. She waited for Anne to leave for college and felt deceitful, watching the red Mini climb the field track away from Glebe Farm, but did not want to distract her during her exams.

Marnie told Roger briefly about the visit to the prison. He was less than enthusiastic.

'You did *what?*'

'Oh God, Roger, you're starting to sound like my sister.'

'Well, I'm glad there's one member of your family with some brains, Marnie.'

'You're supposed to be my solicitor – that's as in *on my side* – I wanted you to sound understanding at least.'

'So tell me what you thought it would achieve to visit Neil Gerard.'

Marnie could not think of anything to say. She sat wondering how she had got herself into that situation. 'I … I … I dunno. I just got talked into it … wanted to do something to help Charles.'

'Did he seem better after the interview?'

She slumped in the chair. 'No … more like suicidal.'

'I rest my case, m'lud.'

'Oh, don't be a smartarse, Roger …'

'You pay me to be a smartarse, Marnie. That's what solicitors are for.'

'I'm *paying you?*'

'Not this time. Don't panic. I don't take money from the criminally insane.'

'So what's your advice?'

'Advice? About what? I've already told you, you can't get a retrial or an appeal on the grounds that you don't agree with a verdict. The only way anyone can get Gerard freed – if he is innocent – is by producing new evidence.'

'But it's the *evidence* that got him convicted in the first place.'

'Believe it or not, Marnie, that's not actually a failing … it's how the system works.'

'He says the evidence convicted the wrong person. There must be some other way.'

'There is.'

Suspicion. 'Honestly? Not a wind-up?'

'No. The other way is … you find who really did it. But don't go thinking the British judicial system always gets it wrong, Marnie. The police are thorough and the courts are fair. The cases that hit the news – like the Birmingham Six or the Guildford Four – are very exceptional. Don't go imagining Gerard as the Little Venice One.'

'I'm not a detective, Roger. I can't go out and find a criminal. I wouldn't know where to begin.'

'Marnie, let me ask you something. You're starting to sound as if you believe Gerard is innocent. Is that what you think?'

Lost for words again. Eventually. 'I don't know. Charles said he'd got a top barrister to look into the trial and read the evidence.'

'Verdict?'

'Safe conviction. You can rest your case again, m'lud.'

'Frankly, Marnie, if I were you –'

'Hang on!' Marnie cocked her head on one side. 'Roger, I can hear a car outside. It might be Anne … maybe she forgot something. I'd better go. Talk to you later. Oh, and … thanks for your advice. See you!'

Putting the phone down, Marnie leapt to her feet and made for the door. She looked out into the courtyard. No Anne, no one at all. Curious. Marnie had acute hearing and was certain she had heard a car. There were no clients due to visit that day, no deliveries for the renovation of the house. Hurriedly she darted outside and at once heard an engine revving. She rushed to the corner of the office barn and looked up the field track, just in time to see the dust from a vehicle at the top of the field.

While she watched, one of the builders came round the side of the house.

'Colin, did you see a car here just now?'

He shook his head.

'Did you hear it?'

'Sorry, Marnie. I was sawing wood out the back.'

For some seconds she stood asking herself who might pay a call on Glebe Farm … and decide not to stay.

• • • • •

Anne rang later in the afternoon. Her last exam was finished and she pronounced it as: *no big surprises*. She would be back at around five and would bring the evening paper plus any stores they needed. Marnie gave her a list of items and promised to have the kettle on by the time she returned.

On the days when Anne was at college the post run fell to Marnie. There were three letters to send off and she pulled open the top drawer to find the stamps folder. Reaching in, she stopped, hand poised in mid-air. There, to one side in the drawer, lay a forgotten business card. An official coat of arms, London Borough of Riverside, Department of Human Resources, Senior HR Officer … Sarah Cowan BA MIPM. At the bottom, after the contact details, was scrawled *private*, followed by a number.

Afterwards, Marnie had no recollection of dialling.

'Human resources, Jackie Mullen.'

'I'd like to speak to Sarah Cowan, please.'

'Who's calling?'

'Marnie Walker.'

'I'm sorry, Sarah's already left for the day. She finishes at four. She'll be back in the office by eight tomorrow. She's our early bird.'

Marnie glanced at the wall clock. Four forty-five.

'Perhaps I can try her at home.'

'I'm not allowed to give out her home number, I'm afraid.'

'That's fine, I've got it.'

Sarah was probably pushing a trolley round a supermarket, like Anne. Marnie hit the buttons. The phone was answered at once as if Sarah had been waiting for a call.

'This is Marnie Walker … we met when you came to Knightly –'

'I remember who you are.' The tone was cool. 'You went to see my brother … in prison.'

'Yes.'

'That was quite a brave thing to do.'

'I don't know about *brave* …'

'You went with Charles Taverner. Why did you go?'

'Charles had some idea that if he confronted your brother, he might be able to persuade him to drop his appeal campaign.'

'I meant, why did *you* go? Neil could see what Taverner wanted, although he thinks – *thought* – Taverner might've believed he was innocent.'

'Why does he – or did he – think that?'

'He'd heard a lot about him …from Barbara obviously … and had the idea that Charles was a fair-minded man … with a lot of qualities.'

'Didn't stop her playing away from home.'

'Perhaps there were some things he couldn't provide. Marnie, why are you ringing me? I assume it's not to discuss my brother's morals.'

'You wanted me to get in touch.'

'That was about the campaign. Is that what you want to do? Could you persuade Charles Taverner to help?'

Marnie looked up at the clock. It was approaching five.

'I haven't got a lot of time to speak just now. When we visited your brother, he hinted that Barbara had had other lovers.'

'So?'

'The inference was that one of them might have … you know.'

'I'm not sure what I know, Marnie. But of one thing I'm positive …'

'Yes, yes … okay. We'll take that as read.'

'It's no small thing. My brother is definitely innocent. Don't be in any doubt about it.'

'Let me ask you something. If you could turn the clock back to the time the police questioned you … knowing what you know now … would you change your testimony?'

'No. It was their mistake not mine. But the consequences were the same. Neil got a life sentence. I can't stand by and do nothing about it.'

'Does your brother –'

'His name is Neil … he's a *person*.'

'All right. Does Neil know who these other people were … her other lovers?'

'I expect so … some of them, probably. Believe it or not, we don't spend time talking about his sex life. That's not what sisters are for. He's very private about that sort of thing.'

'The question is, would any of them want to kill her? And if so, why?'

'Marnie, I never met Barbara Taverner ... you did ... but I got the impression she was the kind of woman who could arouse strong passions. Can you imagine that?'

'I have to go.'

'All right. But please ... do what you can to help us.'

Marnie sighed. 'I wouldn't hold your breath.'

• • • • •

At the end of the working day Marnie rang Charles from the office barn while Ralph and Anne were preparing supper on *Sally Ann*. First she gave an outline of her talk with Roger Broadbent, which confirmed the advice Charles had received from his barrister colleague. It came as no surprise and brought no comfort. Charles thanked Marnie for her information.

'I didn't ring just to tell you about Roger. There's something else. I hope you won't be angry or upset ...'

'I'm sure there's nothing you could do that would make me feel either of those, Marnie.'

'Well ... it's just ... I phoned Gerard's sister. She gave me her card when we saw her that day.'

'Oh?'

'Do you want to revise your opinion of me?'

'No. In fact ... I was wondering about contacting her myself.'

'*Really?*'

'Your turn to be surprised, I think, Marnie. What did she say when you asked your question?'

'She just repeated that he was innocent ... he told the truth at the trial ... they both did ... and she wanted your help to get an appeal.'

'That wasn't all, was it?'

Marnie did not want to tell him she had asked about other lovers. 'It was the main thing.'

'No. I think I know what your main question was, Marnie ... why you decided to ring her. It's been on my mind too, ever since Gerard mentioned it.'

'It just seems so unfair that you, of all people, Charles, should be dragged into a campaign to defend the man who ... This is a kind of moral blackmail. I've almost found myself wondering if it could be a trick.'

'I don't think Gerard is that sort of person. Ironically, he's a bit like me, Marnie. He has standards ... even if he was having an affair with another man's wife. And it may be fair to say that I have to take my share of the blame ... for not providing everything Barbara needed in her life.'

'I wouldn't think fairness came into it, Charles.'

'Well, whatever it is, I've been thinking about the situation and I want to see Gerard again.'

'You're not serious.'

'I am, and I'm going to be totally unfair and unreasonable ... I'm going to ask you … if you'd come with me.'

Marnie was taken aback. She had been trying to get Charles to follow another course and now he was wanting to drag her along with him.

Faced with Marnie's silence, Charles continued. 'He seemed to find it easier to speak to the two of us.'

'You really want me to go with you again … to see him in prison?'

'Yes. Please. I know it's a lot to ask but –'

'Let me think it over, Charles.'

After disconnecting, Marnie sat looking at the phone. Her mind was a jumble, her thoughts a mess. She hated being pulled along like this on all sides. She resented Sarah Cowan demanding help from Charles and herself. Her brother had killed Charles's wife, for God's sake! The police said so, the court said so, an independent barrister said so, her own solicitor said so. All the evidence pointed that way.

Then why did Charles of all people seem willing to keep an open mind? What did he know? Why was Sarah Cowan so confident that Charles accepted her arguments? That was the strangest of all. … *he's a bit like me, Marnie.* What was all that about? A sound across the office made Marnie sit up straight. She began tidying the papers on the desk, slipping them into her pending tray.

'Again?'

Marnie whirled round. Anne was standing in the doorway.

A smile. 'Hi. Supper ready?'

'Again?' Anne repeated.

'Sorry?'

'You're going to visit Neil Gerard in prison … *again*? You've been there with Mr Taverner before? When was this?'

Marnie gave in. 'Sunday.'

Anne frowned. 'Right …'

'I didn't –'

Anne raised a hand. 'I know … I know. You didn't want to make me worry. I know the usual reasoning.'

'I can't even pretend I was going to tell you. Anyway, I expect you would've found out, however I tried to cover up … I'm sorry. I didn't want to get involved, but –'

'Don't be sorry, Marnie. It's interesting.'

'It is?'

'It's interesting that Mr Taverner is visiting Neil Gerard in prison. Hardly what I would've expected. What's going on?'

'I wish I knew.'

'Does Ralph know about this?'

Marnie nodded. Anne crossed the room and took her by the arm.

'Come on, then. We can talk about it over the meal. It's a special supper to celebrate.'

'Celebrate?'

'My last exam. Ralph and I have made my favourite things … apart from raspberries not being in season.'

Marnie reflected on the resilience of the young as they walked arm in arm on the path through the spinney to *Sally Ann*'s docking area in the evening sunlight.

• • • • •

The first course was asparagus in vinaigrette with an account of Marnie's visit to the prison. Both were helped along with a glass of dry white Orvieto and some crusty French bread.

Next, Ralph served them poached salmon in hollandaise sauce with minted new potatoes while each added their speculations on what motivated Charles to take the Free-Gerard-Campaign seriously. They all agreed the salmon was delicious but opinions otherwise varied from the possibility that Charles knew something he was not telling anyone to the idea that his curiosity had simply been aroused.

The crème brûlée arrived on the table without raspberries, but accompanied by a question from Anne. As far as Marnie and Ralph understood the situation, what was their gut feeling about Gerard?

Marnie. 'All the evidence points to him being guilty …'

'There's a *but* coming,' Anne observed. 'I can feel it.'

'Not really … it's just that … I can still see Gerard's face pleading with me as I walked away from the table in the visiting room. And I can hear his sister just now on the phone asking me to help.'

'I count that as a *but*,' Anne said dryly. 'Ralph?'

'Oh … I'm not sure I have enough information to form a valid opinion. I've only got the media accounts to go on. But I have to be influenced by the fact that the courts have judged the conviction to be safe to the extent they've ruled out an appeal.'

Marnie thought that was a typical balanced academic view. She looked at Anne. 'You haven't given your verdict. What do you think?'

'I think … this has been a lovely supper … and it's been food for thought …'

Ralph smiled. 'That's more evasive than my reply.'

Marnie smiled too. 'Is that all? You've at least seen Gerard's sister, which is more than Ralph's done.'

'I was just thinking … now that my exams are over, I wanted to take a few days off … have a breather before I get back to studying.'

Ralph agreed. 'Good idea.'

'So I could pop into the reference library on Monday and check out the newspaper accounts of the trial.'

Marnie looked sceptical. 'I'm not sure you'll find anything new there. The main points in the case could be summed up on the fingers of one hand: Neil Gerard had no real alibi; his sister failed to back him up in court; his fingerprints – and his alone – were found on the damaged pipe joint; he and Barbara had been heard quarrelling that evening; he'd *stormed off in a rage* – according to the tabloids.'

'That's what I was thinking … I might take a look at the serious papers, including the big Sundays.'

Ralph narrowed his eyes. 'I read the reports at the time ... I think you'll find Marnie's right.'

Marnie stood up to put the kettle on. '*The Little Venice Murder*,' she muttered. 'He was condemned by the highest court in the land.'

'But his case didn't even get to the court of appeal,' Anne protested.

'I didn't mean that one. He was tried in the tabloid press and found guilty by public opinion.'

17

The bombshell hit them the next day, Tuesday morning.

Anne had set off in good time to find a parking place near the reference library in town. Alone in the office, Marnie buckled down to a solid morning's work, tidying up designs for clients, instructing the joiner fitting wardrobes in the farmhouse, sketching out a hotel project for Willards Brewery, her biggest contract. Before lunch she had cleared enough of the in-tray to phone Charles. She told him of the discussion on *Sally Ann* the previous evening, without mentioning Anne's researches.

Charles sounded more cheerful. Marnie sensed he was preparing himself mentally to draw a line in the sand, to listen to the voice of reason in his head and walk away from any further involvement in the Neil Gerard affair.

'On reflection, Marnie, I really think the time has come –'

His words were drowned out by a loud crunching of gravel outside, a car skidding. Marnie braced herself for the sound of a crash.

'Charles, sorry … just a … hang on a sec … there's something …'

Marnie heard a car door slam and stumbling footsteps racing across the courtyard. The door burst open.

'Marnie!' Anne gasped for breath. 'Did you hear that just now?' She put a hand to her chest. 'On the radio …'

'What was it? Anne, what did you hear? Sorry, Charles, Anne has just run in … something's happened.'

Anne was struggling to speak. 'I only caught the tail end of it … fiddling with the radio. Neil Gerard … he's hanged himself in his cell.'

• • • • •

There were more than fifteen minutes to the next news bulletin. Marnie rang Ralph in his study on *Thyrsis*. No, he did not have the radio turned on. Molly Appleton in the village shop, usually first to get news on any subject, had been counting in a delivery and had heard nothing. No reply from Beth. No reply from her friend Jane Rutherford in Little Venice. Mrs Jolly had just come in from shopping. It was a nightmare, but at least making phonecalls had used up some time.

The three of them huddled round the radio in the office. The news summary at twelve noon on the BBC. An economic report on the lack of a feel-good factor; the Chancellor would be making a statement to the House. Talks had broken down on the question of greater European Union integration. *Come on!* An earthquake in southern Japan … six point nine on the Richter scale … eight dead and thousands of homes damaged. A ship carrying nuclear waste, listing badly off the west coast of Africa … a potential environmental disaster. The other items concerned rumours of a ministerial scandal, a crisis in the management of the NHS and a shortage of teachers in inner-city schools. No mention of Neil Gerard. *Damn!*

Anne shook her head. 'But I *heard* it … I *know* I did.'

'What were the exact words?'

'I'm not sure. I was on the dual carriageway … thought I'd find some music on the radio. I was pressing buttons to change channels and there was this news flash …

something like *Gerard who was in prison serving life for murder ... bla-bla-bla ... found hanging in his cell* ... I didn't take it all in ... I was in traffic. I thought there'd be more detail, but that's all there was.'

Marnie frowned. 'Odd that there was nothing about it on the national news. What do you think, Ralph?'

'I agree. Of course, it's unlikely that Anne was mistaken –'

'I *definitely* heard it.'

'I'm sure. Then perhaps a suicide in prison doesn't rate national importance. Do you know what channel you were on, Anne?'

'No. I had to concentrate on driving.'

'I was wondering if it might've been a local radio station ...'

Anne agreed. 'I've got a whole load programmed in the radio's memory.'

'Any London stations? Can you get them up here?'

'Yeah ... could've been. I've got Capital something and Metro whatever ... a few like that.'

Marnie turned to Ralph. 'I'm impressed you even knew local radio stations *existed*.'

'I've been interviewed on some of them.'

Marnie grinned. 'Smartarse ... I might've guessed.'

Anne sighed. 'How do we find out about Gerard? I'm *positive* I wasn't mistaken.'

'At the risk of being called a smartarse ...' Ralph glanced sideways at Marnie, 'I think that's quite ... elementary.'

Two minutes later Ralph completed a phonecall. His contact in the newsroom of Radio Oxford had solved the mystery.

'That was Carl Phipps, one of the news editors. He confirmed Anne's story. Gerard apparently attempted to commit suicide this morning. It seems he used his shirt to make a 'rope' and hanged himself from the bars in his cell.'

'God ... so he's dead?'

'No. A warder looked in and saw him. He was unconscious but they rushed him to the hospital wing and revived him.'

Anne went even paler than usual.

'Why wasn't it on the news?' Marnie asked.

'Carl thought national radio and TV would probably run the story on the main one o'clock programmes. Before noon they weren't sure if he'd survive or not.'

A gasp from Marnie. 'Charles! I wonder if he knows.'

She rang Charles's number. He sounded less than reassured. She could guess why and had had the same feeling herself.

'Thank you for letting me know, Marnie. I'm sure he wasn't just trying to get attention.'

'I think it's too soon to make a judgment about that.'

'Oh, I think he meant it,' Charles persisted.

'You can't be sure.'

'Do you believe that? Really?'

'Well … it doesn't look as if they thought he was a suicide risk. I think they have special procedures for that kind of thing.'

'That's what I was thinking. It makes it worse, Marnie.'

'How do you work that out?'

'He wouldn't be considered a suicide risk while he was mounting a vigorous campaign to get an appeal or a retrial. He kept going because he had hope for the future. Something changed that.'

'Let's not speculate, Charles. We don't know all the facts. Something might've happened in prison … bullying … threats …intimidation …'

'Something took away his hope. That's what I think.'

It's what Marnie thought, too.

18

Marnie had always thought Neil Gerard was a fine-looking man. But not that Friday morning. When they approached his bed he was bleary-eyed, as if he had not long been awake. It was nearly eleven. She guessed he had been under sedation.

The previous day he had been returned from hospital to the prison, where the authorities had installed him in the sanatorium for his first night back. Marnie was certain that Charles had pulled strings to obtain permission to visit him, and she had reluctantly agreed to take part. They had met in the car park, and Marnie told Charles this was the last time she would be coming to see Gerard. He accepted her decision and made the point that it was unlikely Gerard would be remaining in the prison where he had tried to take his life. He was sure they would move him, possibly to a secure hospital. And from now on he would be on suicide watch.

Entering the sanatorium, Marnie saw her role as nothing more than moral support. She was determined to let Charles do all the talking. They walked up to the bed. Gerard was propped up on pillows.

'It didn't do any good, did it?' Charles said softly.

Gerard looked and sounded weary. 'I didn't succeed if that's what you mean.'

'You know what I mean. What if they hadn't found you in time?'

'Then I would've succeeded.'

'Doing that didn't help your case.'

'*Case* … I didn't care then and I don't care now … not any more.' He gestured to the chairs beside the bed. 'If you're staying, you may as well sit down.'

Marnie looked at Charles, who hesitated and took the chair next to him.

Charles leaned forward, continuing in the same quiet tone. 'I told you I had the case checked by a barrister. We've taken separate legal advice. We've read all the court reports, including the statement by the appeal judges. It's no good.'

'I'm glad we agree on something. That's why I tried to find a way out.'

'Because you realised there was nothing to back up your story.'

'Because I couldn't stand being kept in prison for the rest of my life … for something I didn't do.'

Charles sighed and sat back in the chair. He looked exasperated.

'But the evidence –'

'What *evidence*?'

'All of it … even your sister not backing you up … what more do you want?'

'My sister *is* backing me up … she's the only one.'

'And this is your way of repaying her?'

'I wasn't trying to repay her. I was trying to kill myself.'

Marnie felt a pain in her head and winced.

Gerard noticed and continued. 'Have you any idea what it's like … to tie something round your neck, push your feet away from the wall and hang … the pain of it … the choking … your tongue starting to swell in your throat –'

Charles looked hastily at Marnie. 'All right, all right … we get the picture.'

'No you don't. You've no idea what it was like. And if you're thinking it was some kind of … *cry for help* – or whatever the cliché is – then you can forget it.'

Charles looked at him steadily. 'You really … really meant to do it?'

'Yes.' Gerard grimaced and cleared his throat.

Charles turned and raised an eyebrow in Marnie's direction. She did not know what kind of reaction he expected and lowered her eyes. And that simple unprepared gesture turned the conversation in a new direction.

'When we saw you before, you suggested that my wife had … other lovers.' Gerard looked up but remained silent. Charles continued. 'How do you know that?'

'What do you mean?'

'It's a simple enough question.'

'Well, we … talked about them.'

'You had rows about them?'

'No. She just told me about them. I suppose you'd call it … pillow talk. Look, I don't think I really want to go into all that.'

'You think it might turn me against you if you gave me the details?'

'Perhaps. Something like that.'

'Believe me, Gerard, it couldn't make me more hostile towards you than I have been already.'

'Then let's just drop it, shall we?'

Marnie was feeling increasingly uncomfortable with the whole situation. She moved as if to get up.

'Don't go, Marnie, please.' Charles reached a hand towards her. 'Please.'

Why do all these big, grown-up men have to have me there to hold their hands? She nodded and sat back.

Charles turned back to Gerard. 'I'm trying to understand your story, your side of things.'

'I don't believe you.'

Charles looked puzzled. 'Is that a luxury you can afford?'

'I'm interested in the truth and, in my case, I suppose you could say it's a luxury.' Seized by a coughing spasm, Gerard heaved himself up onto one elbow. Marnie quickly got up and passed him a glass of water from the table. When he stopped coughing, he lay back against the pillows clutching the glass. 'But I gave up when I reached the conclusion that your visiting me in prison had nothing to do with keeping an open mind or giving me the benefit of the doubt … or maybe helping me.'

'You seem very sure of yourself. I would've thought someone in your position –'

'You're not here to try to help me. You're trying to find out why your wife was …' He swallowed as if he found it difficult to speak.

'*Murdered* is the word you're looking for, I think.'

'No … *unfaithful* is the word. That's what you're looking for.'

Marnie spoke for the first time. 'I don't think this is getting anyone very far.'

Gerard agreed. 'No. Why not get to the point? What have you come for? I'm a busy man. I've got years of thinking ahead of me.'

Charles hesitated. 'Tell me … about the lovers. I find that difficult to understand. You don't talk about other people … other lovers … when you're in a relationship with someone.'

'Depends on the relationship. Maybe not when you're married … but then I don't know … I've never been married. But when you're lovers, it's different. There's a greater freedom and honesty. You have no secrets. You talk about old lovers because the atmosphere between you is more frank … somehow more intimate … more sexy. You're not trying to cover up. Everything comes out in the open.'

The silence that followed was so solid that Marnie stared at Charles, thinking he might have had a seizure. When he eventually spoke, his voice seemed to come from far away.

'These … lovers … You know who they are?'

Gerard made a barely perceptible gesture with one shoulder.

'How many?'

Gerard thought about it for a while. 'Four.'

'Four others … apart from you?'

A nod.

Charles got up slowly and began walking away. Marnie stood. Reaching the door, Charles turned to look back. 'No secrets,' he said.

Gerard shook his head. Charles opened the door and went out, his footsteps sounding along the passageway. Marnie turned to say good-bye for the last time, and Gerard looked up at her, a curious expression on his face. Not quite a smile. A thank-you?

Marnie moved her face closer to his. 'I've got a question for you. What if they weren't just *old lovers* … what then?'

She walked out without looking back and without waiting for an answer.

• • • • •

Charles was already crossing the car park when Marnie went out through the gates. He was plainly pre-occupied and walked head bowed, looking at his shoes. Marnie noticed them, black Oxfords, hand-crafted from fine leather, a discreet reminder of the world that Charles inhabited, a contrast with the drabness of the prison where Gerard would be spending the next thirty years or so. Charles looked up, saw Marnie's Discovery and walked her to it. Neither of them spoke.

Standing with his back to the car, Charles looked at the prison as he had before. 'Marnie, I know what you said … about it being the last time you'd visit …'

'I meant it, Charles.'

'I know. What did you make of what Gerard said back there?'

'I thought you were going to tell him he'd have to abandon any idea of your support. That's what I thought this visit was about.'

'So did I.'

'Did you, Charles? I got the impression Gerard was right about your reason for coming.'

'Do you blame me?'

'I don't see that it would do any good to rake over the past. If you sincerely believe

Gerard was guilty, I think it'd be best to leave it at that. You don't need to know who those other people might be.'

'*If* Gerard was guilty.'

'But you said –'

'I know about the evidence. But what about miscarriages of justice? They do happen, you know, despite all available evidence.'

'So?'

'What if it wasn't Gerard?'

'That doesn't mean it was another lover.'

'Do you believe she had all those lovers, Marnie?'

'I really don't know. Look, you're going to have to believe me on that … once and for all.'

Charles looked at her pointedly. 'I know you're an intelligent woman, Marnie, and I think you're perceptive and – to use an old-fashioned word – *sophisticated*, but you don't seem to understand what this means to me. My wife was allegedly having an affair with another man, and had had – or for all I know – was still involved with others … *four others*, if Gerard's telling the truth. Would you regard that as at least a possibility?'

Marnie took a deep breath and exhaled slowly. 'I suppose anything's a possibility. But if it is true, it may change nothing. It could be another motive for Gerard … jealousy.'

'I need to know what's true, Marnie.'

'But you need to be careful. My solicitor thinks that if you take the spotlight off Gerard, the next most likely suspect is … you.'

'I'd worked that one out already. Tell me, Marnie, what do you think of me … as a suspect?'

No hesitation. 'Ridiculous.'

'Yes, though more to the point, I had an unshakeable alibi. I'm appalled at the idea of needing one, but there it is.'

'I'm not sure where this is getting us, Charles.'

'I'd have thought it was pretty clear. I need to know for certain what happened. I find it difficult dealing with Gerard, but you … At least say you'll think about it.'

Marnie was horrified. 'About *what?*'

'Just talking to him. I'd really value your unbiased opinion. He'd talk to you, I know he would.'

Marnie saw a way of leaving. 'I'll think about it, but I can't promise anything.'

They separated. Marnie climbed in behind the wheel as Charles slipped into the Jaguar nearby. He hit the starter and was away while she was still fastening the seatbelt. *Captains of industry don't hang around*, she thought. She was just pulling out of her slot when a group of pedestrians went by, a small flock. Perhaps a train had deposited a number of visitors who had made their way up to the prison on foot. Taking care where she drove, Marnie reached the car park entrance when more people appeared. One of them, a woman, acknowledged Marnie's holding back with a wave of her hand. She immediately did a double-take and turned towards the car, blocking Marnie's exit. A face came to the driver's window. Two taps on the glass. Recognition. It was Sarah Cowan.

'You've been to see my brother again?'

Marnie pressed a button and the window slid open. 'Yes.'

'I don't know how you have the nerve.' It was said without anger, more in disbelief. 'Why did you come?'

'Charles Taverner wanted to see him … asked me along …'

'But what for? Why?'

'Good question. I'm still wondering. You'll find your brother has a view on it, and I think he may be right.'

'Please don't talk in riddles. This isn't a game for us. Neil has just tried to commit suicide, and one of the reasons was the loss of any hope that he might get at least an open-minded response from Charles Taverner. Why *are* you here?'

'I think Charles wanted to know about the lovers … the alleged lovers, I should say.'

Sarah checked her watch. 'Have you got time for a coffee?'

'No. I must get back. And you've come to see your … to see Neil.'

Sarah looked thoughtful. 'Are you here because you think Neil's right … and maybe one of the others killed her?'

'It's not my affair … I mean it's not my battle.'

'But surely you have an opinion, otherwise you wouldn't keep coming back with Charles Taverner.'

'Look, I've had enough problems in my life without interfering in someone else's. Barbara was a client, no more, no less. Her marriage, her private life, her affairs are none of my business.'

'Is it so easy to walk away?'

Marnie spelled it out slowly. 'I came here because Charles wanted an unbiased presence, just a little moral support. That's all it was. I didn't want to get involved. I still don't.'

'That sounds very judgmental, Marnie. Is that your approach to life … to stay aloof because nothing like that ever happens to you?'

'I'm not judging anyone.'

'That's how it sounds to me. Tell me, Marnie, were you a virgin on your wedding night? And have you never slept with anyone but your husband since then?'

Marnie stared at her and lowered her voice. 'My husband is *dead*.'

Sarah stepped back from the car as if Marnie had slapped her. Marnie let up the clutch and sped away.

19

The phone rang the next morning at eight-thirty. It surprised Marnie. Few people used the office line on a Saturday morning. She grabbed it quickly. There was no preamble or greeting, no introduction. It was Sarah Cowan and she launched straight in.

'I owe you an apology, Marnie. It's been troubling me ever since you went off yesterday. I felt awful. It made me see how unreasonable I've been.'

'It's understandable.'

'Maybe, but other people have a right to their own lives.'

'I can see I probably came across as heartless.'

'Even so, I shouldn't have tried to hang the guilt thing on you like that … as if you had to agree with me – with us – and had to fall in with our wishes.'

'You felt you had nothing to lose by trying.'

'Sure. But that was with Charles Taverner. It had nothing to do with *you*. You just got drawn in by chance … Marnie, are you yawning?'

Marnie's mouth snapped shut. 'Sorry.'

'You've not been sleeping?'

'It's okay.'

'I sympathise. I hardly sleep at all these days. Look, I really am sorry about everything. I'll not trouble you again … that's a promise.'

'Sarah, you genuinely believe Neil didn't kill Barbara, don't you?'

'It's more than that. I *know* he didn't. I know him better than anyone in the world … known him all my life. He's just not capable …'

'In a fit of jealous rage?'

'He knew all along the relationship with Barbara wouldn't be permanent. It was an affair, Marnie. They were both adults … they knew what they were doing.'

'Yeah.'

'Anyway … I just wanted to apologise for what I said.'

'That's all right, Sarah. I appreciate it. So … what are you going to do now?'

'Not sure … but …' A change of tone. Cheerful. 'We've got plenty of time to think of something.'

They said good-bye and disconnected. For the last time, Marnie told herself. It felt like a burden lifted from her shoulders. She reached an instant decision. They had decided over breakfast to work through the morning and travel down to Hemel to start bringing *Perfidia* back in the afternoon. Now, she phoned Ralph and suggested they leave at once. He agreed. Next stop, Anne. Marnie was heading out of the door when the phone sounded. Aware that these days she took calls with some foreboding, she picked it up. Again no preamble, no introduction. None was needed. It was Beth, and her opening words hit Marnie with more force than anything Sarah Cowan had ever said.

'That was you in the paper, wasn't it? Are you *mad*? What did you think you were doing?'

'Paper? What paper? What are you talking about?'

'The front page of the *Sun*? That's what I'm talking about. You standing there with Charles Taverner ... then talking to Gerard's sister ... that's what I'm talking about.'

'Beth, slow down, I don't understand.'

'You made the front page ... and some of the inside pages.' Doubt crept into her voice. 'You didn't know?'

'Of course not. Do I sound as if I knew? How did *you* know? You've started taking the *Sun*?'

'Paul spotted it when he went to pay our paper bill ... bought a copy. I've got it here.'

'The article says it was me?'

'It refers to a *woman friend of Charles Taverner*, but I recognised you straight away ... and your car, that poncy Sloan Ranger thing you drive around in.'

'What's the article about? No, don't tell me. I'll buy a copy. I've gotta go.'

Marnie legged it through the spinney to *Sally Ann*.

'Anne, we're going early. Pack up! We're leaving.'

Absentmindedly Anne looked up from her sketchpad. 'Is it lunchtime already?'

'I'll explain on the way.'

On *Thyrsis*, Ralph was just as engrossed in his work as Anne had been. 'Now?'

'Now.'

• • • • •

In minutes they were driving through the village in convoy, Ralph's elderly Volvo trailing in the wake of the Discovery. A quick halt outside the shop while Anne dashed in to buy the *Sun* – much to the surprise of Molly Appleton – and they were back on the road.

Anne held up the paper. 'What am I supposed to be looking for?'

'Try the front page.'

'Really?' Anne began reading to herself. 'Oh my God ...'

'Sounds like you found it.'

'This *woman friend* ... it's you, isn't it, Marnie?'

'Am I recognisable?'

'Well ... Mr Taverner's clear ... Sarah Cowan's clear ... but you ... you've got the side of the Discovery blocking you ... except for part of your profile. It's unmistakeable, but only if you know who you're looking at.'

'Telephoto lens job?'

'Must be.'

'What does it say?'

'It asks: *Why is Charles Taverner visiting Neil Gerard ... his wife's convicted murderer? Who is this woman talking to Sarah Cowan in the car park? What is going on?*'

'Not bad questions.'

'What *is* going on, Marnie? I don't get it. Is Mr Taverner trying to help Neil Gerard get off ... or make an appeal or something?'

'More good questions.'

'And?'

'There's a café at this roundabout. I'm pulling over. We need to talk, all of us.'

• • • • •

It was a Little Chef, busy on a Saturday morning. Anne had bagged a table, and the three of them sat amid the hubbub while Marnie told them in a lowered voice all the details of the conversations with Neil Gerard and with his sister. Until then she had kept back the information about Barbara's supposed four other lovers, not wanting to perpetuate her involvement any longer than was necessary.

After they had digested the facts, it fell to Ralph to ask the obvious question. 'Marnie, you know I'm always happy to go along with your plans ... even those made on the spur of the moment ... even if I don't know the reason behind them ...'

'Ye-e-es.'

'But why are we actually going to *Perfidia* now? I mean, why couldn't we just stick to our original plan and go this afternoon?'

'I thought ... well, it seemed to me ...'

Anne joined in to help her. 'Were you thinking it'd be best to take the boat in case a reporter spotted it ... and had it under surveillance?'

'Among other things.'

Ralph's turn. Sceptical. 'A quick getaway ... at four miles an hour?'

'Better than taking the risk of leaving her under their noses.'

'But we haven't come with any supplies for the journey.' Anne, ever-practical. 'I just grabbed a few undies and overnight things. Is there food and stuff on board?'

'We'll need to get provisions on the way. In fact, you two could go to the supermarket while I check the boat over.'

The revised plan was agreed and the cars were back on the road again. Following the tailgate of the Discovery from a short distance back, Ralph was wondering what was really going on in Marnie's mind.

• • • • •

By arrangement with the landlord they parked the Discovery at a waterside pub off the main road north of Leighton Buzzard, estimating that they could reach it on Sunday. It was the usual boater's game, two-car relay, with one at each end of the run. Ralph drove them on to Hemel where they sat in the Volvo at a strategic spot, watching for any sign of a concealed reporter or photographer. Satisfied that all was clear, Ralph dropped Marnie at the boat. She opened the side door and climbed aboard as the Volvo trundled towards the town centre. After a count of twenty, her head appeared from the hatch and she re-emerged onto the bank. In less than two minutes she was boarding a cab in the taxi rank at the station.

The plan almost came unstuck at the prison gate. In her haste, Marnie had forgotten the need to have an appointment. But luckily the rules for visitors to the sanatorium were less strict, particularly where it concerned a 'suicide case', and she was known from signing in the previous day.

When Marnie was escorted into the san, Gerard sat up in surprise. As soon as the warder withdrew, she wasted no time.

'I've got ten minutes max.'

Gerard looked perplexed and seemed unable to speak. Marnie rushed forward and seized him by the collar of his pyjamas, speaking urgently in a harsh whisper into his ear.

'You killed her, didn't you? You really did it. Admit it. I want the truth!'

Gerard did not flinch. He spoke calmly. 'No. I had nothing to do with Barbara's death. You don't need ten minutes. You can leave now if you don't believe me.'

Her eyes held his for an age before she released her grip and stepped back. She walked round the bed and flopped onto a chair, deep in thought. Gerard remained immobile.

'You told Charles that Barbara had four other lovers … in addition to you.' Gerard breathed out audibly but said nothing. Marnie continued. 'You see, that's the part I find difficult to believe.'

'Why difficult? I can't imagine that an attractive woman like you finds it hard to believe that an attractive woman like Barbara had lovers. Surely you must've –'

Marnie raised a hand. 'Stop there. Let's get something straight. I'm here to talk about Barbara. My private life is not up for discussion. It's my business and no one else's, especially yours. Are we clear about that?'

'Quite clear. But my point still stands. Why could Barbara not have lovers … if she wanted them?'

Marnie thought of the phantom diary dates, Barbara's meticulous preparation for their meetings. She certainly had one lover. But *five*?

'How long had you and Barbara been seeing each other?'

'Just over two years.'

'And the others?'

'What do you mean?'

'You know who they were, so presumably you must know when they were together.'

Gerard stared at Marnie for some time. She looked at her watch. Misunderstanding his silence, she said, 'She had a lover … I can believe that. But if you're suggesting she had *five* … at the same time …'

'I'm not suggesting any such thing. She wasn't a *tramp*. I was just trying to fit them into a time frame.'

'What I wanted to know was … were any of them still in touch with her? Also, what was the nature of their relationship?'

Gerard raised an eyebrow. 'Meaning?'

'On a sliding scale from *grand passion* to … one-night stand.'

For the first time, Gerard's face muscles relaxed. He settled back on the pillows and smiled. 'You're dressed for boating, I see.'

'Very perceptive … but let's stick with Barbara. My time's running out.'

'Not very perceptive. Jeans and a sweatshirt … the sort of things Barbara wore on the boat. You and Barbara have a lot in common.'

'Look, are you going to tell me about these so-called lovers or do I just leave now?'

'Why the rush?'

'We were seen leaving here yesterday –'

'I know. Sarah told me she'd seen you. She was going to phone to apologise for what she said.'

'She did. But we were also seen by a reporter … and photographed. You're looking at the *Sun*'s new cover girl.'

Gerard started. 'You're kidding!'

'I want to be away before anyone can get a tip-off to the newshounds.'

'Of course. Look, I need to think about it. I'll write out a list of names and try to put some kind of timescale together. Would that help? I'll pass the details on through Sarah.'

Marnie got up.

'Thanks for coming, Marnie. I always thought you believed me.'

She looked at him coldly. 'I didn't, actually.'

'Then why did you come?'

A pause. 'I believed Sarah.'

• • • • •

The first thing Marnie did on arriving back at *Perfidia* was to start the engine. Even if Ralph and Anne returned in less than a minute, it would give the impression that everything had been prepared for the journey. It slightly horrified her that she had become so sneaky. *You and Barbara have a lot in common …* The idea brought her up short.

No! Hell, no! She had no desire to go down that path. Ralph was probably the most intelligent person she had ever met, but he was not shrewd or cunning in the sense of detecting duplicity, and Marnie knew he would never suspect her of trying to deceive him. Would he have known if she had a lover? Probably not. He may not have been the world's most dynamic action man, but he possessed great qualities. He had integrity and valued truth above everything. His world was based on it. It was a good foundation for a life together.

She had checked the butane bottle and connected the gas supply, switched on the electrics and selected the starter battery on the isolator. The fridge was humming. The water pump was growling as it built up pressure. She had ignited the flame in the water heater and tested the central heating system. Everything was up and running, and the Volvo had not yet returned. Marnie went aft and switched off the engine, leaning against the bulkhead. Her motives may have been right, but in pursuing them she had gone behind the back of her lover and her closest friend.

Walking through to the dining area, she dropped onto the banquette and put her head in her hands. *What was she doing? How had she got herself into this mess?* Her life had been difficult enough since leaving the secure job in London and branching out on her own. Did she really want these complications?

Contemplating the irony of trying to resolve one deception by creating another, she lost track of how long she was sitting at the table. It was the rocking of the boat that first made her aware that the shoppers were back from their expedition. They brought the bustle of the outside world with them, both chattering as they swung the bags down onto the galley floor.

'Sorry we took so long, Marnie. I got snarled up in a one-way system. If it hadn't been for Anne's excellent organisation we'd still be in the supermarket –'

'But Ralph's a dab hand with a shopping trolley. You should've seen him … Marnie? Are you all right?'

Marnie looked up from far away and focused on them. 'Come and sit down …' She gestured. 'I want to talk to the two of you.'

Her sombre tone changed the atmosphere on board in a trice. Two serious faces confronted her across the table. She began by recapping on all the events leading up to the time of Barbara's death, including the affair with Gerard and the other lovers.

'That's the story so far.'

'We knew all that, Marnie. You've told us already.'

'There's more. I've … I've been to see him again.'

'You told us that, too.'

'No. It was just now. I went to the prison while you were shopping.'

Anne looked at Ralph. He frowned. 'Was that a spur of the moment thing?'

'I made up my mind on the drive down.'

'That's why you wanted us out of the way.'

Marnie studied Ralph's face. 'Yes.'

'I see.'

'And that's why I'm telling you now. I hate the idea of deceiving you … either of you …'

'What was your purpose in going to see him … and the timing of your visit?'

'It was talking to Sarah on the phone this morning … and then that business with the newspaper. I saw how convinced she was … the anxiety on her face in the photo … how desperate she was.'

'You wanted to see Gerard by yourself without Charles there to influence things.'

Marnie nodded. 'That must've been part of it.'

'I'm glad you told us this, Marnie.' He grinned. 'I knew you were up to something.'

Surprise. 'You did?'

'I had my suspicions.'

'And you're not annoyed with me?'

'I'm glad you explained.' He spotted Anne's list on the table. 'And you can give us the rest of your story later … I'm sure there's more to come. But don't you think we ought to get going before anyone – like a tabloid reporter – sees *Perfidia* and starts getting interested?'

Marnie rose at once from the table. 'You're right. Time for a quick getaway … at four miles an hour.'

By the time Marnie had the engine running again and Anne had pushed off fore and aft, Ralph had Boxmoor Top Lock ready to receive *Perfidia* on her run through the Winkwell and Bourne End locks up to Berkhamsted and, beyond that, the long pound of the Tring summit.

• • • • •

They estimated the run at around twelve miles and seventeen locks, and even with Ralph preparing most locks in advance, it took over eight hours. When they cleared the last of the Marsworth flight there was still daylight and travelling time ahead of them, but Marnie had other ideas. Entering the Tring Cutting, she eased back and pulled over in a secluded spot with steep slopes, overhung with trees. While Ralph and Anne made *Perfidia* secure on mooring pins Marnie inspected the boat, turning the knob to grease the stern gland, switching to leisure battery, checking the bilge pump was turned off, *the little things Barbara as a good boatwoman would have done routinely*, she thought to herself.

They felt rejuvenated and pleasantly tired after the long spell of exercise. On any other evening they might have set off for the nearest canalside pub, but this was an exception. They were eating on board. Having been responsible for the refurbishing of several of the pubs along the canal, Marnie was known in the area. *Perfidia* was now an infamous boat, and canal users took note of passing vessels. Marnie feared it was possible that together they could excite comment, and word of their presence might get out. Ralph was not convinced of the danger. He took the view that most people never gave the waterways a thought and would not go looking for Marnie – the unidentified *woman* – or even *Perfidia* – on the canal, obvious though that might seem to the group of them. Alone on their remote mooring, Marnie was confident that no one would come looking.

After hours of rapid walking along the towpath and working the locks, Ralph muttered that he would welcome a change of clothes, and he was packed off to the shower room. Marnie and Anne meanwhile made supper. Anne offered to make a tuna pâté and toast as a starter; Marnie prepared a vegetable stir-fry with basmati rice. Yogurts were keeping cool in the fridge. An opened bottle of Aussie Shiraz stood breathing quietly on the workbench. A perfect meal for the end of an enjoyably strenuous trip.

Ralph had been thinking through the situation during his shower and launched straight in as soon as they began eating. 'Visiting Gerard like that, Marnie … you did the right thing if you really believed his story.'

Marnie took a sip of wine. 'Do you think Gerard's innocent?'

'Is that really the point here? Does it matter what I believe?'

'It matters to me, Ralph.'

His turn to sample the wine. 'All the evidence suggests otherwise.'

'Damn … what about you, Anne?'

'I think I'm out of my league on this one. I've only seen what's been in the papers and on TV.'

'And you've met Sarah.'

'So? I'd do all I could to stick up for my brother if he was in trouble.'

'Would you have lied to help him … if he was accused of murder?'

Anne fingered her glass. 'Probably …'

'But Sarah didn't,' Ralph observed.

Anne looked up. 'No, but … she didn't think she had to, did she?'

'Ah … now that's the point.'

Marnie shook her head. 'We're going round in circles … covering the same old ground again. The trouble is, there's no evidence to go on. What if Gerard produces these names … her other lovers?'

'Producing names won't prove anything ... not in itself. You'd need much more than that to get the police to re-open enquiries.'

They finished off the pâté, and Marnie got up to tackle the stir-fry while Ralph cleared the first course debris. By the time Anne had put out the rice, Marnie was serving vegetables from the wok. The air over the table was laced with steam and the smell of soy sauce. Before taking her first mouthful Marnie made a pronouncement.

'I think you're right, Ralph. Nothing's going to make any difference.'

It was the next day, a Sunday morning in spring. A quiet stretch of canal under an overcast sky, with only a solemn heron looking on from a distance. Not a sound from the outside world, no birdsong, not even church bells ringing at the early hour when Ralph and Anne untied ropes and pulled out mooring pins.

They made steady progress throughout the day, cruising through open countryside that Marnie always found surprisingly remote, given how close they were to the huge city to the south. Ralph again spent most of the time walking from one lock to the next, but shortly after Ivinghoe he was caught by a sudden shower and took shelter under the bridge by Horton Wharf.

He ventured out to work the lock, envying Marnie in her waterproof jacket and rain hat. Once they were in clear water again he stepped onto the gunwale in the bridge hole and was delighted to be welcomed on board with a change of sweater and a mug of coffee reinforced with brandy. The rest of the journey passed without incident. They left *Perfidia* by arrangement at a boatyard in Leighton Buzzard.

They walked along to the pub car park and collected Marnie's Discovery. Driving back to Hemel, they picked up Ralph's Volvo. Within half an hour they were motoring down the high street in Knightly St John in convoy and turning off the road to take the field track home.

Marnie swung in first and slotted the car straight into its place in the garage barn. Ralph pulled into the next bay, and they were lifting their overnight bags from the car boots when Angela came round the corner.

'Hi! You gave me a surprise there. Did you forget something?'

Three pairs of eyes focused on her while their owners tried to make a connection.

'Say again,' Marnie urged.

Angela spoke slowly and clearly. 'When I heard you the first time I came out to say hallo but you'd already gone.'

'The *first time* ... when was this?'

'Five or ten minutes ago, at a guess.'

'It wasn't us.'

'What made you think it was?' Ralph asked.

'I ... mm ... I'm not sure. I knew you were expecting to be back about now and I ... just assumed it was you.'

They ushered Angela into the office barn where Anne prepared tea. Marnie took her seat opposite Angela.

'Okay ... what did you see ... or hear?'

'I heard a car outside.'

'What colour ... what make?'

Angela shook her head.

Ralph joined in. 'What about the sound... anything?'

'It was just ... a car.'

'Think carefully. Could it, for example, have been a diesel ... sounding like a Land

Rover?' Angela looked doubtful. Ralph continued. 'Or perhaps it might've been a more powerful car … with a loud engine?'

'Sorry. I didn't notice anything special about it.'

'And you didn't catch a glimpse of it through the window?'

'No … 'fraid not. I'd just got back from evensong and I was changing my clothes upstairs. I don't normally parade in front of the window in my underwear.'

While Ralph struggled to untangle his thoughts about female vicars and underwear, Marnie took over.

'You say you heard it from upstairs. How?'

Angela pondered, frowning. 'Gravel … I heard it on the gravel.'

'Going quickly?'

'No … quite slowly, come to think of it. It surprised me a bit because you always just turn straight into the barn, don't you?'

'Where was your car?'

'I'd just left it in the courtyard for a few minutes. I'd carried in a box of new hymnbooks. They were heavy and I didn't want to have to lug them too far.'

'So the driver wouldn't have seen your car in the courtyard until he drove round the office barn.'

'That's right.'

'And whoever it was, they decided not to stay.'

Angela look worried. 'Do you attach any particular significance to that, Marnie?'

'I'm not sure.'

• • • • •

There was no pretext this time. Marnie simply told Ralph and Anne that she wanted to phone Sarah. She left them putting supper together in the galley on *Sally Ann* and returned to the office barn to make the call. Predictably she got the answerphone. Her first reaction was to hang up, but she decided to leave just a brief message.

'Hi. It's Marnie Walker. Could you give me a ring when –'

The phone was snatched up. 'I'm here. These days I screen all incoming calls … media attention, you know.'

'I can imagine.'

'You've been to see Neil again.'

'You too?'

'I go every Saturday and Sunday, especially since … I'd go every day if I could. You're phoning me about those names.'

'Names?'

'Neil promised to let you have the names of Barbara's lovers. He's given me a list. I was going to send them by e-mail … unless you want me to read them out now?'

'No … e-mail's fine. I'm really phoning you about something else. Have you been here today?'

'Where's here? Where are you phoning from, Marnie?'

'From home … from Glebe Farm.'

'I've never been there … don't even know where it is. How could I?'

That was a blow. If the visitor had been Sarah, it would have been the simplest explanation. But if it wasn't her ... Sarah's voice cut into her train of thought.

'Are you still there, Marnie?'

'Sorry ... er ... yes.'

'Has something happened?'

'A car came down here this afternoon and left as soon as it got close enough to realise someone was around.'

'Is that unusual? Cars come past my house all the time.'

'We live at the end of a farm track down a slope ... it's a few hundred metres ... you have to cross a field to get here.'

'So ... if it wasn't me, who was it? That's what you're thinking?'

'Right.'

'My guess is the media. They're out looking for you ... the woman from the paper?'

'But how did they know I lived here?'

'Easy. You were followed.'

Marnie decided this had gone far enough. 'That must be it.'

'I'm sure that's the solution, Marnie.'

'Yeah.'

Sarah promised to copy Neil's list of names and e-mail it that evening. They disconnected.

Before walking back to the boat through the spinney, Marnie made a tour of inspection. She believed Sarah. Why shouldn't she? Everyone believed Sarah. *I've never been there ... don't even know where it is.* She looked into the barns. She went to the back of the farmhouse, checked behind the cement mixer and the shed. She looked in the small patio gardens of the three cottages. No one was lurking.

As an afterthought she examined the grass at the edge of the gravel for tyre tracks, but Angela had gone over the ground when she drove her car out of the courtyard. And anyway, Marnie wondered, what could she have deduced from tyre tracks?

Standing at the back of the office barn, she ticked off the possibilities in her mind. A courting couple looking for somewhere secluded to be alone together? All the locals knew Glebe Farm was occupied, and the couples who were the two most likely candidates in the area had now become her tenants. A stranger who had got lost? No one would think of taking the field track to go anywhere.

Through the trees she caught a glimpse of lights twinkling fifty metres away. With the day beginning to fade, they had switched on the cabin lights on *Sally Ann*, nestling in her docking area. It was a welcoming sight, and Marnie set off like a mediaeval traveller seeking shelter on the road. As she walked she itemised four certainties that were clear to her.

One. This was the second time in the past few days that someone had made the journey down the field track to check out Glebe Farm and then left in a hurry.

Two. Such a thing had never happened before they got involved with Neil Gerard. And the Taverners.

Three. No one had followed Marnie home. They arrived there before she did.

Four. Someone was watching them.

21

Monday morning and Marnie's first task was to fire up the computer and open the e-mails. There it was, third in the list of seven that had come in since yesterday. Sarah Cowan. She double-clicked on the sender's name in the in-box. A short message with the paperclip symbol to indicate an attachment.

Hello Marnie

Here is Neil's list, as promised. I've told him I can't really see what you or anyone else can do about them, but he said you wanted to know who they were. If this makes Charles Taverner feel more inclined to give Neil the benefit of the doubt, maybe it will do some good. Anyway, it's up to you to take whatever action you think fit, if any.

Thanks for your interest,

Sarah

Marnie double-clicked on the attachment, and the list appeared. Sarah's typing was neat and precise. The list was numbered with the four names and a few lines of notes under each one. Two of the names were unknown to Marnie. One was famous. The other was quite a surprise.

1. Ian Stuart

Owner of marina in Docklands at Bermuda Reach. He is very well-off. Barbara said he fancied himself as a lady's man. They had a relationship a couple of years back. From what she said, I think they may have had some contact recently.

2. Clive Adamson

A businessman and former colleague of Charles. I'm sure Barbara had known him for a long time. Not sure she even liked him, but was attracted by his 'dynamism and energy'. Charles definitely disliked him and thought him unscrupulous. Interestingly, he seems to have treated Barbara as just another girlfriend among many. He dropped her, which is not usual.

The famous name leapt off the page.

3. Piers Wainwright

The artist. Barbara met him at the opening of a one-man show at the Weatherly Gallery in Bond Street. Charles commissioned him to do a portrait of Barbara. You can imagine how the sittings went. I think it was about three years ago and lasted only a few months.

The fourth name was the surprise.

4. Mike Brent

Manager of Little Venice. I think this may have been more of a flirtation that turned into a 'fling' than a real relationship. Not really in her class. (Do I flatter myself here?!) Barbara gave the impression she had seen him quite a lot while pottering about on *Perfidia*.

A cacophony of thoughts and impressions crowded into Marnie's mind. She herself had had relatively few lovers. There had been the usual propositions starting at the age of fifteen that had all been rejected. There was the customary run of boyfriends at college. But then she had met Simon. From that day on she had been a one-man woman. After they split up she threw herself into her career to the exclusion of all else, with the passing distraction of being pursued by a colleague of her brother-in-law, a lecturer at UCL. And then Ralph had come along.

But Barbara. She was a different breed. Marnie had known a number of men who were predators. Was Barbara a female equivalent? If this was the recent list of her conquests, how many others had figured in her life? And why? Marnie thought she could probably guess. Curiosity and possibly boredom, dissatisfaction with the physical side of her life. Presumably dissatisfaction with Charles.

This was high-stakes gambling. Had Barbara not cared about losing the life of ease and luxury that Charles provided? On reflection, that answer was easy as well. She never thought Charles would find out. She was too clever to give the game away.

But that was no concern of Marnie's. The question now was what to tell Charles, if anything.

• • • • •

Anne walked up to the shop in the late morning to pay for last week's newspapers, overlooked in all the movement at the weekend. She was glad of the exercise, the fresh air to clear her head after three hours of non-stop studying.

Molly Appleton looked up from the counter and called across to her husband, Richard, immured in the glass box that was the domain of the sub-postmaster.

'Look who it is ... ten minutes too late. Hallo, Anne. Guess who was in here just now?'

'Hi. No idea ... Brad Pitt ... Keanu Reeves? Am I warm?'

'Ronny!'

'Oh? I thought he was away on his gap year.'

'You mean you didn't know he was coming back? Perhaps he wanted it to be a surprise for you. Hope I haven't spoilt it.'

Anne's expression betrayed her bewilderment. 'I'm not sure I follow ...'

'Well, you two being ... sort of friends ... and him being so keen on you ... I thought you'd have been in touch while he was in Canada.'

'Oh, I see.'

Molly raised a hand to her mouth. 'Have I spoken out of turn? I am sorry, Anne ...'

'That's all right. I haven't really had any contact with Ronny since last summer.'

'I'm sure he'd be pleased to see you.'

'Right.'

Anne paid the paper bill and said a cheery good-bye. She did not feel cheery. Had Ronny Cope been talking about her to the Appletons? The truth was, she had no desire to see him. They had parted as less than friends the previous year after a row in which he more or less accused her of leading him on and being frigid when he tried to get friendly.

But it occurred to her that it would be best to see him before he had a chance to make any false assumptions about their non-relationship. The element of surprise could be useful in this. If Ronny was at home, he would be alone. His father was a commuter, his mother worked mornings, his brother would be at school. The small 'executive development' known as Martyrs Close was like a ghost town at this time of day. Anne would pop in, say a friendly word or two and pop out ... cordial ...

neighbourly … but nothing more.

Martyrs Close was on the other side of the church, and Anne turned smartly in at the lych gate to take the path through the churchyard.

Back down the high street, Molly Appleton was taking the opportunity to check the shop's window display – unchanged in living memory – and watched Anne veer off towards the church. With a look of satisfaction she went back inside and gave a knowing wink to her husband.

• • • • •

Ralph sat on the corner of Marnie's desk and read the list of names that she had printed from the computer. He had come to the office barn for his morning coffee and found Marnie on the phone to a boatyard near Blisworth. She was negotiating for a slot in their schedule and, while waiting for the owner to consult his programme, she had signalled to Ralph to pick up the print-out. A lucky cancellation made it possible for the yard to take *Perfidia* in about two weeks, and they could move her up any time they wished. The yard would black the hull and do whatever was required to the topsides. Marnie scribbled a note for Anne to put in the diary and looked up at Ralph.

'We can take *Perfidia* up to Blisworth the weekend after next.'

'That's the Oxford Conference weekend, remember?'

'You're there for the whole weekend?'

Ralph nodded. 'Starting with dinner on the Friday evening.'

'Then it's either a solo trip or I take Anne.'

'Wild horses …' Ralph murmured enigmatically.

'Yeah. There are some long pounds between locks. Anne can get on with her college work while we travel.' Marnie pointed at Gerard's list of names. 'Do you know any of them?'

'Well, Adamson of course is your classic captain of industry. Accountant by training, I think … made his name over the past twenty years as an asset-stripper.'

'How does that work?'

'Case study. Dolman and Yates … struggling in the early eighties. Adamson went in as special adviser … got half the board removed … sold off two or three subsidiary companies for the redevelopment value of their sites … got the firm refocused and became chairman. Golden handshake after three years … made a couple of million. On to the next challenge.'

'Onward and upward,' said Marnie. 'Better than going bust. I'm impressed.'

'Unlike the company's employees.'

'Oh?' Marnie prepared herself to become unimpressed.

'Production was moved to the Far East, so most people lost their jobs. Adamson refused to negotiate reasonable redundancy terms. Stripped of their powers, the unions couldn't do a thing about it.'

'I wonder what Barbara saw in him.'

'The same as she saw in Charles, no doubt … wealth and power … not bad aphrodisiacs.'

Marnie frowned. 'Charles isn't like that. He's not that kind of businessman, is he?'

'I doubt it. He made a number of shrewd moves during his career. Got an MBA from

Cranfield … put him on the so-called fast track. But he's more the dependable sort … the safe pair of hands. That's what they really like best in the City.'

'That's what Barbara liked, too. In fact, I suspect it's what most women like.' Ralph smiled. Marnie continued. 'What about the other names on the list?'

'Don't know Stuart. Brent we both know, of course …. affable, presentable sort of chap. But Wainwright … that's something I would *never* have expected.'

'Why not?'

'*Why not?* It's like finding out she's been involved with Picasso.'

'He's not that famous, Ralph!' Marnie exclaimed.

'Hockney, then.'

Marnie raised an eyebrow. 'Bit unlikely?'

'You know what I mean. Weren't you surprised?'

'Yes … and no …It's wealthy business people who can afford to commission the best artists. I must've seen the portrait in their house at Templars' Wharf.'

Ralph frowned. 'I didn't think he painted portraits … just landscapes and abstracts.' He stood up and walked over to the kitchen area with his mug. 'The thing is, Marnie. What do you intend doing with this information?'

• • • • •

Anne shut the gate in the churchyard wall behind her. It felt strange being in Martyrs Close again after an absence of several months. For Anne, Ronny had only ever been a casual friend, someone roughly her own age who lived in the area. Since coming to Knightly St John she had had one real relationship, but that was brief and unlikely ever to be revived. Ronny had assumed more than he should. Anne was going to act quickly and decisively to set matters straight.

She glanced from side to side at the houses as she passed by. *Ghost town* just about summed it up. The estate of a dozen or so detached houses, each set back from the street, standing on its own substantial plot, felt like a suburb, completely different from the rest of the village.

Anne took a deep breath as she approached the Copes' house. Ten minutes maximum, then home to Glebe Farm, a sandwich for lunch at noon and back to her project work. Turning onto the drive she noticed that the gravel needed raking. Mr Cope had left in a hurry, running late to catch the 7.22, no doubt. Everything else was neat and trimmed.

She rang the doorbell and while waiting for an answer, she bent down and righted the milk bottle holder that was lying on its side in the porch. Nothing stirred in the house. Her journey had been wasted. Ronny had not come home after all. Reaching out to press the bell one last time, she saw daylight at the edge of the door. She pushed it and it swung inwards. Something was wrong. The churned-up gravel … the knocked-over bottle holder … the open door. Another deep breath.

Stepping into the hallway, Anne stopped and listened. She could hear only her pulse racing. Digging into a back pocket, she pulled out her mobile. Before moving further into the house, she opened the front door wide. Noiselessly she looked into the nearest room – the *executive through-lounge* – and was surprised to see the television and video machine on their stand in the middle of the carpet. An armchair had been pushed aside and on it was stacked the hi-fi and a pile of CDs and videos.

A sound somewhere in the house made Anne freeze. She was not alone. Understanding what had happened, she pressed three nines on the mobile, tip-toed to the glazed dividing screen at the end of the lounge and eased one half of it apart. The dining room was untouched. She crept across to the kitchen door and peeped round it. The kitchen was in chaos. A small TV stood on the breakfast table that was askew in the centre. The workbenches were a mass of broken and upturned bottles and jars, one work area covered in flour as if a snowstorm had struck.

Anne hit the send button on the mobile. The call was answered at once.

'Emergency. Which service, please?'

'Police.' Anne's eyes were attracted by something on the floor behind the table and she squatted down. 'And ambulance. Please come quickly.'

She gave the details of name, address and location, and described what had happened. Her hands were trembling. All the time she was struggling to keep her composure. When she finished the call, promising that she would wait at the scene, she knelt down beside Ronny.

'Oh, my *God* …'

• • • • •

Marnie sat alone in the office. Ralph had gone back to *Thyrsis* to analyse some statistics, and Anne would return from the shop in the next few minutes. She read the list of Barbara's lovers once again, asking herself if somewhere on the page she was looking at the name of her killer. If she really had so many, perhaps there might be others. Other lovers, other suspects. Another life. And Charles, where did he fit into all this?

Marnie swivelled in her chair and looked up at the ceiling. Old beams, ancient oak, pitted and uneven, raised there centuries earlier by men whose lives were less tormented. But perhaps not. A young woman had once hanged herself from one of those beams.

Marnie shook herself mentally and came back to the present. What was she going to do with the list? What should she tell Charles? It could only add to his suffering to delve into Barbara's involvement with these other men. What had Gerard said? Between lovers there were … *no secrets*. But in a marriage some things were best left untold. Perhaps it should stay that way.

The phone rang, and Marnie swivelled round to pick it up. It was Anne.

• • • • •

A light on the instrument panel showed that one of the car doors was not properly shut. Marnie paid it no heed as she gunned the Discovery up the field track, bumping and bouncing on the hard ridges, her foot heavy on the pedal. She was steering with one hand, the other groping to plug in the seat belt between gear changes. Beside her on the passenger seat lay the first aid box that she had grabbed from the cupboard immediately on putting down the phone. Anne's attempt at speaking calmly had barely concealed her anxiety.

Reaching the field gate, Marnie snatched second gear, keeping the car rolling and bucketing out onto the empty road. It was little more than twenty metres to Martyrs Close, and she treated the manoeuvre as one extended right-hand corner, throwing the wheel over, all four wheels biting into the tarmac as she kept on the power. The first houses came into view, and she slowed, realising that she had never been to the Copes' house and was unsure which one it was.

Marnie cursed under her breath as she found she had left her mobile back in the office. A farcical thought came into her mind. She saw herself knocking on doors, asking if by any chance they had been burgled and had a young man lying on the kitchen floor, possibly dying. Then she saw the gravel. Deep grooves had been gouged into it by a vehicle speeding away. The front door stood wide open. Marnie braked heavily, seized the first aid kit and leapt out, not bothering to push the door shut behind her. She raced into the hall.

'In here!' Anne called out from the rear of the house.

Marnie shot forward just as the phone started ringing on the hall table. She ignored it and pressed on towards the kitchen. In the doorway she paused for a millisecond to take in the scene. Anne was kneeling beside Ronny whose face was the same colour as the flour that covered half the room. She had rolled some tea towels to make a pillow for his head and was holding his hand. He lay ominously still. Marnie dropped to her knees and touched Ronny's forehead. It felt cold and damp. She reached for his wrist and began searching for a pulse.

'I ought to know more about what to do in an emergency. Has he been like this the whole time?'

'Yeah.' Anne's voice was strangulated. She cleared her throat. 'Since I found him. I tried to check his pulse, but there was nothing.'

Marnie moved her hand from Ronny's wrist to the side of his neck. His head rolled. Things were not looking good.

'How long before the ambulance gets here? Did they say?'

'Very soon. She didn't give me a time.'

'We need to keep him warm.' Marnie stood up, scouring the room for inspiration. 'The airing cupboard!'

She ran out, and Anne heard her bounding up the stairs. She started in panic. Could the burglar still be in the house? She was on the brink of calling out a warning when Marnie scudded back down the staircase and burst into the kitchen holding a bundle of towels. She unfolded them to reveal two large white bath sheets, which she spread over Ronny, tucking them round his shoulders. They looked like a shroud. The phone started ringing again.

'Did you give them the house number?'

Anne shook her head. 'Just my mobile.'

They caught a snatch of sound somewhere far off. A siren.

'Come on!' Marnie breathed.

They ignored the phone. There was the siren again. Or was it another one, a different tone? Marnie and Anne felt helpless and inadequate. Both resolved separately to learn more about first aid. The phone stopped ringing. Suddenly the siren was very near. A vehicle pulled up hard outside. Doors banged. Running footsteps on gravel and in the hall.

Marnie shouted. 'We're in the kitchen back here.'

Two men in uniform rushed in. Police. Marnie stood up to explain. Before she could speak, the first officer gestured at her.

'Mrs Walker, can you move your car out of the way. We need more room for when the ambulance gets here.'

Marnie headed off without a word. The phone started up again. She climbed into the Discovery, surprised to find she had left the engine running, and parked a short way along the street. Jogging back to the house, it struck her as curious that the policeman had called her by name. She reached the drive at the same time as the ambulance and stood aside while the driver reversed towards the front door. His colleague had already jumped out and was walking purposefully into the house carrying a bag, the word *Paramedic* emblazoned on his luminous jacket.

The ambulance stopped, the driver leapt out and rushed to open the rear doors. He pulled out a stretcher trolley and positioned it at the front of the house before going inside. Marnie followed him slowly, unsure of what she should do. While she was waiting in the hall, Anne came out. They stood together, superfluous now that the experts had arrived.

'Any change?' Marnie asked quietly.

Anne shook her head. The phone started ringing on the table in front of them. Marnie picked it up. It was cordless, and she walked towards the front porch as she spoke.

'Hallo?'

'Who is this?' A woman, her voice fraught and shrill.

'Marnie Walker. Is that Mrs Cope?'

'What's going on?'

'Well … er …'

'What's happening?' It was almost a scream. 'Tell me what's happening!'

'It looks as if your house has been burgled … or rather that someone has attempted –'

'Why is an ambulance there?'

The ambulance? How did she know? Of course. Across the street a curtain was twitching.

'It seems that Ronny may have disturbed the burglar and –'

'Is he all right? What's happened to him?'

'The paramedics are with him now …'

On cue, one of the men rushed out and pulled the trolley into the house. Marnie saw Anne step back into the lounge to leave the hall clear.

'Has Ronny been hurt? Speak to me!'

'I think they're taking him to hospital to … to get him the proper attention.'

'*Hospital?* He's been injured … how badly?'

'I can't be sure.'

'Where did he say he was hurt?'

'Mrs Cope, look … at the moment, it's not straightforward.'

'What do you *mean*? Didn't he tell you what was wrong?'

'He's … he's not able to speak at present.'

'What are you talking about? Oh, no …'

The stretcher rolled past and the men loaded Ronny quickly into the ambulance and slammed the doors. One of them stayed inside with Ronny while the other ran to the front and jumped into the driving seat. The ambulance was on the move in a second, blue lights revolving on the roof. Turning onto the road, the siren began wailing. Marnie was aware of an urgent voice coming from the phone. Anne was escorted out by one of the policemen. She was holding her face in her hands, watching the tail of the ambulance disappearing round the corner, her expression desolate.

• • • • •

If she had not been so sick with worry Marnie would have smiled. It was the typical British response to any emergency. A pot of tea. Marnie had phoned Ralph as she and Anne left Martyrs Close, and the kettle was boiling before they reached the office barn.

Anne told her story, sitting with the mug of tea clasped in both hands, thin and anxious, looking younger than her age, vulnerable like a refugee. Ralph was just telling her that she might have saved Ronny's life when they heard tyres crunching on the gravel in the courtyard. Marnie looked out to see a familiar grey Vauxhall outside the farmhouse. DCI Bartlett and DS Marriner were making one of their visits.

They accepted Ralph's offer of tea, explained that they needed the basic facts and told Anne they would need a statement from her in due course. She told her story again, and the detectives listened to the end without interrupting.

'Why were you at the house, Anne?' Bartlett asked quietly. Marriner flipped open a notebook.

'I went to see Ronny. He's been abroad on his gap year … Mrs Appleton in the shop said he'd come back.'

'He was expecting you?'

'No. I just sort of popped in.'

'Lucky for him that you did. Did he say anything to you when you found him?'

Anne shook her head. 'He was unconscious. I rang 999 as soon as I saw him.'

'According to our records you asked for the police first, then an ambulance.'

'I saw the house had been burgled … then I saw Ronny … on the floor …'

'Did you see anybody leaving the building … or anywhere near it?'

'No one.'

'Weren't you worried that the burglar might still have been there?'

'It looked as if they'd been disturbed … left in a hurry. The milk bottle holder was knocked over … the gravel on the drive was all churned up.'

'That's very observant of you, Anne. Did you see any vehicle on the street … a van perhaps?'

'Nothing. I came through the churchyard, not along the road. Mr Bartlett, how is Ronny? He looked dreadful.'

'Too early to tell. We've sent an officer to the hospital to talk to him as soon as he comes round. Anne, is there anything you can add to what you've already told us … anything unusual or suspicious … anything at all?'

Anne sighed. 'I don't think so.'

'I wonder …' All heads turned as Marnie spoke. 'There has been something suspicious, Mr Bartlett. Twice in the past week or so a car's been down here. It just came and went without stopping … as if wanting to find out if anyone was around.'

'Did you report it if you thought it might be a prowler?'

'There wasn't anything substantial to report.'

Marriner joined in. 'You've no explanation for who it might've been?'

Marnie hesitated for just a second before replying. 'No.'

The detectives made no reaction. Bartlett took up the questioning. 'What sort of car was it?'

'We didn't see it. That's why we had nothing to report to anyone.'

'We? Who else?'

'Angela Hemingway – the vicar – she's staying in one of the cottages. She heard it one time. Before that, I'd heard it.'

'But not seen it. So you don't know that it was the same one.'

'You asked if we'd seen anything unusual, anything at all. No one comes down here for no reason, not normally. Two visits seems an odd coincidence.'

With a nod Bartlett stood up. 'Thanks for the tea. We'll be in touch about that statement, Anne.'

Marnie walked the two men out to their car.

'Can I ask you something, Mr Bartlett?'

'Sure.'

'Is it at all possible that … you might be keeping us under surveillance?'

'Is there some reason why we might want to do that, Mrs Walker?'

'Perhaps in connection with the murder enquiry?' Marnie suggested.

They stopped at the car, and Bartlett turned to face her. 'Let me tell you two things. First, if we were keeping an eye on you, you wouldn't know anything about it. Second, we're not, and for one very good reason. There is no Taverner murder enquiry. It's finished. The murderer is in prison for life … unless he manages to top himself.' Bartlett saw Marnie's grimace. 'Sorry. I should've said until he gets let out on parole, which will probably be all too soon for my liking.'

'It's a lot of years to spend in jail,' Marnie observed. 'I hope you're confident you've got the right man.'

'We are. Don't let his sister's campaign fool you. I've seen it all before. My guess is she feels guilty at not helping him. This was a really sound case. I'd strongly advise against further contact with any of them.'

'I hear what you say, inspector, but you must see that Charles needs to draw a line and rebuild his life.'

Bartlett spoke slowly to emphasise the point. 'There's nothing to stop him doing that.' He climbed into the car and opened the window. 'Everyone involved in a murder investigation is somehow damaged by it, worst of all the victim's loved ones. Take my word for it. You do the design work; leave the policing to us. Stick to the rules, eh?' He pulled on the seat belt and plugged it in. 'And that's another thing you can do – make sure Mr Taverner gets proper security at the vicarage. When we were investigating the death of the previous vicar, I noticed it had no alarm system at all.'

'I'll pass on your advice.'

'And take it.'

Beside Bartlett, Marriner started the engine.

Marnie leaned forward. 'One last question. When the police arrived at the Copes' house, your colleague addressed me by name. If you're not keeping an eye on us, as you put it, how would he know who I was?'

Bartlett smiled. 'That's easy. All our officers know you, Mrs Walker, from past contact. I wouldn't want you to think you're notorious. Let's just say Glebe Farm is like a home from home for us.'

The car reversed out of the courtyard, turned between the barns and drove off up the field track. Marnie watched it go.

• • • • •

Marriner took it gently over the bumps. Nothing put his DCI into a bad mood more than bashing his head on the roof of the car, especially after a conversation with Marnie Walker.

'I know what you're thinking, sir.'

'Yes. She's doing it again.'

'Keeping something back from us?'

'Got it in one.'

'You think she has an idea why someone might be keeping watch on her?'

'Definitely. That's why she asked if we were. She wanted to be able to rule out that possibility.'

Marriner steered carefully round a tussock. 'Any idea who it might be?'

'My guess is it was probably our burglar sizing the place up.'

'Not likely to be anyone else, is it, sir?'

Bartlett held on firmly as the car passed over a series of ruts. 'Knowing Marnie Walker, it could be anybody, Ted. With that woman, who knows what might be lurking in the background?'

22

On Tuesday morning Anne did not turn up for breakfast. Marnie went looking for her and found her working in the office barn. She had had a restless night, the events around the burglary preventing her from sleeping. The only solution was to be active. She had got up at dawn and started drafting a statement on the computer while all the facts were fresh in her mind.

After a shower and breakfast her spirits had revived and she went straight back to the desk to check the draft and print off a copy. Marnie watched her from across the office, impressed as ever with Anne's level of concentration.

Anne was on the phone when the first call of the day came in, so Marnie picked up the receiver. Charles Taverner. He announced that he was coming to the vicarage and asked Marnie to see him. They agreed a time to meet at the house. When Marnie disconnected, she heard the familiar piping of Anne's computer as it linked up to the Internet.

'Checking for e-mails, Anne?'

'And sending one.'

'Oh?'

'I've just been on to the hospital. Ronny's regained consciousness.'

Marnie breathed out audibly. 'Thank goodness. You did well to get them to tell you about him. They're usually strict about releasing details of patients.'

'They were. But I asked them if a woman police officer was there, and the nurse said she'd just come back on duty. I asked if it was Cathy Lamb, and they let me speak to her. She told me.'

Marnie grinned. 'How did you know that, Holmes?'

Anne twirled an imaginary moustache. 'Elementary, my dear Watson ...'

'Well?'

'She's the only woman DC I know, so I just guessed.'

Marnie laughed. 'A brilliant deduction! So what's the e-mail you're sending?'

'My statement. Cathy gave me the address ...' Anne raised a finger and struck the keyboard. '... and there it goes.'

'Are you planning to visit Ronny, Anne?'

A hesitation. 'Dunno. I suppose so. I was worried when I saw him lying there like that. I thought he was ... well, he didn't look good, that's for sure. Ronny's a bit of a problem, but ... yeah ... I'll drop round and see him ... just a short visit. Do you want to come?'

Another hesitation. 'Not this time. I've got a meeting with Charles Taverner.' *And I've got problems of my own ...*

• • • • •

Marnie had the feeling with Charles that he was always moving the goalposts. He did it again. She had been on the point of leaving Glebe Farm for the vicarage when he rang from the car on his mobile. Could they meet instead by Stoke Bruerne bottom lock? It was a reasonable enough request. He had been sitting in the car for a couple of hours and wanted a walk in the fresh air before going over the house. A stroll along the towpath was ideal therapy. But Marnie suspected Charles had in mind to get her away from the decorating project to talk about another subject. What he did not know was that Marnie had her own concern, and it was pulling her in several directions at once.

She walked out to the car, pulled open the door and took a decision. *Damn!*

• • • • •

Marnie arrived first and was staring at the weed growth on the lock gates, watching the water splash over the top and through the gap in the middle, when she heard the broad tyres of the Jaguar rolling down the access road. Its paintwork was shining like new as it drew alongside the Discovery, putting it to shame with its light coating of dust from the field track. Marnie fixed a welcoming smile and raised a hand.

'Good of you to come, Marnie. Hope the sudden change wasn't a nuisance. Such a nice day, I thought it'd be good to stretch a leg.'

'You'll be able to do this more often when you move up. Do you have a firm date yet?'

'A few weeks … assuming you tell me everything's ready when we do the inspection.'

'No problem.'

'Good. And thank you, Marnie. Your handling of … well, of everything … has been most impressive. I don't know what I would've done …'

'There is one thing. There's been a burglary in the village, and the police have advised on the need for an alarm at the vicarage.'

'Oh?'

'Someone we know actually interrupted the burglar and got clobbered for his pains … a young man, a friend of Anne. He's in intensive care.'

'*Good lord!* You'd think that out here in the country … still, crime is everywhere.' He turned and looked at the Jaguar.

Marnie nodded. 'Yes, and with a car like that on the drive …'

They set off slowly along the path in the spring sunshine.

'Can you see to it, Marnie? Can you organise an alarm or do you want me to get a specialist to come and advise on a system?'

'I can deal with it locally if you wish.'

'Excellent. We have a very elaborate security system at our house in Templars' Wharf.'

'I saw it … the CCTV camera … the monitor in the kitchen …'

'Oh yes. Intruder alarms everywhere, motion sensors, dead locks on doors and windows. God knows what we'd have done if the place had caught fire and we had to get out in a hurry!'

'Perhaps something a little less … *elaborate* … for the vicarage?'

'Probably.' His voice was suddenly vague as if his mind was already moving on.

Marnie knew the signs. 'I'll get onto it at once. I'm not sure how long it takes to –'

'Marnie … there's something I wanted to ask you …'

'I know.'

'I thought you probably did.'

'I ought to tell you that the police officer who mentioned the need for an alarm also gave me his views on Gerard's appeal campaign. He was involved in part of the case.'

'What does he think?'

'That the case against Gerard was rock solid.'

'And now that you've been with me to see Gerard, is that your view?' Marnie shrugged. Charles continued. 'That business about the lovers … I've been thinking about it … perhaps it was just a blind. I was wondering about going back and confronting him … challenging him to produce names … facts … not just random accusations.'

Marnie wanted to bite her tongue off, but she failed. 'I did.'

Charles stopped abruptly. 'What did you say?'

'I did just that … confronted him … demanded names …'

'How did he react?'

'At first, evasively. But then he agreed to think about it and let me have some names. They arrived by e-mail yesterday … names and a few notes on each one.'

Charles stared into the distance. When he spoke his voice seemed to come from far away. 'How many?'

'Four.'

'Four lovers … *Jesus Christ!* Oh, sorry, Marnie. Four … in addition to himself.'

'Yes.'

'Over what period of time?'

'A few years, it seems.'

'Dear God …'

Charles turned and began walking on. Marnie followed slowly in his wake, wishing she had no part in this, wishing she had never returned to the prison or asked for the names. Beyond the lock was a line of mooring bollards for boats waiting to go through. On that morning the place was deserted. There, the river Tove passed culverted under the canal to emerge in a clump of trees, and a line of fencing protected the edge of the towpath from the drop down to the river level a metre or two below. Charles leaned against the fence, looking down to the stream. Marnie stopped beside him, resting her back against the ironwork, facing the opposite way towards the canal and the fields beyond. All around them was pastoral tranquillity and peace, light clouds dappling shade and sunlight on the landscape.

'Charles, I really am sorry. I only wanted –'

'Thank you, Marnie. You acted for the best, I know that.'

'Would you like some time to yourself? I could join you at the house in, say, half an hour?'

Charles shook his head slowly. 'All the professionals think it's a solid case,' he said quietly. 'On paper it seems that way to me, too. But what did Gerard say? … *The trial was perfectly fair … just wrong.*'

'It sounds like you've come to agree with him, Charles.'

'Haven't you? Isn't that why you went back to see him … to get the names?'

'I don't know. I think perhaps I wanted it to be him ... didn't want there to be any lovers.'

'I wanted that too ... more than anything. But now that you've got the names, they won't go away ... And they could be suspects. Do you have them with you?'

'Yes.'

For a full minute Charles said nothing. Marnie waited for him to ask her to hand over the list. When he spoke it was as if he was changing the subject.

'I have to accept the loss of the most important person in my life ... a whole part of my life has gone for ever.'

'Barbara was very special,' Marnie agreed. It sounded lame to her ears, but she realised that many expressions of emotion appeared banal and trite.

Another silence. It seemed to enclose them in a glass box and shut out the world. No birds were singing, no sounds of traffic penetrated to where they stood. Everything in the universe seemed centred on them, and Marnie could feel the weight of it pressing in. Through the heavy air she sensed that Charles felt it too. When he spoke again his voice came to her like a memory or a dream.

'I'm almost sixty, Marnie. I'll never experience anything like it again. I'll never be in love with anyone, never know what it feels like to have that kind of relationship. All the excitement and apprehension of making love with someone for the first time ... building a bond with another person ... another woman ... all of that's gone.'

'I understand.' Marnie felt impatient with herself at making these feeble mutterings. She was unaccustomed to having this kind of frank conversation with a man old enough to be her father.

'Do you, Marnie? I often wonder if women really understand what men think. To me, life is about women. We're attracted to them. That's the system ... that's how it works. When that part of our lives comes to an end ... well, that's more or less it, really. If I were twenty years younger, perhaps some day I could make a new start. As it is, in that timespan there's a good chance I'll be dead.'

Marnie could feel his pain. 'That's why you want matters resolved.'

He nodded. 'Putting my affairs in order ... unfortunate choice of words, in the circumstances.'

'It's understandable, but you mustn't give up on life, Charles.' *Damn! Another cliché.*

'Getting at the truth isn't giving up, Marnie. You know that.'

'I do, but I worry about the pain it could cause you, and in the end you might find that the police and courts have been right all along.'

'That's a risk I'll have to take. But somehow ... I'm not ready to give up yet.' He gestured. 'Those names, Marnie.'

She pulled out the paper. He read slowly, a deep frown creasing his features. Pronouncing each name, his tone registered a reaction. 'Stuart ...' Comprehension. 'Adamson ...' Distaste. '*Wainwright!* ...' Amazement. 'Brent ... *Brent!*' Bewilderment.

He re-read the notes. 'These comments are Gerard's, presumably? They're his own words?'

'I assume so. They seem to be, unless Sarah paraphrased what he told her.'

'Interesting ... At least it would be, if it wasn't so bloody awful.'

'You had no inkling of these relationships, Charles?'

'Of course not. It's hardly something Barbara would tell me about, is it?'

'I meant now ... in hindsight. Looking back, you can't think of anything that made you wonder ...?'

'No. Nothing. Barbara covered her tracks all right. What about you, Marnie?'

'I told you, she never confided in me like that. It was all strictly business.'

'But now that you know ... was there nothing, no hint, no careless word?'

'Truly not, Charles.'

'What did Gerard say? Between lovers there are ... *no secrets*. But why would a lover want to know this kind of detail about her past, any more than a husband would?'

'I think he explained that.' Marnie had no desire to go into Gerard's reasons. The fact that it made the affair more frank, more intimate, more sexy was not something she wanted to drag up at this point. 'Anyway, it's all past history now.'

'You think so, Marnie? Barbara and I never talked about such things when ...'

Marnie knew what he meant. 'At moments of intimacy with your husband, you're not necessarily trying to ... spice things up in that way. You're building a long-term relationship.'

'That's not what I meant.'

'Oh?'

'No. You see, Barbara and I had an affair for about a year before I split up with my first wife.'

'Your *first* wife?'

'We were both married at the time. We both got divorced and remarried.'

'I didn't know that.'

'It was in all the papers ... not about the affair, but that we were ... second time round.'

'I see.' Marnie's mind was racing. 'Did your first wife know you were having an affair with Barbara?'

'Yes.'

'And did her first husband know about you?'

'What do you think we talked about as grounds for divorce, Marnie?' He frowned again. 'Why are you so surprised? It's what happens.'

Lights were flashing and bells were ringing in Marnie's brain. 'Presumably your divorce wasn't one of these modern no-blame arrangements ... it wasn't amicable?'

'Are they ever? It cost me a million in settlement, plus the house.'

'And do you ever have contact with your first wife ... or Barbara's first husband?'

'Of course not. What's that got to do with anything? I don't follow you.'

Marnie pointed at the list that Charles was holding. 'You think those might be our only suspects? I'm getting the feeling we could have two more.'

Charles saw the light. '*Jesus!*'

• • • • •

The inspection of the vicarage, the main reason for Charles's visit, was an anti-climax after their conversation by the canal. They walked round the house together, Marnie ticking off items from her clipboard schedule, Charles trying to sound enthusiastic about the design.

The tour lasted barely half an hour, and Marnie had only one point left on the list by the time they returned to the hall.

'Is that it, Marnie? It's all just as I expected. You've done a wonderful job.'

'There's only one more thing: the intruder alarm. I'll get onto it.'

'Good. I suppose it's necessary. Such a pity to need that sort of thing out here in the country. Violence is all around us, it seems.'

'Inspector Bartlett was quite insistent on it.'

'Bartlett,' Charles repeated. 'Oh yes … the policeman who's also *quite insistent* that Gerard is guilty.'

'I think he's got a point, Charles … about the alarm. There's at least one family in the village who'd support him on this.'

'That poor young chap. Of course.' Charles turned towards the door. 'I'm sure Bartlett's right about the alarm, but as for his other views, I wonder …'

Marnie did not react. They walked out onto the drive, and she locked the door behind them.

Charles looked up at the handsome facade of the house. 'There is one other thing you could have put on your list, Marnie. You were going to order the sign with the name on.'

'You want me to go ahead with that?'

'Of course. *The Old Rectory*, just as Barbara wanted.'

'I thought you were going to hold back on that for a while, in view of what Angela said about the church's rules.'

'Look, Marnie, I've paid them top rate for the house, my wife has been murdered, my life virtually ruined. Let's get things in perspective. What I call the house is none of their business. The church authorities have no real power over me. If they say anything, I'll tell them it's a kind of memorial to Barbara. That'll shut them up.'

· · · · ·

Marnie spent much of the afternoon on the phone letting her fingers do the walking. *Yellow Pages* listed dozens of companies marketing security systems. She was puzzling over which ones to approach when Anne returned from the hospital with the news that Ronny was being moved from intensive care to a regular ward. He would spend a night or two under observation and probably be sent home at the end of the week.

'What was the verdict?'

'Severe concussion but not a fracture of the skull …three cracked ribs, lots of bruising. They think he was hit with something heavy like an iron steak pan and then thrown across the kitchen. He hit the edge of the workbench with his chest.'

Marnie grimaced. 'Can they do anything for his injuries?'

'Lots of rest and painkillers. He'll be in bed for a couple of weeks, they said.'

'So will you be trotting round with grapes to mop his brow?'

'Maybe.' Anne spotted the open directory 'What're you looking for?'

'Burglar alarms for Charles. There are loads of firms doing them … all with accreditation from various bodies. I hardly know where to start.'

Anne read the entries over Marnie's shoulder. 'Will Geoff know?'

'Our electrician? Not sure. I think these are installed by specialists.'

'George Stubbs has an alarm system,' Anne said thoughtfully. 'There's a box with a blinking red light on his wall. Might be worth asking him for advice. And there's Mrs Frightfully-Frightfully at Hanford Hall. I'm sure she's got one.'

They had given the Georgian house in the next village a makeover the previous year for their client, Mrs Dorothy Vane-Henderson. Anne's nickname for her had stuck.

'That's brilliant, Anne. Which reminds me, Charles Taverner sends his thanks for your stencil design. I think I'm becoming superfluous round here. You're the one with the ideas. All I get is ...'

'What?'

'Neil Gerard and his campaign.'

'I thought you were dropping out of that.'

'I am. Definitely.'

'I believe you. I mean, I'm glad to hear it.'

Anne climbed the wall ladder to her room to read up on Art Deco graphic design for one of her college projects. She lit a joss stick and angled the desk lamp over the place where she habitually sat by the end of the bed. Lowering herself onto her giant bean bag, she wriggled to a comfortable position, her back against the foot board, and opened the first book. Normally she would have been pleased to receive a compliment from Marnie. But that day she knew that although her alarm suggestion had been sensible, it was not exactly ground-breaking. Marnie's mind was focused elsewhere, and Anne did not have to be brilliant to guess where that was.

Marnie settled down with the telephone and a mug of coffee. Her mind was on motion sensors and remote keypads when Charles Taverner rang at the end of the afternoon.

'Marnie, I've been thinking about your Inspector Bartlett and what he said.'

My inspector Bartlett! 'Yes? I'm gradually sorting out the alarm suppliers. It's more complicated than I imagined.'

'Oh yes.' Charles sounded less than enthusiastic. 'I meant about Gerard's campaign.'

'Oh yes.' Marnie tried to sound dismissive.

'Look, do you think it might be worth –'

'Charles, I told you, I don't want to get involved in that. I meant it. Really.'

A pause. 'I respect your wishes, Marnie. Of course I do. But despite the evidence I can't help thinking that Gerard seems a steady sort of person ... so does his sister. I'm ... giving them at least the benefit of the doubt.'

'Very generous of you, but what does that mean ... in practical terms?'

'I suppose it means finding out about the ... the lovers.'

'If you think there are grounds for re-opening the case, Charles, you should get in touch with Chief Inspector Bruere. He's the officer responsible for the investigation.'

'But don't you see, Marnie, that's precisely why he's probably the last person to contact. To him, it's a case solved, a crime statistic with a successful outcome.'

'True, but I'm sure that if he discovered grounds for doubt, he'd want to look into the matter.'

'We don't have *grounds for doubt*. All we have – at the moment – is a list of names.'

Marnie did not like the use of *we*. 'Short of employing a private detective, I don't see what you can hope to achieve … unless you throw your weight behind Sarah Cowan's campaign. That would get the police jumping.'

'I don't have enough evidence to be able to do that, Marnie.'

'Quite.'

'Not at this stage. That's why I thought you might be able to help.'

'I'm sorry, Charles. This is outside my scope. I've been involved in police investigations, sure, but always on the outside. I don't know the first thing about what to do. And to be brutally frank, I have a business to run here, clients, deadlines …'

'I know … I know. Unreasonable of me to ask you. This whole thing has become an obsession with me. I need to sit down quietly and work out what to do for the best. Your idea about a private detective might be one way forward.'

'Think carefully before you do anything, Charles. That's my advice. You might find you're going round in circles and only causing yourself even more pain.'

'I've thought of that, Marnie. But whatever Barbara did, she was still the most important person in the world to me. Every time I think about her I feel a great weight in the pit of my stomach … knowing I'll never see her again … So, she had the odd affair … I don't think I'd have cared, as long as she came back to me in the end.'

• • • • •

That evening after supper, after Anne had gone back to her reading, Marnie and Ralph sat out on the stern deck of *Sally Ann* in the spring warmth, picking at a bunch of black grapes, cups and saucers on the picnic table between them.

'Charles said a strange thing today, Ralph. He thinks life is about women. What do you think?'

'About *women*?'

'About men being attracted to them. He said that's how it all works.'

'Mm …I would've thought there were one or two other things as well. But I suppose he's right … up to a point. Of course the time aspect is important.'

'You mean, having recently lost Barbara, she must be uppermost in his mind at the moment?'

'Not just that, Marnie. I was thinking about time in the sense of lifespan. For many men I think sex – which is probably at the heart of what you're talking about – assumes great importance at some time in their life. It's the driving force. Then for many it settles back into a kind of support role, depending on how their relationship works out.'

'People develop … relationships develop? Is that what you mean?'

'Fundamentally, yes. I can see what Charles was getting at. It sounds as if he was very much in love with Barbara … to use a rather unfashionable phrase.'

'Why unfashionable?'

'Some people regard it as an outdated concept. We see so many marriages fail. We regard nothing as quite as enduring as people used to think. Perhaps we trust our feelings less these days.'

'Do you see us like that, Ralph?'

'I'm speaking objectively ...' He smiled. '... as a pedantic academic, not personally. I suspect I'm rather old-fashioned. I know I've been lucky to have a second chance at a loving relationship ... and it's become central to my life.'

Marnie reached out for a grape. 'Yes. That's exactly how Charles felt.'

'Then you can imagine how devastated he felt to lose Barbara ... and how shattered to find she had betrayed him.'

• • • • •

Later in the shower on *Thyrsis*, turning slowly under the hot jets, Marnie pictured Gerard's list of names and tried to imagine what those men meant to Barbara. And somewhere in the background she had an impression of ghostly shapes lurking in the shadows, unseen, Charles's first wife ... Barbara's first husband. What part might they have played in all this?

Through the hissing of the shower she could hear the voices that had haunted her all day. *The trial was perfectly fair ... just wrong ... What are rules for, if not for breaking? ... More frank, more intimate, more sexy ... No secrets ...*

Social scientists call it synchronicity. Most people would call it coincidence. For the tabloids it would be a double whammy. To Marnie it felt like the hand of fate gripping her throat.

Wednesday morning was like any normal working day until the phone rang. Marnie was waiting for a delivery date for bathroom fittings for the main farmhouse and was opening the diary as she reached across the desk to take the call. Sarah Cowan was trying to sound relaxed but her voice was tense.

'I've got some news, Marnie.'

'Is your ... is Neil all right?'

'Yes. Did the e-mail get through to you okay?'

'Yes, it did.'

'And you were able to open the attachment?'

'No problem.' Marnie realised that Sarah's pretence of having news had given way to the real reason for her call. 'I showed the list to Charles Taverner.'

Sarah gasped. 'You did? What did he say?'

'Not a lot. He was curious about them, of course, but he knew nothing of the relationships.'

'He *never* suspected *anything*? I find that hard to believe, Marnie. He must've had *some* inkling. Nobody's that clever that they *never* let anything slip.'

'Well, I'm only telling you how he reacted.'

'Is he ... I mean, do you think he's going to do anything about the list?'

'What can he do?' Across the room the fax machine began ringing. It was the perfect get-out. 'Sarah, that's the other phone. I'm alone in the office. I'd better go.'

'Right. Oh ... my news. They're moving Neil to another prison.'

Sarah blurted it out as the ringing stopped, and the fax began stuttering. Marnie felt a wave of relief wash over her. It was selfish but *so* good.

'Really?' She was thinking rapidly. Gerard was a convicted murderer. He could go to Dartmoor, perhaps, or that other place on the Isle of Wight. Or maybe Broadmoor, the secure hospital, since he had tried to commit suicide. All of them further away.

Sarah's voice cut into her thoughts. 'They told him last night, and he just rang to let me know. It's amazing.'

'But probably not a surprise, seeing as how he –'

'No, I mean it's amazing where they're sending him. He's moving to a prison up at Milton Keynes. That's not far from you, isn't it? Apparently they have a unit there ...'

Sarah continued speaking, but Marnie no longer heard. The name Milton Keynes was echoing in her mind, drowning out every other sound. This was a disaster.

And the morning was about to get worse.

• • • • •

After ending the call with Sarah, Marnie sat thinking over the implications of having Neil Gerard on her doorstep. It was as if the enemy was moving in to surround her. Sarah would be coming up every week to see her brother. Charles would be moving house in just a short while. The pressure on Marnie would grow.

When the phone rang again, Marnie was astonished to see that half an hour had passed. She dreaded answering it.

'Walker and Co, good morning.'

'Marnie? Didn't you get my message?' It was Neil Jeffries from Willards Brewery, the main contact with her principal client. He sounded tetchy.

Neil! She could not even escape the name. 'Hallo, Neil. Sorry, I've been … What can I do for you?'

'As I explained on your answerphone …' He paused to emphasise the point. 'I wanted you to ring me back about an important new commission.'

Sometimes a lie was the simplest way out. 'I've only just got back into the office … haven't even had time to check the phone. I'm sorry if it needs urgent attention. How can I help you?'

'The company has just agreed terms for a contract to create a wine bar and restaurant in London, in Docklands.'

Marnie perked up. She loved that kind of project. 'Adaptation of an existing building?'

'Conversion of a warehouse complex … built around 1820 … ground floor and basement with waterside terrace …' He sounded as if he was reading from the brief. 'Two-seventy square metres inside for the restaurant plus kitchens … ninety-five for the wine bar. I thought you'd have been keen.'

'Certainly am. What's the rush?'

'Just the usual … pressure from the board to get things moving. Can you give this priority?' He tried to make it sound like a question. 'Everett Parker Associates will be the project architects … your old firm.'

'E-mail me the brief and I'll get onto it. Whereabouts in Docklands is the building?'

'It's at … hang on …' There was a shuffling of paper. '… Bermuda Reach. It's not a big development, but it's quite exclusive, apparently.'

'Bermuda Reach,' Marnie echoed dully.

'You've heard of it, Marnie?'

'Oh yes, I've heard of it.'

'You'll need to contact the owner of the marina to arrange a site meeting. He'll show you round. His name is …' There was the sound of pages being turned again. 'Just a mo … it's here somewhere …'

Marnie could see the name on the print-out of Neil Gerard's notes on the desk in front of her. 'Ian Stuart,' she said.

'What was that?'

'The owner … it's Ian Stuart.'

'Ah yes … Ian Stuart. Would you like his phone number?'

Would she like it? She'd prefer to throw it in the bin and forget the whole project. 'Just e-mail it to me, Neil, with the rest of the stuff.'

'Is everything all right, Marnie? You don't sound overjoyed. I thought these Docklands jobs were right up your street.'

'Just trying to contain my excitement …'

Moments later they ended the conversation and disconnected. Marnie sat staring at Gerard's list of names. Only then did she see that Ralph had come into the office. He looked enquiringly in her direction from the doorway. Turning her head, Marnie spotted Anne descending the wall ladder from the loft.

'Hi! Are we all ready for a cup of …' Anne glanced from Marnie to Ralph. 'What's up?'

Marnie outlined that morning's news, starting with Gerard's move from Hemel to Milton Keynes. Agreement that this was a Bad Thing was unanimous.

'Then Neil Jeffries rang.' Marnie shook her head slowly.

'Nothing wrong is there?' Anne looked concerned. 'We're bang on target with all the Willards' projects.'

'He wants us to start on a new job in docklands … wine bar and restaurant … Bermuda Reach …'

Ralph looked as if he was not following the reason for her lack of enthusiasm.

Anne was totally bewildered. 'That goes down as good news in my book, Marnie … even *great* news. What's the problem?'

'The owner is Ian Stuart.'

'Ah …' Ralph understood.

Anne looked blank. 'Who's he?'

Marnie realised at that point that Anne was not up-to-date on the Gerard front. She replied slowly. 'He is the problem.'

• • • • •

After the coffee break Marnie was alone in the office again. She was convinced she had given a reassuringly confident outline of the situation, at least as far as Anne was concerned. It was important not to cause her anxiety when she had studies to pursue.

For the second time that morning Anne descended the loft ladder from her room over the office.

'Hi again.' Marnie aimed at a breezy carefree style. 'What brings you to these parts?'

Anne jumped down from the third rung of the ladder. 'Problems with concentration … noise disturbance …'

Marnie was baffled. 'That you can't concentrate, I can understand – there's a lot happening just now. But noise?' Marnie cocked an ear towards the door and the building site beyond. 'I can't hear anything.'

'Not *my* problems of concentration, Marnie … *yours*. You've been sitting there immobile ever since I went up to my room … half an hour ago.'

Marnie was aghast. 'Is it that long? This is turning into the incredible shrinking day.'

'Longer. And I can't get on with my work because I can hear your brain clanking like a steam hammer.'

'Oh …'

'It's no use. Whether you like it or not, you need me to help you with this Gerard thing.'

'But you've got projects to do for college and –'

'I'm well ahead with them. I've got the whole summer term to do them and I've got everything worked out. Easy …'

Marnie stretched and yawned. 'I give in.

Anne pulled her chair over to Marnie's desk and sat down, notepad at the ready. 'So … follow-up …'

'Follow-up to what?'

Anne sighed. 'To the phone call you're about to make to Charles Taverner, of course. He probably doesn't know about Neil Gerard's move to our friendly local jailhouse.'

'Where they have a unit to help stop people killing themselves?'

'That's the one.'

Marnie pressed the conference button on the phone so that Anne could listen to the conversation. She made the call and Anne was right. Charles knew nothing of the planned move. But he quickly grasped its significance.

'That means he'll be just down the road from –'

'I spotted that, Charles.'

'Mm … and his sister rang you up to tell you … interesting.'

'There's something else. Willards want me to do a restaurant job for them … at Bermuda Reach.'

'You'll be dealing with Stuart?'

'You guessed.'

'*Very* interesting.'

'It's just a coincidence, Charles.'

'Then here's another one. We have a buyer for *Perfidia*.'

'Since when?'

'Since Mike Brent rang me earlier this morning.'

'Mike Brent?'

'We'll be needing to liaise with him about delivering the boat back to Little Venice once the refit's completed.'

'You mean *I'll* need to liaise with him, presumably.' Marnie noticed that Anne was writing on her pad. 'Is he in a hurry?'

'I understand his customer's willing to wait. Can you check details with him, Marnie?'

'I'll probably get Anne to contact him to agree a timetable.'

'*Anne?*'

'She is part of the firm. You were telling me just recently how much you admired her work.'

'Of course. But I thought you might … no, you're right. You must organise things as you see fit, Marnie.'

• • • • •

Charles had barely managed to conceal his disappointment, but Marnie was determined not to relent. She would see Ian Stuart simply as part of her job with

Willards and no more. Reading Stuart's contact details from the e-mail she picked up the phone.

It seemed like old times. Across the room Anne was pressing the buttons of a familiar number, the BW office in Little Venice. She asked for the manager, Mike Brent, and was connected at once.

'Anne, good morning, what can I do for you?' Brisk but friendly.

Anne was trying to imagine him as a lover ... as Barbara Taverner's lover. 'I'm phoning about *Perfidia*. Mr Taverner's told us about the offer.'

'Right.'

'You know we've got some works to do on her ... exterior painting, internal redecoration, new carpets, curtains. The thing is, will your customer wait or do you want us to bring the boat back as she is?'

'There's no rush. The new owners are away visiting family in New Zealand, and I've told them she's being refitted inside and out. Jock's done all the mechanical side, hasn't he?'

'Everything up to the new standards. She'll be like a new boat when we've finished with her.'

He chuckled. 'I don't doubt that. Seeing the way Marnie transformed *Sally Ann* – that old tub – oh, sorry, no disrespect.' He laughed. 'She's a lovely old girl, but you know what I mean.'

'*Lovely old girl* ... is that the boat you're talking about or Marnie?'

More laughter. 'Ah! I'm digging myself into a hole here.'

Anne was beginning to think of Mike Brent in a new light. She realised that she lacked the experience in the ways of the world to be able to reach a mature judgment, but here they were laughing together in friendly uncomplicated banter, and there was no doubt about it, he did have an attractive voice and a warm personality.

'Anne, are you still there?'

'Oh, yes ... I, er ... I was wondering about timescale. When will your client want *Perfidia* back in London?'

They talked over practicalities, agreed they would keep in touch in the next few weeks and liaise again about delivery. When Anne hung up, Marnie was ending her conversation on the other phone.

'Thanks. I look forward to meeting you. See you soon.'

For a few seconds after ending their calls, they looked at each other across the office.

'You go first, Anne.'

'No hurry. The clients are abroad till the end of next month.'

'Good. So we complete the work?'

Anne nodded. 'Yep. Part of the deal.'

'How did you find Mike?'

'Nice. Friendly as usual. I could imagine someone liking him.'

'You mean Barbara.'

'Yes. Of course, he's quite old – must be about forty – so I can't judge how anyone would feel about him, but he comes across as very pleasant to talk to.'

'And he does run everything at Little Venice,' Marnie added. 'To someone with a boat, that could be seen as part of his charm.'

'You mean, Barbara might have wanted to keep him sweet … she might've just been using him?'

'No. A woman like Barbara wouldn't need to go that far to get what she wanted from a man … any man.'

'Then what did you mean?'

Marnie shrugged. 'His position gives him a certain modest importance in the field he works in. Women like a man with authority.'

'What about Ian Stuart?'

'He acts like a man with authority, that's for sure. I've arranged to go down to see him tomorrow. And that's another thing for sure. We're going together.'

Thursday morning and a subdued journey on the train to London. Marnie had none of her customary enthusiasm for the start of a new project, even one in Docklands. She read and reread the brochure about Bermuda Reach that Stuart had faxed to her and the brief sent by Jeffries from Willards. This job had too many complications, too many associations with her dead friend. And there was the small detail that the man she was going to meet was now on the list of suspects for the murder of that friend. She tried not to shudder.

As usual she did everything possible to conceal her anxiety from Anne who was sitting opposite her, nose buried in a book about the art and craft movement in Germany. And as usual …

'Marnie, you haven't turned over a page since we passed through Tring.'

'I'm … I'm thinking. I do that from time to time, you know. It's a sort of habit. And the amazing thing is … the more I do, the easier the job seems to get. Strange, isn't it?'

Anne smiled like an indulgent mother. 'So you're thinking about the restaurant job?'

'Of course I'm not. I'm worrying myself simple about meeting someone who could've …' She fell silent. Anne had raised a finger to her lips.

'You're raising your voice, Marnie.'

Marnie leaned forward. 'You know what I mean … what I was going to say.'

'Yes, I certainly do.'

'Honestly, Anne, it's like working with Svengali going around with you.'

Anne chuckled. 'Look, we're just going to a site meeting, like any other job. We're getting the tube to East London, then trying out the DLR –'

'The what?'

'The Docklands Light Railway. You know it, Marnie. It's new … ish … trains without drivers … all run by computer –'

Marnie looked aghast. 'We'll never be seen again!'

'It'll be *fun*.' Anne emphasised the last word.

'I believe you.' Marnie sounded unconvinced.

'Good. The DLR will take us within a short … ish … walk of our destination.'

'How short is *ish*?'

'Seven or eight minutes.'

'Assuming we're not mugged or raped,' Marnie added helpfully.

Anne nodded. 'Or carried off into white slavery.'

'That's nice. I'm glad I invited you along, Anne. You cheer me up.'

'All part of the service.'

• • • • •

Ish turned out to be an accurate assessment by Anne. The DLR deposited them – without a driver in sight – safely in the heart of Docklands, and they walked unmolested through streets undergoing wholesale redevelopment. Marnie was looking at her watch to check their timing when she felt a tug at her sleeve. When she looked up, Anne pointed ahead. There it was, an imposing sign announcing Bermuda Reach, with the coat of arms of the colony on one side and the logo of Stuart Developments on the other.

It was typical of Docklands and not unlike Templars' Wharf, but on a smaller scale. Even so, it was a development worth millions. Here and there workmen were busy, and vans were dotted round the site. To Marnie's eye it looked as if the finishing trades were predominating. She imagined that in six months everything would be clear and all the works completed. Willards would be urged to have the restaurant finished in that time, which would put more pressure on Walker & Co.

As Marnie and Anne aimed in the direction of the office, clearly marked with a blue and white board, breaking sunlight danced on water in the marina where a few boats were already occupying their berths. There was not a narrowboat in sight, but high-quality American Grand Banks and British Nelson boats were much in evidence.

Bermuda Reach was in the customary Docklands shape of an oblong surrounding the marina basin, with one of the shorter sides partly open to give access to the Thames. On one side stood a warehouse that had been converted to offices. Two sides were residential blocks divided into flats and loft conversions, with an extension of modern houses in a terrace on the short end by the marina entrance. It all blended seamlessly into the riparian landscape. Marnie felt envy of the architects and designers who had brought the place to life, but excited at her part in completing the picture.

The door to the office stood open, and Marnie looked inside. She smiled as she reflected that these prestige developments in Docklands were unlike normal building sites. The furniture looked like Conran originals, and seated at a chrome and glass desk was a strikingly pretty young woman in a black silk shirt and cream trousers, speaking persuasively on the phone. Marnie withdrew a business card from her wallet and placed it on the desk beside a nameplate inscribed, Amanda Gilbert-Reeves.

Without interrupting her call, the young woman gestured towards the front door and mouthed, 'Press the bell' before pointing upwards. Marnie rejoined Anne who had waited outside admiring the view. Her attention had been captured by a low-slung silver Aston Martin two-seater, its hood down, revealing impressive quantities of dark red leather. Parked against the backdrop of bijoux residences and white cruisers, it looked like part of a fashion shoot.

Marnie found the doorbell and pressed it as instructed by Miss Gilbert-Reeves. The intercom clicked.

'Marnie Walker for Ian Stuart.'

A metallic voice replied, 'Come on up,' and a buzzer sounded.

They stopped at a spacious first floor landing smelling of fresh paint and sawn timber. Daylight flooded down on them from glazed panels in the roof. Somewhere nearby a man's voice could be heard, speaking on the phone. After a few seconds he said good-bye, the phone was put down and almost immediately a door opened. Ian Stuart was exactly as Marnie had imagined him, only more so.

She had barely two seconds to form an impression of the man who was master of everything around them, and whose mistress had been Barbara Taverner. Tall, with blond wavy hair and a square jawline, he seemed younger than she expected. This may have been the effect of his suntan, which probably proclaimed a recent trip to the Caribbean. His clothes proclaimed City businessman, from the blue and white striped shirt, the red braces attached to dark blue pinstripe trousers and shiny black Chelsea boots.

He bounded forward, hand outstretched, pronouncing his name. His expression was earnest and pre-occupied, but relaxing into a smile. As Marnie introduced herself, Stuart became aware of Anne, and the smile receded.

Marnie was turning towards her friend when Anne extended her right hand and spoke in a firm clear voice. 'Anne Price. Designer. Marnie's colleague on this project.'

Faltering for a second, the smile clicked on. 'Oh ... right. Hi. Ian Stuart.'

His large square hand enveloped her thin fingers, and Anne's face remained inscrutable. If she felt any discomfort from the encounter she did not show it.

Stuart's office was untidy, with folders and bundles of papers and plans piled on the desk, on the filing cabinets and on every visible – or rather *invisible* – surface. In one corner a coffee machine was set up on a table, with plastic cups in a dispenser and sachets of sugar in a basket. On the floor below it lay a sports bag. Ian Stuart with his broad shoulders and deep chest was a fitness freak. Marnie was amused to see a mirror hanging on the wall beside the machine.

'Shall we have coffee?' Stuart asked smoothly.

Marnie and Anne thanked him and immediately sat down. Their eyes met briefly while Stuart tugged at cups and pressed buttons in the corner behind them, muttering instructions to himself as he did so.

Surprise. The coffee tasted like coffee. While they sipped it, Stuart gave them a tour of the site, his finger guiding them across a plan spread out over the papers on the desk. Speaking in short staccato phrases, he radiated energy and enthusiasm for his work.

Marnie found her concentration lapsing. Uncharacteristically she was watching Stuart instead of studying every detail of his exposition. Even more uncharacteristically, she found herself wondering what kind of lover he would be. The words, *swept me off my feet* came into her mind. She tried to imagine Barbara held in those powerful hands, her slim body gathered up in those strong arms. Perhaps Barbara liked having that kind of treatment. Perhaps she liked having it in all ways. Marnie heard Barbara's voice: *Variety is the spice of life ...*

'Marnie, shall I take your coffee while you dig it out?'

Anne was talking to her. Marnie had not been paying attention. Time to flannel.

'I was just wondering ...' She passed her cup to Anne, hoping for more help. Stuart was looking at her expectantly.

Anne again. 'I think you put our draft *timetable* in the blue folder.'

Draft timetable, great. 'No, Anne, it's in the red one. Blue is for the briefing papers.'

'Oh yes, of course.' Anne turned towards Stuart. 'Sorry, you were asking about our best completion date.'

Marnie consulted a document encased in a transparent folder. It looked impressively efficient. 'I'd normally expect anything up to about six months from brief to handover on a job of this size ...'

'Not unreasonable ...' Stuart murmured. '... but we were rather hoping ...'

'Could get it down to four ... if ... we get rapid decisions when we put forward our scheme design and depending on availability, of course.'

'Good … good …'

Marnie took a last sip of coffee and stood up. 'Right. Shall we do the Grand Tour?'

While they inspected the building, Marnie bombarded Stuart with questions and was impressed with his command of every aspect of the development. While she made copious notes, Anne photographed the restaurant, the bar and its terrace from every angle.

'Don't worry about the terrace,' Stuart called over. 'It'll just be teak decking with steel balustrade.'

'We'll want to be sure the whole scheme blends in together,' Marnie explained. 'Are you an architect yourself by training, Mr Stuart?'

'Ian … do call me Ian. No. Merchant banking. Came to work in the City, saw the opportunities opening up … started my own company …'

'And never looked back,' Marnie completed his sentence.

Stuart looked thoughtful. 'Something you should never do … look back.'

Half an hour later, Stuart was opening the door of a cab summoned by his secretary to take Marnie and Anne back to Euston station. He leaned in to speak to the driver. 'Put it on our account, Kenny.'

'That's kind of you, Ian.'

'No trouble. We like to look after our colleagues … and friends.'

As they shook hands, Marnie glanced up at the nameboard. 'What's the connection with Bermuda?' She hoped it had nothing to do with the slave trade.

'None at all. There is no connection. It used to be called Tannery Dock. I thought Bermuda Reach sounded more appealing, more in tune with the aspirations of our clients, so I changed it for the brochures and put up signs with that name on.'

'No objections from the borough council?'

'Nobody even noticed it, tucked away down here. I'd paid good money for the place, so I decided I could call it what I wanted.'

Ian Stuart and Barbara Taverner … *birds of a feather*, Marnie thought.

●　●　●　●　●

Settled comfortably in their seats on the train home, there was none of the usual talking over of the project that was now underway, none of their usual excitement. Anne pulled out her book to settle down for a read; Marnie was staring out of the window. When they did speak, both began at the same time. They grinned at each other.

'After you, Anne.'

'I was only saying I liked Bermuda Reach … *very* smart. I can't wait to see your design.'

Marnie smiled broadly. 'I'll keep it in the *blue* folder, of course.' They burst out laughing. None of the other passengers noticed. Everyone was too occupied with their mobile phones. 'You saved my bacon there. As soon as we get back to the office, I'm going to commission a statue of you to take pride of place in the courtyard.'

'Well, you did seem to have wandered off into a world of your own.'

'My mind was on other things. Do you think he noticed?'

Anne shook her head. 'Probably too busy worrying about his hairstyle. Did you see that mirror on the wall?'

'Yes. Thanks for your presence of mind, Anne ... the *blue* folder ...' They laughed again.

'What was the document you were looking at actually, Marnie? I didn't think you'd worked out a detailed timetable yet.'

'I hadn't. I was consulting the travel expense forms that you printed off this morning.'

They laughed out loud. Again no one noticed. Everyone was staring at their mobiles. The train had gone into a tunnel.

25

Marnie may have learnt nothing about the relationship between Stuart and Barbara on the visit to London, but it had brought her one positive outcome. It had led her back to focus on what she did best. She was able to concentrate for almost the whole of Friday morning on the interiors at Bermuda Reach. And for almost the whole of that morning she managed to distance herself from the Gerard case.

On one side of the office barn was a workbench over which the wall had been fitted with corkboard. Here she pinned up the plans given to her by Stuart and around them Anne's Polaroid photographs. On the bench she laid out swatches of materials and colour cards of paint and emulsion. For a few hours she immersed herself in light, shade and texture, moving from subtle pastels to bold statements in strong colours, from sandy shades to stark black, white and grey. She was edging towards understated neutral tones that blended with the teak decking of the terrace, when she caught sight of the architect's name in the corner of a drawing and remembered she had not yet spoken with Philip Everett.

With no need to look up the number of the firm that had employed her for nine years, she picked up the phone and pressed buttons automatically. Philip was available and they talked over the project. His own inclination was towards a bolder treatment to counter-balance the broad expanse of the grey-brown waters of the Thames and the low-rise buildings on the far bank. The conversation moved to a close.

'How did you get on with Stuart?'

'All right … knows what he wants … a good client in that respect. And Bermuda Reach is an absolute goldmine. He's got a good eye for an opportunity.'

Philip chuckled. 'He's got a good eye for a lot of things, Marnie. I think you were wise to take Anne along for the meeting. Or perhaps you didn't know about his reputation?'

'A woman doesn't need to know about someone's reputation, Philip.'

'No, I suppose not. Anyone can see he fancies himself as a real lady-killer.'

Marnie froze. She could feel the hairs rise on the back of her neck. A *lady-killer* … It was a common enough expression, quite harmless. But it suddenly brought the whole Barbara Taverner affair flooding over her and she felt as if she was drowning, sucked under the grey-brown waters flowing past Bermuda Reach.

'Marnie? … Hallo? …Can you hear me? …Marnie?'

She swallowed and cleared her throat. 'Sorry.'

'Are you all right? What's happened?'

'It was … nothing … sorry, Philip.'

'Marnie, I've known you for a long time. It wasn't nothing. Did something I said upset you?'

'No, of course not … well, yes … in a way … Look, I am sorry … perhaps we can talk a bit later …'

It was absurd, but she felt tears running down her cheeks. She pressed the button to disconnect the call and slumped down at her desk, dropping the receiver onto the surface and with head in hands she closed her eyes. For some minutes she sat motionless and was taking deep breaths trying to compose herself when she felt a hand touch her shoulder. Anne had silently descended from the loft and stood beside her. There was no need for words between them. Without a sound Anne withdrew, and moments later Marnie became aware of the heady aroma of brandy close by. She heard the glass being pushed towards her.

'Here, Marnie. This might help.'

A paper tissue was pushed into her hand, and she wiped her eyes. 'This is ridiculous,' she murmured, but took the brandy and sipped it gratefully.

'No prizes for guessing what this is about,' Anne said gently. 'What brought it on?'

Before Marnie could answer, Ralph came into the office. He kissed the top of Marnie's head.

'Philip's just phoned me. He was really worried about you ... couldn't understand what had happened. He said one minute you were talking about the job, then without warning you suddenly went all strange and hung up on him.'

'Lady-killer.' Marnie spoke quietly, her chin over the brandy glass. 'He said Stuart was a lady-killer. I know it's stupid, but it caught me completely off-guard.'

'I knew it had to be that. I promised I'd investigate and let him know how you were.'

'Did you tell him anything?'

'I came straight over. But I'll phone him back and explain.'

'It's all right, Ralph. I'll talk to him ... least I can do.'

Marnie finished her brandy and asked to be left alone to talk to Philip. A good and trusted friend, he had helped Marnie to establish her business when she left London. She had been head of interior design at his company, and he had provided her biggest client, Willards Brewery. He was also a good listener, and once she had started to explain, she brought out the whole story without being interrupted.

'... so seeing Stuart was more than just a site meeting, Philip.'

'I can see that. And what I said about him must've been –'

'You weren't to know. It just caught me on the hop.'

'Thanks for being so frank with me, Marnie. You know I won't breathe a word of this to anyone.'

'You don't have to tell me that.'

'So ... Clive Adamson and Piers Wainwright ... how do you propose getting in touch with them?'

'I don't. Charles can sort that out.'

• • • • •

It had to be done, and Marnie left the call to Charles until just before the lunch break. With a feeling of relief she listened to his answerphone.

'... and leave a message with your name and number after the tone. Thank you.'

Did anyone else hear the messages, she wondered. Did Charles have a secretary who dealt with his calls, or was this purely a private line? It was a different number from the one she had used when phoning Barbara. Marnie realised how little she knew of Charles's private life. She decided to play safe.

'It's Marnie. I've had a site meeting at Bermuda Reach – with the owner – and I need to talk to you. I'm in the office all day or you can reach me over the weekend. Bye now.'

Marnie hesitated before hanging up in case Charles was using the answerphone to screen his calls. After a few seconds had elapsed she replaced the receiver.

26

The next morning Anne wanted nothing more than a quiet start to a quiet weekend. At breakfast they had planned their day like any normal Saturday: tidy up the week's loose ends in the office, pack a picnic lunch and head off up the canal on *Sally Ann* for a relaxing afternoon. It was worth a try, but it turned out differently.

Anne's first duty was to look in on Ronny – newly released from hospital – before visiting the village shop to fetch a few provisions and pay the weekly newspaper bill. She had picked him a bunch of spring flowers from the overgrown wilderness behind the farmhouse. As she was ringing the doorbell she heard the sound of tyres on gravel and turned to find Ronny's younger brother returning from his paper round. He flipped a leg effortlessly over the saddle and leaned his bike against the porch.

'Hey, Anne, that's funny. I was just thinking of you.'

'Oh? Why's that?'

'Something in one of the papers, the *Sun* I think it was … or the *Globe* …'

'What was it?' she snapped. 'Sorry … I mean, can you tell me what it was … please?'

'Well, it wasn't really about you … it was that bloke who bought the vicarage … the one whose wife got –'

'I know who you mean, Paul.'

'I saw their photos …'

'Mr Taverner … and Marnie?'

'*Marnie?* No. Taverner and the murderer … wotsisname?'

'Neil Gerard?'

'That's the one. They were on the front page.'

'What did it say about them?'

The front door opened behind Anne but she paid no attention to Mrs Cope.

'Er … well, I just saw the headline …'

'Hallo, Anne.' Mrs Cope tried to attract the attention of her visitor.

Anne spun round and thrust the posy of flowers into Mrs Cope's hands. 'Hi. These are for Ronny. I'll come back later.' She rattled the words off like a machine gun. To Paul she barked, 'Can I borrow your bike?'

Before he could reply, she grabbed it and raced up the drive. Rounding the churchyard wall, she left Martyrs Close and accelerated up the high street. The bike clattered on the pavement outside the shop as Anne dismounted on the run and almost went sprawling on the ground. Keeping her balance, she pushed open the door and made a lunge at the rack of newspapers.

'That's funny …' Molly Appleton began.

'*The Sun*,' Anne interrupted breathlessly.

Molly pointed. 'On the end … if there's one left.'

Anne saw the photo on the front page. An actress from a TV soap. Definitely not male. No doubt about it.

'*The Globe!*' Anne shouted.

'None left. The last one went just two minutes ago. You wouldn't believe it –'

'Sorry, Mrs Appleton … gotta go.'

She went. Before she had reached full speed, the plan was forming in her mind. Back at Glebe Farm Anne would collect her Mini and drive to the nearest garage on the main road. They sold papers. On the way down the field track she made a mental note to increase Paul Cope's Christmas box at the end of the year. In fact, she would commission a medal. He deserved it for delivering the papers down and up that treacherous slope in all weathers.

In the courtyard of Glebe Farm Anne attempted a smoother descent, lifting her leg over the saddle to glide like a ballerina in *Swan Lake*. But the classical ballet takes no account of cobblestones. She was vibrated off the pedal and managed a good impression of a dying duck as she landed in a heap outside the office door.

Inside, she was surprised to see Marnie and Ralph huddled together at Marnie's desk.

'Just getting my car keys,' Anne blurted. 'I've got to get a –'

She stopped, mouth open. Marnie was holding up a newspaper. On the front page, side by side, were two men, familiar faces. Beside them in large print was the headline: *The Odd Couple*.

• • • • •

Saturday's plans were jettisoned. Ralph's task for the morning had been to check out his cottage near Oxford, and he had called in at the shop for a packet of Polo mints on the way. Seeing the headline in *The Globe*, he had bought the paper – the last copy – and rushed back to Glebe Farm.

Marnie wasted no time in phoning Charles. She pressed the speaker button on the phone so that Ralph and Anne could hear the conversation. As usual the answerphone cut in.

'It's Marnie. Listen, if you're there, pick up the phone. It's very important. I must talk to you before –'

'I'm here, Marnie. I was shaving. What is it?'

'Did you learn anything new from Neil Gerard yesterday? You were out visiting him when I rang you.'

'Nothing of any substance. He still maintains he's totally …' He paused. 'Wait a minute … how did you know where I was yesterday?'

'You're on the front page of *The Globe* … both of you. You're being described as the *odd couple*.'

'Christ!'

'They're wondering why you're spending so much time visiting the man who … well, visiting Neil Gerard. There's speculation about whether you're going to back his campaign for an appeal or a retrial.'

'Oh, God …'

'Are you going to do that, Charles? Is that what this is all about?'

'I don't know … Everything's just …' His voice faded.

'I need to know, Charles. I'm stuck in the middle and I haven't a clue about what's going on.'

'Well, yes, I did go to see him yesterday … just before they moved him up to near you. I wanted more information about Barbara's … other men. He was quite forthcoming … told me roughly the times when she was seeing them … I've written it all down … things she'd said about them … things she'd said about me. He was –'

'Charles, with respect, that isn't the top of our agenda just now. The report in the paper has changed all that.'

'But it's given me information I needed. Frankly, Marnie, that is top of my agenda.'

Marnie sighed with impatience. 'Look, the *Globe* is running a story. They won't be running it alone from now on. The other tabloids will be wanting their piece of the action. At any minute they could be camping on your doorstep. Hell, Charles, I shouldn't have to tell you this.'

'You're right, I should get away.'

'Unless you want to be hounded day and night, yes.'

'You don't think involving the press might lead to more public interest in the case, further evidence being uncovered?'

Ralph leaned towards the phone. 'Charles, this is Ralph. I have to say that would be a very risky strategy. You'd be laying your private life wide open to exposure in all the media. Even the broadsheets would take this one up.'

Marnie again. 'It would be as painful as when the trial was running.'

'Yes …'

'Where are you now?'

'Templars' Wharf. Most of my stuff is over at the new penthouse, Bermuda Reach. The house here is almost empty.'

'Your clothes and personal things?'

'At the penthouse.'

Ralph joined in. 'Is it widely known that you've bought the place in Bermuda Reach, Charles?'

'Not as far as I know. We didn't get round to organising house-moving cards because of what happened.'

'Then that's probably the best place to go at once.'

Marnie shook her head. 'But only to pack things for a trip. You'd soon be tracked down to Bermuda Reach. You've got to get right away, Charles.'

'But –'

'Don't say you've got nothing to hide. You wouldn't want every part of your life to be hung out on the line for everyone to inspect. That's what would happen.'

'Damn the bloody press!'

'Yes, but don't let them damn you.'

'Marnie if I send you my notes, will you read them and see if there's anything worth following up? Will you do that for me?'

'I don't know, Charles …I might just make things worse.'

'So I just run and hide like a dog and that's it. I never get to find out if Gerard is telling the truth.'

Ralph and Anne were staring at Marnie. She put her head in her hands, elbows on the desk, defeated. 'Send me the notes and I'll have a look at them,' she murmured slowly.

'I can send them by fax. Gerard said he might be able to provide more details. I was going to go back to see him some time …'

Anne looked alarmed.

Ralph cut in. 'You're asking a lot, Charles. This is putting a huge strain on Marnie. You probably don't realise. What if she visited him and got targeted by the press herself?'

'There's no need for anyone to know about Marnie, Ralph. I think it was just bad luck that someone recognised me at the other prison. No one will link Marnie with Gerard.'

'We can worry about that later,' Marnie said. 'For now, you have to disappear … the further away, the better. Any ideas?'

'Not sure. Maybe the cottage in France. I could drive there … avoid the airports.'

'That would probably be wise, but don't go in the Jaguar, or in Barbara's BMW. They're too conspicuous. Perhaps you could hire something like a Ford or a Vauxhall.'

'Good idea.'

'You'd better get going.'

'Yes. Thank you for everything … all of you.'

The phone clicked off. The three of them sat quietly with their private thoughts. It was Anne who broke the silence.

'Oh well … I suppose that's it.'

Marnie nodded. 'I don't like the way he said, *no one will link Marnie with Gerard*, rather than *no one would* … He's taking me for granted … as usual.'

Ralph frowned.

Anne did one of her theatrical sighs. 'I think I'd better put in an order for a false beard and dark glasses. Sounds like you're going to need them.' She stood up and headed for the door. 'I'd better take Paul's bike back. He'll be needing it.'

Marnie looked up. 'And you should look in on Ronny while you're there. Wish him well from me.'

'I will. And there are other things I have to say … so he doesn't have the wrong idea.'

• • • • •

Anne was soon back and found Marnie reading through notes on fax paper. There was less information than she expected, just one page of extra details. It took only two minutes to go through the comments. Ralph and Anne read them over her shoulder, after which they sat down.

Marnie tapped the first item with her finger. 'There's nothing very enlightening here. Look at this about Clive Adamson: *might go back some years* … What does that tell us? *They met through his involvement in my company* … So what? *He is younger than me, older than Barbara. Gerard thinks the affair must have lasted about a year.*' Marnie shrugged. '*He moved to new company, had less time for social life* … This is not exactly … ah, wait a minute … *may have hurt Barbara* …' She repeated, '*… may have hurt Barbara* … I wonder what that means.'

'I would've thought it meant she was distressed when they split up,' Ralph suggested.

'Probably. I don't suppose it meant they indulged in S and M and it went too far.'

Anne looked up, curious.

'It was through Charles that she met Wainwright, too,' Ralph observed.

'You think that's significant?'

'Only in the sense that it probably meant he hadn't suspected anything between Barbara and Adamson. He'd hardly be introducing her to a man with Wainwright's reputation with women if he thought she might be susceptible.'

'You see that as a sign that Barbara was good at covering her tracks.'

'Partly, although we already knew that. I wonder if it's a sign that Charles might be rather naïve.'

'Or very much in love with his wife and unable to imagine she'd be unfaithful.'

'Why did he introduce them?' Anne asked. 'I'm getting confused.'

Marnie looked down at the notes. '... *I commissioned a portrait.*'

'Oh, yes ... she had that strange name for him ...'

Marnie read further. '... *called him "an English Michelangelo" because of his strong physique* ... He seems to have been her bit-of-rough – *hard drinking, unkempt, tempestuous* – as well as an acknowledged genius. That could be quite an attractive mixture to some women.'

'I think I'd find that rather scary,' said Anne. 'But then, what do I know?'

Marnie consulted the paper again. 'She might've agreed with you, Anne. It seems like she could only manage him for a short time ... *a matter of a few months*, it says here ... *he didn't like it when she dropped him* ... That's interesting.'

'That she dropped him or that he didn't like it?' Ralph asked.

'Maybe both.'

'And Stuart came next, isn't that right? Charles's notes don't reveal whether she left Wainwright to start a new affair with him, do they?'

'Not specifically, but there can't have been much time between her breaking off with Wainwright and starting up with Stuart.'

'Or between any of them,' Anne added.

Marnie agreed and read on. 'Charles – or rather Gerard – describes Stuart as a *quite different type – English public school, Cambridge, City, "old money" ... Barbara perhaps grudgingly admired him for his achievements –*'

'Meaning his wealth, presumably,' Ralph interjected.

'No doubt, and his looks too, I expect ... the playboy image ... handmade shirts, gold watch, Aston Martin ...'

'I wonder ...' Ralph began. 'Did they all pursue Barbara, or did she go after them?'

'That isn't clear from the notes. Charles has written: *Stuart had an eye for younger women, always surrounded by them ... liked to cultivate dashing image.* That's it.'

Ralph sat back in his chair. 'I can't quite see Mike Brent in with this lot. He's the odd one out. What did Gerard write before about him not being in Barbara's class, or something like that?'

'What are you getting at?'

'I'm not sure I'm getting at anything really. It's just that he stands out from the others as being more ... ordinary. Perhaps to someone like him, the affair might've meant more. He might've been more upset when they split up.'

'You're assuming they did split up, Ralph.'

'Gerard says they had ... though he did mention that Barbara had had contact with Mike quite recently, didn't he?'

'He also thought they might've had a one-night stand rather than a full-blown affair.'

'Are you thinking there might've been some overlap, Ralph ... the possibility of jealousy or rivalry?'

Ralph shook his head. 'I'm not really suggesting anything. We don't have enough evidence – if you can call those notes evidence – to be able to arrive at any kind of firm conclusions.'

'You're right. I don't think these notes add anything material to what we knew before, apart from a rough timescale.'

'It's like chain smoking,' Anne said. 'She hardly put one out before going on to the next.'

Marnie and Ralph looked at her. It was a compelling image.

'And what do they tell us about her?' Ralph wondered.

'That her life with Charles didn't fulfil all her needs?' Marnie suggested. 'That's been my feeling all along. Unless ... unless something happened between her and Charles about five or six years ago that led her to look elsewhere for excitement.'

'You don't think it might be that old line about marriage? A woman marries a man thinking she can get him to change ... but he doesn't. A man marries a woman thinking she'll never change ... but she does.'

Marnie smiled grimly. 'We'll never know ... not now.' She re-read the notes.

Ralph steepled his fingers against his lips, thinking. He made a gesture across the desk towards Marnie. 'Whatever they tell us, those comments don't give us anything like the whole picture.'

'No ... and only Barbara could answer our questions.' Marnie laid the paper on the desk. 'Although ...'

'What is it?'

'I was just thinking ... Gerard could tell us more. He might feel able to say more to us than he could to Charles.'

Ralph looked concerned. 'Are you serious?'

'I don't know ... no ... or perhaps ... I don't know what I think ...'

Anne stood up and went to switch on the kettle. 'Oh well, he's only just moved. You can afford to wait a few days to decide what you want to do ... if anything at all. He'll be settling in first in his new cell.'

'What did you say, Anne?'

The sharpness of Marnie's tone made Anne look round in surprise. 'I only meant there was no need to rush into anything. He's only just moved to the new prison. No one would expect –'

'Anne, you're a genius.'

Anne looked surprised. 'True. Could you just remind me in what particular way?'

• • • • •

The new city of Milton Keynes is the most modern in Europe and its planners laid it out on a spacious grid pattern, each intersection forming a roundabout. While Marnie drove along the V roads – vertical, running north-south – and H roads – horizontal, running west-east – Anne gave directions and followed their progress with a finger tracing the route on the street map. Their goal was the nearby prison, presumably as modern as the town itself.

With one of her lightning decisions, Marnie had phoned the prison to ask if a visit to Neil Gerard was possible that day. An efficient voice informed her that visiting that afternoon began at two o'clock. No appointment was necessary. Anne had not been surprised at Marnie's proposal. It was typical of her to seize the initiative. Anne had insisted on coming as navigator. They took Ralph's old Volvo as camouflage.

Marnie had only half-reluctantly agreed to Anne's presence, but had insisted that Ralph stay behind. On arrival in the prison car park Anne pointed to a corner slot at the end of a row and asked Marnie to drive forwards into the space. They split forces. When Marnie was inside with Gerard, Anne was to stay in the car and keep a lookout for any journalists or photographers. Marnie would switch on her mobile as soon as she exited the prison gates and ring Anne for clearance to return to the car.

Anne climbed into the back of the Volvo, slipped on a baseball cap and settled herself low in the seat. For extra cover, she had brought a book, hoping she would look like a child waiting for its parents to return. Under the peak of the cap, from her vantage point she could keep the whole car park under surveillance without it being obvious to an outside observer. Moving around to get comfortable, she looked at the other cars to see if any of them contained a passenger. As far as she could tell, every one was empty.

Bringing both feet up onto the seat, she rested the book against her knees and looked over them to scan the area. All clear. Beside her, the mobile lay ready. Now it was up to Marnie.

• • • • •

Marnie's first impression on seeing Neil Gerard again was that he seemed thinner than before. In the hospital bed it had not been obvious, but now in the visitors' room, in grey shirt and trousers, with matching complexion, he looked like a man recovering from a long illness.

He rose stiffly when she entered the room, shook hands and offered her a seat. His grip was feeble, his hands cool. He waited until she had taken her place before sitting.

Marnie was determined to keep proceedings business-like. She deliberately refrained from asking how he was feeling and came straight to the point. On the table she placed Charles's extra notes.

'So you're following up the leads?' His voice too was more subdued than before.

'There's nothing to follow up here, nothing of any substance.'

'I suppose not. But how do you talk to a man about his wife's infidelity? It's not easy. I know he's more interested in finding out about Barbara than in helping me, but he's gradually realising that it amounts to the same thing. He knows I didn't kill her, I'm sure of that. He must want her killer found and punished. At the same time he's torturing himself with thoughts about what she was doing during the latter years of their marriage.'

'You're doing the same,' Marnie said. 'You're wondering about her affair with Mike

Brent, if she was being unfaithful with him at the same time she was involved with you.'

A hesitation. 'Yes.'

'Do you suspect him?'

'Yes … definitely … but I have to suspect all four of them.'

'What about the others?'

'*The others?* What do you mean?'

'Barbara's ex-husband, Charles's ex-wife. Couldn't they be suspects too?'

Gerard frowned. 'They're past history. No one harbours a grudge that long, surely … assuming they had a grudge.'

'Who knows what's happened in their lives since you all split up? Resentment can bubble up at any time. You don't know how they might be feeling.'

Gerard breathed one word slowly under his breath. '*Jesus …*'

'Possible?'

'I dunno.' He tapped the paper. 'Can't we deal with these ones first?'

'We?'

'I've been dreading you saying you're going to drop the whole thing …'

'I've had a meeting with Stuart and we've been in touch with Brent.'

It was a simple statement but it made Gerard jump. 'You have? What did you find out?' His eyes were staring.

'Nothing really.'

'You must've learnt *something*, gained *some* idea …'

'I couldn't exactly haul them down to the precinct and beat a confession out of them, could I?'

'I'm serious, Marnie.'

She leaned forward and lowered her voice. She hoped it sounded menacing. 'So am I. What do you expect me to do? I don't have any experience, any resources – apart from these few scrappy notes – any authority to do *anything*.'

To Marnie's surprise, Gerard countered in the same tone. 'And what do you think *I* can do from in here? Can't you imagine what it's like? You're supposed to be intelligent and sensitive. Why don't you –'

'I need more information. If you want me to do more than I've done so far, you've got to give me more to go on.'

Gerard shook his head. Far from it being a gesture of resignation, Marnie had the impression that he was wrestling with something inside him.

'What is it, Neil?'

He said nothing, stared in front of him as if looking into his memories.

'Neil … talk to me. I can do nothing if you hold back on me. Only you can give me the information I need if I'm to stand any chance of helping you.' Marnie could hardly believe she had let herself be dragged in this far.

'No.'

Marnie felt impatience well up inside her. She began pushing the chair back. 'Then if you can't talk to me, there's nothing –'

'Barbara will have to tell you herself.' He spoke so quietly that Marnie was sure she'd mis-heard him.

'What did you say?'

'You need to hear the story in Barbara's own words … from her own lips …'

Marnie felt the skin prickle all over her body. The world seemed suddenly shut out and distant. She felt suspended between the present and infinity. Into her mind floated words from a poem she had discovered the year before in a notebook of verses written by Simon, her late husband:

> … *And you will sleep with roses round your head,*
> *Kissed by the lips of poets long since dead …*

She had stepped out of time and place and heard herself speaking, but was unable to make out the words. Absurdly she wanted to ask herself to repeat what she had said.

'Are you all right, miss?' A hand was touching her arm.

She looked up. 'How can she speak to me from beyond the grave?'

'Pardon? Are you feeling all right? Would you like a glass of water?'

'What?' She was looking up at a man in uniform. Her eyes moved across to where Neil Gerard was sitting, one hand reaching for hers.

The guard gestured to Neil to move back. 'You've gone very pale, miss.'

'No … I'm fine … really I am … thank you.'

'I think it's probably time you were leaving.'

'Just two more minutes.'

'Are you being threatened?'

'Oh, no. It's nothing like that.' She attempted a smile at Gerard. 'Sorry. I haven't had much to eat today … too much rushing around …'

The guard withdrew, keeping watch on Marnie as he walked away.

'What was that about?' Gerard asked.

'That's *my* question. You tell me. What did you mean about Barbara?'

Gerard leaned forward again, glancing at the guard, careful not to get too close. 'I'm not sure this is a good idea, Marnie … but I don't think I have any choice …'

• • • • •

Marnie walked briskly across the car park without touching the mobile and pulled open the car door. Her speed took Anne by surprise. She scrambled out from the back and slipped into the front passenger seat, grabbing the safety belt and jiggling the catch to make it engage as Marnie gunned the engine into life.

'Blimey, you were quick! Wasn't he in? Don't tell me he'd popped out for a spot of shopping and a quick half down the pub?'

No reply. Anne looked at Marnie.

'What's up? Hey, you look as if you've –'

'Don't say it. I almost feel like I have seen a ghost.'

'Has something happened to Neil Gerard?'

'No, it's not like that.'

'Did he come up with anyone else who could help?'

'In a manner of speaking …'

'Someone we know?'

Marnie let in the clutch and drove for the exit.

'Yes … Barbara Taverner.'

It had been another of Marnie's decisive moves. Ralph was overruled. He would be spending the day in Oxford having Sunday lunch with the warden of his former college, discussing future collaboration. Anne would accompany Marnie to London. Early that morning there was little traffic as they sped down the motorway in light drizzle. Anne had been ominously quiet since Marnie had outlined the plan for the trip.

The drizzle eased off and Marnie gave the screen washers one last squirt before switching off the wipers. 'You're thinking this isn't a good idea, aren't you?'

'I don't know. I did at first, but ...'

'Changed your mind?'

'I ...'

'Come on ... what is it? If you're worrying about me, it's too late. I've decided I'm going to find these tapes, listen to them and only then take a final decision. If they don't give us any substantial details, that's the end of it.'

'And if they do?'

Marnie overtook a van, using the wipers and washers again to clear spray from the windscreen before replying. 'That's the big question. I'm keeping an open mind until I've heard the story.'

'Mm ...'

'Anne, you could've opted to stay behind. I don't want to drag you into something against your will.'

'I know ... but I had to come. I didn't want you going off on your own.'

'Why not? It's only a matter of finding some tapes in Gerard's flat. We'll be in and out in ten minutes.'

'I'm glad you think so, Marnie. Are things ever that simple?'

'You think it'll take longer to find them?'

'That's not what's on my mind.'

'Then why don't you just tell me what's bothering you?'

'I ... I suppose I'm scared.'

'*Scared?* What of? The flat's unoccupied ... we know where to find the key ... we know what we're looking for ... No one's going to be there. What's there to be scared of?'

'I can't quite describe it.'

'Are you worried we might discover someone else is the murderer ... and they could try to ... stop us?'

'I had thought of that, and I suppose it's part of it. You seem to have come round to thinking that Gerard's innocent now, so – if you're right – someone else must be guilty.'

'That follows, but if we did find out anything, I'd hand it straight over to Inspector Bartlett and let him get on with it. Don't be in any doubt about that. I know my limitations.'

'That's fine.'

'So is that it?'

'Not quite. There's something else … I'm finding this new development with the tapes kind of … well, spooky …'

A voice from beyond the grave, Marnie thought. *Spooky* is the word. And so it was, as they reached the outskirts of the capital and Marnie took the roads across north London to Neil Gerard's flat that they prepared themselves mentally. Barbara Taverner was about to re-enter their lives.

* * * * *

Londoners are not early birds, and on a cool Sunday morning the traffic was sparse as they made their way through empty streets of drawn curtains. In another hour or two life would return to the huge city, but by then Marnie and Anne would be heading for home up the M1. At least that was the plan.

As usual the traffic lights conspired against Marnie and stopped her at every intersection. The two of them had been silent since their earlier exchanges when Anne took up the theme once again.

'Gerard can't be leaving his flat empty for the next thirty years, or however long he's going to be in prison, can he?'

'I think he's decided to keep it for the time being. Like an act of faith. To sell it would be an admission that he's staying inside for life.'

'That puts a huge burden on you, Marnie. Does he realise how unfair he's being?'

'It's only natural … he's entirely focused on his own needs just now. In a way it's all rather pathetic … pinning his hopes on his sister's campaign … relying on me to find evidence that will get him freed.'

'And these tapes are somehow going to do that … provide this extra evidence? I don't get it. What are they exactly?'

'That's what we're here to find out. I've been wondering if they're like love letters, only recorded on tape instead of being written down.'

'I've never had a love letter, but I can't imagine what might be in them that can possibly prove anything.'

'Neil was vague about their exact contents. He said they were Barbara talking about her life, their relationship together … past relationships as well. It was just pillow talk, he said, but it might reveal something.'

'*Pillow talk* … That sounds a bit old-fashioned. Marnie, why did she make the recordings?'

'According to Neil she said she was too lazy to write. Seems it was her way of extending their affair, adding some extra spice …It is an odd thing to do, that's for sure.'

'Do you think she was an *odd* person, Marnie?'

'You mean *odd* like … deviant?'

'Maybe.'

'I think she liked to live life in the fast lane … You might think that's another old-fashioned term?'

'But she doesn't seem to have been an old-fashioned kind of person, does she?'

'Whatever she was – and the more I think about her, the less I realise I knew her –

we're about to find out. This is Neil's street. We're looking for number thirty-two.'

Marnie turned the big car into the side street and almost at once both she and Anne gaped in unison. Fifty metres ahead of them the road was blocked. Two police cars and a number of unmarked cars filled the street. Blue lights were revolving, people in uniforms were milling about. A small crowd had gathered on the pavements. *This is becoming a habit*, Marnie thought.

'Something tells me we won't have to look too far to find number thirty-two,' said Anne.

Marnie stopped the Discovery in the middle of the road between parked cars and began to get out. Anne followed. 'Are you just going to leave the car here?'

Marnie shrugged. 'I don't think anyone's going to be moving. Anyway, I just want a quick look.'

Anne was proved right. Number thirty-two was the centre of all the activity. They walked quietly along the pavement until they were as near as possible without being obtrusive and attached themselves to the back of the onlookers. Gerard's flat was on the ground floor of a spacious Edwardian house that had been divided up like most of the properties in the street. Uniformed officers were coming and going through the front door. Some others in plain clothes were standing in a group outside talking earnestly together with a woman. Marnie was aching to know what was going on, but did not want to draw attention to their presence.

To Anne she said casually, 'I wonder when it happened.'

A man standing beside her turned. 'It was the woman opposite. She was up in the night to feed their new baby. She went to open a window ... saw a light on in the front room.'

'She thought that was suspicious? Couldn't it have been the person who lives there?' Marnie asked innocently.

The man lowered his voice. 'Not really. He's inside ... I mean in prison ... for life.'

'Oh?'

'You've heard of the Little Venice murder? That was him, Neil Gerard.'

'Gosh ... So no one's living there at the moment?'

'No. He's kept the flat on ... says he didn't do it.'

'And now someone's broken in?'

'The burglar got away before the police could get here, but he got the usual things first.'

Marnie's heart sank. 'The TV and video ... hi-fi ... that kind of stuff?'

'Yeah, all that. Gerard was into music ... had a huge collection of CDs and tapes ... hi-fi equipment ... all cleaned out now, I reckon.'

Damn! Marnie was struggling to phrase her next question when she felt a nudge in her side. Anne nodded pointedly towards the front of the house. Marnie froze. The woman talking with the police officers was Sarah Cowan. Slowly Marnie turned away, muttering a non-committal remark to the man. Anne followed. They walked at an unhurried pace back to the car and had almost reached it when they heard urgent footsteps behind them.

'Marnie!'

They turned to find Sarah Cowan bearing down on them, her expression a mixture of anger and bewilderment.

'What are *you* doing here?'

Marnie hesitated, unsure how to reply. She knew she looked as guilty as if she had committed the burglary herself. 'That seems to be your usual way of greeting me, Sarah.'

'I said what are you *doing* here?'

'I know it must look odd –'

'*Odd?* My brother's flat has a break-in and the next minute you're on the scene. What's going on? And don't tell me you just happened to be passing.'

'Tell me about the burglary. What's been taken?'

Sarah tossed her head impatiently. 'What d'you think? What they always go for, of course.'

She doesn't know about the tapes, Marnie thought. *She doesn't realise the importance of what's happened here*. Sarah's suspicion returned.

'Are you going to tell me exactly why you've come here at this hour of the morning? You must've set off ages ago.' Her eyes narrowed. '… unless you were here already.'

Marnie took Anne by the sleeve and began to lead her away. 'We're doing something for Neil. That's all I can say.'

'Funny he didn't mention it to me! What is this thing you're doing?'

'I can't tell you just now.'

'Why ever not? Look here, Marnie, I want to know what you're up to.'

'I told you.'

'You told me *nothing*. Maybe you'd better explain to the police. I'm sure they'd be interested to know.'

Marnie looked her straight in the eye. 'You made the wrong assumptions once before, Sarah. Don't repeat that mistake now.'

Sarah was left staring after them as Marnie and Anne got into the car and reversed up the street. She was still standing where they had left her when Marnie turned into the next road and accelerated away.

Anne breathed out audibly. 'Phew … That was awkward.'

'It's more than awkward. We've lost our chance of finding the tapes.' Marnie was glancing nervously in the rear-view mirror, expecting that any minute a police car would come after them with siren wailing.

Anne broke into her thoughts. 'What do we say if the police catch up with us?'

'That's easy. We tell them the truth. We're doing nothing illegal. We have the owner's permission to retrieve his property from his flat.'

'So why didn't you just tell Sarah what we were doing?'

'That's a good question, Anne. The simple answer is … I'm not sure … instinct, perhaps.'

'About what?'

'It's hard to explain … I found myself wondering why Neil hadn't told his sister about what we were doing for him. Why shouldn't she know? After all, she's leading his campaign. And yet he isn't confiding everything in her. It made me think of client confidentiality. If he wanted his sister to know about it, then it was up to him to tell her, not up to me.'

They pulled out onto a major road. The traffic was still very light, and no other car was following them.

'I've got another good question,' said Anne. 'Where are we going? Oh and a follow-up: what are we going to do now?'

'Easy.' Marnie paused for effect. 'I haven't a clue. And while we're on questions, try this one. Was this a straightforward burglary ... or did the intruder know what they were looking for? Were they doing the same as us? Did they just beat us to it?'

Anne looked anxiously over her shoulder. 'Well, at least the police aren't following us.'

'No. But our old friend Chief Inspector Bartlett might be making plans to camp out on our doorstep back home at this very minute.'

'Great ... though he could be in for a surprise ...'

'You mean, me telling him the plain and simple truth, without keeping anything back?'

'Exactly. He'll probably pass out with shock.'

Marnie thumped her friend gently on the arm. 'You're a great comfort, Anne, you know that?'

'Seriously, Marnie, what *are* we going to do now? Charles Taverner's got us into this, and everything's gone wrong.'

Marnie paused again, but this time it was not for effect. 'Charles Taverner ...' she repeated thoughtfully. They stopped at traffic lights, and Marnie leaned forward, resting her forearms against the wheel. She remained there immobile for several seconds. Anne watched and waited.

The lights changed. Marnie pushed the car into first gear and accelerated off.

'Anne, what tape do we have in the cassette player?'

Anne pulled it out and read the label. It was handwritten. 'Carly Simon ... Greatest Hits. You want me to play it?'

'Is it the original?'

'No. It's a copy. You know we always keep the originals at home and make copies to use in the car in case they ...' Her voice faded away.

'Like we make back-up disks of all our computer files in case they get lost or damaged ...' Marnie added. '... at least everything important.'

Anne sat bolt upright. 'You think Barbara might've kept copies of the tapes?'

Marnie steered the car into the side of the road, pulled on the handbrake and switched off the engine. She blinked rapidly a few times. 'Those tapes were meant to add spice to their relationship,' she said quickly. 'If Barbara gave a set to Gerard, it's logical that she'd keep copies for herself.'

'So where are they now?' Anne asked.

Marnie ran a thumbnail over lips. 'They're not on *Perfidia*. She must've kept them at home.' In her mind Marnie saw again the small TV and music room at Templars' Wharf ... Barbara's den, the bookcase stacked with records, videos, CDs ... *and cassette tapes.* 'Charles said everything had been cleared out and sent over to the new penthouse. I bet that's where they've gone ... if they still exist ... Bermuda Reach.'

Marnie dug into the door's pocket and picked out the mobile. She turned it on and sat staring at it.

'Who are you phoning?' Anne asked. 'Not Charles Taverner?'

Marnie shook her head, switched off the mobile and thrust it at Anne. 'I don't think so. Before I said anything to him about this, I'd want to know exactly what was on those tapes. Probably best if he never knows about them. He should certainly never hear them.'

She reached behind her and grabbed the shoulder bag on the back seat. Rummaging in it, she fished out the bunch of keys belonging to *Perfidia*. One by one she identified them, muttering to herself. 'Boat ignition, side door, steerer's door ... Templars' wharf ... vicarage ... ah ... *yes*. This must be it.' She started the engine. Hesitating momentarily, she made up her mind, engaged first gear and moved off.

'So where are we going?' Anne asked.

'Bermuda Reach. Where else?'

• • • • •

Marnie parked the Discovery one street away from the marina and they walked to the edge of the development. It was still barely eight o'clock and no one was stirring, only two cats slinking along the quay after a night on the prowl. There was no Jaguar limo, no Aston Martin roadster. They were steeling themselves to go forward when a movement on the far side caught their eye. They eased back into the lea of the nearest building to observe. It was a security guard in uniform on patrol, walking towards the lodge beside the entrance road. Marnie signalled wordlessly to Anne and they withdrew.

Back at the car they sat and went over the options. Marnie thumped the wheel.

'*Damn!* I really don't know what we're doing here. I never asked to get involved in this crazy scheme.'

Anne nodded. 'I suppose there's no point mentioning that we made a special effort to get up with the cockerel to be here.'

'I'll strangle that bloody bird when we get back.'

'So will I ... we'll take turns.'

Marnie's face cracked into a grin. 'It's not funny, Anne.'

Anne laughed weakly. 'I know. That's why we're not laughing.'

'And don't ask me what we're going to do next.'

'Of course not.' Pause. 'But ... since you mention it ...'

Marnie fiddled with the clasp on the shoulder bag in her lap. On impulse she opened it and looked inside, pulling a business card from one of the slots intended for Visa and MasterCard. 'Bloody Ian Stuart,' she muttered.

'That's two bloodies in two minutes. Angela would be shocked.'

'Then she shocks easily.' With nothing better to do, Marnie read Ian Stuart's card. She stiffened.

Anne craned her neck to see. 'What is it?'

Marnie raised a finger and shook her head. She did the thumb against the lips thing, a sure sign she was plotting. 'Have you still got the mobile?'

Anne handed it over and Marnie pressed buttons, reading them from the card. When she finished, she gave the card to Anne. At first she could see nothing out of the ordinary. It was designed purely for the Bermuda Reach development. Company logo, name, site office, contact numbers. But there, in small print at the bottom, was an additional phone number:

Site security (24 hours)

Marnie's voice was calm and relaxed when she spoke into the mobile. 'Good morning. This is Marnie Walker of Walker and Co. Are you currently on duty at Bermuda Reach? … Good. My company's handling the restaurant/wine bar design. I need to check some details. I'm down in London and I'd like to do it before heading out of town this morning after breakfast. Would that be convenient?' She listened and pulled a face. Anne edged closer to listen at Marnie's ear.

'… only authorised persons on site. Those are my instructions.'

'But I told you, I do have authorisation. We're handling that contract.'

'Sorry, miss, but you're not on my list. I can check for you but not until Monday.'

'I don't understand. Ian … er, Mr Stuart … said I could have access at any time.'

'But your name isn't on my contractors' list. I'm sorry.'

Marnie bit her lip. 'We're doing the work for Willards Brewery and they –'

'Willards? You should've said. Just a minute.' Pause. 'What did you say the name was?'

'Marnie Walker.'

'Walker and Co? That's fine. You're on their list. When do you want to come? I'm only on duty for the next half hour.'

'I'm staying nearby, so I'll come straight away.'

She disconnected and clenched a fist. '*Yes!*'

They sat for a count of five minutes – it seemed like an age – working out their plan. Just as Marnie was reaching for the ignition key, Anne spoke.

'Marnie, does the penthouse have its own garage?'

'There's a block for residents' cars round the back on the service road. It's carefully camouflaged with a terrace garden on top. Why?' As soon as she phrased the question, Marnie knew the answer. If she had a spanking new Jaguar, she'd want to keep it in a garage, too,

Anne did not bother to reply. She had another question. 'Do you know where Charles Taverner's staying at the moment?'

'He said he was going to leave and go to their cottage in France. Immediately.'

'Are you sure he's actually left?'

'No.'

'So what if –'

'I don't know. Maybe I should ring him …'

'Where?'

'Here, I suppose. I'd hang up if he answered the phone.'

'He could get your number with one-four-seven-one.'

'I can withhold it.'

'But didn't you say he used the answerphone to screen calls before taking them?'

'*Damn!*' Marnie breathed out impatiently. 'This is getting too complicated.' She turned the ignition key. 'Come on, let's just do it.'

They drove calmly to the marina and pulled up at the lodge. The security man came out and walked round to the driver's side, eyeing Anne with interest.

'Good morning. Miss Walker? You didn't say you'd have someone with you.'

'Hi.' Very casual. 'My assistant, Anne Price. She should be on your list. We were both here the other day seeing Mr Stuart.'

She gave him their two business cards. He read them and handed them back with a faint smile. 'So you're both staying down in London.'

'We're a busy firm. Shall I park over there by the flats? I don't want to disturb people more than necessary. We won't be long.'

'There aren't many people to disturb. They go away a lot at weekends, and some of the flats are still unoccupied.'

'I see. Well, we'll get on. We have to be back in time for a lunch engagement.'

Marnie drove on. Anne snorted indignantly as they parked close by the entrance to the residences.

'Did you see the way he looked at me, Marnie? And you.'

'I don't care if he does think we're a couple of dykes, as long as he lets us in and we find what we want. Come on. First we've got to wander over to the restaurant and look busy. Bring your notepad or something.'

They mooched around inside for several minutes before venturing back out. Standing in the restaurant doorway, Marnie could see across to the lodge. Inside, the security man seemed to be reading his newspaper. They stepped out and walked unobtrusively along towards the car, keeping close to the buildings, Marnie fingering the Taverners' bunch of keys at her side. She was ready for the door leading to the penthouse, praying that the security man would be engrossed in stories about priests and choirboys or sightings of Elvis in Rotherham.

The easy part was turning the key of the front door and entering the lobby. The lift was on the ground floor but they climbed the stairs.

'What if the security man comes looking for us and finds us here?' Anne asked.

'We're calling in on our client, Charles Taverner, as we happen to be in the area.' It sounded quite convincing, Marnie thought.

'What if Mr Taverner's in the penthouse?'

'I could tell him the same.' A shade less convincing.

'Then we find the tapes and sit round listening to them … like a townie version of *The Archers* … an everyday story of city folk?'

'Hell, Anne, I don't know. But we're about to find out.'

Breathing heavily they arrived on the topmost landing. Marnie could feel her palms sweating as she slid the key into the lock.

'Actually, you're right, Marnie. If we found Mr Taverner here, you could just tell him the truth and it would be okay, wouldn't it?'

Marnie hesitated. 'Yeah … I suppose so.'

Anne spoke softly. 'That's not the real problem, is it?'

Marnie stopped turning the key halfway round. 'The real problem being …?'

'If we get in and find the flat empty but the burglar alarm switched on. If we set off the alarm, the security man would be over here in a flash and the police would be on their way and –'

'Thanks, Anne. I get the picture.'

Marnie drew a deep breath, the key clicked and she pushed the door. There was no tell-tale peep-peep from an activated alarm, no motion sensors winking from the corner of the ceiling. The penthouse flat exuded the unlived-in smell of new joinery and fresh paint. They walked on woodblock flooring into a spacious living area that spanned the building, giving views on one side down to the river and on the other to the marina.

Furniture stood around in groupings, everything covered with dust sheets. Boxes marked *Pickfords Removals* were piled up in the corners. The whole flat was flooded with light from curtainless windows. Marnie relaxed and looked into the other rooms. The place was unoccupied. Its uncompleted condition explained why Charles was not yet staying there. Her interior designer's mind was longing to draw up plans for the decor and finishes, but she forced herself to concentrate on the task that had brought them there.

'The views from up here are *fabulous*,' Anne said. 'You can see all the way down the river to Canary Wharf.'

'Great. But for now we have to focus on finding boxes of tapes, right? I reckon we can stay for ten minutes, no more, before the guard gets curious about where we are.'

'They've got labels on,' Anne observed. She began reading out loud. 'Clocks … candlesticks … here's one labelled *statues*. Never seen that before. When we moved we had labels like *tea set* or *kitchen things*.'

'Try that room over there, Anne. It's got built-in shelving, might be a place for books and music. I'll try this one.'

Marnie drew a blank. She had chosen a bedroom, though there was no sign of a bed.

'Bingo!' Anne called from her room. Marnie hurried across.

Anne was kneeling beside an open box. 'What are we looking for exactly?'

'Neil said she'd used boxes for recordings on the Deutsche Grammophon label. They should be easy to spot … yellow labels, two *m*'s, no *e* on the end.'

'You think Barbara would use the same system for hers?'

'It's a starting point.'

The search was not as simple as they had expected. The collection was substantial and highly eclectic. It took all their efforts not to spend time reading the labels. The Taverners' taste ranged from grand opera to hits of the 60s and 70s, from New Orleans jazz to boxed sets of the works of the classical masters. One by one they opened the cartons, peeling back the tape that sealed them, hoping they would be able to leave them looking untouched after they left.

'Ah …' Anne murmured. 'Yellow labels … Deutsche Grammophon … two *m*'s, no *e* on the end.' She looked up. 'I think I might've found some.'

'Check the insides. I'll keep on looking here.'

Anne flipped open a number of the box-lids. 'Marnie … plain tapes inside, just numbers on the labels. What do we do with them?'

Marnie continued her search. 'With luck, we can just take the box and stow it in the car. That's why I parked outside the door.'

Anne delved further. 'Most of this box has those tapes.'

'Mm …'

'Marnie?'

'I heard you. Try another box.'

'No. Marnie … listen.' Anne crawled towards the window and looked down. She gasped.

'What's up?'

'Red Jaguar … it's stopped next to your – oh no.'

'Charles?'

'Yeah. I suppose we'll have to come clean.'

Marnie got up and ran to the side of the window. She peered round fleetingly. 'He's going over to the security lodge.'

'What do we do?'

Marnie looked at Anne's open carton. 'We can hardly wander out carrying a Pickfords' box.'

'Can't we just explain why we're here? He's bound to find out anyway.'

Marnie shook her head. 'I'm not ready to tell him yet. I don't want him to know about the tapes until I've listened to them first.'

'But –'

'Cram as many as you can into your bag. I'll do the same. Try not to make it look bulky.'

With a shrug, Anne did as Marnie said, carefully fitting the tapes into her shoulder bag. She grabbed everything from the box indiscriminately until it was empty. As she worked she became aware of an overwhelming necessity to go to the loo.

'Marnie, I think I need to –'

'So do I. Don't think about it. No time. Just grab what you can and stack the box under the others in that pile. Let's go!'

Out on the landing, Marnie pulled the front door quietly shut. A sudden thumping sound followed by a low hum made them jump. The lift was travelling up from the ground floor.

Marnie pointed. 'The stairs. Come on! We can avoid him.'

They raced down on tiptoe, one hand grabbing the rail, the other fighting their shoulder bags that were banging about, rattling their bizarre contents. Reaching the ground floor, they heard the change of sound as the lift arrived at its destination some way above them. Marnie had the Discovery's tailgate open before they could draw breath. She yanked up the flap to the under-floor compartment and they pushed their bags into the well. They tried to look unhurried as they climbed in, panting.

'That was close,' Anne muttered. 'I still need the loo.'

Marnie was letting in the clutch before Anne had the seat belt fastened. 'I think I'm beyond physical things. I'll never need the loo again.'

Anne permitted herself a smile. 'Don't make me laugh, Marnie. It could be fatal.'

Unhurriedly Marnie drove towards the site exit, preparing herself for a cheerful relaxed wave at the security man if he looked up when they passed. She would absolutely not be stopping, short of him lying in the road in front of her. She swallowed. The man was emerging from his lodge at the moment she changed up to third. She raised her gear-change hand to wave. He did the same, but it was a command not a sociable gesture, and he stepped out in front of the car, blocking the roadway. Marnie pressed the button to lower her side window for a friendly word. As she did so, her stomach turned over. Behind the security man, another man was appearing from the lodge. It was Charles Taverner.

'Did you get what you wanted, miss?'

'Yes, thanks.' The least said the better. Marnie smiled to conceal her rapid breathing.

Charles moved forward. 'I thought the car looked familiar. Marnie?'

'Morning, Charles.'

'What was it you wanted?'

'A few details.'

Charles looked puzzled. 'Details of the penthouse?'

The security man looked puzzled. 'You mean the restaurant, sir.'

'*Restaurant?*' Charles repeated. 'What's the restaurant got to do with it?'

'I came in the week to see the owner of the whole development …' Marnie stared pointedly at Charles. '… *Ian Stuart.*'

Charles suddenly got the picture. 'I see … of course.' As the security man turned to look at him, he added, 'I misunderstood.'

'But everything's fine?' said the guard.

'Yes.' A chorus from Marnie and Charles.

Charles walked round to the passenger side of the Discovery. The security man went back to the lodge. Anne lowered the window for Charles to speak but Marnie got in first.

'Why are you still here, Charles?'

'That's what I was going to ask you.'

'I thought you agreed to get away.'

'I'm going, but first I wanted to leave some things in the flat. So are you going to explain why you're here, Marnie?'

'I needed to clear up some more details.'

'But the restaurant's all locked up. I don't understand.'

'You're just going to have to trust me on this, Charles.' *Those words again!* Trust was in short supply these days.

'I'd like to, Marnie, but I think I need something more to go on. Why should I trust you? I mean, why do you say I need to?'

'You have to trust me because if you can't – or you don't want to – then I'm walking away from the whole business with Neil Gerard, here and now.'

'So this is about Gerard, not the restaurant.'

'I'm not saying any more. The choice is yours. You can deal with Gerard alone …
and I'll pass the design projects on to one of the team at Everett Parker. I mean it,
Charles. I'm not joking. I've had just about all I can take of this.'

'Very well, Marnie. I trust you, of course I do, though I haven't any idea what you're
doing.'

'That's what trust is about, Charles.'

Marnie wished she had not said that.

• • • • •

They drove in silence until they reached the M1 and settled down to cruising speed.
Both were thinking about the strange cargo hidden in the back. It had been an
unsatisfactory and unsettling journey. All Marnie's instincts told her she should drop
the crazy plan of helping Neil Gerard. They also told her it was too late. As usual she
felt guilty about dragging Anne into her problems. She gave her friend what she hoped
was a reassuring smile.

'You all right?'

Anne nodded.

'Sure?'

'Mm. I'd still like us to stop so I can use the loo.'

It was enough to lighten the atmosphere. Marnie gave her friend a genuine smile.
'Sure. There's a service station just up the road.'

'That's the best news of the morning.'

'Absolutely.'

'By the way, Marnie …'

'What?'

'We don't actually have a cockerel.'

Marnie's brain struggled to make the connection and finally succeeded. 'I know …
and it's just as well … for his sake. He had a lucky escape there.'

• • • • •

There was a spring shower that night. Marnie got into bed with Ralph on *Thyrsis*
feeling more cheerful than she had been all day. She loved the sound of the rain on
the window. It reminded her of squally nights when she was a child and she used to go
to Beth's room and snuggle up with her sister, feeling cosy and safe.

On their return from London they had taken the decision not to listen to the tapes.
It required no effort of willpower; they had had enough of them for one day and
wanted to spend their Sunday in more agreeable pursuits. Anne had found a cardboard
box for them and volunteered to sort through it the next morning and make a
catalogue of the numbering system. She would assemble the whole *Deutsche
Grammophon* set in whatever order Barbara had listed them.

As usual Ralph was sitting up reading through the work he had completed that day.
Still wearing her silk dressing gown, Marnie climbed onto the bed and sat cross-legged
beside him, running both hands through her hair. Ralph looked up.

'Marnie, I've been wondering … Why didn't you just tell Charles the truth? You
had every right to be at Bermuda Reach. You were following up what he'd asked you
to do.'

'That's what Anne said.'

'I think she had a point. What's your answer?'

'I don't know.'

'Do you really mean that? Can I suggest a reason?'

'Go on.'

'You don't trust him.'

'Neil Gerard?'

'Charles.'

'Why do you say that?'

'Can you think of a better reason? Your list of suspects is growing by the day. You've got Gerard's list of Barbara's four lovers – former lovers – plus Gerard himself, of course.' Ralph held up his fingers to count. 'Then you've added the two ex-spouses and now Charles. That makes eight.'

'How could I think that about Charles?'

'It's not unreasonable. You're casting him in the role of the jealous husband … always the obvious suspect in a case like this, I'd imagine … which is why I'm sure the police must've investigated that possibility. And they decided he had nothing to do with Barbara's death.'

'Why is he pursuing this when Gerard is already in prison?'

'Sorry? You've jumped ahead of me there.'

'You're saying I don't trust Charles because I regard him as a suspect.'

'That's how it seems to me. It could explain why you haven't told him about the tapes. I'm assuming it's not just to spare his feelings. After all, he's going to know about them sooner or later.'

Marnie shifted onto her side and stretched her legs. 'So if he is a suspect, why take all this trouble when Neil Gerard is convicted and serving time, and everyone's convinced he's guilty?'

'Well … a number of reasons … could it be to justify his action if he did it? Or possibly as camouflage, a smokescreen to keep in contact with Sarah and her campaign, to know what she's up to … and maybe influence it?'

'You think it's all smoke and mirrors, Ralph?'

'No. Personally I don't. I've come round to thinking that Charles is just trying to get at the truth.'

'However painful that might be?'

'He's suffering already. However much it hurts, certainty is less agonising than doubt.'

28

Marnie was surprised when Anne arrived promptly for breakfast at seven thirty on Monday morning. She had fully expected her to be late, guessing that she would want to make an early start on cataloguing the tapes. Marnie reflected that she was wrong about so many things these days.

Ralph greeted her. 'You're bright and early.'

Anne hopped down the steps into the cabin on *Sally Ann* and checked the toast under the grill. As usual at that time the boat smelled of coffee. The table was set with a cloth of blue gingham. Marnie was pouring orange juice. It was an inviting start to the week. Putting the carton back in the fridge, Marnie looked up at her friend. Anne was wearing pale blue jeans and a yellow T-shirt. Her short blond hair was brushed and gleaming, freshly dried from the shower, her pale complexion touched with pink from the brisk walk through the spinney.

'Ralph's right. You remind me of that line from Shakespeare … *golden lads and girls* …'

'From *Cymbeline*,' Ralph commented. 'Better not to complete the quotation, though.'

'Not if it spoils the illusion,' said Anne, putting the first rounds of toast in a basket and loading more slices onto the grill pan.

'You look as if you slept well,' said Marnie. 'I half expected you to be absorbed with the tapes this morning. Knowing you, I thought you'd be doing them before breakfast … thought I'd have to come and find you.'

'No need. I did them all last night. I couldn't bear waiting any longer.'

'You *did* them?'

Anne sipped her orange juice. 'Separated them out from the other tapes in the box – there are more than twenty of them – put them in order … made a list of all the numbers, four to a page so you can write notes on the contents if you want.'

'*How many?* … blimey, that's a lot. Did you … listen to any of them?'

Anne shook her head. 'I was curious, but once I'd got them organised I didn't want to do anything else. I'm not even sure I want to hear them at all. But I've done my bit.'

'Are the numbers in chronological order, are they dated?' Ralph asked.

'No … just numbers 01, 02 and so on. I thought maybe Mrs Taverner had gone through them afterwards to sort them out.'

'Why do you think that?'

'It looks as if they were all done together, same style, same pen, a felt-tip. They look all of a piece … the sort of thing I'd do on a rainy day, like sorting my CDs out, putting the loose ones back in their cases.'

'So she went over them systematically.'

'That was the idea,' said Marnie. 'She was wanting to *extend the experience*. Where are they now?'

'The tapes are up in my attic under the bed. The list's on your desk.'

'Thanks, Anne. This morning I've got to prepare for my afternoon meeting in Hanford. We might get a chance to listen to one of the tapes at lunchtime before I set off.'

Marnie was wrong about that, too.

• • • • •

The phone was ringing when Marnie reached the office just before eight. It had to be a bad sign. She was right. When Marnie picked up the receiver the caller began without any introduction.

'I think I've done the wrong thing again. I shouldn't have interrogated you like that.'

'That's all right, Sarah. It was an odd situation. I don't blame you. It's an odd season.'

'I was just so surprised to find you there. One minute the police are asking me if I had any suspicions about who might burgle the flat, the next thing I turn and see you in the crowd … I mean at *that time* on a Sunday morning … and you live fifty miles away.'

'Why didn't they accept it was just a common burglary?'

'It was all very tidy … just a few things missing … the VCR, mini hi-fi, CDs, tapes … a few other bits and pieces.'

'The burglar was travelling light?' Marnie suggested.

'Marnie, what *were* you doing there? I can't work it out. It couldn't have been a coincidence.'

Marnie hesitated. 'I can't tell you that. You'll have to ask Neil for an explanation.'

'*Neil?* What has Neil told *you* that he wouldn't tell *me?*'

Marnie thought, *if he hasn't told you, perhaps he has a reason.* 'I'm not saying he won't tell you. I am saying it's up to him what he tells anyone. As for me, I'm treating everything he's told me as confidential for the time being.'

'Er …'

'What?'

Sarah spoke slowly. 'That might be tricky.'

'I understand that. All you've got to do is ask Neil and I'm sure he'll explain.'

'It's not Neil.'

'Go on.'

'It's your own fault, Marnie, you should've talked to me instead of making a run for it. What was I supposed to think?'

'What have you done?'

'The police saw me talking to you and asked who you were and what we were talking about.'

'You told the police you suspected I was involved in some way? How could you think that?'

'I didn't. I just told them I knew you but had no idea why you were there.'

'Did you give them my name?'

'I'm sorry, Marnie. I wasn't thinking. I'd been dragged out of bed to attend the burglary at Neil's flat and –'

'Sarah, you have to tell the police that my presence was *not* suspicious.'

'I think it's probably too late for that, Marnie.'

Muttering to herself, Marnie ended the call and put the phone down. She looked up to find Anne standing at the foot of the loft ladder and Detective Sergeant Marriner in the doorway.

• • • • •

Marriner took a sip of his coffee and put the cup down on the desk. 'Very nice. Thank you, Anne.' He looked at Marnie in a not unfriendly way. 'All you have to do is persuade me that your presence at the scene of the burglary wasn't suspicious and I can get back to filling in my crime statistics forms.'

'I'm glad to provide light relief from your chores, sergeant.'

'That doesn't answer my question.'

'The truth is I was on my way to Neil Gerard's flat ... with his agreement ... at his request.'

'Why so early?'

'I wanted to be in and out before people were around.'

'Like our burglar.'

'For slightly different reasons.'

'What were your reasons, Mrs Walker?'

'I admit I had gone there to try to find something.'

'What was it?'

'All I can say is it was something for Neil Gerard.'

'That surprises me. Why ask you to find it when he could easily have asked his sister?'

'That was his decision. You'll have to ask him.'

'We have. He said he had nothing to say.'

Marnie was stunned. 'He wouldn't explain why I was there?'

'He said he couldn't. Shall we start again?'

'I know we've had our ups and downs, sergeant, but you can't believe I'd do anything illegal.'

'Our *ups and downs*, as you put it, generally involve you not telling us everything you know. Once it nearly cost you your life.'

'I want to tell you the truth, but it's not as simple as that.' Marnie got up and walked over to the window. 'I can say that I was going to Neil Gerard's flat to try to find something he thought might help his appeal campaign.'

Marriner folded his arms. 'The campaign being run by his sister ... who has keys to the flat ... who can go there without hindrance whenever she wants?'

'Yes.'

'Then why not get her to do it?'

'That's what I don't know.'

'This *something* ... could it be evidence? Withholding evidence is quite a serious matter, Mrs Walker.'

'Not actually evidence, no, I don't think so. Neil thinks it might be a pointer to what happened.'

'We're not getting very far, are we?'

'Mr Marriner, in my working life I respect client confidentiality. I don't talk about my clients or their projects to outsiders without their consent. I'm treating this the same way.'

Sergeant Marriner stood up and walked slowly to the door. 'Tread carefully, Marnie.

This isn't the same thing as interior design. Think about it ... the police aren't involved in your usual work ... nor are potential murderers ...'

• • • • •

Marnie found concentration difficult that afternoon and hoped her clients did not notice. The young couple, Steve and Tricia Keating, who had recently bought a small manor house on the edge of Hanford with a view to reviving it were full of enthusiasm. Owners of a thriving and growing business, Marnie saw them as younger versions of Charles and Barbara. During the meeting she found herself wondering where their lives would lead them. She hoped she had managed to appear positive when discussing options.

On arrival back at Glebe Farm she was faced with a stack of messages from Anne who had worked on her college projects in the office so that she could man the phones. It was the end of the afternoon before any opportunity arose to listen to the tapes. Marnie waited until Anne had gone off to post letters at the village shop before walking through the spinney to *Sally Ann* and loading the first tape into the cassette player.

She sat at the table, a pad in front of her with the pages printed by Anne for note-taking, prepared to listen objectively and try to spot any clues as to what happened that led to Barbara's death.

At the first sound of Barbara's voice Marnie was startled at the clarity of the recording. She spoke softly, her words intended for one person only, a warm intimate tone that the close confines of the cabin made even more close, even more personal. It was as if they were sitting together over a late-night drink. Marnie settled down and listened, feeling like an interloper, as Barbara spoke directly from beyond her grave.

29

The first tape.

Well here we go, darling

This is meant to be a surprise for you

I thought it up in the cab on the way back here

Let's see if it works

I'm not sure how this will turn out but if it does it'll keep us closer together at times when we're apart

Isn't this cosy?

I want you to imagine me here

It's a beastly night – I hate the autumn

I was huddled up in the taxi coming back from your place, splashing through the traffic

It's still raining outside – can you hear it on the window pane?

I want you to imagine me sitting here on the seat, looking down at the river

Everything's lit up like a film set with this big black band where the river runs through the middle

I'm wearing my dressing gown – it's Japanese silk … blue and gold

I'll have a shower soon but I'm not ready yet to rinse you away

I've been thinking about the things you said

Usually I don't pay any attention to what men say, especially on an afternoon like we had today

You probably think women like to hear men talk about how wonderful they are and all that jazz

Flattery is easy and it's cheap

I mean … it doesn't cost anything

It doesn't have to be cheap in the other sense – don't let me put you off saying things

But most of the time, frankly, I'd rather be complimented on the way I dressed

At least that would reflect on something I'd done rather than on something that I just happen to be by chance

So here I am, alone in a big house on a rainy evening

Charles is off on one of his interminable meetings followed by an interminable dinner at the conference centre

If the rain keeps up like this it'll ruin his golf tomorrow

I notice you never criticise him, never have a harsh word for him

That's good

Whatever he might be, it's not for you to say it

I could call him a self-absorbed workaholic driven by ambition

He wouldn't recognise himself in that description … he'd be horrified

I could say he spends more time with his laptop than he does with me

But I don't ever want you to do that … to criticise him

And you never do, so that's good

I wonder about you sometimes

Wonder why you always ask so many questions

It's like the third degree being with you – not always but on days like today ...

I don't mind talking about the past

Don't mind talking about other people who've been part of my life ... if it turns you on

And it certainly did that (she chuckled)

Just so long as it doesn't grow into a subject for jealousy ... argument

What's gone before is over and done with

Ian ... Clive ... Piers ... they were then ... now is now

Then doesn't matter, now does ... for now

What I'm saying is, don't spend too much time looking back to the past

Or trying to push into the future

Stolen moments like ours are one day at a time

Maybe a stolen season

Who knows?

Who can tell?

You were wrong to say I keep you dangling

That makes it seem like I have a plan of some sort

You were wrong to ask if there was anyone else in my life ... in my bed

And even more wrong to get sensitive when I reminded you that Charles is in my life, yes, and in my bed too

What did you expect me to say – no ... I am exclusively yours, now and forever?

You mustn't expect me to lie

I wasn't laughing at you when you talked about commitment

I was laughing at the idea, the way you put it

It's usually the woman who wants commitment

The man is usually thinking about what to say so he can get laid

Afterwards he's thinking about keeping his hands untied

It's funny but most of the men in my life have been obsessed with themselves

Sex was just an extension of that

I'm starting to think ... well, it's possible you could be different

Yes, that's what I said – in an unguarded moment perhaps – but it's true

When you said how was it for you, I got the idea that you meant it

I only laughed because it's such a cliché

Every woman knows it only means: how well did I perform in the sack?

It's another male ego thing

It means, how good was I compared with other men you've slept with?

That's all it means

No, not even that

It's more like: tell me I'm better than all the others

Or rather, tell me I'm much better
Just don't ever expect me to tell you
Even if I could remember
Even if it was possible to compare anything like that
But you have to realise you're not the only man in my life
You have to understand that ... and accept it
You ask me about others
So I tell you
And you say it's because I – because I have feelings for you
I warned you of the dangers of that kind of conversation
But you insisted
And to be fair, you do seem able to take it
But don't misinterpret what I said about Charles
Of course I would never talk to him that way
You don't need me to tell you why
Think about it
Work it out, I know you can
You may not like the reasons
I can't help that
There are lots of things I can't do anything about
Don't expect that to change
But if it's any comfort to you I will say this
You're the only man who's ever made me laugh in the middle of trying to make the earth move (she laughed)
Silly expression – where did you say it came from?
Oh, yes ... Hemingway ... For Whom the Bell Tolls?
Sure, I'll get round to reading it some time
But you know I'm not really the bookish kind of girl
You'll have to find the relevant pages and read them to me
I know you'd enjoy that
I don't do things on paper
Don't even write letters
That's why I'm sitting here looking out at the rain – it's easing off now – talking into these machines
It's not quite like talking to myself
I'm not even really sure why I'm doing it
I put it down to your influence
If I'm honest I'd probably admit I like the idea of extending our afternoon
You understood I had to get back
You didn't make a fuss
That's good

Charles is going to phone any time now
I'm going to be here when he does
Remember that
I'm always going to be here
I'm glad you didn't turn funny when I told you why I had to get back
It's just part of reality
Don't lose sight of that
Right, it's time to slip out of the dressing gown and into the shower
Time to wash you away
Down the plug hole with you! (her laughter again)
I'll listen to this in the morning
If I decide it's too awful, too cringe-making, you'll never hear it
Good night
Sweet dreams …

30

There was a click and the tape went dead. Marnie fast-forwarded to the end and turned it over. Side two was blank. A fresh tape for each recording. She checked the note paper that Anne had printed for her. The last number was twenty-four. So presumably, two dozen assignations. Over what period of time? There was no mention of any date … an autumn evening. But when?

Marnie reached for the note paper and under the heading *Tape One* she wrote:

Timing – how long was their relationship?
When did it start?
Mention of Ian, Clive and Piers – how long were those affairs?
No mention of Mike Brent – when did that start?
When did it finish? (if it did finish)

The next question was what to do with the tapes. Marnie wanted Ralph to hear them so that she could get his views. But Anne? The fewer people who heard these the better. Marnie sat back in the chair and looked up at the ceiling. Three things immediately became clear.

One. The contents of the tapes would be heard by no one else, except Ralph, assuming he wanted to listen.

Two. Neil's reasons for not wanting his sister to hear them were obvious. They were too intimate. He wanted no one else to be privy to these secret thoughts.

Three. Marnie was amazed to realise that Neil Gerard trusted her more than anyone. He was willing to share Barbara with no one but her.

She stood up and went to the *cellar*, the cupboard in the galley where she kept the wine and spirits. She pulled out the bottle of Courvoisier and poured a measure. To her notes she added:

Barbara mentions "these machines"
Two recordings, one for Neil, one to keep for herself?
Why?

Marnie had thought she knew why, thought it was an intimate way of maintaining contact. She sat for some minutes thinking about that. It was certainly an original idea. Could she, Marnie, have imagined making tapes of that kind for a lover? No. But then she had never had a clandestine affair with a married man.

Strangest of all, it flew in the face of the rules programmed into girl babies at birth. Reveal to a man that you're keen and there's a good chance he'll get bored, take you for granted and start looking for the next conquest that proves he really is God's gift to womankind.

What did it tell her about Barbara? She was imaginative. She had a sultry kind of style. How would Neil feel about getting a tape like that? Marnie tried to put herself in his position. How would any man feel? Excited, definitely … anxious to see Barbara again – and soon. Flattered. It could do amazing things for his ego. Marnie doubted that was the reason for making the tapes. She sipped the cognac. There could only be one reason. It was becoming more obvious by the minute.

Marnie's concentration was broken by the ringing of her mobile. It was Anne, just returned from the post run.

'Can you come back to the office, Marnie? You've got a visitor.'

'Who is it?'

Anne told her, but she could have guessed.

•   •   •   •   •

Marnie was back in the office barn in a few minutes, having stowed the box of tapes under the bed in the sleeping cabin on *Sally Ann*. She wasted no time, anxious not to have Chief Inspector Bartlett coming to look for her. He was standing in the middle of the office with DS Marriner when she opened the door. He wasted no time on idle greetings.

'I'm disappointed in you, Mrs Walker. I thought we'd reached an understanding that you were going to be open and frank with us.'

Marnie knew from his tone it would be a waste of breath to offer them tea. 'That's right. But I explained to Mr Marriner that –'

'We don't accept *client confidentiality* as a valid reason for keeping things from us if we ought to have access to them.'

'I was going to say that I'd gone to London to retrieve certain objects belonging to Neil Gerard.'

'The *objects* being?'

'Love letters from Barbara Taverner.'

Bartlett frowned. This was not the answer he expected. 'What?'

'That's why Neil didn't want his sister to get them for him. I understand they were of a very intimate and personal nature. He obviously couldn't have them in prison, and he wanted them put away somewhere safe.'

'Are you telling me the truth?'

'Yes. Absolutely.'

Bartlett turned sharply to look at Anne. She returned his gaze without flinching. Back to Marnie.

'Then how did Gerard think they could help with his campaign?'

'Hard to say. Maybe he hoped they'd show how close they were, he and Barbara. Personally I don't think they would've proved anything. They were just old love letters after all. Now we'll never know ... unless you can find them in the flat.'

'He presumably told you where to find them?'

'Of course. They were concealed in his collection of CDs and tapes.'

'*Bloody marvellous!*' Bartlett fumed.

Marnie was surprised at his reaction. 'What difference does it make? Old letters ... they can't be considered as evidence of anything. And in any case, you got your conviction. Neil Gerard's inside for life.'

'You're missing the point, Mrs Walker. If anything should come to light that has relevance to the case – anything at all – then we want to know about it first. We don't want it suddenly popping up on the front page of the *Sun*.'

'If we'd found the letters, that would never happen, Mr Bartlett. Client confidentiality, remember?'

'And what if your *client* thought it suited his campaign to release them via the press? Thought about that?' He turned and walked quickly towards the door, Marriner following in his wake. Pulling on the handle, he looked back. 'If you discover anything that might be material to the investigation, you'll inform me, right?'

'That's a promise, inspector.'

'I'll remember that. Be very careful not to meddle in police business, Mrs Walker. It could lead to trouble … and you don't need me to remind you it could be dangerous.'

'Are you starting to think Neil Gerard might be innocent?'

'No, but I've been around long enough to know there are few certainties in our business. Just watch your step, that's all I'm saying.'

The detectives went out leaving Marnie and Anne staring at the door in silence.

•   •   •   •   •

Ralph and Anne had been surprised when Marnie announced that they should "dress for dinner". Ralph remarked that his dinner jacket and dress shirt were at the cottage in Murton. Anne lamented that her Balenciaga evening gown had been sent back to Harrods for alterations; the hem had been catching on the heels of her hobnail boots. Without argument they had been happy to change into jeans and sweatshirts. They were going for a tootle on *Sally Ann*.

'I had to do something *active*,' Marnie declared. 'This Neil Gerard thing is getting me down.'

'No better way to clear the head than a trip on a narrowboat,' Ralph agreed. 'Full ahead both … cylinders?'

'I think it would be a good idea if we untied her and reversed out of the docking area first, don't you think?'

He grinned. 'Good point, cap'n. I'll pass the word to the bos'un to er … do whatever bos'uns do.'

Anne was already untying and stowing the mooring ropes. *Sally Ann's* engine was thumping away steadily beneath the stern deck as Marnie pushed the heavy gear lever into reverse, and the boat slid out across the main line. She turned her bows north and they picked up to cruising speed for the journey towards Hanford, half an hour or so up the canal.

When Anne emerged after five minutes in the cabin bearing a tray containing three glasses of Pimm's and a bowl of green Provençal olives, the cares of life 'on the bank' began melting away.

'*Yes!*' Marnie exclaimed. 'Good decision, bos'un.'

Ralph agreed. 'I knew they did something important, these bos'uns.'

Reaching their goal, they tied up on the opposite bank to the towpath alongside a field extending down to the tiny River Tove, invisible in its channel meandering through pasture land. As always, Marnie found it extraordinary that just a short journey on the boat could distance her from the worst of her worries, even if only for a temporary respite. Her lover and her friend both understood this and both knew there was more to the decision to take the boat for a trip than the simple need for a breather on the canal.

They took the remains of their drinks with them to the galley where Anne, at Marnie's request, had begun preparations for a variation on a *salade niçoise*, using pieces of hot smoked salmon instead of tuna and hard-boiled quails eggs, on special offer in the supermarket. As usual they divided up the tasks. Ralph supervised the cooling of the boiled potatoes, Jersey Royales – another offer at Waitrose – and the French beans, plus the warming of a baguette in the oven. Marnie and Anne chopped and prepared little gem lettuce, salad onions, cucumber and cherry tomatoes.

'Mm …' Anne breathed in deeply, groaning and stretching out her arms. 'It smells like mid-summer in here. I'm getting hungry.'

Ralph checked that the wine, a dry rosé from the Loire valley, was at optimum temperature in the fridge. It was a perfect meal for a mild spring evening to lift their spirits and boost morale.

Marnie looked up from mixing the *vinaigrette*, her expression serious. 'I want to tell you about the tapes. We've got a few minutes before things are ready. I want to get it over with so that we can enjoy supper. Why don't you sit down and I'll explain.'

When they were settled, Marnie leaned back against the workbench. 'I've listened to the whole of the first tape. I told Bartlett we'd been looking for love letters from Barbara. That wasn't too wide of the mark. She doesn't actually talk in those terms, but they are very personal and private. Once I'd got over my initial curiosity I felt quite uncomfortable listening in.'

'Which no doubt explains why Gerard didn't ask his sister to find them,' Ralph said.

'I think so.'

'He obviously has a great deal of faith in you, Marnie.'

'I can't think why. He hardly knows me. Anyway, the tapes make it clear – at least the first one does – that they were very close. No one does that sort of thing for someone they're having a casual affair with. Barbara talks about their relationship on all sorts of different levels … the things they'd said, things they'd done … She talks about Charles, too … seems very loyal to him – yes, I know she was involved with Neil but … somehow it reminded me of that old song … *I'm always true to you, darling, in my fashion* … you know the one?'

Ralph nodded. 'Does anything you've heard so far make it clear why she was having the affair – *affairs* – even though she was obviously not planning to leave Charles?'

'She mentions how hard he works, how much of his time it takes … his ambition. It's obvious there were times when she was lonely.'

'Presumably she wasn't thinking of ending the affair with Gerard, otherwise she wouldn't be starting to make tapes …'

'And going on to make two dozen of them.'

'Sounds like you've got a lot of listening to do, Marnie.'

'Part of me wants to get the whole story, but another part wants to hold back. I don't want to treat their relationship like a spectator sport.'

Ralph stood up to bring the conversation to a close. 'One thing is clear. You must be the only one to hear the tapes, Marnie.'

'I want you to hear this one, Ralph.'

'No. Gerard trusted you. It wouldn't be right.'

'Just this first one. I need to be able to talk things over with you, to get matters sorted out in my own mind. We can't do that if you've never heard what they're like.'

'Let's eat. We can decide on that later.'

• • • • •

The evening had clouded over and a light rain was falling when Marnie ran the first tape that night in the sleeping cabin on *Thyrsis*. She and Ralph listened without speaking as Barbara's soft voice spoke of that rainy autumn night, while the raindrops spattered the roof and windows of their boat making an eerie accompaniment to her words. Marnie was struck again by the intimacy of Barbara's tone and the power of her imagination at coming up with the idea of making the tapes. Ralph lay back on the bed propped up on one elbow thinking as he listened that Barbara was extraordinary, that he personally had never known a woman who would do such a thing.

At the end Marnie switched off the cassette player and pressed the rewind button. 'Thanks for listening, Ralph. Now you can see why I wanted you to hear that for yourself. What did you make of it?'

'I've never heard anything like it. Have you?'

'No. I remember that when Simon and I were first seeing each other, he'd phone me late at night for a chat. The conversations were in that sort of vein … sometimes a bit more amorous. But then he was a man. This seems to have been entirely Barbara's idea.'

'Dreamt up in the taxi on the way home,' Ralph observed.

'Apparently.'

'There's no reason, of course, why women would be unlikely to make such tapes. It just seems somehow out of character. I don't know why. It was interesting to hear it … and sad, too.'

'I wanted you to listen because I wanted to know what you made of it … just for a second opinion, really.'

Ralph thought back to the time of his marriage, that had ended when his wife died in her thirties several years previously. 'Well … sometimes Laura used to read poetry to me … in bed …'

'It's fine, Ralph. You don't have to explain about –'

'No, it's all right. You recall she was a specialist in mediaeval literature. She liked reading ancient love poems by candlelight.' He grinned. 'Once she burned incense in our bedroom to go with a particularly passionate series of poems by a troubadour from Provence. You wouldn't believe it … we were up half the night –'

'Actually, I think I can imagine the rest, Ralph,' Marnie interrupted, smiling, putting the cassette player on the shelf above the bed.

'I don't think you can, Marnie. You see, we were up coughing and sneezing for hours because of the incense. We ended up sleeping in the living room, Laura on the sofa, me on the floor.'

'So not the ultimate aphrodisiac, then?'

'Quite the opposite. We both looked like zombies in the morning.'

Marnie slipped off her bathrobe and slid naked under the duvet. Ralph emulated her and reached up to turn out the light. In the darkness the sound of the rain against the windows made them both think of an autumn night, a solitary woman in an empty house by the river in Docklands. Ralph reached across and pulled Marnie towards him.

'You wondered what effect that tape would have on Gerard, Marnie. Speaking personally, there's not much doubt of the effect it's had on me …'

• • • • •

In her attic room above the office Anne could barely hear the rain, her only window being little more than a slot in the end wall. She sat up reading in bed, resting against plump cushions, red, blue and emerald green. Table lamps on either side of the bed gave a cosy glow to the room, accentuated by the sloping roof beams and the oriental rugs lent by Marnie. Her book was on the early period of the Bauhaus, one of her favourite college projects.

Her eyes had begun to droop and she lay back breathing in steadily prior to turning out the lights and moving the cushions away ready for sleep. A sudden thought jolted her awake, eyes wide open. With a last flurry of energy she pulled back the duvet and crawled towards her book case. Running a finger along the spines, she found what she was looking for and drew out a thick volume, a prize she had won at school. Sitting cross-legged on a rug, she thumbed through the *Complete Works of William Shakespeare*, blinking to bring the small print into focus. She opened the book wide and flat, making a lap for it in her nightdress, and found what she was seeking, *Cymbeline*.

Unfamiliar with that play, she rapidly scanned each page, following the lines with a finger until it came to rest on the key words she was looking for. She read the whole speech to herself and understood what Ralph had meant when he suggested it would not be desirable to recite the end of the quotation. The words were a beautiful elegy. At any other time she would have found them poignant and moving, but in the dimly-lit attic on a rainy night, with thoughts never far from the tragedy that had overtaken Barbara Taverner and was dragging them all along in its wake, they filled her with foreboding.

… golden lads and girls all must
As chimney sweepers come to dust.

31

Tuesday morning seemed like a return to normality. Ralph was writing a lecture in his study on *Thyrsis*, like a mediaeval monk in his cell. Anne was sitting on her giant beanbag on the floor of the attic, mapping out the Bauhaus project, surrounded by text books and notepads. Marnie was at her desk checking the diary. For the coming weekend she had noted: *Perfidia to Blisworth boatyard*, and wondered how long it would take to move the boat up from Leighton Buzzard. In pencil for Friday she had made an entry: *Ralph to All Souls – symposium – back Sunday*. What a difference to her previous life in London, she mused. Then, she had had a regular office routine and a regular social life. Compartments. Simple. Now, she had the business to run, Anne's education and future to take into account, Ralph's career to follow, all of it circumscribed by activities on the canal. And now, lately, everything was dominated by the Barbara Taverner affair. Listening to that voice on the tape had almost brought Barbara back to life. She was certainly back in Marnie's life. *What are you going to tell me, Barbara?* she wondered. *Are you going to tell me who …*

The ringing of the phone made her jump. She composed herself rapidly.

'Walker and Co, good morning.'

'Marnie. It's Mike … Mike Brent.'

Number four on the list of suspects, she thought. 'Hi, Mike. How're things?'

'Fine. Just wanted to check where we are with *Perfidia*.'

'She's booked in at the boatyard for hull blacking and partial repainting next week. My redec will add another week or two.'

'Where is she now, exactly?'

'Does that matter?' Marnie bit her lip. She had not intended to sound confrontational. 'Sorry, Mike, I meant … are you concerned about her?'

His voice was flat. 'No … just curious, that's all. I didn't mean to imply –'

'Of course you didn't. And I didn't mean to be snappy. Sorry. She's at Leighton Buzzard, Mike.'

'Right. It's just that … Well, I was wondering …' He paused. 'Did you get any people gawping at her on your travels?'

'Some, yes. What's on your mind?'

'The name. It occurred to me it might be an idea to change it … while she's out of the water. People can be funny about … you know.'

'That's why you asked where she was. You were wondering if she was safe?'

'There are strange folk about, Marnie. See a famous – or *infamous* – name and they can do silly things.'

'Like vandalise the boat?'

'Maybe. Also, if I'm being honest …I'm a bit anxious about our customers.'

'You think they might pull out?'

'I imagine them coming back from the other side of the world, telling their friends they're buying a boat. They tell them it's called *Perfidia* … people say, *hey, isn't that the boat in Little Venice where that woman was murdered?*'

'It could put them off.'

'It would put *me* off, Marnie. If the name could be changed, now's the best time to do it. You'll have her in the boatyard.'

'Actually, Mike, Braunston have already raised that with me. I'm going to discuss it with Charles. I'll see what he says.'

'Good. Thanks. You might mention that the offer from the people on their world trip is the only one we've had.'

'Really?'

'Yep. All the other enquirers have withdrawn as soon as I tell them the name or they see the boat. Not surprising, really …'

• • • • •

The morning still felt like a normal day when Marnie climbed into the Discovery and set off for a site meeting at a pub near Whilton Marina, the scene of a refurbishment project for Willards. On the journey she mulled over the question of the name of the boat. *Perfidia* was a fine craft, but would she herself buy it with that name, with that association? She would certainly understand the reluctance of potential buyers to invest a substantial sum in a vessel however attractive, tainted with an aura like the *Marie Celeste*, with the albatross of the Ancient Mariner hovering over it.

The meeting was purely routine – Marnie had carried out so many of these projects that she could do them in her sleep – and on the way home she took the decision to ring Jane Rutherford in London. Jane was a professional artist who lived on a houseboat in Little Venice. Well known for her watercolours, she was even more famous as a signwriter and teacher of signwriting.

'Jane, hi, it's Marnie. Are you well?'

'Great. You?'

'Not bad. Can I talk to you wearing your signwriter's hat?'

'Go ahead.'

'Nothing definite, but how would you be fixed if I needed a sign done?'

'Mm … Pretty booked up, but that's normal. You want to spruce up old *Sally*?'

'It's a client's boat. We're taking her out of the water for the next few weeks.'

'Bull's Bridge?'

'Not actually. Up here at Blisworth.'

'I see. Er … would I know this boat by any chance?'

'Everybody knows this boat. That's the problem.'

A pause. '*Perfidia*?'

'You guessed.'

'I take it this would be a change of name?'

'If I can persuade Charles Taverner it would be a good idea. I don't know if you'd fancy a few days in the country, but you could stay with us while you did it.'

'Get back to me when you know for sure and I'll see what I can do. Tell me, Marnie, have you spoken to Mike Brent about this?'

'Mike raised it with me.'

'Can't say I'm surprised.'

'You've heard he's only had one offer for the sale?'

'I didn't know that. No, it's just that … well, he took Barbara's death quite badly. Did you know he'd been down with flu around that time? Had a really bad dose … off work for about two weeks. Came back when all the fuss was going on and they arrested that man.'

'Neil Gerard.'

'Yes. The Barbara thing really got him down. He was *so* depressed.'

'Were they particularly friendly?'

'She was pretty popular … especially with the men, of course. But generally, too. I liked her … a real character … down to earth … no nonsense, for all the glamorous image they went on about in the papers.'

'And Mike?'

'I think he had those post-flu blues … you know how low you get after influenza. He couldn't seem to shake them off. When I saw him he was very glum, almost …'

'What?'

'I was going to say it was almost as if he was *heartbroken*, but that wouldn't be quite right. That'd be too personal. But he was really upset.'

'Did he say anything?'

'He said he couldn't bear the thought of seeing *Perfidia* around, always reminding him of what had happened. Was it his idea to change the name?'

'Yes. He rang this morning and suggested it.'

'Let me know when you've got a decision, Marnie. I'll see what I can do. A few days in the peace and quiet of the country would be very welcome.'

They certainly would, Marnie thought as they ended the call.

• • • • •

Back in the office Marnie was welcomed by the inevitable line-up of yellow post-it notes stuck round the edge of her monitor. Nothing exciting. No shocks or surprises. She scanned them quickly while Anne made tea for the builders and took the tray out to the farmhouse site. Marnie organised the messages in priority order, dialled Everett Parker Associates first and was put through to Philip Everett without delay.

'Hi, Philip. You're wanting a progress report on the Bermuda Reach project, presumably?'

'No. Listen, Marnie. Ian Stuart rang this morning while I was out … wants me to phone him back … apparently he wants to know if we have problems with the project.'

'Why should we?'

'You tell me. He wants to know if the fact that you went back to look around … *on a Sunday morning* … means we're having some sort of difficulties. Were you there on Sunday?'

'Yes.'

A pause. 'And?'

'Er …'

'This isn't about work, is it?'

'No.'

'So what is there at Bermuda Reach that makes you go all monosyllabic on me?'

'It's ... it's a bit tricky to explain.'

'Marnie, I'm going to need more than that if I'm to sound convincing when I speak to Ian Stuart ... our *client*, remember?'

'Yeah. Phil ...'

'Whenever you call me Phil, I know there's going to be one of those *We've known each other ten years* conversations in which I'm supposed to trust you. Am I right?'

'It really is a difficult situation.'

'But not connected with the restaurant project.'

'No.'

'Good. So that's that out of the way. What else is there? Ah ... Has this got something to with ... you know ...'

'Yes.'

'How?'

'Charles Taverner has a penthouse there. I needed to look in and get something ... while he was absent.'

'But you must've told a different story.' Philip waited, listening to air. 'Help me, Marnie, I'm struggling here.'

'I have known you ten years, Phil. I can't lie to you. I was looking for some of Barbara's things. Listen ... it's possible Neil Gerard may be innocent.'

'Wow! And you didn't want Charles Taverner to know about it until you had whatever it was you went to get?'

'Exactly. I found what I was looking for. It implicates other people.'

'Can you tell me who they are?'

A pause. 'Ian Stuart is one of them.'

'*Bloody hell!* Who else?'

'Phil I –'

'Marnie, I don't want to put my foot in it. Also, I need to know if any of our other clients are likely to be carted off to the nick without paying us.'

'You know Piers Wainwright?'

'You're kidding!'

'Ever heard of Clive Adamson?'

'Don't think so.'

'Then there's Mike Brent. He's the manager of Little Venice.'

'Don't know him.'

'That's the lot.'

'And one of them could be ...'

'Not necessarily, but they may be implicated in some way.'

'So I have to cover for you being at Bermuda Reach on Sunday.'

'Yes. It's important Ian Stuart doesn't get suspicious.'

'Mm ... Right. Checking dimensions wouldn't sound terribly convincing ... What did you tell him you were doing?'

'He wasn't there. I told the security guard I was checking details, I think.'

'Details … Well, suppose I said I was thinking of hanging sail material as a lining for the interior ceilings and wanted to continue that outside to create awnings over the terrace that looked like sails?'

'Sounds like a good idea. Are you thinking along those lines?'

'As of now, yes.'

'Are the ceilings high enough to accommodate that?'

'That's what you were checking.'

'Great, Phil.'

'With one small reservation. I only have floor plans of that part of the building, no elevations or sections yet. It'll look odd if I send someone round to measure up after you've already been to do it.'

'Yeah … Wait a minute. Anne took her usual load of Polaroids. We can probably get the scale from them. It'll be close enough for now. I'll get her to post them to you.'

'Marnie, you have a devious mind.'

'Makes two of us. Thanks, Philip.'

Before tackling the more routine calls, Marnie dialled one number that was longer than the others. While she was waiting, Anne returned with the empty tray and went back to her desk.

'Where are you, Charles?' Marnie muttered to herself. She was listening to the intermittent single buzzing note, the France Télécom ringing tone. It was her third attempt at getting through.

'Still no reply?' Anne asked, looking up from her pad.

Marnie put the phone down. 'I expect he's out having lunch somewhere.'

'I've been thinking. I'm sure it's a good idea, changing the boat's name.' Anne made one stroke on the paper in front of her, put down the pencil and sat back. 'But wouldn't it be better to wait till we've got her back in London? Jane could paint the new name down there.'

'I think it's an old tradition on the canals. You change a boat's name when it's out of the water.'

'Why's that?'

Marnie shrugged. 'Dunno. I suppose it's like relaunching her with a new name … a new identity for a new owner. Or maybe it's just a superstition. You can never tell with waterways and boats … these old customs.'

'D'you think Mr Taverner will go for it?'

'Possibly. I think he's probably past caring … just wants the boat out of his life.'

Anne looked down at her work. 'Marnie, I've finished the outline for the stencil for the conservatory. Do you think he'll still be interested?'

Marnie stood up and walked across the room. She looked down over Anne's shoulder. 'Hey, that's really good. How many of these designs have you done now?'

'Seven or eight. It's taken me a while to get it right. What do you think?'

'They've all been good. Any one of them would be fine.'

'I like this one best. I think it's got the right balance between the grapes and the size of the leaves. Perhaps I'd better wait till Mr Taverner's approved it before I cut the stencil.'

'Just do it. Go ahead. He'll accept.'

'Great. I'll make a copy of the design, just in case I make a mess while I'm cutting it out. Would it disturb you if I did it here this afternoon?'

'Course not.' Marnie wandered over to the window and looked out. 'In fact, you'd be doing me a favour. It'd be helpful to have someone here in the office to handle any phone calls.'

'Okay. I was going to pop round to see Ronny some time today. I can do that later on.'

'Sure?'

'No probs. What's this … another meeting? I haven't got it in the office diary.'

'That's because I've only just thought about it.'

'Ah … No prizes for guessing, then.'

• • • • •

Marnie was one of the first to be led into the visiting room, and Neil Gerard showed no surprise at seeing her. They shook hands, both recognising that the atmosphere between them had changed. Neil waited for Marnie to be seated before taking his chair.

He smiled ruefully. 'Couldn't keep away?'

'How are you finding it in here? Is it better than the other … place?'

'A holiday camp.' He lowered his voice. 'Actually, it's quite interesting, Marnie. Would you like to guess which prison has just about the worst record for inmate suicides in England?'

'You're kidding.'

'Check it out. Home Office statistics will confirm it, if you don't believe me.'

Marnie stared at him across the table, incredulous. 'But I thought …'

'I think there's something you need to understand, Marnie. A life sentence is the replacement for the death penalty. Many people argued that hanging was more merciful than spending the rest of your life in prison. They had a point. It's a lifetime in hell.'

Marnie shuddered. 'But you are going to stick it out, aren't you … whatever happens?'

'Tell me why you've come, Marnie. Although I suppose I know. You've listened to the tapes.'

'The first one.'

'I think you need to hear them all. Did …' He made a gesture in the air. 'Your … er … partner hear it?'

'Ralph.'

'Ralph. Yes. Sorry.'

'He didn't want to listen to them at all … thought they were too private.'

'Fair enough.'

'But I persuaded him to listen to it. Perhaps I shouldn't have, but I needed another perspective. He's got very good judgment.'

'So have you, Marnie. You decide what you think's best.'

'The police know I went to your flat.'

He nodded. 'Sarah told me. She also said you wouldn't tell her why you were there.'

'I'm treating this whole matter as client confidentiality. I'm afraid Sarah didn't like that.'

'I told her you went to get some tapes. She concluded that they were stolen. I saw no reason to disabuse her of that idea.'

'As your sister, she must've thought you didn't trust her.'

'I couldn't let Sarah listen to them. It just seemed … Look, I'm not prudish, it's not that … not *just* that. But somehow they're too private for someone so close to me to hear … someone who really matters to me.'

'Thank you.'

'Sorry, Marnie, I didn't mean it to come out like that. What I meant is … you could listen to them in an objective way … a *neutral* way … like … er …Ralph. If anything comes of all this, that will be the time for Sarah – and no doubt the whole country – to hear them. If nothing comes of it, then you and Ralph will walk out of my life and that's an end to it.'

'I understand that.'

'So what about the police? What did you tell them?'

'That I was trying to find some love letters from Barbara.'

'Love letters …' He smiled. 'That's not far from the truth. So they don't know about the tapes?'

'No. We can decide what to do when I've gone through them all … provided I'm not thrown in gaol for concealing evidence. Neil, do you think there are … I hate to use this silly word … *clues* in the tapes about who might've killed her?'

'It's hard to remember. She did speak about those other men. I hope you don't find this all too distasteful. I just hoped you'd be able to form an opinion about our relationship and see if anything Barbara said might suggest a possible line of enquiry.'

'There's something bothering me. I wonder why you didn't consider using them in your defence to show what your relationship was like. If this examination had happened at the time of your trial, perhaps things would've turned out differently.'

'It's naive, I know, but because I'm innocent I never thought I'd be found guilty. The evidence struck me as too flimsy.'

'You couldn't produce an alibi, Neil … even from your own sister.'

'All the same, I never for a moment considered using the tapes like that.'

'But you would now.'

'This is a last resort, Marnie. I haven't got anything else. On the one hand, those tapes are all I have remaining of Barbara. It would feel like a betrayal to go public on them. On the other hand, the real murderer is out there. I know it's corny, but I don't think Barbara will ever be at rest until that person is found. Nor will I, of course.'

Marnie stared at him. A strange feeling was coming over her. She had tried to resist it all along, but now she realised she had started to believe Neil's story. Perhaps it was the effect of listening to the tape. Perhaps that was his plan, to draw her in despite herself. But she knew that her doubts were slipping away.

'I'm going to do all I can to help you.'

Neil stared back. He blinked a few times. 'I don't want anyone else to hear the tapes, Marnie.'

'But they might provide evidence of something. Isn't that what you're hoping?'

'I just hope they might in some way give an insight ... a hint, an idea ... anything that might lead to Barbara's killer.'

'If they do, they'll have to be turned over to the police. If they're used in evidence they'll become public.'

'Even so ... I don't want our relationship to be turned into nothing more than a soap opera. Britain has become a voyeuristic society. I don't want Barbara to become part of that. It would be the final betrayal.'

• • • • •

At supper Ralph mentioned that a colleague had e-mailed some material that was relevant to the weekend symposium, and he wanted to incorporate it into the paper he was presenting on Saturday morning. If no one had any other plans he would like to deal with it that evening. Anne chimed in that she would be keen to make a start on her next summer project, a study of the life and work of the architect, Le Corbusier. Marnie was happy to comply. She could hear the call of the unheard tapes stowed under the bed and wanted to continue Barbara's story.

As she set up the cassette player in the saloon on *Sally Ann* after the others had gone, she wondered if they had deliberately given her this opportunity. She pressed the *play* button and made herself comfortable. Moments later she heard the quiet almost husky voice and drifted back through time and space to probe into Barbara's private life.

32

The second tape
> *Don't be alone*
> *Come and sit here beside me*
> *Better still come and lie with me here*
> *[There was a long pause]*
> *Intimate – that's a good word*
> *You said it was one of your favourites*
> *Said it was the word you always thought of when you thought of me*
> *Say it softly*
> *It's the only way to say it, really*
> *Breathe out and say it*
> *Intimate*
> *Hold onto that word for a few moments*
> *Think about it*
> *You can almost touch it, almost smell it*
> *[A long sigh]*
> *I could never speak like this with Charles*
> *He wouldn't understand*
> *He's a good man*
> *I've never known anyone better*
> *But this kind of thing isn't his scene … not his forte*
> *Not like you*
> *[Another long pause]*
> *You said you weren't sure about the tape I gave you …*
> *Maybe not a good idea, you said*
> *What if Charles found it?*
> *Do you think I hadn't thought of that?*
> *Charles never goes through my things*
> *It would never occur to him not to trust me*
> *But I liked your idea … Deutsche Grammophon boxes*
> *Very highbrow*
> *An affair of quality*
> *I've got loads of them … cassettes, I mean*
> *Who knows … perhaps we'll need a lot*
> *Perhaps just a few*
> *Who can tell?*
> *And don't come over all sensitive*
> *I don't want you getting all intense*

There'd be no fun in that

One of our ground rules, remember?

Coming back to your question

You know the one I mean

I told you it was out of order

We're not going to talk about things like that

If we're not going forward, we're not going anywhere

But some subjects are out of bounds

You agreed

So that's it

[Another pause, another sigh]

Why is it always raining when I do these tapes?

It's been fine all week and now there's a real storm out there

I got drenched running from the taxi to the house

If I go down with double pneumonia I shall blame you

[She laughed]

If I die of it, I'll come back and haunt you, so be warned

[More laughter]

You wouldn't want that

It might cramp your style when you pursue your next conquest

And what was all that frankness thing about?

I didn't want to know about Judy or … Sonya, or whoever it was

Although once I got used to the idea, I have to say …

Well, it did spice things up a little

How many have there been in your life?

Don't answer that

Yes, do

It doesn't really matter … I can't hear you anyway

And another thing … why did you want to talk about them?

You can't be getting tired of me already

You demonstrated that all right

And you ask a lot of questions

I'm not sure it's a good idea to tell you about my past

It's no concern of yours really

I may decide to talk about it … I may not

You'll have to wait and see

I haven't made up my mind yet

But you won't find out by pestering me

So don't try

You don't want to get me annoyed … believe me

You said we shouldn't have secrets from each other

Why not?
A woman should be a creature of mystery
Oh … it's getting late
I need my beauty sleep
But first [laughter] it's plug-hole time for you
I think it'll be a soak in the tub tonight
All those bubbles
Wash you away
I might burn one of those joss sticks you gave me
Light a candle
Very atmospheric
Just like … you know
[A pause]
I'm yawning
Time to go
Good night, sweet prince
Good night
Good night …

33

'Did you get your paper written?' Marnie came into the sleeping cabin from the shower wearing her bathrobe. 'Are you all ready for the symposium?'

Ralph looked up from his notes. 'More or less. I've just added some more bullet points, a few more slides. I can *ad lib* from them. That's how I usually do my talks.'

'Good.'

'How about you? Did you listen to any more tapes?'

Marnie sat on the bed. 'Just one. I can only manage one at a time. Mind you, I went through it twice.'

'And?'

'Do you want to hear it?'

Ralph shook his head. 'No. The first one was enough. I got the flavour.'

'If anything, this one was even more intimate than the first. *Intimate* seems to have been one of their favourite words.'

'Did you learn any more about their relationship?'

'Not much. They were obviously very close … but we knew that.'

'Anything about Charles?'

'Praise from Barbara, again. She said she'd never known anyone better … said he trusted her and wouldn't go searching through her things.'

'So no risk of him finding the tapes, presumably. Anything else?'

'I get the impression Neil was trying to get Barbara to say how committed she was to the relationship.'

'The L word?'

'Could be. She warned him off becoming too intense about things.'

'You know, Marnie, I'm not sure you're going to find anything of great significance in those tapes. I can't see any real *evidence* coming out of them, can you?'

'Not if they just carry on in the same vein, no.'

'Perhaps you should try a different approach.'

'Such as?'

'Maybe take a whole day and listen to them all in one session.'

'Phew! That could be a mind-blowing experience.'

'But it would concentrate your attention … give you an overview of everything. Then you could home in on any tape that might be of special interest. Might be the best way to complete the task.'

'Mm … I see what you mean. But when can I afford a whole day? We've got to bring the boat up this weekend and I'm under enough pressure from work as it is.'

Ralph leaned back against the pillow and slotted his notes into their folder. 'Perhaps you should start with the last tapes and work backwards from there.'

'I hadn't thought of that. My idea was to see how their relationship developed over time.'

'That's why I suggested tackling all the tapes in one long sitting. You'd get a concentrated view very quickly. Still … I suppose speed isn't the main consideration in getting the task accomplished. Neil has all the time in the world. A day or two won't make much difference one way or the other.'

Marnie turned and stretched out beside Ralph, propping her head on her hand. 'I'm not so sure about that. Time's weighing very heavily on him. You know what he said today? The prison where they've moved him has the worst record for suicides in the country.'

'Really? I thought they had a special programme for –'

'That's not all. He said a life sentence was *less* merciful – in some ways – than being hanged … said it was a *lifetime in hell*.'

'That was one of the arguments used against abolishing the death penalty, of course.'

Marnie screwed up her face. 'But it had to be abolished. It was *barbaric* … cruel … mediaeval. And mistakes were made. Innocent people were hanged.'

'All reasons why it was abolished. But a life sentence was never intended as an easy option.'

Marnie rolled onto her back. 'I'd never really thought about it like that. But I've seen the effect it's having on Neil. Of course it's better like this. At least we have a chance to get him freed … if we can prove he's innocent. It would all be different if he'd been … executed.'

'Better not to think about that, Marnie.'

'No. I keep thinking that for Neil every day is another day in hell.'

'You're right. It's a slow dreadful life in place of a quick dreadful death.'

Marnie was beginning to worry about Charles. She rang the house in France on and off throughout Wednesday. No reply. Fearing that she might be dialling a wrong number, she checked it more than once and even rang the operator to check the regional code. By Thursday she was systematically trying all his numbers in rotation. Nothing. Ralph suggested calling his business number in the City. A secretary explained that he was away from the office, and she was not sure when he would be returning. She offered to take a message. Friday morning followed the same pattern. Ringing tones and silence. No response to her message. *Where are you, Charles?*

On the other two evenings that week Marnie had settled down on *Sally Ann* to listen to more of the Barbara tapes. It was the mixture as before, and she wondered if Ralph had been right. Maybe it would be better to blitz the whole set and identify what tapes, if any, held useful information. The only noticeable change in tone was a gradual increase in tenderness. There was no mention so far of any third party except Charles. The words *wild goose chase* had begun flitting across Marnie's mind.

Just before noon on Friday Marnie and Anne packed their kitbags for the trip on *Perfidia*. Ralph packed a suitcase for his weekend in Oxford. They gathered on *Sally Ann* for lunch. Marnie mixed tuna with mayonnaise to fill warmed pittas, plus the remains of salad from the fridge. Anne added squeezed lemon juice into sparkling mineral water. Ralph prepared a cafetière of coffee.

In half an hour they were ready to climb into Ralph's venerable Volvo for the journey to Leighton Buzzard. Before locking the office barn Marnie gave final instructions to Angela about feeding Dolly. At the last minute she left Anne and Ralph at the car to rush back into the office to check the answerphone. No red light. No word from Charles.

• • • • •

As they drove south Marnie asked her companions if they thought she should notify the police about Charles's apparent disappearance. The consensus was that he was a grown man, free to go where he pleased and that they had no legal right or obligation to question his whereabouts. When Marnie pointed out that he was supposed to be at his house in the Dordogne, Ralph asked if she seriously thought they had grounds for concern that would persuade the French police or Interpol to organise a manhunt. She answered with a sigh.

Perfidia lay safely at her mooring alongside the boatyard in Leighton Buzzard. No vandal had damaged the boat, not so much as a pigeon dropping was visible on the paintwork. Ralph kissed Marnie and Anne good-bye, wished them a safe journey, and they agreed a rough time for their rendez-vous at Blisworth on Sunday evening. A brief call in at the boatyard office to pay the mooring fee, ten minutes to check the boat's systems and they were on their way. Thoughts of amorous tapes, potential suspects, a missing husband, concern for a man unjustly imprisoned for life, all of these cares were set aside as *Perfidia* eased her way quietly through the water.

The first lock was upon them in minutes. Marnie jumped onto the bank and went ahead to operate the machinery. While she waited for the chamber to fill, she looked back at the boat and saw Anne holding her in mid-channel, waiting to enter. A sudden thought struck her as she looked at the thin pale blond girl who had become such an important part of her life. *How bloody thoughtless of me!* A wave of guilt swept over Marnie and she was cursing herself inwardly when Anne called out and made a gesture at the gates. The chamber had filled, and the gates were parting as the water pressure reduced. Marnie pulled on the balance beam, and Anne slowly brought *Perfidia* in through the narrow opening, careful not to nudge the other gate. Marnie looped *Sally Ann*'s bow-rope over a bollard and set to with the paddles. Anne held the boat close to the side of the chamber with the rope, feeding it out as *Perfidia* descended. Marnie needed no prompting from Anne this time and leaned back against the beam so that the gate began to swing open as soon as the water reached the lower level.

Stepping onto the counter, she stowed the windlass in its slot by the door and turned towards her friend. 'Anne, I am *so* sorry.'

'That's all right. I could tell you were thinking about something and I saw the gate move.'

'No, not that. I just realised … here we are at Leighton Buzzard and it never occurred to me you might want to look in on your family. Typical! I'm so bound up in –'

'Marnie, that's fine. We've got a long journey ahead of us and we've got to make progress.' Anne grinned. 'If we turned up at our house, mum wouldn't let us leave without wanting to feed us. We'd never get away.'

Marnie shook her head. 'Even so –'

'No. If I'd wanted to do that I could've said something.'

'But –'

Anne pointed ahead. 'Tight bend coming up. Why don't you take over here while I go down and make coffee. There's a few miles before the locks at Soulbury.'

Marnie spent the time while Anne was below resolving not to be so obsessive. All the time concentrating on the long bend, she straightened her back, breathed in deeply and became aware that they were passing through a gentle but beautiful landscape of meadows and woodland. Anne emerged with a tray of coffee and biscuits.

'Look at all this, Anne. I suppose this is your home county, isn't it?'

Anne handed her a mug. 'Practically my back yard.'

'There's a bridge round here somewhere. I remember it's where we first met.'

'In circumstances I'd rather not remember.'

Anne was fifteen at the time, her father had been made redundant, and she had been running away from home to ease the family finances.

'I've still got that sketch you did of *Sally Ann* under the trees.' She laughed. 'You made her look really charming.'

'She's a lovely boat,' Anne protested.

Marnie nodded. 'What do you think of *Perfidia*?'

'A very fine craft.'

'Yes, she is. Even now she looks better than most other boats, but when her hull is freshly blacked, we've done some touching up and maybe got her a new name painted on, she's going to look like new.'

'Yeah.' Anne's tone was flat. 'I used to like this boat a lot.'

'Not any more?'

'The further we get dragged into the Barbara Taverner affair, the more I'm getting to dislike everything connected with it.'

Marnie was taken aback. 'I can understand that but It's a pity. *Perfidia*'s a beautiful boat, not an old tub like *Sally Ann*.'

Anne stared at her. 'That's just how Mike Brent described her … *an old tub*.'

'Mike Brent? When did he say that?'

'He was teasing me on the phone when I talked to him about moving *Perfidia* and doing the works on her.'

'That's typical Mike. You know I can sometimes understand why …' She stopped herself. 'No. I've made a vow not to be obsessive. I'm banning all mention of what you call the Barbara Taverner affair. Let's just enjoy the trip.'

Anne made a face. 'You … *obsessive*, Marnie? Whatever gave you that idea?'

• • • • •

They were a good crew and worked calmly and unhurriedly together, neither needing to speak where managing the boat was concerned. Each took turns at the tiller in the long pounds, though Marnie usually handled the locks. Although both were slim, Anne's slight frame did not allow performance on paddles and balance beams to match her willingness to share the work. The best way, literally, for her to pull her weight when they encountered the locks was in steering.

They ate up the miles, travelling without incident, heading north away from the Chiltern Hills. Light cloud cover and intermittent sunshine with only the lightest of breezes was perfect boating weather, and they met numerous craft enjoying their weekend on the water. Both noticed that other boaters sometimes looked thoughtful when they read the name on the side, and often they attracted a second glance. Or a third.

Unlike the crew on a sailing boat, often remaining in close proximity with each other, the crew of a narrowboat can spend lengthy periods of time apart. On several occasions Marnie opted to walk on to the next lock rather than waste travelling time bringing *Perfidia* into the bank for her to jump aboard. Each lock required around ten or fifteen minutes to operate, and even a short flight of three might result in an absence ashore of up to an hour.

Despite her resolution, Marnie inevitably found her mind wandering. The hypnotic effect of watching water pouring into or out of a lock triggered trains of thought from which she could not hide. Even when she lay on a balance beam and closed her eyes in the sunlight, the rushing of the water seemed to float her mind back to the subject that occupied almost every waking hour. Her only consolation was that she was able to keep her thoughts to herself without imposing them on Anne.

Marnie began to realise that although she probably now knew as much as anyone about the Barbara Taverner affair, her knowledge had only left her with a new set of doubts and questions. She was certainly no nearer to working out which suspect might have been Barbara's killer, or even if she had the killer's name on the list of candidates.

What if it was not one of them at all? Could it have been a prowler or a stalker or a burglar, someone with a drug habit who knew Barbara and Charles were wealthy and might have money or jewellery on board? No. She dismissed that idea as ridiculous. That kind of intrusion would have resulted in more conventional spontaneous violence. Marnie shut out the idea.

The names of the people involved in the case, even peripherally, whispered themselves in her head in harmony with the gushing water in the locks. More than any others, two names persistently rose to the surface. The first was her preoccupation for the past few days. *Where are you, Charles?*

It was not that she believed he had killed his wife. Marnie was coming to realise that her anxiety was about what he might do to himself. Now she regretted telling him to go away. Who knows what action a tormented man might take when alone and far from home with only his thoughts for company? She kept telling herself that he was mature and practical, an intelligent person unlikely to succumb to a fit of depression. Even while thinking that many highly intelligent people had taken their own lives under emotional stress, Marnie suddenly saw the truth. Charles's whole approach to the question of his wife's death was absolutely clear. His only concern was to find Barbara's murderer *beyond any doubt.* That was why he had persisted in his contacts with Neil Gerard. That was why he would not commit suicide. What had Barbara said about him? ... *self-absorbed* ... *driven by ambition* ... His sole ambition now was to remove all doubt about what really happened that night the previous winter. *It would never occur to him not to trust me.* Poor Charles. He must be bleeding inside at the thought that the woman who was at the centre of his whole life had betrayed him. Only certainty would bring some measure of understanding. And only then would he be able to get on with his life.

Marnie felt better now that she had rationalised the position. But then she realised that he could have met with an accident on his journey, and anxiety began hovering over her again.

Clearing the lock at Stoke Hammond, Anne signalled to Marnie that she wanted to talk. They conferred on *Perfidia's* stern deck, poring over the cruising guide.

'How far do you want us to go this evening, Marnie?'

Marnie ran a finger along the route on the map, noticing that Anne had been writing notes on her pad. 'What did we make the total journey ... about twenty-nine miles, fourteen locks ... that's forty-three lock miles, say roughly fourteen hours or so?'

Anne nodded. 'That's what I reckoned.'

Marnie looked around them, thinking out loud. 'Only one small lock before the outskirts of Milton Keynes ... then afterwards one at Cosgrove ... another long run past Glebe Farm to the Stoke Bruerne flight ... then the tunnel, and it's not much further after that. What are you thinking, Anne?'

'We've got plenty of time. Whatever we do this evening is a bonus. I was just thinking it would be nice to tie up somewhere quiet for the night.'

Marnie returned to the cruising guide. 'Somewhere near Willowbridge?'

'Fine.'

With Anne once more at the tiller, Marnie prepared the mooring ropes for their arrival. She walked through the boat and emerged in the cratch. For the next twenty minutes she was on the lookout for a suitable spot to tie up for the night. Alone again, she allowed her thoughts to wander. They settled very soon on the other name that had been going though her mind. There were questions relating to Sarah Cowan that would not go away.

The more she thought about it, the more she found the position of Sarah intriguing. If under questioning she had simply said that her brother had looked after her during the night in question, that would probably have been an end to it. A solid alibi. By default, her evidence had played a major part in convicting Neil. Marnie reminded herself that they had explained all that. Even so, it felt somehow unsatisfactory. And there was more. Marnie wondered if Neil had become suspicious of her. He had given his reasons for not wanting Sarah to hear the tapes. But was that the truth? If this was his last resort, would he really not want Sarah – the organiser of his appeal campaign – to help him? The tapes were intimate, sure, but Sarah was a grown woman. There was nothing in the tapes that would cause Neil serious embarrassment. Marnie was an outsider whose discretion he valued. She could understand that. But Sarah was his sister and keeping it in the family was a certain way of guaranteeing that the details of the relationship with Barbara would remain private.

And then there was the burglary of Neil's flat. Could that have had something to do with Sarah? Who else could have known what to take? But that was wrong. Sarah did not know about the tapes … according to Neil. Marnie shook her head. It was all very confusing. So what did she know for certain about Sarah?

She had failed to support Neil's account by giving him an alibi.

Neil was unwilling to share the tapes with her.

She would know where to look in the flat if somehow she knew about the tapes.

Was there anything else? Not really. Sarah was doing all she could to run Neil's campaign. By her commitment she had persuaded Marnie to keep an open mind. She was fighting gamely for her brother's freedom. Marnie could see the face that had confronted her in the prison car park. She could see Sarah glaring at her in the street on the morning of the burglary. The burglary … It had been Sarah who had told the police about Marnie's presence there. She had not hesitated to implicate Marnie. More confusion.

Her head still full of doubts and questions, Marnie became aware that the boat was slowing. A long whistle drew her attention back to Anne. Marnie turned her head and saw Anne pointing at the bank. It was a good place to moor. Marnie gave a thumbs-up, and Anne brought *Perfidia* gently into the side.

• • • • •

'What were you thinking about, back there?' They were eating supper in the dining area, and Anne asked the question while pausing to let a knob of butter melt on her corn on the cob. '… as if I couldn't guess.'

'At the lock where you had to wake me up?'

'Yes.'

Marnie thought back. 'Your guess is probably correct.'

'But what in particular?'

Marnie attempted a smile. 'I thought we weren't going to talk about … you-know-what.'

'But it's on your mind the whole time, and I don't want just to be left guessing.'

'Well … I was wondering about Charles … where he is, what he's doing, how he's feeling. Everyone goes on about Neil, but we mustn't forget that Charles has at least as much right to our sympathy. He's the completely innocent party in all this.'

Anne frowned. 'I've been thinking about that, too, and …'

'Go on.'

'I don't like to … it seems unkind.'

'You're wondering how much Charles is to blame for Barbara looking for solace outside their marriage?'

'Yes. Something must've been wrong. I mean, Barbara wouldn't just suddenly have got curious and felt like having a lover … *lovers* … would she?'

'No. But you can never judge how things are inside someone else's relationships. There are too many imponderables that you just can't know.'

'Is that what you were thinking about?'

'Not quite. I was thinking that suspicion is the worst part of this whole affair.'

'You suspect Charles, you mean?' Anne was incredulous. 'I thought you saw him as the victim … as *a* victim.'

Marnie picked up the corn and gnawed it thoughtfully. 'I was thinking about Sarah.'

Anne started on her corn. 'So was I.' Marnie waited. Anne wiped her mouth with the napkin. 'While you were having your shower and I was putting the corn on the stove, for some reason I began thinking about Sarah not backing Neil up. I mean, why be so pedantic about it? Why not just say he was there looking after her?'

'We've been over all this, Anne.'

'I know, but then I wondered why he didn't trust her about the tapes and why she told the police she'd seen you at the scene of the burglary.'

'I know. We've said all this before.'

'But I'd never thought about it this way. Hasn't it occurred to you …all the time her reaction is to push the police in the direction of somebody else?'

'What are you suggesting?'

Anne stared down at her plate. 'It's funny how doing routine things makes your mind wander … you, operating the locks … me, beating eggs in a bowl for an omelette …'

'Anne, I'm not following. What do you mean?'

'Suppose Sarah wasn't really as bad that night – the night of the murder – as she said she was. Suppose she slipped out when Neil was asleep on the sofa. She didn't vouch for him. If he was sleeping, he couldn't vouch for her.'

Marnie stared at Anne across the table without speaking.

'Am I being silly, Marnie?'

'*Silly* isn't a word I'd associate with you.'

'But you think I'm off target.'

'I can't see how your argument fits together. Why would Sarah want to harm Barbara?'

'Jealousy?'

'He's her brother. That would be too extreme a reaction, surely.'

'What about anger? Because of Neil, Barbara was being unfaithful to her husband.'

'So?'

'Hadn't Sarah's husband left her for another woman?'

'Mm … How could she know what to do on the boat?'

Anne shrugged. 'I dunno. But she lives alone; she must know about how things work … gas pipes and all that.'

'How did she even know where Barbara was that evening?'

'Neil might've told her. Barbara was more likely to let a woman on board *Perfidia* than a man.'

'That's a point. And you're thinking she's running his campaign out of a sense of guilt, because she didn't believe they'd pin the murder on Neil?'

Anne sighed. 'Not really. I suppose it's all too absurd. Perhaps *silly* is a word you ought to apply to me.'

'Nonsense.' Marnie smiled. '*Obsessive* perhaps, but not *silly*. Have you been having thoughts about any other aspect … or any other suspect?'

Anne paused. 'Mike Brent.'

'*Really*? Why Mike Brent in particular?'

'I don't know any of the others.'

'Of course. What were you thinking about him?'

'He's … well, the odd one out, isn't he?'

Marnie nodded encouragement and returned to her corn while Anne continued.

Another shrug. 'I mean, the others are all quite rich or powerful … and the artist is famous. Mike Brent is none of those. I suppose he's got a good job, but why would Barbara be attracted to him?'

'You yourself said he came across as pleasant and friendly. Attraction is a very personal thing. Opportunity also plays a part, doesn't it?'

'Actually, Marnie, I don't think I'm very well qualified to judge. At my age anyone over thirty – oops, sorry, forty – seems old, and I can't imagine what it's like.'

'Barbara was over forty. Didn't you think she was stunning?'

'Like a film star.'

'There you are, then.'

'But men …'

'What about Ralph? He's over forty.'

'He's great … really lovely … but …'

'You can't imagine him as a romantic lead.'

'He's as old as my dad.'

'Okay. Let's get back to Mike Brent. What were your thoughts about him?'

'If they did have a relationship … I could imagine it being a bigger deal for him than for the others. Rich or famous people must have more opportunities. Mike is more ordinary. He might feel stronger about Barbara because he might not expect to get involved with someone like her.'

'So if she tried to end the affair – if it ever was an *affair* – he might be more upset, more inclined to react violently?'

Anne stood up to clear the plates. 'He might feel more desperate.'

Marnie ran a thumb across her lips. 'I think you've got a point there.'

35

By their normal standards Marnie and Anne were up late on Saturday morning and sat down to breakfast listening to the eight o'clock news headlines on the radio. Both had slept soundly after the hours spent in the fresh air the previous day. Although they were well rested, the world seen through the portholes was colour-washed a pale grey by low cloud cover, and there was a subdued atmosphere in the cabin.

Anne studied the cruising guide while munching Weetabix and announced that the first lock was less than two miles ahead at Fenny Stratford. Marnie declared that she would walk that distance along the towpath to blow away the cobwebs. As soon as the table was cleared she set off at a brisk pace armed with her windlass while Anne guided *Perfidia* away from the bank and settled down to the boat's moderate cruising speed. For several minutes they were travelling in close proximity, but as Anne slowed to pass moored craft, Marnie began to extend her lead and was soon striding away into the middle distance. Half an hour later Marnie pushed open the gate of the shallow lock to admit *Perfidia* and very soon climbed aboard for the long uninterrupted journey round the varied landscape of Milton Keynes.

Taking turns to steer, Marnie decided to interrogate the answerphone back home in the office barn before going below to make their morning coffee. Using the mobile she quick-dialled the number, a pencil and notepad lying in expectation on the roof of the boat beside her. Anne noticed Marnie's expression cloud over.

'What's up?'

Marnie pulled a face. 'That's odd. No messages.'

'Nobody loves us.'

'Possibly not, but yesterday was a working day, and there are always calls on Friday afternoons. I'd have expected half a dozen messages at least.'

'True. Was the machine working properly?'

'Yep. The voice told me I had no messages.'

'Were you expecting anything important, Marnie?'

'I was hoping maybe there'd be something from Charles.'

'Mm …'

'What's that supposed to mean?'

'Well … it was you who said he should go into hiding.'

Marnie looked crestfallen. 'I'll make coffee.' From the stern door, she turned back. 'Anne … does it seem to you like … Barbara's starting to seem unreal, like when you get back to work after a holiday and everything seems so far away and long ago that it might never really have happened?'

'That's exactly how it feels.'

'I only met her twice …'

'But she's back, isn't she? She's come back to you in the tapes.'

'But that isn't real. It feels like I'm just clinging on to her by my fingertips.'

Marnie turned and backed through the door to go below. Anne concentrated on steering the boat. It seemed to her that neither Marnie nor Barbara was going to let go of the other.

• • • • •

The excitement of the afternoon was to stop at a marina in Milton Keynes for a pump-out and to take on water. Feeling under no time pressure, they stopped again for a stroll round the village of Great Linford and tied up outside a pub a short distance further on to take lunch in its canalside garden. It surprised both of them that they managed to avoid talking about Barbara and Charles or Neil and Sarah for so long.

Anne looked up from a cheese and pickle sandwich, fingering a crumb in the corner of her mouth. 'You know, Marnie, this is going to be a real test of endurance ... or willpower.'

Marnie looked puzzled. 'Piece of cake. I've done this journey single-handed in the past, no problem.'

'Not what I meant. We'll be passing Glebe Farm about two hours after we leave here.'

'So?'

'Even money says you'll have to stop to check the answerphone in the office barn.'

'You shouldn't gamble. You'll lose your shirt.'

'Wanna bet?'

'Hah ... hah. Forget it. I've already checked the machine ... did it when I went to the loo when we arrived here.'

Anne shook her head. 'Have you always been like this?'

'Focused, you mean?'

Anne flashed the Death Stare. 'Were there any messages?'

'Two. Beth wanting a chat. Jane Rutherford wondering if we'd reached a decision about repainting the name on *Perfidia*. I'll ring them tomorrow night.'

'Did they say when they were phoning?'

'Both rang this morning.'

'Mm ...'

'That's right ... no calls at all on Friday afternoon. Odd.'

'Are we actually going to continue past Glebe Farm or do you want to call in for the night at home?'

'Might as well carry on. Isn't that what you'd like?'

'Sure. So come what may and whatever you say, I just keep steering us past Knightly. Are those my orders?'

'If you like I'll put them in a sealed envelope only to be opened once we've cleared the territorial waters of Wolverton.'

Anne laughed. Later, as they resumed their journey and the afternoon wore on, her estimate proved to be correct. In little more than two hours they cleared the lock at Cosgrove and travelled on through pleasant Northamptonshire fields and meadowland, making their approach to Knightly St John. Leaning against the bulkhead beside Anne, Marnie seemed relaxed. But it came as no surprise to Anne when Marnie reached into her pocket and pulled out the mobile. Anne rolled her eyes while Marnie pressed buttons and raised the phone to her ear.

'Hi Angela, it's me, Marnie.' She paused briefly to poke her tongue out at Anne. 'How are things? Everything okay back at the ranch?'

'Nothing to report, really. I'm just going over tomorrow's sermon ... bane of my life, sermons.'

'No visitors … commotion … excitement?'

'Well, there was one thing …I'm not sure if I handled it very well.'

Marnie became serious. 'What happened?'

'Dolly brought me a mouse.'

'Was it dead?'

Anne, unable to hear the other half of the conversation, looked startled.

'Very. She just came into the cottage and dropped it on the kitchen floor.'

'What did you do?'

'Told her she was naughty, picked it up in a tissue and put it in the bin.'

'That wasn't the right thing to do.'

Anne mouthed, *what is it?*

Angela sounded glum. 'I thought not. What *should* I have done?'

'You should've eaten it – preferably swallowed it whole.' While Angela made yuck-yuck noises at the other end, Anne's expression went through three shades of horror. Marnie continued. 'Then you should've praised her hunting ability and given her a saucer of milk as a reward.'

Anne laughed quietly and helplessly at the tiller.

Angela replied in mock – or possibly real – horror. 'Marnie, you're *dreadful!*'

'She was only showing her gratitude to you for looking after her.'

'Please tell her not to bother in future!'

'We'll be passing Glebe Farm in the next ten minutes, but we're not stopping. We'll probably spend tonight up by Hanford. We're well up to schedule.'

'Right. I'll bring the mouse down for you, if you like.'

'Great. Dig it out of the bin. I'll give it to Anne as a tea-time treat.'

More grimacing from Anne.

'Oh … there was one other thing. You had a visitor yesterday evening, Friday.'

'A visitor?'

'Ronny Cope came down on his bike. He's up and about again. Came to see Anne.'

A pause. 'She'll be pleased. I'll tell her.'

Predictably, Anne was not pleased.

• • • • •

It felt strange to navigate on past *Sally Ann* and *Thyrsis* at their moorings, seeing them as other boaters saw them. The approach was round a long curve, following a contour line in gently sloping ground, and their first view of home base revealed the pair nestling by the bank close up to the spinney, *Thyrsis* on the main line, *Sally Ann* at right angles in her dock. The boats formed a charming yet protective scene, as if they presented a defensive barrier against outside intrusion. *If only*, Marnie thought.

Now that the spring foliage had sprouted, it was impossible to see through the trees to the Glebe Farm complex beyond. The sight of their home base never failed to make Marnie happy. Turning to Anne, she was surprised at the look on her friend's face. Anne smiled in understanding and recognition, but for half a second, Marnie had caught her registering anxiety and concern.

Anne turned her attention back to steering, concentrating on negotiating the bridge ahead, aiming to pass under the arch of the simple brick structure. With one fluid movement she suddenly pulled the control lever into reverse and applied full power to bring *Perfidia* to a halt, decisively raising a hand to wave to an oncoming boat to keep going. She reversed half a length back from the bridge to create a passing space and held *Perfidia* in neutral while the other craft came by.

Anne acknowledged the thanks of the steerer, pointed towards the bridge and called out, 'Clear ahead?'

'All clear,' came the reply.

She lined *Perfidia* up for a second run and pushed the accelerator forward. Marnie glanced back and saw the couple on the stern deck looking across at the moored boats. The woman pointed and the man was nodding as Marnie felt Anne tap her arm, and she moved over in response to keep her head clear of the brickwork as they entered the bridge hole.

• • • • •

That evening they moored at the foot of the land rising towards Hanford Hall, the house of their client, Mrs Dorothy Vane-Henderson, scene of a highly successful and profitable redecoration contract.

After supper they took their coffee out onto the bank and sat on picnic chairs to admire the view as dusk came down. The rounded hillside and the scattered flock of sheep reminded Marnie of the paintings of Samuel Palmer, and she talked about his life and work while Anne listened, enthralled.

They spent a quiet night in the depths of the countryside, and Marnie drifted off to sleep with only occasional bleatings from the field above floating in through the half-open porthole in her cabin.

• • • • •

It rained in the early hours of the morning, but the sun was already burning off the clouds as they slipped their ropes after breakfast and set off for the Stoke Bruerne flight. In her role as navigator, Anne estimated an hour and a half to the first lock and she was correct to within five minutes.

They worked steadily up through the seven locks and had been underway over three hours by the time *Perfidia* crawled past the cluster of buildings beside the canal museum and found a mooring space long enough to tie up for their early pub lunch break.

When it was time to go they donned jackets and woolly hats, with a golfing umbrella and powerful handlamp at the ready, in preparation for the passage through Blisworth tunnel. Untying the bow rope, Marnie checked that the headlamp was in working order and gave a thumbs-up to Anne in the stern. Two minutes later they lined up for the gaping mouth of the tunnel, felt the chill air surrounding the entrance, flicked on the headlamp and slid into the darkness. Only two boats came towards them during the passage, and they emerged into daylight after thirty-five minutes, pleased to be back in fresh air, relieved that they had avoided the showers of water spraying down on them from the overhead ventilation shafts.

Within two miles Anne was lining up to take the right-hand Gayton turn, Marnie standing halfway along the gunwale, ready with a centre rope. Rounding the bend they found boats triple-banked against the wharf.

'Where can I put her?' Anne called out.

Marnie began pointing. 'On the outside of ...' Her voice faded. Her hand lowered itself slowly.

Anne waited, expecting further instructions. 'Marnie?' Still no reaction. 'Marnie!'

Then Anne saw it. Parked close to the boatyard's office stood a cherry red metallic Jaguar. As she looked on two things happened at once. The driver's door opened and out stepped Charles Taverner. At the same time a horn sounded from an approaching boat. Anne realised she had drifted across the canal, blocking the channel. She quickly raised a hand and accelerated lightly to gain steerage, easing *Perfidia* to the side, leaving space for the oncoming boat to pass.

Anne apologised to the other steerer, who smiled and nodded. 'Piccadilly circus here,' he called out good-naturedly.

Marnie meanwhile had regained her composure and was indicating a space where Anne could bring *Perfidia* alongside another boat to tie up. Attaching short ropes to the nearest boat at bow and stern, they crossed the two inner boats to meet Charles on the bank. His expression was calm but he was not smiling.

• • • • •

As usual Anne sat in the back on the journey home. The interior of the Jaguar was so quiet she had no difficulty hearing the conversation between Marnie and Charles in front.

'I was going to ring you on your mobile to tell you about the change of plan, Marnie, but –'

'Which change did you have in mind? There seem to have been quite a few.'

'What do you mean?'

'I thought you were keeping out of the way in France, staying at your house in the Dordogne. I've been ringing you for days.'

Charles breathed out audibly. 'No. It wasn't on. There were too many associations ... memories ... I only realised it fully when I got there ...'

'Suppose you start at the beginning. How is it that you're here to meet us? Where's Ralph?'

'Ralph,' Charles repeated vacantly. 'Oh yes ... I rang you on Friday afternoon to say I was getting ready to come back. Just before I left, Ralph phoned to say he'd picked up my message. We talked and he explained about coming to meet you here. But there was some change to his programme at the seminar that meant he'd be later than he'd thought. I offered to come instead. It seemed the obvious solution.'

'But you live in London.'

'Not any more. I arranged with Harrods to move everything up to the Old Rectory. I called by just now to check. Everything's in place. I'm now officially a resident of Knightly St John.'

'That was sudden.'

'I've made up my mind about a lot of things, Marnie. The trip to France helped me to see clearly what I had to do. It was a good idea of yours. Oh, by the way, your mobile seems to be switched off. I told Ralph I'd ring you to let you know what was happening.'

Marnie tut-tutted. 'It ran out of charge. Did you have to wait long at the boatyard?'

'No.'

'So what about France?'

'The house was too full of memories, so I took myself off to the coast ... found a good hotel at Arcachon the other side of Bordeaux, right on the seafront. Went for long walks on the beach ... huge sand dunes there ... space to think. It just all became clear to me. After that I was bursting with impatience and frustration. I had to get back ... to hell with the consequences.'

There was an interval while Charles overtook a line of lorries and negotiated a roundabout. Marnie wondered if Charles's conclusions were in line with her own.

'Are you able to tell us what you concluded on your walks?'

'It's easy. But first, Marnie, tell me about Neil Gerard.'

'What about him?'

'What do you think of his story? You've been travelling on the boat. That gives you time to think. My guess is, you've reached conclusions of your own.'

'I ... I tend to believe his account of what happened.'

'Was Barbara in love with him, do you think?'

'That's hard to say. From everything I've heard I'm pretty certain she was completely loyal to you ... despite the circumstances.'

Charles said nothing for some minutes, and the Jaguar purred along the open road. Anne sat in silence, touching the leather upholstery, hoping her jeans were not making any marks on the seat, or her trainers any stains on the carpet.

Charles suddenly spoke in a firm voice. 'I believe him too. He didn't do it.'

'I only said I tended to think he –'

'I know. But I'm convinced he didn't.'

'Do you intend doing anything about it?'

'That isn't the next question.'

Marnie was bewildered. 'What is?'

'I expected you to ask me why I'd decided he wasn't guilty.'

'Okay. Why did you decide that? And why are you so certain?'

'You go first. I'd be interested to know your reasons.'

'Well ... I can't really explain, Charles.'

'You're not telling me it's all just intuition. Women can't use that argument these days; it's old hat.'

'I mean literally I can't explain ... not yet, anyway.'

'It has something to do with your visit to Bermuda Reach that Sunday morning when I found you there?'

'Possibly.'

'You're being very enigmatic. When will you tell me about that?'

'I'm not sure ... maybe never.'

'Marnie, that isn't an answer.'

'I'm sorry. It's the only one I have at present.'

They turned off the dual carriageway on the minor road to Knightly St John. Passing the Old Rectory, Anne suddenly spoke.

'Will you still be wanting the frieze in the conservatory and the kitchen now that you've moved in, Mr Taverner?'

'Definitely, Anne. Can you arrange for it to be done?'

'I'll do it myself.'

Marnie pointed at the field entrance. 'You can drop us here, Charles. No need to bring the car down the track. We've only got light kitbags.'

'Nonsense. But I do have one more favour to ask, Marnie. Could you come round the house with me and check what still needs to be done? We can drop off your bags and leave Anne to settle in at Glebe Farm.'

Marnie understood his meaning.

• • • • •

It was strange to open the door of the Old Rectory and find it furnished again. Marnie recognised a small hall table from Templars' Wharf. The surprise was to notice the vase of freesias beside the telephone. It brought an unexpected woman's touch to the entrance.

'You said Harrods did the move, Charles?'

'Loaded up in London early on Friday morning, drove up and had all the furniture in place by evening.'

Marnie sniffed the flowers. They were real. 'They think of everything.'

'What? Oh ... the flowers ... that would be Ellen's idea. She has a marvellous eye for detail.'

'Ellen?'

'I persuaded my old secretary to come out of retirement to supervise.'

Marnie had a vision of an elderly lady in a pale blue twin set, grey hair gathered back in a bun, fob watch hanging on a chain round her neck. They moved from room to room. Apart from the odd packing case, the house looked as if it had never been furnished any other way. Returning downstairs, Charles led Marnie into the drawing room and invited her to sit down.

'I'm glad to have a few minutes alone with you, Marnie.'

'You wanted to tell me your reasons for believing Neil Gerard.'

'I said it was easy, but in fact it's a mixture of a lot of elements. Oddly, one of them is rather intuitive, or more accurately it's about personal judgment and experience. To be successful in business you have to be a good judge of character. Gerard has always struck me as a straight sort of person ... reliable ... honest ... you know that. He's no choirboy, but neither is he the type to help himself to the collection or steal the church silver.'

Marnie nodded. 'I agree.'

'Once I'd settled on that point, the rest fell into place. His non-alibi is believable. Paradoxically, his sister's story backed him up in my view. If it had been too definite, that would be *more* suspicious. The tampering with the gas system ... no. This was supposed to be a crime of passion. You don't kill someone in a fit of anger by messing about with gas valves or joints or whatever.'

'That's right. Too premeditated.'

'Quite. For me, the last straw was the suicide attempt. That was no cry for help. You don't hang yourself hoping someone might happen to come by … too risky. That was the real thing.'

'But he could've known when the officers did their rounds.'

Charles shook his head. 'No. I enquired. The timing is random. Significantly, he strung himself up just after an inspection. Every now and then they do a quick follow-up tour without pattern or warning. He couldn't have known they'd come round so soon that day. He intended to kill himself.'

'Could've been remorse,' Marnie suggested.

'That's possible, I suppose. But the timing … he did it just after I refused to help with the appeal campaign.'

Marnie shrugged. 'I'm not sure if that necessarily proves anything.'

Charles continued. 'There's something else … something you don't know about. He sent a letter to his sister.'

Marnie sat up in her chair. 'A letter? A suicide note?'

'He thanked her for her help, asked her to forgive him, said he was innocent and that he couldn't stand being in prison any longer.'

'How do you know this? He's not mentioned it to me.'

'I contacted Sarah.'

'Have you seen the letter?'

'Not yet.'

'But you believe her.'

'Absolutely. She's as honest as he is.' Charles began to get up. 'I should've offered you a cup of tea, Marnie, or perhaps something stronger.'

Marnie waved him back. 'No, that's fine. I ought to be getting home. Do you have everything you need? What about provisions?'

'All taken care of by Ellen. There's enough food in the fridge to withstand a siege. Before you go, Marnie, I wonder if you have any news of any of the people on the suspects list?'

'No further progress … if in fact they *are* suspects. I don't think there's much I can do in that direction, being realistic about it. What about the ex-spouses?'

'You can rule one of them out. I spoke to my first wife on the phone. She's happily living in Florida with her second husband … and their three children.' Charles emphasised the last part of the sentence. 'She was on an anniversary cruise in the Caribbean with her husband at the time of the murder.'

'And Barbara's ex-husband?'

'Don't know. I think he's also abroad somewhere, but …' A shrug.

'It's not easy to investigate things when you've no authority or resources, is it Charles?'

He stood up. 'Worth trying, though.'

They crossed the hall, and Charles opened the front door. Marnie had insisted on bringing the Discovery up from Glebe Farm behind Charles's Jaguar, and he walked her out to it.

Marnie scuffed the surface of the drive with her shoe. It seemed to be rough concrete that had been laid many years before. The church commissioners did not go in for extravagant finishes. 'Here's a job that still needs doing. I don't think you've yet decided how you want it surfaced.'

'What do you think would be appropriate, Marnie?'

'Nothing too *smart*, I think. In the country block paving always looks to me as if it's come out of a catalogue.'

'What about simple tarmac, then?'

Marnie looked doubtful. 'Maybe … or something more rural. Rolled hogging might be more in keeping, though it tends to pot-hole after a time. Cobbles would look nice or maybe gravel would be best … pea shingle, perhaps. But you need to be vigilant.'

'Vigilant. From the security point of view, you mean?' He smiled. 'I can always rely on my military training. Gravel never lets anyone get close to the house without making a sound.'

'I didn't mean vigilant in that way. I meant you have to keep weeds from growing through it.'

'Ah, yes. Perhaps there's a local chap who'll help look after the garden?'

'I'll put a card on the notice board in the shop. There's bound to be someone.'

'Kind of you, Marnie. But I'm imposing on your goodwill. That would be rather outside the remit of an interior designer.'

'Put it down to help from a friend and neighbour. Anything else, while we're talking business?'

'The name plate?'

'Of course. I'll make enquiries and get that put in hand. You still want it to be *The Old Rectory*?'

'Absolutely.'

'That reminds me, Charles. *Perfidia*. It's been suggested to me that now might be a good time to change the name.'

'Why?'

'It's a tradition on the canals, I gather, that you change the name when a boat is out of the water. *Perfidia* will be coming out for hull blacking.'

'I still don't follow.'

Marnie hesitated. 'It's not going to be easy to sell her with her current name. There's only been one offer, and the people haven't seen her yet. They're in New Zealand.'

Charles frowned. 'I'm not sure … perhaps I should think about it.'

'The point is – and I'm sorry there isn't a pleasant way of saying this – she's rather an infamous boat with her present name. A number of potential purchasers have withdrawn when they saw her.'

'Just because of the name?'

'That's what I've been told.'

Charles walked a few steps away, looking down as if inspecting the surface of the drive. He turned back. 'No. I can't do that. *Perfidia* was Barbara's boat. She loved it … it was part of her. That was the name she gave it. It stays the same.'

'That's your decision?'

'The *infamy*, as you put it, will soon be forgotten. It won't bother these people from the other side of the world. And if it does, we'll sell her to somebody else. I don't want to keep the boat for obvious reasons, but I'm not going back on Barbara's choice of name. You know how insistent she was about names, Marnie.'

'Very well.' Marnie opened the car door. 'Charles, would you like to eat with us tonight? I'm sorry it sounds like an afterthought.'

'It's a kind thought, Marnie, but thank you, no. I have plenty here and in any case I've got a number of phone calls to make after being away. One of them will be to Sarah Cowan.'

'You've made up your mind.'

'I have.'

• • • • •

That evening Ralph asked Marnie if she was going to listen to another tape. The thought had been prompted by a light rain falling after supper. But she had had enough of Barbara's business after a whole weekend of it and opted for an early night. A read in bed was what she most wanted. She placed a few design magazines on the duvet in the sleeping cabin on *Thyrsis* and set off for a hot shower. When she returned in her dressing gown Ralph was checking his seminar notes.

Marnie sat on the edge of the bed. 'There's been something bothering me all evening.'

Ralph put his papers down. 'What is it?'

'Two things, really. Charles said his first wife now has three children.'

'Is that significant?'

'It was the way he said it … as if that's what she'd always wanted. I wondered if there was a problem with Charles in that regard.'

'A fertility problem … or not wanting children on his part?'

'Either … both … I dunno.'

'But she has a family now, so it's no longer an issue. She also has a solid alibi, if that's what you were wondering.'

'I was wondering more if that was an issue between Charles and Barbara … a reason why she might have been playing away from home.'

'Not something you can really ask him.'

'No.'

'And the second thing? You said you had two things on your mind.'

'Charles mentioned his *military training*. Do you know anything about that?'

'*Military training*?' Ralph looked thoughtful. 'No. That's new to me. I know he was at Cambridge … read history, I think. Do you want me to find out about his background?'

'Can you do that?'

'Leave it with me.'

Marnie stretched across the bed and kissed him. 'I've missed you this weekend.'

'Same goes for me. Are you really planning to read all those magazines?'

'That's a leading question.' Marnie turned onto her side, dropped the magazines on the floor and began loosening her bathrobe.

Ralph leaned forward, took her face in his hands and kissed her for several seconds. Deftly removing the satin robe and turning back towards him, Marnie was surprised to find his expression serious.

'What's the matter?'

'I've had something on my mind as well.'

'I thought I'd just worked out what that was.'

A smile crossed his face, but only briefly. 'Now probably isn't the best time to talk about it.'

'Now might be the best time to put it right. What's the matter? Come on, spill the beans.'

'It occurred to me that if Charles goes public in his support for Neil Gerard's campaign – and there isn't much point in him doing so if he isn't going to make some sort of publicity about it – there might be consequences for us … for *you*.'

'In what way?'

'Well … if whoever did the murder found out that you were helping him, it could put you in danger.'

'Oh, I thought of that long ago. No, I'm sure no one's going to be interested in me. I'm very much in the background. Don't worry about it. In any case, I think my part in that business is more or less over now. I've done all I can do.'

'Just be careful, Marnie.'

'I will … promise … cross my heart … I always hold myself back. Well … nearly always. Talking of which, are you really planning to read all those notes?'

36

Ralph was surprised to find Marnie still in bed when he returned from his morning walk along the towpath. He came into the sleeping cabin, flushed from his exertions, breathing deeply.

Lying flat on her back under the duvet, Marnie groaned. 'Oooh ...'

Ralph knelt by the bed and pulled back the cover to reveal her face. 'What's up, Marnie, aren't you well?'

'Done something to my back,' she drawled.

'Your back? What can have caused it? Did you lie awkwardly in the night?'

'It could've been working the locks over the weekend.' Her voice was weary.

'Ah, yes.'

'But probably not ... I'm paying the price ... Remind me to enter a nunnery straight after breakfast.'

'Oh ... right ... I'll put it in the diary. I daresay Anne will be able to produce a list of local institutions ... *Yellow Pages* should help. You'd better stay where you are this morning. Should I call a doctor?'

'A vet.'

· · · · ·

Marnie had not moved when, ten minutes later, Ralph re-appeared on *Thyrsis* with a breakfast tray.

'Easy-to-eat breakfast for the invalid,' he announced cheerfully.

Another groan from Marnie, but with a grateful edge to it.

'Anne sends greetings and will be over to see you shortly ... if you survive breakfast. Can you sit up at all?'

'Not without fatal consequences ... but I'll try.'

Ralph supported Marnie's shoulders and helped ease her up the bed. He propped her with pillows.

'Orange juice, coffee and a croissant. No skill required.' He helped slip on her nightdress. 'Can you manage?'

'Yeah. This is a real drag, Ralph, I'm sorry.'

'Shall I cancel my meeting in London? I can stay here today.'

'No, no. Your meeting's important. I'll work something out.'

'I expect Anne already has a plan.'

'Good. She can tell me about it when she brings the list of nunneries.'

Ralph smiled. 'That's a good sign.'

'You think so?'

'You didn't mention the vet.'

· · · · ·

'No probs.' Anne brushed crumbs from the duvet onto the tray and took it through to the galley. Seconds later she was back, armed with her notepad. 'Seriously, Marnie, do you want me to phone the doctor's?'

'He'll only tell me to rest. It's a bind, it really is. This is the trouble when you're a very small outfit like us. Perhaps you could change the message on the answerphone … ask callers to ring my mobile number.'

'No need. I'll man the office. I can handle some of the enquiries and take messages for the rest. If necessary I can get them to phone you on the mobile or get you to ring them back. Easy peasy.'

'You've got college today, Anne.'

'Only a couple of tutorials about my projects. I can rearrange them for later in the week. I'm so far ahead with the work, they won't mind.'

'If you're sure … I don't want you to get behind with your –'

'Don't worry about it. I work twice as fast as anyone else and do twice as much. Honestly. What would you like to do, Marnie?"

'I thought I'd go for a jog, do some aerobics and maybe –'

'Marnie!' Mock severity.

'Well, there's not much I can do, is there? All I can do this morning is just lie here and hope it wears off.'

'Mm … I know … shall I bring the radio through? At least that would give you something to listen to … take your mind off things.'

'Radio?' Marnie looked thoughtful. 'There's a thought.'

Anne turned to leave. 'I'll go and fetch it.'

'No … not the radio, Anne. Could you lend me your walkman?"

37

There was a faint hiss as the tape began turning, the husky voice, quiet and slow.

You were in a funny mood this afternoon

What was all that about?

You know the rules

I don't do games, I don't do French

French anything [a laugh]

Sometimes I can't make you out

You really are the strangest man

You get all energetic, all that passion, as if you haven't seen me in years

I know it's been a couple of weeks, but we both knew I'd be going away for a break

I know you don't begrudge Charles the odd holiday

That's the thing about being a workaholic ... he works a lot

And then you lie there, babbling on ... in French

Mon dieu!

Maundering

Yes, there is such a word, even if you say you don't know it

I speak English too

Actually, it was nice that you didn't try to confuse me with the French

I was always quite good at it at school, you know

I can still get by

One of my shopping languages

I'm not bad at Italian ...I mean, I know how to pronounce Versace and Gucci

Useful for life's little essentials

I understand American, too ... Fifth Avenue American, of course [another laugh]

You said my French accent was good

Who was it you were quoting?

Ah yes ... Baudelaire

Tu mettrais tout le monde dans ta ruelle ...

See? I do remember

You said I'd forget it as soon as I got home

The other poems by him that you quoted were pretty crude, I thought

And that one about the rotting carcass ... ugh!

What did you say it meant ... the ruelle one?

Something like ... you'd let everyone into your bed?

That's when you started to come over all strange

It's always a sign that something odd's on your mind when you start stroking my hair

I thought you'd gone round the bend when you said that about ... other men

Every man in the world should have the experience of sleeping with me!

Huh! [a prolonged laugh]
Whatever made you think of that?
For the wonderful experience, you said
It would make the world a better place, you said
That was nice
They'd be smiling when they swept me up afterwards and dumped me in the bin!
Seriously, I'm not sure it was a good idea, talking about …lovers
Other lovers
First, it's none of your business
Second, I can see it getting out of hand … you getting jealous
You said you aren't the jealous kind
It's possible
You could be the exception
The only one
In my experience all men are the jealous kind
It would add spice to our relationship, you said
Up till then I hadn't felt inadequate
At least you didn't ask me to compare you with them
That would've been fatal
The end
I mean that
Don't ever ask me anything like that
Somehow … I don't think you would
So perhaps you are exceptional
For most men, that's the only thing they'd want to know
Tu mettrais tout le monde dans ta ruelle …
Well I wouldn't
I'm very choosy
But like a lot of women, I don't always choose well
Ian … Ian Stuart … there's a joke
He could give Narcissus a bad name
Ian was in love … I told you
He was really sincere
I've never known a man more in love … with himself
And believe me, I've known a few
Men are just as vain as women
In all ways
And mostly, with less justification
A flabby man looks in a mirror and sees a flat muscular torso
A slim woman sees herself in a mirror and worries if her bum looks big
It's true

We may be vain, but we're vain worrying about our faults

We usually don't have illusions about ourselves

Any attractive woman could give you a list of her weak points

But Ian ... he thought he was the cat's pyjamas

It was weird, seeing him again after all that time

Turning up to view Bermuda Reach, seeing that la-di-dah secretary and then ...

Out came Ian, trying to look all dynamic

I'll swear he had highlights in his hair

Then he saw me

He didn't know whether to pretend we hadn't met or we had [a laugh]

I saw the looks he was giving me

The nonchalant way he gave me his business card

I know what he was thinking

He looked surprised when I handed it to Charles

My husband is more likely to need it than I am ...

Huh!

His tan went two shades deeper

Oops ... getting late

Just time for a shower before Charles rings from ...where is it?

Can't remember

Ellen knows more about Charles's movements than I do

She controls his life

Nobody controls mine, not even you, my darling

Time for you to go down the plughole

Until soon

Bonne nuit

There was a muffled whispering sound, the swish of blank tape running and then a click as the machine was switched off.

38

Listening to the tape on Anne's walkman made the experience seem even more real, more intimate. Marnie could hear Barbara taking every breath while she spoke. She could imagine the expressions on her face. It still felt like voyeurism, but Marnie had become accustomed to that now and just found the experience interesting. There was no point in wondering how Barbara would have felt about her listening in on her private life. And Neil obviously did not worry about it. Perhaps he even thought it enhanced his image in Marnie's eyes to have her know how closely he was involved with such a beautiful woman.

Marnie rewound the tape, shifting position in the bed to try to ease her back. Perhaps the pain was diminishing. She adjusted the earphones and ran the tape a second time.

• • • • •

She must have dozed off. Something roused her. Voices. It took some seconds to recall what was happening, lying there in bed with daylight seeping into the cabin. She took out the earphones and wriggled under the duvet. A twinge in the back. Outside on the canal people were calling to each other. A friendly exchange between boaters passing the moored craft, *Thyrsis* and *Sally Ann*, dead slow. They were speaking English to each other, Marnie thought idly. She frowned. Of course they were speaking English. What else?

Then she realised. She had been dreaming. She had been in Neil Gerard's house. Although she had never seen the inside, she could imagine every detail, the bookcases, the hi-fi, the comfortable well-worn furniture, rugs on a polished wooden floor. Barbara was there. Like Marnie, she was wearing a bathrobe, hers was in pale blue silk, with golden thread tracing a floral pattern on the back.

They were speaking French, all three of them. Marnie struggled to remember the conversation. What was it about? *Les amants* … lovers. Barbara thought the word ought to be *aimants* … from the verb *aimer, of course, my dears*, she had said.

The voices outside were receding. Marnie tried to sit up and turn round to look at the clock on the shelf, but her back was too tender. She became aware of the walkman she was holding in her left hand. She flipped open its lid. The tape inside had reached the end. Barbara's hypnotic voice must have lulled her to sleep. Marnie closed the lid, pressed the rewind button and fitted the earphones back in place.

Making an effort of concentration, she listened to the tape again. It was strange, like overhearing someone on the phone when you only get one side of the conversation. The references to French were open to all sorts of interpretation … French kissing, French letters, doing it French-style. It seems to have been their theme for the day. Why Baudelaire? Marnie had never read any of his poems at school. She recalled they were supposed to be very explicit. That must have been why Neil was quoting them to Barbara, to enhance their sex life.

Then there was mention of *other lovers*. The Baudelaire poem seemed to have sparked that off. Or perhaps they had been talking about that beforehand, and Neil branched out to the poem about putting all the other people in Barbara's bed. Pillow talk. And Barbara's instincts had told her this was not a good idea. Perhaps she was right and it had fatal consequences.

Barbara certainly had Ian Stuart to a tee. *Highlights!* Yes, definitely a possibility. Not just a holiday in the Caribbean. So she had seen him in the recent past, though it was clear she had no intention of picking up where they had left off.

Not much mention of Charles this time. But Ellen? How had Charles referred to her? … *I persuaded my old secretary to come out of retirement* … Could there be a touch of jealousy in what Barbara said? No. Marnie was sure Barbara did not do jealousy. She went her own way. Perhaps a little resentment, nothing more.

Marnie reached the end and was fumbling for the stop button when she thought she caught the indistinct echo of a sound after the *Bonne nuit*. She rewound for a second or two and pressed play. There it was again. Another rewind. Something or nothing? One more time. As soon as she reached the *Bonne nuit*, she rolled the volume control to maximum and this time she heard clearly. Another rewind to be certain.

Thank you for today, my darling.

It was heavenly.

The words had been whispered quickly as if Barbara did not want to say them out loud, as if she was only giving them the faintest chance of being heard. Would Neil have detected them? Oh, yes. Marnie was in no doubt about that. She was sure he would listen to the tapes over and over again. If he was a hi-fi enthusiast, she was certain he would also listen to them on headphones, probably expensive high quality equipment, not just a little thirty-pound walkman. He would want Barbara inside his head.

So what was the purpose of the whispered message that set it apart from the rest? Gone was the conversational tone, the banter, the assertiveness, the air of independence. Here was a direct expression of tenderness, the kind of language that Marnie herself might use in intimate moments with Ralph. What had Ralph called it? *The L word.*

●　●　●　●　●

Thyrsis rocked gently. In the pale light of the cabin, Marnie turned her head towards the porthole, wondering if she would catch a glimpse through the net of a boat passing. But it was Anne coming on board. She pushed open the cabin door and came in backwards, holding a tray.

'Meals on Wheels, or rather Meals Afloat,' she announced cheerily. 'How are you feeling?'

Marnie pulled out the earphones. 'Not bad.'

'Good. I've brought you some soup and a sandwich … brie with cucumber.'

She set the tray down on the bed. The soup smelled wonderful, and a yellow gingham napkin covered the bread basket. Beside them stood a glass of sparkling water and an egg cup containing a single daisy. Marnie smiled at the sight.

'This is a nice surprise. I was expecting mid-morning coffee.'

'I'll forward your complaint to the management. But it is half past twelve, so lunch is in order.'

'Is it so late? I had no idea.'

'You were dozing when I came over with coffee, so I thought I'd better let you sleep.' Anne noticed the walkman. 'Did you listen to the tape?'

'Yes.'

'Do you want me to bring you any more?'

'No. I must try to get up when I've had this.'

'I've been through all the post and I've done some letters for you to sign. All routine … invoices, reminders, the usual stuff.'

'Thanks. I hope you've been able to get on with your college work.'

'No probs. Now eat up. I'll be back soon.'

'Before you go, can you help me to get up? I need to visit the bathroom.'

Anne supported Marnie's back while she manoeuvred out of bed. 'Can you manage from here on?'

'Sure.'

Anne passed her the mobile phone. 'You'd better take this with you. If you get stuck in the loo, ring me. I'll send in the Seventh Cavalry.' She laughed. Before leaving, she turned in the doorway. 'Oh, a couple of phone messages, I meant to tell you. Mike Brent rang. I told him we'd got *Perfidia* to Blisworth. He was pleased about that.'

'Did he mention the change of name?'

'No, but … well, I told him Mr Taverner didn't want it changed. I thought I'd better let him know, seeing that he'd raised it with you. Was that all right?'

'How did he react?'

'He seemed surprised … said he thought it'd been agreed. I just said you'd asked Mr Taverner about it, and he was adamant. Mike was quiet for a moment or two, then said it was a pity. I told him you'd tried to persuade Mr Taverner, but he wouldn't budge. I hope I did the right thing.'

'Did Mike say anything else?'

'Er … oh, yes, he said he might talk to Mr Taverner himself.'

'That's fine, Anne. We'll carry on as before … no action unless Charles tells us otherwise.'

'Okay. There was one other message. Philip rang. He wants you to phone him back when you're up and about. Nothing urgent, he said.'

• • • • •

The trip to the loo was more of a struggle than Marnie had expected. After two unsuccessful efforts to stand, she even thought of taking up Anne's offer of the Seventh Cavalry. Her sense of personal dignity forced her to persevere and at the third attempt she wobbled to a vertical position, smoothed her bathrobe around her and staggered back to the sleeping cabin. To her surprise, Anne was sitting on the bed.

'You look to me as if you need a doctor, Marnie.'

She got up and helped her friend to reach the bed. Anne supported Marnie while she swivelled her legs, lowered her back against a pile of pillows and pulled up the duvet.

'There are some magazines on the floor under the bed. Would you like to read them … help pass the time?'

'I shall die of boredom if I lie here much longer.'

'Let me fetch the radio … and what about some music cassettes to play on the walkman?'

Marnie nodded in resignation.

'Do you think you'd be able to run an eye over my project work, Marnie? I'd really like to know what you think about them so far.'

'Of course. Absolutely.'

'Thanks. I'll go and fetch the folders. If you think of anything else you need, ring me in the office barn and I'll bring it down. You've still got your mobile handy?'

'Yep.'

When Anne had left the boat, Marnie reached into the pocket of her bathrobe and pulled out the phone. She was wondering whether to ask Anne to bring some clients' folders to look through her own projects, when another idea came into her mind. She pecked out a familiar number on the keypad.

'Hi. Philip Everett, please. It's Marnie Walker.'

Philip was talking to colleagues in the meeting room, and Marnie left a message. Within less than ten minutes he returned the call.

'Anne said you were in bed with your back, Marnie. What's happened to you?'

'Probably overdid the locks at the weekend. We brought *Perfidia* up from Leighton Buzzard.'

'A hazardous business, boating. Well, you've got to get better by next week.'

'What's on next week?'

'I have an invitation for you. Would you like to come with me to the opening of the new extension to the Spice Quay Centre?'

'Where's that?'

'Spice Quay is *the* new financial quarter in Docklands, downstream from Tower Bridge, south side.'

'You have a connection with it?'

Philip sounded pained. 'Marnie … it's one of *our* projects. Are you so far removed from London that you don't keep up with things any more?'

Marnie could feel her face redden. 'Oh, Philip … I'm spending so much time worrying about … other things … that I'm losing touch with reality. Tell me about Spice Quay … great name.'

'It's a great place. My best job ever. Seriously. It's an extension to a converted Victorian warehouse. The whole thing will be the HQ of Findhorn Asset Management.'

'Stockbrokers?'

'Something like that, part of the Findhorn Banking Group. We've been nominated for a Civic Award for this.'

'Congratulations. I'd love to come … if I'm able to walk around by then. It'll be a pleasant break from my other concerns.'

'Er … not actually. That's partly why I'm inviting you.'

'Oh?'

'Remember you told me about Clive Adamson?'

'Ye-e-es.'

'He'll be there. Turns out he's chairman of the parent company. I've only dealt with the team at FAM, but his name is on the invitation as the big cheese. That's why I thought of you.'

'That's really *weird* ... what a coincidence.'

'Would you like an even bigger coincidence? They've just bought a painting to hang in the boardroom ... by Piers Wainwright.'

'You're *kidding*!'

'It's a riverscape of how Spice Quay looked in the nineteenth century at the height of its days as a busy dock, when it got its name.'

'Will the painting be in place for the opening?'

'That's the plan. And so will the artist. You'll be able to kill two birds ... sorry, Marnie, I mean you'll get to see them both. Are you up for it?'

'I suppose so ... if I'm up for it.'

• • • • •

The afternoon passed more quickly. Marnie was astonished at how much work Anne had carried out on her college projects. She had taken as her theme the development of European design roughly between the Franco-Prussian war of 1870-71 and the second world war. The sheer volume of material she had produced was incredible, ranging from the Art and Craft movement in Britain and its spread throughout Europe via *Art Nouveau* and *Jugendstil*, to the influence of the *Bauhaus* and the international style.

Anne had included biographies of key players and a wealth of illustrative material to demonstrate how development had taken place. Marnie thought the project was well up to university standard, not just an A level project. Here was not just an assembly of facts taken from other people's books, but a well-argued and attractively presented exposition of a key period in architecture and design. The biggest surprise was how much Marnie learnt from the dossier.

When Anne arrived with tea in the middle of the afternoon, Marnie heaped praise on her.

'No wonder you don't feel under pressure on this. It's virtually finished.'

'Not really. I want to turn it into a whole presentation now, a complete package. I'm going to make it into a book, like those big art books in the shops, with an illustrated cover, graphics, title pages, footnotes, acknowledgements and an index ... oh and a bibliography. I'm thinking of adding a whole section of illustrations showing what buildings and artefacts looked like before William Morris and his friends came along and how they changed over the decades up to people like Charles Rennie Mackintosh, Le Corbusier and Frank Lloyd Wright.'

'He was American, surely, rather than European.'

'But he was part of the same trend. Anyway, his mum's family was Welsh.'

Marnie stared. 'I didn't know that.'

'Your tea's getting cold. How's your back feeling?'

'Not so bad. The rest has done me good. So has your project ... helped take my mind of things.'

'Good. Are you up to making some phone calls?'

'Sure.'

Anne gave Marnie a list and a small pile of folders. 'I think this is all you'll need.

Apart from that there were a few other calls. Ralph rang with a very curious message … something about … a nunnery? Does that make sense?'

Marnie grinned. 'Yes. An in joke.'

'Okay. Beth rang. She'll phone you tomorrow. And Mr Taverner phoned to say he'd been contacted by Mike Brent and had confirmed no change to the name, *Perfidia*. No need to ring him back. He'll be out tomorrow … speak to you later in the week.'

'Okay.'

'I told him you were likely to be resting at home tomorrow,' Anne said pointedly. 'That's right, isn't it?'

Marnie smiled. 'Yes, mummy.'

After Anne had left, Marnie lay back against the pillows, wondering how she would ever cope without her closest friend. She hated herself for having lied to her.

39

Marnie waited till Ralph had gone for his morning walk the next day before she attempted to stand. Only a slight niggle as she swung her legs out from under the duvet. She bent forward, pressed down on the mattress with both hands and straightened up. A wobble, but she steadied herself against the cabin wall and took two steps. Muttering thanks for her deliverance, she tottered towards the bathroom.

When Marnie headed for breakfast on *Sally Ann*, a little more slowly than usual, Ralph and Anne applauded her entrance. She replied with a thumbs-up.

'So it's … *back* to normal.' Ralph grinned.

Marnie groaned and threatened a relapse. Anne gave him the Death Stare. He cringed.

By late morning, with Marnie promising to take it easy, Anne set off for an afternoon at college, armed with her project folders. Ralph was surprised when Marnie rang him in his study on *Thyrsis* and asked if he could bring his work over to the office to man the phones after lunch. Believing that she was going to spend the afternoon in bed, he readily agreed, telling her he was glad she was being sensible. He should have known better.

She had already put her shoulder-bag in the Discovery before Ralph appeared for lunch. After they had eaten and she eventually walked towards the door, Ralph was concentrating intensely on a paper he was preparing on the implications for global resources of growth in the Chinese economy. He glanced up and wished her a good rest before returning to his analysis. It was a minute later, hearing the car leaving the garage barn, that her words registered. As she walked out she had spoken quickly.

'A woman's gotta do what a woman's gotta do.'

By the time he reached the door, the Discovery was halfway up the field track.

• • • • •

Marnie parked as close to the prison entrance as she could. The car park seemed unusually full for a mid-week afternoon, and there appeared to be some kind of demonstration in progress at the far end. She hoped it would not result in her being turned away after she had taken so much trouble to escape from Glebe Farm to be there.

Her anxiety was unfounded, and she was allowed in, passing in the corridor a number of visitors who were already leaving. She was later than she had hoped and knew she would have barely twenty minutes to talk.

When Neil entered the room with his escort, he looked very surprised to see her. He noticed that she sat down stiffly and carefully.

'Marnie …' Concerned, he reached across to take her arm and steady her. 'Are you all right?'

'Pulled something in my back. It's nothing.'

When they were settled he looked into her face. 'I wasn't expecting you.'

'Look, Neil, I haven't got much time. I've been listening to the tapes and I need to know more about Adamson and Wainwright. I'm going to an event next week, and they'll both be there.'

'Will Charles be there?'

'No.'

'But aren't you with him?'

'Charles? What do you mean … *with him?*'

'He was here just a couple of minutes ago. I'd only just gone back to my … room when they fetched me out again. I thought he'd forgotten something.'

'I had no idea he was even here. He didn't mention it to me.'

'I'm amazed you didn't pass him on your way in. Wait a minute … you mean you don't know about his proposal?'

'I don't know a lot of things. Tell me about it.' She looked at her watch.

'He's going to announce that he believes I'm innocent and he supports my appeal campaign. Isn't that great?'

'Yes, it is. But I came here on my own to find out whatever you can tell me about those other men.'

'I only know what's on the tapes, Marnie. I've never met them personally. I've seen Wainwright on TV … the South Bank Show, the odd exhibition opening, that sort of thing. I don't even know what Adamson or Stuart look like. I've met Mike Brent a few times, of course.'

'So far I've come across the odd mention of Stuart and Adamson on tape. Is there much more? I feel like I'm prying into Barbara's – and *your* – private life like some kind of voyeur without learning anything.'

'She talked about them several times. You've got all the tapes, presumably. You'll find out what she thought about them. It might give you an idea … an insight … some sort of feeling for their relationships.'

'I don't know if this will really get me anywhere, Neil. I feel uncomfortable sticking my nose in like this. You may agree to what I'm doing, but I don't think Barbara would've been happy about it.'

Neil paused, staring at Marnie. 'If it helps in the slightest way to find who killed her, she'd approve. Take my word for it. I knew her better than anyone in recent years. Surely you can tell that from the tapes.'

• • • • •

Marnie felt she had wasted her time. She was no wiser than when she had arrived. All she had was more questions, more doubts. Why had Charles left the message that he was going to be out today without saying where he was going? Didn't he trust her? The whole business was unsatisfactory. She was being pushed into doing things without ever getting the full story. What did Neil imagine the tapes were going to reveal, apart from a load of intimate details that Marnie had no right – and no desire – to hear? She comforted herself with the thought that Charles was now assuming more direct responsibility and from now on he would be taking a leading role in the campaign. *As long as he leaves me out of it, that's fine,* Marnie muttered to herself.

At the entrance she reached into her pocket for the car keys. Pulling them carefully out of the tight jeans for fear of jolting her back, she looked up to find herself confronted by people wielding cameras and recording machines. At the centre of the hubbub, a few metres away was Charles Taverner. Their eyes met.

'Marnie!' He went towards her.

'What's all this?'

'I made my announcement. I've just given an interview for television.'

'You didn't mention that when we spoke.'

'Spur of the moment this morning. I just picked up the phone, rang the newsdesk at the BBC and said I was coming here today to tell Neil Gerard that I was supporting his campaign.'

'That seems to have got them jumping. Shouldn't you get back to the paparazzi? Your public awaits you.'

'They've finished now.'

Marnie saw that most of the journalists and photographers were moving away. One or two lingered, casually observing the conversation, then they too went off.

'So what happens next, Charles?'

'To tell you the truth, I'm not really sure. Neil thinks I should write to the Home Secretary and protest my belief in his innocence.'

'What about your buddy, Chief Inspector Bruere? Are you going to contact him?'

'I think I should probably concentrate on the higher authorities ... politicians, the judiciary.'

'Charles, I don't want to be a kill-joy, but the *higher authorities* are going to want to know what evidence you have to prove Neil's innocence. Do you have any evidence ... other than a gut feeling?'

'You have to start somewhere, Marnie. Perhaps you'll be able to turn up something from your enquiries.'

'But –'

'I have to take a stand, Marnie, do what I believe to be right. And I don't care if it does sound melodramatic. More than anything I want the real killer to be found, caught and put away forever. I'm engaging the best criminal lawyer I know to try to get the case re-opened.'

They both realised Charles was gripping Marnie by the arms. Marnie turned to see if any journalists were still around, but they had vanished, no doubt rushing off to e-mail their stories back to base. Charles released his grip.

'Sorry. This is a very strange situation, Marnie. I've never had an experience to prepare me for what I'm doing at this moment. But I do believe what I said with total conviction.'

'Okay. For what it's worth, I agree with you.'

'And you'll go on helping me?'

She sighed. 'If I can. I told Neil a while ago that I'd do what I could. It's just that ...'

'What, Marnie? Are you afraid you might be in danger?'

'No. I'm afraid I haven't got a clue what to do. Our best bet is if you can have the case re-examined. But something tells me the police aren't going to be overjoyed at having their crime statistics damaged, or having Neil's conviction declared unsafe. I don't think they're going to be on your side.'

'On *our* side, Marnie.'

'Right.'

• • • • •

After enduring lectures from Ralph and Anne, Marnie explained about her meeting with Charles. With much tut-tutting of disapproval at Marnie's 'escape', they sat down in the saloon on *Thyrsis* to watch the early evening news. The lead story was a government reshuffle and bitter recriminations from ousted cabinet members. Charles's declaration made the number two spot.

He spoke thoughtfully and confidently in front of the camera. His points were simple and clear. The evidence was largely circumstantial; the identification of the killer was made on a dimly-lit towpath by a neighbour who *expected* the man returning to be Gerard; interference with the gas system was not the weapon for a crime of passion; the lack of a strong alibi was not in itself proof of guilt. Moreover, Charles had taken the trouble to get to know Gerard and his sister over recent months. It would have been easy for Sarah to back up her brother's story. Charles was convinced they were both telling the truth. He was convinced Gerard tried to kill himself when he lost all hope of a retrial or an appeal. He urged the authorities to re-examine the case.

A junior minister from the Home Office stated that the authorities had already conducted a comprehensive review of the proceedings and had found that the investigation and trial had been carried out thoroughly. It remained the government's view that the conviction was safe.

The BBC's legal correspondent pointed out that Charles Taverner had an influential circle of acquaintances and friends and it was likely that he would be taking counsel's opinion, if he had not done so already. Standing outside the Old Bailey, the Central Criminal Court in London, the correspondent had ended his report with the speculation that this issue was not simply going to fade away.

40

On Wednesday morning Anne was up at the village shop by the time the two newspaper boys were filling their panniers for delivery. She bought a copy of every paper, dumped them on the front seat of the Mini and sped back to Glebe Farm.

Charles made the front page, in varying sizes of article, in each paper. The story of a victim's husband coming to the aid of her convicted killer was irresistible. He almost made the leading item in two of the tabloids but he had chosen to speak out on the same day as a pop singer chose to reveal she had had silicon implants. Editors have their priorities. All except the heavyweight broadsheets ran a series of photos, including shots of Barbara, *Perfidia* in Little Venice, Charles making his announcement outside the prison and the well-known image of a bewildered Neil being led into court. Predictably, the tabloids resurrected the headline, *The Odd Couple*.

Opinions were divided on whether a re-opening of the case was likely. One tabloid vowed it would mount a campaign to secure a retrial and invited its readers to write in if they had any evidence that might prove to be relevant. Marnie voiced the opinion that this would result in thousands of letters. Most of them would come from misguided cranks, an enormous amount of work for the paper's staff and a waste of time. Ralph commented that that was not the point.

'Then what is the point, Ralph?'

'To sell newspapers.'

'Silly me.'

Scouring every batch of photos, Anne made an exclamation from the inside pages of the *Express*. She held it up. There was a shot of Charles and Marnie outside the prison. It was a long-distance picture, the two of them in profile, and it looked as if Charles was either reaching out towards Marnie or had just released her from his grip.

'That's me all right. Charles was trying to convince me of his sincerity. Do you think I'm recognisable?'

Ralph peered more closely at the photo. 'It depends how hard anyone is looking at you.'

Or *for* you, he thought.

• • • • •

For all of Wednesday Marnie was grounded. Ralph had to return to Oxford for meetings and he made Marnie promise to stay at home and rest. She protested that her back was now fine, but agreed nonetheless to his demand. Anne announced that she would be working from Glebe Farm that day and was posted as watchdog. She would be at her desk in the office to ensure that Marnie was sensible.

On his journey to Oxford Ralph should have been focused on the setting up of the International Working Group on the Global Economic Situation. It was to be based at All Saints College with Ralph as chairman, and in the shower that morning he had dreamt up an acronym for it, I-GES. He was sure it would appeal to his American colleagues. Many of them frequently began their sentences with *I guess* … He had felt quite pleased with it. Given the amount of speculation involved in any forecasting, it had a subtle irony. But now, trundling down the A43, his thoughts were entirely on

Marnie. As usual, he conducted an interrogation of himself to sort out the issue.

Did Charles's decision to give public support to Gerard's campaign have tangible consequences for Marnie? Answer: probably. No, definitely. It made any action by Marnie of potential interest to the actual killer.

How had circumstances changed? Before, Marnie might have been casually coming into contact with the suspects, if they were suspects. Now, the killer would be on his – or her – guard. If he – or she – suspected that Marnie had an alternative agenda … Ralph did not like to contemplate the risks.

Did that put Marnie in direct danger? Answer: possibly. Why not definitely? Because the killer might not make the connection between Charles and Marnie. How many people knew that Marnie was working on projects for Charles? How many people knew that Marnie and Barbara had had meetings and were becoming friendly? How many people knew that Marnie had been visiting Neil Gerard in prison?

Ralph gave his full attention to negotiating the big roundabout over the motorway and slotting into the heavy but fast-moving traffic on the approach road to Oxford. By the time he was able to steer his thoughts back to Marnie, he had the situation in perspective. Everything depended on whether Marnie could preserve her anonymity.

Was she in immediate danger? Perhaps not.

Was she likely to do anything that might place her in jeopardy? On past performance … yes. Ralph was sure that if he pointed out the dangers of the situation, Marnie would just laugh.

Was there any way she might become identified with Charles and his campaign? Tricky. Too many variables to judge. But one thought would not go away. There she was in the paper. Admittedly it was probably just an opportunistic long-range shot with a telephoto lens. It was grainier than the other images, but this time she was more recognisable than the earlier pictures in the other prison's car park that had only shown part of her profile.

Ralph turned off the by-pass and headed towards the city centre through tree-lined suburbs. Before devoting all his efforts to the one-way system, he was comforted by the fact that Marnie's name did not appear in any of the articles or captions. The only person mentioned was Sarah Cowan. As far as she was concerned, the more people who knew of her intentions, the better. Her name was no secret.

• • • • •

The truth was that Marnie, for all her protests, was glad to sit in the office and get on with some routine work. The back was still tender, every now and then giving her a reminder that all was not well. She smiled to herself when she saw the carafe of water topped by its inverted glass – a Victorian night-stand set found in the antique centre overlooking the canal at Weedon – and the box of painkillers beside it. Anne's attention to detail. Going through her files and phone messages, Marnie tried to work out how she had given herself the injury in the first place. Was it the exertion of working the locks on the way up from Leighton Buzzard? Or was it the exertions in bed with Ralph the night they arrived back? It was probably a combination of both, one coming on top of the other, so to speak. That thought made her smile again.

'Glad to see you're on the mend.'

Marnie looked up. Anne was standing by the desk grinning down at her.

'On the mend?'

'You've been sitting there smiling for the past ten minutes. Must be a good sign. You've had a droopy mouth whenever you thought I wasn't looking your way up till now. What were you thinking of?'

'Oh, you know ... just odd things.'

'Mm ... I did wonder.' Another grin. 'Well, don't have a relapse, but here's the post. I've slit the envelopes, but I thought you might like some gentle exercise, so you can take the letters out.'

She put the pile of correspondence on the desk and went to switch on the kettle. Marnie's spirits rose with the first item. It contained a cheque from Willards. In their early days that company had been the lifeblood of Walker & Co, but now, with a bigger portfolio of clients, it was just one contributor to their prosperity. Two or three bills were followed by a more substantial envelope, thick vellum with an embossed coat of arms on the flap. Marnie pulled out a card, the invitation to the opening of the new finance building. She read:

Mr Clive Adamson

Chairman and Group Chief Executive
and the Directors and Management of the Findhorn Banking Group
have pleasure in inviting
Ms Marnie Walker Dip AD, MA, FRSA
to the opening of the Spice Quay Finance and Trading Centre

It looked impressive. The whole text was printed as if written by a calligrapher, including Marnie's name. And someone else had an eye for detail; they had taken the trouble to check her qualifications. Here was no dotted line on which a minion had scrawled the name in ball-point pen.

She quickly slipped the card back into its envelope and dropped it into her bag. Anne knew that Clive Adamson was on Neil's list of ex-lovers and potential suspects. There was no point in causing her to worry.

'Anything interesting in the post?' Anne called from the kitchen area.

'A cheque ... no ... *two* cheques.'

'Hurray! We can eat this month.'

Anne brought coffee and sat beside Marnie while they went through the follow-up action from the day's post: cheques for banking, invoices to send, bills to pay, phonecalls to make, orders to confirm, clients to contact. A typical day in the life of a small but successful interior design company.

Anne happily gathered up the empty envelopes and took them away with her notepad. She would have a busy hour before getting back to college work. Freed from basic administration, Marnie was able to concentrate on her designs. She checked her own jobs-to-do list and remembered to write a postcard for the shop notice board to fill Charles's vacancy. *Gardener/handyman wanted for general duties – apply to Marnie Walker at Glebe Farm ...*

Across the office Anne was writing out a paying-in slip for the cheques that she would bank later in the day. She was happy as always with any task related to running

Walker & Co, but one cloud smudged her horizon. Her eyes strayed to the waste-paper bin beside the desk. Into it she had dropped the detritus from the morning's post, the unwanted leaflets, unsolicited junk mail and envelopes. She knew one item was missing and her thoughts returned again and again to the thick cream envelope with the coat of arms that had been included with Marnie's letters. She had double-checked the pile without making it obvious and now she was wondering what it could have contained that Marnie did not want her to see.

• • • • •

Marnie waited until Anne went back to *Sally Ann* to make sandwiches for lunch. She pulled the card out of her bag and pressed buttons on the phone.

'Judith Gross, good morning.'

'Good morning. Is that the chairman's secretary?'

'It is. Head of secretariat.'

'My name is Marnie Walker. I'm replying to –'

'Ah, yes, Ms Walker. I remember your name. You were one of our later additions.'

'That's why I'm ringing. As it's rather short notice for next Tuesday, I wonder if you'd mind me accepting the invitation by phone rather than in writing.'

'Of course. I'll put you on the acceptances list.'

'Do you need me to confirm that by fax?'

'That won't be necessary. Is there anything else I can do for you?'

'I was just wondering about directions to Spice Quay.'

'All those details are on the reverse of the invitation. We have our own car park in the building. Would you like me to reserve you a space?'

A pause. 'I haven't decided how I'm travelling yet, but a provisional space would be helpful.'

'That's no problem, Ms Walker. I'll allocate you space number … let me see … one forty-one, that's the first floor level. Perhaps you could let me know eventually if you don't require it.'

Marnie felt a fool. In her haste to conceal the invitation she had not thought to check the reverse of the card. That efficient woman – head of secretariat, no less – would think her incompetent. Marnie's attempts to prove her wrong were to have dire consequences.

• • • • •

The treatment had worked. Marnie had to admit to herself that Ralph had been right. In the shower that night she let the hot jets play down her back. She rocked forwards and backwards inside the cubicle, hands on hips, and tilted her torso from side to side. No pain, not so much as a twinge. Blessed relief.

She had already told Ralph about the invitation and listened to his misgivings about getting further involved in the Gerard affair. She gave him the reply she had prepared in advance. It was just a function, loads of people would be there. It was a good opportunity to get a glimpse of Clive Adamson and Piers Wainwright, and Charles could obviously not be there. She would be nothing more than a pair of eyes. There was no possibility of danger, and in any case she would be with Philip. Good, solid, reliable Philip.

For once, Ralph was not sitting in bed reading his notes. He was standing by the porthole looking out at the canal. He turned and kissed Marnie lightly when she came into the sleeping cabin.

'I'd offer you a penny for your thoughts, Ralph, but you might give me a lecture on the exchange rate mechanism.'

He laughed. 'Dangerous beasts, economists. How's your back?'

'Talking of dangerous beasts?' She grinned. 'It's good.'

Ralph made a face. 'So not just working the locks, then.'

'Suffice it to say that I'm wearing a nightdress tonight,' she said primly, underlining the point by removing her bathrobe and draping it at the end of the bed.

Ralph climbed across to his side under the opposite porthole and held the duvet back for Marnie to get in.

'How was *your* day? How did the inaugural meeting of I-GES go?'

Another face. 'They didn't like the acronym. I was overruled.'

'But you're the *chairman*,' Marnie protested. 'Couldn't you impose your will on the rest of them?'

'It's meant to be a democratic body and … well, they did have a point.'

'Which was?'

'They thought American colleagues wouldn't appreciate the subtle irony – not their kind of thing, subtle irony …'

'Really? So what did you go for?'

Ralph cleared his throat. 'Oxford Research and Analysis, the Global Economy.'

'Catchy little title. Trips nicely off the tongue. You're not serious, are you?'

Ralph nodded. 'Bit dull, isn't it?'

'I think your idea was much better. It had a more … hi-tech ring to it.'

'Thank you, darling. Your loyalty is most commendable.'

'Don't mention it. But why Oxford Research and … whatever?'

'It gives the acronym, ORAGE.'

'That is good? In what way is it better than your idea?'

'It's French for a storm.'

'I know what *orage* means.'

'They thought it sounded more dynamic.'

'And I bet you spent half the day discussing the title and acronym. Am I right?'

'Of course. What are committees for? Though, actually, I did have time to follow up your question in the lunch break.'

Marnie looked puzzled. 'I had a question about the global economy?'

'You had a question about Charles Taverner … his background.'

'Yes! And?'

'Rodney Forbes was there today. He's got a personal chair at Manchester, but he was at Cambridge at the same time as Charles Taverner. Same college, same rugby fifteen.'

'Great!'

'It appears Charles was on some kind of army scholarship. And on graduation he took a short-term commission. It was part of the arrangement.'

Marnie looked thoughtful. 'Interesting ... though I'm not really sure why.'

'Actually, Marnie, that isn't the most interesting part.'

'There's more?'

'Mm ... Rodney's pretty sure Charles was on the staff of a General ... something to do with logistics or communications or something like that.'

'I'm not sure I follow.'

'As far as Rodney recalls, the General, and consequently Charles, were in the Royal Engineers.'

41

Anne gave Marnie an old-fashioned look when she took her breakfast in bed the next morning. Marnie grimaced, struggling to lever herself upright.

'I don't know why you're looking at me like that,' she said through gritted teeth.

'I'm not saying a word.'

'But?'

'But when Ralph announced that your back was dodgy again, it did occur to me that you might have … exerted yourself unwisely a little too much?'

Anne packed pillows behind Marnie's back. Marnie swept a hand in a gesture that encompassed the whole cabin.

'Look around you, Anne. Do you see chains hanging on the walls? … whips lying about? … discarded fishnet tights? – Ralph's, of course.'

Anne laughed. 'Well, whatever the cause, Ralph and I have taken an executive decision.'

'I know. You don't have to tell me. I've got to stay here and rest.'

'We're sending for the doctor.' The tone brooked no argument.

'Nonsense!'

'You could have a slipped disc or something, Marnie. You need proper medical attention.'

'But –'

'It's been decided. Ralph's phoning the surgery first thing. Eat your breakfast and afterwards I'll fetch you a bowl and some water so you can brush your teeth.'

'Yes, matron.'

'And a flannel to wash your face.'

'Yes, matron. Any chance Ralph might pop back to give me a bed bath?'

Death stare. Exit of matron.

• • • • •

A visit by the doctor was promised for that afternoon. In the meantime Marnie would stay in bed, Ralph would work in his study close at hand and Anne would man the office. As far as the outside world was concerned it was business as usual at Walker & Co.

Mid-morning, Anne arrived on *Thyrsis* to make coffee. She brought with her the post and some routine letters for Marnie to sign.

'I've slit them open for you, all except one that's marked *personal*.'

'Oh? What could that be?'

'It's postmarked Watford. There's not much inside.'

'Oh, it's probably from that new Willards restaurant. I suppose it might be a note of appreciation for the decor from the manager. She seemed very pleased when we spoke on the phone the other day.'

'I thought it might be from British Waterways,' Anne muttered. Her attention was now focused on checking through the rest of the correspondence as she added vaguely, 'They're in Watford.'

Marnie ran her thumbnail under the flap. 'Only one way to find out.'

Sitting at the foot of the bed, Anne was collecting into a pile the letters that required answers when she realised that Marnie's silence had lasted more than the few seconds needed to scan the contents of the Watford envelope. Looking up, she was surprised to see the colour had drained from Marnie's face.

'What's up?' No reply. 'Marnie, what is it?'

She reached forward to touch Marnie's arm but withdrew quickly when Marnie winced with pain.

'Sorry, but what's the matter? Is it that letter?'

'It's nothing,' Marnie croaked.

Marnie went to put the note back in the envelope but she fumbled and it slipped to the floor. She tried to catch it and winced again. Anne was on it the moment it touched the carpet. Picking up the message she found it was a piece of lined paper torn roughly from a pad. Even if it had not fallen face up, she was determined to read it. The words stared up at her from the page.

KEEP OUT OF THE NEIL GERARD CAMPAIGN
MIND YOUR OWN BUSINESS
I KNOW WHERE YOU LIVE
• • • • •

Marnie told Anne it was just like going to the dentist with toothache. The minute you arrive there, the toothache disappears. So it was with the visit by the doctor. Soon after lunch Marnie needed to visit the bathroom. Not wanting to disturb Ralph or drag Anne through the spinney, she slipped her legs out from under the duvet and planted her feet tentatively on the floor. There was a niggle in the small of her back but not a full-blown pain. She managed to walk slowly along the passageway and make her visit with neither undue discomfort nor mishap. Feeling proud of herself, and not a little relieved at her improvement, she called to Ralph and suggested he cancel the doctor. A block of ice would have been more receptive to the idea.

Sooner than they expected the doctor came to Glebe Farm and seemed amused to be calling on a patient in a narrowboat. He examined Marnie's back while she lay face-down on the bed. Next he asked her to perform some movements. He delivered his verdict concisely and rapidly.

'Probably just back strain, not severe enough to be a slipped disc. Physiotherapy would help and that can be arranged at the medical centre. You'll need to ring the surgery for an appointment. In the meantime, rest the back as much as possible, no heavy lifting or undue exertion.'

He left as quickly as he had come.

Anne emerged from the study to escort him through the spinney while Ralph came in for an update. He listened to Marnie's account before commenting.

'Well, that should help. Physiotherapy usually works wonders. One of my postgrad students at All Saints plays rugby for the university. They have their own physio who travels with them on tours. Just a young woman, manipulating all those brawny blokes. Amazing. But she certainly keeps them in shape.'

'I wonder how much she had to pay to get the job.' Marnie smiled.

'You're feeling better, obviously.'

'Scarcely any pain at all now. I'm not sure I even need the physio.'

'But you're going to take it,' Ralph insisted. 'And you're going to get as much rest as possible. I'll do the shopping this afternoon on my way back from …' He looked thoughtful.

'What?'

'Nothing … just something I remembered.'

* * * * *

Marnie decided she should stay in bed more often. She spent most of the afternoon going through all her projects and was amazed at how much she achieved simply by being away from the phone.

When Anne took her tea she brought the box of tapes at Marnie's request and set them down by the bed. She left the walkman on the shelf within easy reach.

42

Marnie was anxious to know more about Adamson and Wainwright before the Spice Quay opening the following week. She looked through the tapes and wondered if she should take up Ralph's idea of starting again with the most recent ones. But she felt unhappy to disturb the flow of the narrative and flipped open the next cassette in the series. Slotting it into Anne's walkman, Marnie was surprised to find herself looking forward to being in Barbara's company again, however bizarre the circumstances. It was as if Barbara was back in touch after being away on a trip.

'Hallo, Barbara,' she whispered. 'I miss you. What are you going to tell me today?'

Marnie was startled and she felt her face tingle when Barbara seemed to answer her directly.

Darling, you know what I'm going to say

There's no need to be upset

They were lovely flowers but you know why I couldn't take them

No, I told you I couldn't say I'd bought them for myself

Not a bouquet like that

Charles would know they were too exquisite, too romantic

The sort of flowers only a man would buy for a woman

And I'm sorry about the holiday idea

Of course I'd love to go away with you, but it's just out of the question

Charles would think it entirely out of character

I'm not the sort of person who goes on holiday by herself

Even for a weekend, you said

Especially for a weekend

Charles would think it very suspicious after I've chided him so often for going away and leaving me in London

In the end, Charles offered to take me on some of his business trips

Bad idea … a disaster

It was so boring

Now I know why all these big business types get so much money

It's compensation for the dull lives they lead

They had a board meeting all morning

I asked Charles what they'd talked about – bored meeting, I called it

I had room service for breakfast and lounged by the pool with magazines till lunchtime

They played golf all afternoon – I went for a walk – I saw them playing in the distance

Never could see the attraction of trying to knock a ball down a hole

Can you understand why they do it?

The high point of the day was supposed to be dinner

I got stuck next to some boring old fart from central purchasing

What do these people talk about with their wives?

What do their wives see in them?

The short answer is of course ... money

Couldn't be anything else

The last time I went with Charles it was for what he called a 'working weekend'

That just means two whole days of it instead of one

That's when I met Clive Adamson

He latched onto me immediately

He had loads of charm, seemed sharper than the others, more lively, more interesting

He seemed genuinely interested in what I had to say

So I yakked on because he actually paid me some attention

Of course I knew why he was so attentive

There's usually only one reason why men listen to a woman

Sorry, darling, you being the exception

But frankly I was past caring

He seemed at least to have some notion of life outside the latest performance figures

In fact I don't think I can remember anything on which he didn't have some knowledge

He was the one who introduced me to boating

He had this cruiser – just short of being a gin palace – that he kept on the Thames near Shepperton

He invited me to go for a trip one day

I said do you mean Charles and me?

What do you think? he said

He'd left Charles's firm by then

So it meant we could go on the boat when Charles was at his next 'bored' meeting

That first time we just cruised up and down the river

The boat was a powerful thing – twin engines, big diesels

He opened it up for me just to see the acceleration

I nearly ended up on the deck

The weather was beautiful

We stopped at a restaurant for lunch

Clive was being careful not to blow it

I didn't give him any signals and he was canny enough not to push things

I liked that

So few men know how to behave – you being the exception again, darling

I don't know why I'm going on about Clive Adamson

Except I didn't feel like talking about other people today

Not when I was with you

You seemed disappointed about me not taking the flowers

And about not going away for a trip together

I thought it would be a bad idea to start going on about ... you know

Anyway, we made up for it later, didn't we?

I'm glad you were cheered up in the end

I suppose that's why I'm rambling like this now

You know Adamson and I had a fling

Charles never knew

It lasted about two years, I suppose

Of course, we didn't see each other very often

He had a business to run … big business – very big business

Always wheeling and dealing in the City

But I can't pretend it wasn't fun while it lasted

Sometimes we went on the boat, sometimes for trips out in his car

He always had beautiful cars … Mercedes, Bentleys, Jaguars

That's one of the reasons I persuaded Charles to get the Jag

Sorry, darling, Jaguar

I know you don't like me to call it a Jag

Essex girls call them that, you said [she laughed]

Do you know what Essex girl dabs behind her ears when she's out for a good time?

[shriek of laughter] *Her ankles!*

Oh dear, I expect you'll tell me off for that

Never mind, darling, I'll make it up to you

Where was I?

Oh yes, the Jaguar

Clive's was a sort of metallic champagne, I think he said it was

Charles would never have a car that colour

Too flashy for him – but I liked it

And that's how I met Piers

Clive wanted to take me to an exhibition, an outing in his latest car

I said no at first – didn't want to risk being seen out with him in public

Clive said none of Charles's cronies would ever go to an art gallery

Anyway it was a private view, just art world people

Clive liked that sort of thing – lots of interests, as I said

So I thought what the hell – anything to get out and do something

It turned out to be a one-man show

It was great – Piers had done these huge canvases

Some were abstracts – loads of complex shapes and colours

The New Psychedelia, he called them

And some were scenes of the river – to Londoners that only means the Thames

That's what had attracted Clive

Piers said the river wasn't London's artery, it was London's soul

They had an argument about whether a soul could be made of dirty water

Piers insisted the soul was always made of dirty water

He said it wasn't transparent at all – because of all the impurities that go through it

He said that's why people always prayed for their souls to be purified

Personally I think they'd both had one glass of bubbly too many

But it was fun, yes, I was with a businessman and it was fun

Amazing

I suddenly realised I was enjoying myself for the first time in ages

I was on the periphery of their conversation but at the same time in the centre

I knew they both fancied me like mad

I could feel it in the air

It was stupid, I know, but it was a marvellous change

Virtually all Charles's other colleagues were as boring as pigswill

And before you start getting any ideas there was never any … overlap

I'd finished with Clive long before – well some time before – I took up with Piers

Or perhaps it was Clive who finished with me

I never did know why … he just became more and more difficult to see

He protested it was too much work

He'd taken over some big outfit that was struggling

It had world class potential, he said

He sold off some parts to pay for restructuring and that was the last I knew

I got most of my news about him from Charles who was a tiny bit jealous, I think

Jealous of Clive's business success, I mean

He said he got control of the bank with hardly any effort or opposition

People thought it was a lame duck, but Clive saw the potential

He brought in some whiz-kids, threw out the old guard – bingo!

Millions – what he'd always dreamed of

I was seeing Piers by then, so I heard about him from that side as well

Piers was made, became the fashionable artist almost overnight

Everyone was talking about him

And it was all down to Clive

Clive commissioned paintings, sculptures

He'd seen the potential in Piers, too

Piers said there were countless talented artists

The art schools churned them out by the hundred every year

But it's getting someone who recognises your talent that really counts

The best customers are the rich ones

Piers said that, but it could just as easily have been Clive

With Piers's works on display, Clive made the bank look impressive and successful

Every visitor to HQ saw these vast works of art

It was like having Michelangelo to work for you

That was how Piers described it … modesty was not one of his virtues

And for a bank, the thousands they paid Piers were just loose change

And tax-deductible

Piers resented that … being classed as a business expense

He hated the idea of being 'tax efficient', part of Clive's marketing strategy
But he loved the exposure and the extra commissions it brought him
So that's how he became the most fashionable artist in London
He gave me one of his smaller river paintings … knew I loved boats and the water
And he did a portrait of me
He never paints portraits, but he made an exception in my case
Charles was delighted, never suspected there was anything between us
He was too busy with his own business concerns, of course
And I was always there when he was around
I think he thought I was always there when he was at work
He thought I was always out shopping … doing lunch with my girlfriends
His type of man thinks that's what women do
I said perhaps when he was out, he was doing lunch with his girlfriends
He didn't like that
I saw straight away he was upset that I should even joke about that sort of thing
I backed off … never said anything like that again
He's too good to upset
Perhaps it's one of his insecurities
I'm sure all men have them
Clive and Piers had their egos … fragile sometimes
They worry about how they perform … in some key departments
Not just in their professional lives
You don't have any misgivings like that, no hang-ups about inadequacies
And you shouldn't have, my darling

• • • • •

The tape ended abruptly. Marnie opened the walkman to see if it had snapped or jammed, but it was still intact. She wound it back and ran the last sentences again with the same result.

She rewound to the beginning and listened to the whole tape again. It was obvious that Neil was trying to extend their affair. Flowers … a holiday together … or at least a weekend away. Marnie was well aware that men tended to become possessive the longer a relationship lasted. Neil needed a reminder that this was not an available option. Perhaps that was why Barbara had spoken at length about Adamson and Wainwright. She seemed to find it easier to talk about them on tape rather than in person.

Adamson. He had dumped Barbara, not the other way round. She displayed no particular distress or bitterness. *Don't be stupid*, Marnie thought. Barbara was hardly going to pour her heart out to a lover about the loss of someone else. But it must have upset her – or at least bothered her – at the time. Why had he abandoned her? If she knew, she was not saying. But she did not know; Marnie was sure of that. Her tone made that clear.

Wainwright. Enough detail there to form an impression. Barbara moved in lively circles, luxury cars, swish receptions, artists, moneymen, the fast lane. Marnie would see that side of life herself at the Findhorn opening. She wondered about running another tape, but listening so intensely was tiring.

She raised the lid of the walkman and ejected the tape, absentmindedly fingering the machine. Odd that Barbara had broken off so abruptly. Had something happened? Had Charles suddenly come home unexpectedly and interrupted her? Were the memories so strong that she could not continue? Odd. The tape began and ended with the same word … *darling*. Marnie shrugged. It was a term of close endearment, but it was … what did Ralph call it? … *debased coinage* … devalued with overuse. People used it carelessly all the time … taxi drivers, market traders, especially people like – no. Barbara never used it, at least not in Marnie's hearing. With her it was always, *my dear* or even, *my dears*.

Outside was the sound of footsteps on cobbles, someone walking near *Sally Ann*. Marnie looked at her watch. Almost five-thirty. Minutes later *Thyrsis* swayed slightly and Ralph breezed into the cabin. He looked pleased with himself.

'You look pleased with yourself.'

He kissed Marnie and sat cautiously on the bed, reaching into his pocket. 'I am … very.'

'One trip to Waitrose and you're the new Mrs Beeton,' Marnie sighed languidly.

'That was routine. This …' He produced an envelope. '… is inspiration.'

She knew it would be good.

'This had better be good. Show me.'

He handed over the envelope and sat back. Marnie's initial reaction was a slight feeling of tension. The last time she had opened a good quality envelope with a coat of arms on the flap it had given her a jolt.

'Oh … it's like a book token … or a gift voucher.'

'That's what it is. On the way back from town there's this new place just opened … Roselawn Country Retreat and Health Club. The voucher is for a full day of self-indulgence and relaxation. You can have a sauna, steam bath, jacuzzi, aromatherapy and a whole load of things I've never heard of. They've got a pool, a gym – out of bounds to you at the moment – a jogging trail … everything, really. And if you like it, I'm going to give you a year's membership for your birthday.'

Marnie imagined herself being cosseted for a day, covered in essential oils, pampered from head to foot, relaxing by the pool wrapped in a fluffy white dressing gown,. She saw the whole thing in her mind in soft focus and was fantasising about Gianfranco the club's masseur when she remembered her benefactor.

'Come here so I can show my gratitude. Then I'm going to ring for an *immediate* appointment.'

43

The decor of Roselawn Country Retreat was a fanciful version of Greco-Roman, with handmade tiles of terra cotta, statues and amphorae evoking the classical age. There was a smell of fragrant massage oils in the air. To a designer it felt just this side of OTT, and from the moment she entered the classical portals to receive her fluffy white dressing gown, Marnie loved it.

Her personal trainer for the day was a young woman called Toni with honey blond hair and a Pepsodent smile, who looked as if she had just popped in from winning the Women's Singles title at Wimbledon. She asked Marnie a series of health and fitness questions, checked her height and weight – *ooh, you're spot-on!* – and worked out a programme taking Marnie's back problem into account. Marnie floated from the steam room to the swimming pool where she gingerly – and successfully – attempted a length or two of breast stroke. Her strong point that day was relaxation, and she buckled down to give it everything she had.

At lunchtime she found herself by the pool in the company of several women of about her own age who had evidently come as a group. They sprawled on recliners, drinking herbal tea. Like some of the others, Marnie picked up a newspaper and skimmed through it while partly joining in the conversation. The day was proving to be a brilliant success until Marnie turned a page to see her own face staring out at her. She jumped so hard that her teacup tipped over in its saucer, splashing the hot liquid over her white gown. Amid consternation in the group, a member of the staff arrived in seconds, whisked the paper out of Marnie's hands, dropped it on the floor and led her away. With Marnie apologising for her clumsiness, and the trainer asking if she had been hurt, they went into the locker room.

Within two minutes Marnie was back in the group with an even whiter dressing gown and a fresh cup of camomile tea. But those were not the only changes. Her return was greeted in tones of only muted concern. She sat down surrounded by an awkward silence. Then she remembered the newspaper.

A brave face and an embarrassed smile. 'Sorry about that … a sudden twinge in the back, I think.'

Murmurings of agreement and sympathy. Not very convincing. Marnie wondered how long she could stay before leaving without further embarrassment. Inside, she was cursing, deeply disappointed that her wonderful day of pampering should be ruined, that even here she should be pursued by the Gerard affair. She was taking a sip of tea when one of the women spoke.

'Was that you … the photo in the paper?'

Their eyes met. Marnie nodded.

The woman continued tentatively. 'It says you're involved with Charles Taverner, helping Neil Gerard get an appeal. Is that right?'

'Yes,' Marnie breathed her reply. She set aside the cup and began swinging her legs off the recliner. A twinge slowed her down. 'I'm sorry if I've spoiled your day. I'll go and –'

'Do you believe he's innocent?' It was a different woman.

'Look, it's a complicated business and I'm not sure I should –'

'But do you?'

A pause. Marnie looked at their faces. 'I do actually, yes.'

'Well, I've never thought he did it.'

More murmurings, this time sympathetic.

Marnie, incredulous. 'Really?'

A third joined in. 'I read all about the trial and I certainly didn't believe it.'

Marnie was amazed to hear herself say, 'But it was conducted strictly according to the law, and all the correct procedures were followed.'

'Then why are you supporting him?' The first woman again.

'There are … factors … things I can't talk about.'

'Evidence?'

Marnie frowned. It was a good question. What hard evidence did they have? 'All I can say is … we're working on it.' More amazement from Marnie at what she was saying. Who did she think she was … Sherlock Holmes?

'Are you a private detective?' A fourth woman, wide-eyed and impressionable.

'No … just a kind of friend of Barbara's husband.'

'That's what they're hinting in the paper.'

Marnie's cheeks reddened. 'No! Nothing like that. Barbara and Charles were clients of mine.'

'So you and Charles are not –'

'Definitely not.'

One of the others said, 'The papers always try to get that sort of angle.'

Marnie was keen to steer the conversation away from that angle. 'So why do you all believe Neil's innocent?'

The first woman answered for the group. 'I know we don't have the evidence and we don't know all the ins and outs of the case, but he's just not the type. He strikes me as somehow too sensitive, too gentle to have hurt her, let alone kill her.'

'That doesn't make for a strong defence case,' Marnie said.

'Okay, but you have to rely on your own judgment. There's something about Neil Gerard … he just seems a decent kinda guy. *And* he tried to kill himself that time.'

'You don't think it could have been out of a sense of guilt?' Marnie as devil's advocate again.

Much shaking of heads.

'Despair,' said the first woman.

'Do you all feel the same way?'

A woman who until then had said nothing summed up their feelings. 'We all know it's the quiet ones who can be the most unpredictable, but Gerard comes over as sincere. I could go for a man like that. You're going to find you've got more popular support for his case than maybe you imagine. Good luck with your campaign.'

'Thank you.'

The impressionable woman spoke. 'So who did it?'

The one who had summed up chided her. 'You can't expect her to answer that.'

'But it's a good question,' said Marnie.

'And no doubt – even though you can't say – you have a good answer.' The woman smiled. 'At least, I hope you have.'

· · · · ·

Anne stretched and yawned. She had spent three hours studying without a break apart from the odd interruption from the phone. That was the trouble with projects that were really interesting. She decided against coffee. An irritation behind the eyes warned of a headache coming. *Fresh air's what I need*, she thought. She switched on the answerphone and set out for the towpath.

Twenty minutes later she was back in the office barn. She listened to three phone messages, none of them urgent, and made a list for Marnie. The project folders on her desk beckoned, but she knew she should be disciplined and take an hour off. The walk had made her restless, and she was not yet ready for lunch. She wondered how Marnie was enjoying her day at Roselawn Country Retreat and pictured her at that moment probably lying beside the pool sipping something cool to the strains of soft music.

Anne climbed the loft ladder to her room, where the light seeping through the window slit was always dim. She switched on the lamps. The low wide bed stacked with pillows and cushions, the Oriental rugs, the table lamps, some of them covered with chiffon scarves to create pools of pale colour, everything combined to create a restful atmosphere that to her mind was magic. It always brought her a sense of peace and security, hidden away from the world.

Her restlessness began to seep away and she thought that Marnie could easily have come up to this room if she wanted to relax. For Anne, this was her country retreat. Soft music was needed. She settled on the bed and pressed the eject button on the cassette player. The tape was a collection of hits from the Seventies. No. Much as she enjoyed those old songs, Mink de Ville, Suzi Quatro and Kandidate were not likely to create a feeling of relaxed harmony in her life at that moment. Perhaps … something orchestral. But what? Her collection of classical music was limited. The 1812 Overture or the set of Beethoven Symphonies was not what she needed. Inspiration came to her. She had the rest of Barbara's cassettes in the box under the bed. Many of those were regular music tapes, and they were all classical.

Sorting through, she quickly found the perfect choice … *Karelia, Finlandia, the Swan of Tuonela* … Sibelius was just what she needed. She fed the tape into her machine, pressed the play button and lay back. In the subdued light she became conscious of the sound of her own breathing. She breathed in deeply and rhythmically and felt herself start to wind down. Surprising how loud your own breath sounds in a confined space, she thought. Her breath started to quicken despite her efforts.

The first doubts came when she realised the music had not started. Groping towards the cassette player, she ran a finger over the controls. The play button was definitely depressed.

'The machine isn't working,' Anne said quietly, exasperated.

'Yes,' came the reply.

The word hung in the air. The sound of breathing grew louder. Anne froze, her hand suspended between the bed and the machine.

'Yes … yes …' More breathing, quicker now. Sounds of groaning.

Anne lay there, mouth open, eyes open.

'Oh, my *God* ...'

•   •   •   •   •

Marnie had not felt so good in a long time. The day had been a great success and she knew exactly how she would be able to show Ralph how pleased she was. The final treatment had been an aromatherapy massage. True, it had not been given by a handsome Italian masseur. There was no Gianfranco, but the trim young woman with curly hair who provided the service revealed herself to be an expert in deep massage techniques and spent many minutes working on Marnie's lower back. Afterwards the whole area felt tender, but the aches and twinges had gone.

'You won't thank me tomorrow, Marnie. It'll probably ache for much of the day, but by Sunday morning you'll be blessing my name. Just take it easy till then and don't put undue strain on it for a few days. No locks, okay?'

She changed carefully into her outdoor clothes, grabbed her bag and checked her mobile as she made her way out to the car park. *You have one missed call. You have one message.* Sitting in the Discovery she played the message.

'Marnie, it's Charles. Can you ring me back when you get this. Better still, can you call round to the rectory? Something has come up. Thanks.'

She phoned to say she was on her way and started the engine. She suspected he did not want to discuss the curtains in the drawing room.

•   •   •   •   •

'The sun's over the yardarm. Fancy a snifter, Marnie?'

Marnie declined and accepted a tonic water. The healthy living ethos of Roselawn had not yet worn off. When they were settled in the conservatory, Charles came straight to the point.

'Sorry to tell you this, Marnie, but there's a photo of you in one of the papers. It's a clear one, no doubt about who it is. You're easily recognisable.'

'I know. I'm on page five ... probably too old to make page three now.' She smiled.

'You *know*? How do you know? Not the sort of paper you and Ralph would buy, surely?'

'Nor you,' Marnie countered.

'Oh, I get everything at the moment ... broadsheets, tabloids, the lot. I want to keep an eye on what's being reported.'

'I saw it just now at the health club. Is that what you wanted to talk to me about?'

'I wanted to warn you that you might get noticed, might get bothered by the media. I didn't want this to happen at all.'

'I doubt they'll track me down here, Charles.'

When they had finished their drinks, Charles escorted Marnie to the front door.

'Health club, did you say?'

'Roselawn Country Retreat. I think it's pretty new. Very lavish development altogether.'

'Don't suppose they have a golf course?'

'They do. Eighteen holes, I think, with a professional coach. I've probably got details about it somewhere. Would you like me to dig them out?'

'Thanks. You're not a player are you, Marnie?'

''Fraid not. I was having a day off, getting treatment for a back problem.'

'You have all my sympathy. I picked up a back injury doing my army training.'

'What regiment were you in?' Marnie kept her voice casual. It was meant to sound like a polite enquiry.

'Mainly Royal Engineers. Did a short commission after university … just a three year stint.'

'I didn't realise you had an engineering background.'

'Not really. I was attached to the staff of a General but it was just part of my overall training.'

'So you aren't an expert in technical matters.'

'In technical …' Charles spotted the implication at once. His expression saddened. 'No Marnie, I'm not … especially not in matters regarding gas systems.'

'I'm sorry, I didn't –'

Charles waved his hand. 'That's fine. You have every right to keep an open mind on all aspects of the case. And while we're being open and frank with each other … Marnie when are you going to tell me what you were doing at Bermuda Reach that Sunday morning when I found you there?'

'Possibly never.'

'But –'

'You're going to have to trust me, Charles.'

'The way you trusted me about my Royal Engineers background … which I never concealed from you?'

Marnie thought for several seconds. Charles waited without speaking for her reply.

'Charles, can we go back to the conservatory? This may take a few minutes.'

He nodded.

'And can I change my mind about that drink?'

• • • • •

Charles was a good listener. He sat nursing a tumbler of straight malt while Marnie gave him as much detail as she felt necessary about the tapes. From time to time he looked alarmed and seemed on the brink of interrupting, but he controlled himself throughout the narrative. Marnie tried to make the tapes seem like a series of monologues, a kind of diary, but he frowned at the idea and it was clear that he dismissed it. When she reached the end of the story Marnie took a long sip of her weak gin and tonic.

Charles spoke softly. 'I see why you tried to conceal the truth from me, Marnie. Thank you for that. And thank you for taking this on board. It can't be very pleasant for you.'

'Apart from the one tape that Ralph heard, I've taken a decision … no one else will ever listen to them … no one.'

Charles flashed her a look. 'You don't think –'

'No one, Charles … for their own good … and for the sake of Barbara's privacy.'

For a full minute neither spoke. Marnie finished her drink and set the glass down, ready to leave.

'There isn't a day when I don't think about Barbara,' Charles began quietly. 'For the first month after her death I wept bitter tears every day for her loss. I hated Neil Gerard with a deep loathing. I wanted to hit him … to kill him with my bare hands.'

'That's understandable, Charles.'

'Of course. But then I found my attitude changing. What if Sarah Cowan was right? What if it wasn't some kind of trick to get him off? That's why I so much wanted you to see him, Marnie. The opinion of another woman, an intelligent woman, would be invaluable to me.'

'I realised that.'

'I wanted to know what a woman might see in Gerard, whether you'd have insights into how Barbara might be attracted to him.' He shook his head despairingly. 'I wondered how I'd feel if I came across a letter from either of them, or a note of some kind. I never imagined for one moment that Barbara might have made tapes like that.'

'Did she ever do anything like it before?'

'Never … to my knowledge. But what do I know about her any more? What did I ever know?'

'You have all your other memories.' It sounded pathetic, but Marnie was desperate to comfort him.

'Mm … I suppose so. I don't know when I began to realise that I *had* to know who'd killed Barbara. It had to be *utterly* certain. And I realised that I did have doubts about Gerard. So did you, didn't you?'

'Not until you put doubts in my mind.'

'But you had an open mind, Marnie, and I knew I could trust you. It seems Gerard shared my opinion. He felt he could rely on you to be discreet and impartial.'

'I can't think why you both elevate me to this position … like some kind of oracle.'

Charles acted as if he had not heard her reply. 'I just want the truth. Ultimately that's all I'll be left with. At my age you start to ponder what it's all about.'

'Not just at your age, Charles. Anyway, it's not as if you're old. You're barely sixty.'

'But what do I have to look forward to? There isn't a morning when I don't wake up aware of the cold empty space in the bed beside me … a space that no one else will ever fill … could ever fill. All that part of my life has gone forever.'

'It's too soon to be saying that.' She saw him wallowing in self-pity and she wanted to pull him out of it. 'Your life will move on … once this is all behind you.'

'Marnie, I know I'm walking steadily towards a lonely old age. It's like sleep walking into a swamp, only it's a swamp out of which there's no returning. That's what it means to grow old … like an illness without a cure. The only way to cope is to have someone to share your life with.'

'I can understand you feeling –'

'Now, the only way I can cope is to know for certain that the person who robbed me of Barbara is found and put away for the whole of their life. It isn't easy to accept that Gerard might be innocent … not after hating him so much for all these months. But I can only hate him if I know he's guilty.'

'You don't hate him for having had an affair with Barbara?'

'It's hard to stomach, of course. But surprisingly I think I could cope with that. I knew she would always come back to me. Having heard the tapes could you believe that, Marnie?'

'I'm sure she would.'

'You really mean that?'

'Yes.' She answered a little too quickly and hoped she had not betrayed her feeling that Neil had become ever more important to Barbara.

When Charles showed Marnie to the door he hesitated before opening it.

'This has been a painful conversation, Marnie. You will let me know if you come across anything important?'

'Of course I will.'

'I'm glad you were so frank with me. What made you change your mind?'

'I expected they'd come out sooner or later, anyway. I wanted you to be forewarned.'

● ● ● ● ●

The effect of Roselawn had worn off by the time Marnie arrived back at Glebe Farm and it showed. Anne was in the office, working at her desk.

'Tough workout, Marnie? You look all in.'

Anne's voice was tense, but Marnie felt too shredded to notice.

'No, the health club was fine. I've just been to see Charles. I … told him about the tapes.'

'The tapes,' Anne repeated in a flat voice.

'He kind of pushed me into a corner and I ended up talking about them.'

'Do you feel like a drink?'

'Just had a G and T.'

'And you were *driving?*' Anne sounded surprised.

'The gin tiptoed through the glass on stilts.' Marnie noticed Anne's expression and found it difficult to read. 'Anne, I only had to drive down the field track. You know I don't –'

'It's not that, Marnie. I've got a confession to make, too.'

'What do you mean?'

'I … I listened to a tape … a Barbara tape … accidentally.'

Marnie looked stunned.

'*Accidentally?* How?'

Anne took a deep breath. 'It was in the box under my bed.'

'But those were just ordinary music tapes.'

'I know, that's what we thought.'

'Didn't it have a label?'

'On the box it just said Sibelius … it had a Decca label or CBS … something like that.'

'On the tape itself?'

'No. It was dim … I didn't see any writing on the cassette … just stuck it in the player.'

'So you heard Barbara talking to Neil … her pillow talk?'

Anne shook her head. 'No.'

'Then how did you know it was her?'

'There wasn't much talking of any kind …but it was her all right … or rather *them* …'

Marnie frowned. 'You mean … they were …?'

'Yes.'

Marnie looked incredulous. 'She actually recorded them … *together?*'

'Uh-huh.'

'My *God* …'

44

Marnie opened one eye in bed on Saturday morning after Ralph had crept out for his customary walk. She did not feel like greeting the day. It had been an uncomfortable night, her back throbbing, dreaming she was sticking pins into a witch's doll – a trim little doll with curly hair. She yawned and heard a voice in her head, *You won't thank me tomorrow, Marnie … but by Sunday morning you'll be blessing my name.* Marnie squirmed, trying to make herself comfortable. *Well, you were right about the first part, lady,* she thought. How to survive Saturday, that was the question.

When Ralph returned from his walk he brought Marnie a breakfast tray. She groaned and resigned herself to another day in bed, or a morning at least.

'Can I sit with you while you have breakfast?'

'Of course, Ralph. But you don't have to keep me company. I know you have work to do.'

'I want to talk to you.'

'I'm in demand these days. Didn't you see the queue?'

'I want to talk about the note you received on Thursday … and didn't mention to me.'

'Ah … Anne told you?'

'Who else? I'm sure you would've got round to speaking about it some time.'

'I'd almost forgotten about it.'

'What are your thoughts?'

'I think you're about to tell me yours. Am I right?'

'You go first.'

'I suppose the key question is … which of the suspects knows where I live?'

'And the answer?'

'Ian Stuart certainly does; I gave him my business card. Clive Adamson must know it too; his office sent me the invitation by post.'

'What about Mike Brent?'

'I don't think so, but he could easily get it if he wanted to. He knows we live up here somewhere by the Grand Union.'

'Wainwright?'

'No. I doubt he even knows I exist.'

Ralph looked thoughtful. 'I think your assessment is right.'

'And what do you think yourself?'

'To tell the truth, Marnie, I don't think there's much we can do. No doubt we should probably inform the police.'

'I'd rather not involve Inspector Bartlett in any of my business, if it could be avoided. He's hardly going to post guards down here to protect me, is he? It would only convince him that I'm concealing information and bring me more hassle.'

Ralph agreed. He cleared away the remains of breakfast and helped Marnie to her feet. Feeling moderately refreshed after visiting the bathroom, with face washed and hair brushed, she let him ease her back into bed.

Two boxes were tucked under the bed, one containing Barbara's 'love letter' tapes, the other the apparent music cassettes. Anne had brought the latter from her attic to *Sally Ann* before supper the previous evening, having no desire to have them under her roof for a minute longer. At Marnie's request Ralph pulled out the two boxes, set them on the duvet beside her with Anne's walkman and left her to it.

Marnie examined every one of the tapes they had assumed were music. Checking every case against the labelling on the cassette inside, Marnie found that they all matched. Only one was not what it seemed. It had been perfect camouflage, perfect except that Anne had stumbled upon it by accident, fumbling in the semi-darkness of her attic room.

Perhaps it was the continuing discomfort of her aching back, or the weariness following a night without rest, but Marnie could not face listening to another of Barbara's intimate monologues. She remembered a friend telling her that after his mother died he had rushed home from the hospital to listen to her voice on the answerphone. She had left a simple message just before entering hospital for the last time, and it had become a precious though tenuous link, a few final words before dying. Hearing Barbara's voice was almost as if she was brought back to life, but Marnie found it hard to listen to words that were never meant for her ears. In that moment she arrived at a decision.

Seeking solace in music, she slotted a Mendelssohn cassette into the walkman and lay back, soon to be lulled to sleep by the Hebridean Overture, the sounds of the sea lapping around Fingal's Cave.

• • • • •

On Sunday morning Marnie woke after a restful night. She turned over without stiffness or pain, muttered a silent *thanks, Curly* and placed her face close to Ralph on the pillow.

'Are you awake?' she whispered.

'Mm.' Ralph put an arm round her and began to pull her closer until he remembered the back. 'Sorry.'

'I've come to a decision, Ralph.'

He still had his eyes closed. 'Nunnery?'

'Apart from that.'

'Tell me.'

'I'm not going to listen to any more of Barbara's tapes … ever again … and certainly not the one that Anne discovered.'

'Good decision.'

'You really think so?'

'Mm … Shame about the nunnery.'

Returning from the bathroom, Marnie realised that her back was free of pain. In the entrance to the sleeping cabin she bent down slowly and touched her toes. Another murmured thank-you to the curly girl.

Ralph observed the performance with both eyes open. 'Is this the sign of another decision being taken? No nunnery after all?'

Marnie gave him the heavy eyelids treatment. 'Actually, I have reached another decision. I'm going to visit Neil this afternoon, tell him I'm packing the tapes up to await his release from prison. Anne can stow them away in her attic.'

Ralph was up on one elbow. Marnie joined him in a chorus of, 'Is that wise?'

'Seriously, Marnie you might be seen.'

'I'll just go in with all the other friends and relatives. No one will know who I am or which inmate I'm visiting. There's no risk at all.'

• • • • •

All the Sunday papers were running the story of Charles Taverner coming to the defence of Neil Gerard. They were now universally known as *The Odd Couple*. Combined with the title, the *Little Venice Murder*, it was a gift to editors.

Anne picked up an armful of papers at the village shop and transported them back to Glebe Farm in the Mini. It was a cool overcast morning, and they sat at the breakfast table reading the different accounts of the story. There was little variation. Charles was quoted with reasonable accuracy, mainly because he had issued a detailed written statement and sent it to all the newsdesks by e-mail. Most comment centred on the uniqueness of the situation. It was the first time in British legal history that the husband of a murder victim was leading the call for a retrial of his wife's alleged killer.

All the now familiar arguments were set out, and several articles observed that Charles was apparently basing much of his judgment on his own personal assessment of Gerard's character. He actually seemed to believe that the man who had been having an affair with his wife was essentially a good person. Apart from some speculation that Charles might be some kind of born again Christian – along the lines of, *love thine enemy* – the reports treated this aspect with total bewilderment. It made his claim of innocence all the more plausible.

Another strange aspect of the reporting was that no blame seemed to be attached to the police for their handling of the case. The Metropolitan Police issued no comment but it was noted that there were no calls for public enquiries, no suggestions of police incompetence. All the papers paraphrased Neil Gerard: *everything was done by the book … they just got the wrong man*.

Where the reports differed was in their treatment of the story. Some took the opportunity to rehash all the background with a full account of the murder and the trial and numerous photographs of all the participants. It was in one of the tabloids that a whole page was devoted to *The Key Questions* under the heading, *If Neil Gerard did not commit this murder, then who did?* On the opposite page a link to the questions was made with photographs, each one bearing a question as its caption. In a line-up at the bottom of the page there were four photos under the heading, *What part do these women play?* There was the witness from the neighbouring boat in Little Venice alongside Sarah Cowan, both obvious choices. The surprises were the two other pictures. Third in the row was Ellen, full name Ellen Samuels, described as Charles's former secretary – *my old secretary … out of retirement*. This was no doddering old biddy. She was a handsome woman with fine bone structure and an intelligent confident expression.

Marnie was horrified but on reflection not really surprised to see her own picture staring out in fourth place. Her caption was short and to the point. *Who is this mystery woman?*

• • • • •

Neil greeted Marnie in the visitors' room as if he was now expecting her to bring good news but not taking anything for granted.

'Good to see you, Marnie, and thanks for everything you've done … you and Charles, of course.'

Marnie felt a slight shock to hear Neil refer to Charles by his first name. Charles always called him Gerard. Surnames seemed more appropriate.

'I haven't really done anything … certainly nothing that's brought results.'

'You've given me hope.'

This was awkward, and Neil's change of expression told Marnie he knew something unwelcome was coming.

'Is anything wrong, Marnie?'

'It's just that … I've been going through the tapes … they're not telling me anything that could ever be used as evidence.'

'I see. They don't give you any ideas about what might've happened?'

Marnie shook her head. 'How could they? Sure, she mentions her lovers, but not in a way that I could use to prove anything. In any case, you wouldn't want them to be played in a court of law if you get a retrial.'

'No.' He pondered for some seconds. 'So you're not going to do anything further with the tapes.'

'That's right.'

'There's something else, isn't there?'

'You're very –'

'Perceptive … sensitive? That's what Barbara used to tell me.'

'I know. I feel like I was there.'

'What is it, Marnie? Don't tell me that after all that's happened you've come to bring bad news.'

'We found another tape … not labelled like the rest.'

Neil looked puzzled. Then his expression hardened. 'You've found … you listened to … my *God* …'

'Why are you surprised? It was in the box with all the others.'

'Well, you heard it, Marnie. It must be obvious why I'm surprised.'

'I haven't heard it, actually.'

Neil was stunned. '*Jesus!* Not … *Charles?*'

'No, not Charles. I have an assistant, a friend who works with me. She's just eighteen. She came across it by accident.'

Alarm. He blurted out, all in a rush. 'Is she trustworthy? That tape's dynamite. If one of the tabloids –'

'Neil, your secret is quite safe. But you really shouldn't have let us come upon it without warning.'

'She said she was going to destroy it, Marnie. There was only one like that. She asked for it back … said it was just an experiment. I didn't know she'd recorded it at the time … and I certainly didn't know she still had it.'

'Can you think why she kept it?'

'No. *Hell*, no. I'm *amazed*. She made so much fuss about it when we listened to it together … said she realised it wasn't a good idea. It was one of the earlier tapes she had brought with her to liven things up.'

'Liven things up?' Marnie regretted saying it as soon as she had spoken.

'Yes. It did, but you can only do that sort of thing once.'

'What did you think of it? I mean, did it strike you as out of character?'

'I didn't like it as much as the others.'

'That's not what I meant.'

Neil's eyes wandered across the room, focused on some distant place. 'There was a song she liked … we both liked … *What a lady, what a night* … you know it?' Marnie nodded. 'That was one of my favourites. Whenever I heard it, I thought of her. That's what she was like, that's what it was like to know her, to be with her.'

'I know all this, Neil. But the time has come for me to pack up the tapes. I don't want to hear any more. I don't think they'll do anything to help your case. It's moved onto a different plane. Charles is leading the campaign now. He'll do it with lawyers … letters to influential people … MPs, ministers, judges. No one will be able to ignore him.'

'You're walking away?'

'It's out of my hands now. It's not as if I'm going to stumble on some clue that's going to solve the case. That kind of thing only happens on television.'

'So that's it.'

'I wish you the best of luck and I look forward to following progress on your campaign. In the meantime I'll keep the tapes safe until you tell me what to do with them. But in practical terms, I think my direct involvement is over.'

• • • • •

Before stepping out of the prison door, Marnie pulled on a headscarf and put on her dark glasses. It reminded her of film stars trying to disguise their looks in old movies, and the thought made her smile. She knew it was unnecessary, but she had promised Ralph she would do it and had even agreed to use his car rather than her own. Behind the tinted lenses her eyes were scanning the whole area as she walked towards the Volvo. There were no journalists to be seen, only the usual movement of visitors arriving and leaving.

The man holding the camera with the long telephoto lens was concealed behind a van about fifty metres from the prison entrance. The wind-on mechanism whirred softly as he carefully shot every person using the doors.

45

Monday morning felt like the first day of a new era. May had started as Marnie hoped it would continue, with bright sunlight filtering through fresh leaves in the spinney and few clouds to obscure the sky. She had walked confidently along the path through the trees on her way to the office barn. The burden of pursuing Neil Gerard's campaign had been lifted from her shoulders, and she knew what was meant by having a spring in your step.

Now free of back pain, she spent the whole day in a burst of energy, making sure that nothing was left undone from last week and that all was prepared for the week to come. Anne gave assurances that her college work was well ahead of schedule and it was no problem for her to spend Tuesday in the office while Marnie went to the Grand Opening in Docklands. This was all the more important since Ralph would also be attending a meeting at Senate House in the University of London.

Opening the *To Do* folder when she reached her desk, Marnie had one jolt of panic when she read the heading of the first message: *Perfidia*. But it was only Anne's reminder about checking on the renovation works with the boatyard.

'Have you dealt with this, Anne, or is it something I need to sort out? They're taking longer than I expected.'

'And I know why.'

'Really?'

'Yep. They stopped working on *Perfidia* to finish another boat.'

'Cheek! I hope they had a good reason.'

'A deadline. They had to get this other boat ready for launching this weekend just gone.'

'That was urgent?'

'It was the last weekend in April.'

'So?'

'The boat's called *April Lady*, so they were under pressure.'

Marnie laughed. 'Well, I just hope they've made up for lost time, that's all.'

Anne checked her own progress folder. 'They've retiled the bathroom … replaced the carpet tiles with the strip wooden flooring throughout. They were varnishing the floors last week, so that should be finished by now. Not sure if the curtains have been made and fitted. I'll ring that woman, if you like.'

Marnie hesitated. 'I'd like to see it, make sure it's all up to scratch. Perhaps I should chase up the curtains.'

'Let me do it.'

'Are you sure you've got time, Anne?'

'Of course I have. Marnie, it's no big deal. It's not as if the boat's being rebuilt. Leave it to me. You can go off on your jolly tomorrow and forget *Perfidia*. Enjoy your champagne and canapés and just relax. There's nothing to worry about.'

• • • • •

It was starting to feel like old times. Marnie and Ralph caught the London train with nothing to concern them but a routine visit to the city. Marnie would be chatting about design and architecture in Docklands; Ralph would be chairing a committee in Bloomsbury. They bought coffee on the train and sat back to read through their working papers. Marnie studied the brochure about the Spice Quay Finance and Trading Centre, based on an article in the Architects' Journal; Ralph read his agenda and notes.

After a while Ralph looked up and smiled at Marnie. 'Don't often see you looking like that.'

'Like what?'

'All dressed up. You look really smart … understated elegance.'

She was wearing a cream jacket over a navy blue shirt and skirt, with gold ear-rings and a gold chain round her neck.

'So I'm usually scruffy?'

'You're usually *casual*. Jeans are fine, but you look good dressed like that.'

'Thanks.'

Ralph lowered his voice and leaned forward. 'You know, Marnie, you've got lovely legs.'

'Thank you, kind sir.'

He had an unmistakable twinkle in his eye. He leaned further forward. '*Really* lovely legs.'

'And a slightly dodgy back,' she reminded him pointedly.

'Ah, yes … Will you be checking out any nunneries while you're in the capital?'

'Just a few.'

Returning to her papers, Marnie came upon the invitation. Her heart quickened when she saw the name at the top, *Mr Clive Adamson, Chairman and Group Chief Executive* … She told herself to relax. This was a day out with Philip Everett, an old friend. She probably would not even get near Clive Adamson. All that was in the past. She turned the invitation card over and saw the map on the reverse. There was a note about parking arrangements. Parking!

Marnie reached in her bag for the mobile and pressed buttons, reading the numbers from the card.

'Good morning. Is that Judith Gross?'

'Speaking.'

'This is Marnie Walker. Short notice again, I'm afraid, but I'll not be needing that parking space.'

'No problem, Ms Walker. I'll take you off my list.'

'Do you want my space number? I've got it written down. Just a moment …'

'No. That's all right. I don't need it. We've decided it's simpler if people just park where they wish, as long as they keep to the same floor. Thanks for letting me know.'

Marnie and Ralph went their separate ways from Euston. They would probably travel back on different trains and arranged to phone Anne when they knew what time they would arrive at Milton Keynes Central.

• • • • •

In the taxi Marnie rang Philip on his mobile. He was already at the venue, and they agreed to meet in the entrance. While she was paying the cabbie, Philip appeared at her side.

'So ... what do you think of it?'

Marnie craned her head back to inspect the Centre. The exterior cladding was bronze reflective glass, twelve or so storeys high, and as if pre-arranged a jet airliner flew past from London City airport, its image flickering across the surface as it gained altitude.

'Impressive. Are you pleased with it, Philip?'

They made their way up the steps and through security, where Marnie showed her invitation and was ticked off the guest list.

'It's my tallest building so far. You wouldn't believe which major partnerships we beat in the competition to get this contract.'

'You did it all in-house?'

Philip ushered Marnie towards the lifts. 'With the usual consultants.'

She scanned the entrance. 'Who handled the interior design?'

'Faye led the group ... your protégée. Do you like it?'

Marnie had groomed Faye Summers as her deputy, and she had taken over as head of the interior design group when Marnie left the firm two years before.

'The only thing that bothers me is the green.'

Philip looked puzzled. 'Green? What green, Marnie? The Findhorn colours are blue and gold.'

'On my face.'

Philip chuckled. 'You can't expect me to farm out all our lucrative contract work to you. I've got to keep something in-house to stop your old team from being idle.'

They took the lift to the top floor, which had been divided into hospitality suites. When the doors opened, Marnie and Philip stepped out into a spacious reception area. A hundred or more guests had already arrived and were milling about, conversing with glass in hand. Marnie remarked that the noise level was just a moderate murmur. Philip pointed to the floor. The blue and gold Findhorn logo was featured in the design of the thick carpet. Covering the whole space, it had the effect of absorbing sound and inducing lowered voices.

They had barely advanced two paces when a uniformed waiter approached, offering a glass of champagne from his tray. Philip guided Marnie through the throng. On the side overlooking the river, a wall of glass opened onto a terrace with uninterrupted views over the Thames and the City. Before they went out, Philip stopped Marnie on the threshold.

'Just look out for a moment and take in the scene.'

Away to their left Tower Bridge rose up from the river with glimpses of the Tower of London, the skyscrapers of the City and St Paul's cathedral beyond. The broad river swept past far below them, curving downstream between banks lined with desirable residences, and the less opulent housing of the East End beyond. Templars' Wharf was down there somewhere. For Marnie it seemed like a distant memory. Little had she known ...

'Well?' Philip interrupted her thoughts.

'A stunning view.'

'Now turn around and look back.'

Marnie did as he asked and found herself gazing across the reception area above the heads of the growing number of guests at a vast painting hung over the lifts. It was almost a mirror image of the view she had just had from the terrace. But it was treated in a powerful, distinctive style.

'Piers Wainwright, I presume?'

Philip nodded. 'And he's here somewhere in the crush. If you want to meet him, like you said –'

'That was then, Philip. It's not really a priority now.'

'Oh … okay. That was rather the point of wangling you an invite, though … meeting Piers Wainwright and Clive Adamson …'

Marnie touched his arm. 'Of course, and I'm really grateful. To be honest, I came mainly because I wanted to see your amazing new building. If there's any chance of a look around, even if it's just –'

Philip touched her hand, his attention suddenly focused over her shoulder. Marnie half turned to see a woman easing her way carefully but determinedly through the multitude.

'Sorry, Marnie, I've an idea my presence might be required. I'll show you round later on.'

The woman smiled as she joined them. 'Mr Everett, the chairman wonders if you'd be able to join him. He thinks it might be a good idea to make his speech now. There's a minister from the treasury who's on a tight schedule and, er …'

'Certainly. Oh, this is my colleague, Marnie Walker. You were kind enough to fit her in.'

'Ms Walker, yes, of course. I'm Judith Gross. We've spoken on the phone.'

Marnie had relieved Philip of his champagne flute and was too encumbered to shake hands. The two women nodded at each other, and the head of secretariat whisked Philip away with an apologetic smile. A minute later while Marnie was depositing their empty glasses on a side table, there were calls for silence and the chairman stepped onto a dais behind a bank of microphones at the far end of the area. For the first time Marnie became aware of camera crews. Floodlights were turned on and Clive Adamson began his speech. It was the usual list of thanks and acknowledgements, including a special mention for the minister who had given up time in his busy day.

Clive Adamson was not what Marnie had expected. Unlike the suave, self-aware Ian Stuart, Adamson's style was understatement. He reminded Marnie of an American senator, with gold-rimmed glasses perched on a long nose, hair brushed back, a neat and tidy man dressed in a formal grey suit like an accountant. A wealthy accountant. Marnie wondered what had made her think of a senator. Then she understood. Adamson had a forceful way of speaking, of giving emphasis to certain words as if to underline them, like a media presenter. The restrained style of dress disguised an assured character, confident of his position and influence. When this man spoke, he knew people listened.

Laughter broke out around her. Marnie had been observing the man and was only vaguely aware of his speech. He had referred again to the minister, made some comparison between the hothouse of Westminster and the glazed building they were celebrating that day. Marnie wondered if Philip would appreciate the joke, when she felt herself jostled by a movement beside her. She took a small step sideways to make space and heard a quiet voice in her ear.

'This is a delightful surprise.'

She looked round. A suntanned face, blond hair, white teeth in a vulpine smile. Ian Stuart was grinning at her, offering another glass of champagne. As a reflex, she took it.

'Mister Stuart.'

'Ian. I wasn't expecting to see you here, Marnie.'

'I'm with the architect … my old firm. And you?'

'Let's just say I was part of the planning and development team. My company negotiated for the site.'

While they were talking, Stuart manoeuvred Marnie towards the terrace. A round of applause greeted Adamson's mention of Philip Everett … *of Everett Parker Associates, the architects who have made it all happen. In particular I'd like to mention …*

'I wanted to ask you, Marnie … that day you came back to Bermuda Reach …'

Marnie felt her jaw muscles tighten. 'Yes?'

'Did you get what you wanted?'

'What do you mean?'

Stuart took Marnie by the elbow and walked her out towards the edge of the terrace. 'Have you seen the view from up here? We were restricted on how tall a building could be erected on this site. But it's still an awful long way down.'

'You can let go of my arm, if you like, Ian.'

'Sorry. Where was I? Of course. Did you get all the details you wanted for your plans … for the wine bar … the ones you came especially to measure up?'

'Oh, yes … thank you.'

'Funny that.'

'In what way?'

'Two days later someone from your *old firm* came along to do exactly the same thing. Rather poor communication, wouldn't you say?'

The sound of more applause was heard in the background.

'But they're *architects*. They'd be measuring different things for a different purpose. Also I wanted to think over some ideas for the colour scheme. I always do that *in situ*. It's the only way … you get to see how things look in real daylight.'

Marnie knew she'd made a mistake as soon as she spoke. She hoped Stuart would not notice. But he did.

'At that time of the morning … for a restaurant and wine bar … with windows facing south-west?'

She stammered. 'It … it was the only time I could be there. I just wanted –'

'What are you doing out here?' It was a hard voice, stern and unfriendly.

Marnie's head snapped round. The sudden arrival of a newcomer had taken both of them by surprise, but Stuart only reacted with his habitual wolfish smile.

'Piers, you old bugger.' He moved forward to shake hands, but the other man turned it into a hug.

So this is Piers Wainwright, Marnie thought, realising at once that she was in the presence of two men who had both slept with Barbara Taverner. That brought her tally to four so far, including Charles and Neil. A bizarre statistic of which they, presumably, were unaware. Or were they?

She only had a moment to assess the artist, but she immediately felt the magnetism of the man. Slightly less tall than Stuart, and not nearly as good-looking, he had a strong face with strong features, his head shaved in a number one, a fashion statement and a concession to thinning hair. Though not bulky, he looked muscular and fit. In black silk shirt and well-cut black trousers, he stood out from the other men present as if he did not play by their rules. He seemed in every way the opposite to Ian Stuart, except in being successful and probably rich.

The artist released Stuart from the hug, holding him at arm's length by the shoulders. He glanced at Marnie but made no apology for his interruption.

'So what are you doing out here?' The tone was different now, bantering but more friendly. Wainwright had a pleasant voice without the regional accent that Marnie had expected.

'Why shouldn't we be?' Stuart was trying to assert himself now, but he was on the defensive. 'We were … admiring the view.'

'*Precisely*. Instead of idling away your time out here, you should be in *there* looking at my painting. That'll tell you what the view is really about.'

'It's about power and domination.' Marnie cut in. She was growing impatient with being ignored while her companions indulged in boy talk. 'Two faces of the City linked by the common thread of the river.'

Stuart blinked and stared at her. Wainwright's eyes narrowed momentarily.

'Which? The view out here or the painting in there?' He put the question like a challenge.

Marnie stared him out. 'Both … of course.'

Wainwright let go of Stuart and moved towards Marnie. She folded her arms, determined that he was not going to hug her. To her surprise, he bowed.

'I'm Piers –'

'I know who you are.'

'My fame precedes me.'

'The signature on the painting is more than big enough to be legible.' Marnie was surprised by her assertiveness. Or was it aggression?

'And if I was painting you, what name would I give the portrait?'

'You don't paint portraits, but the name is Marnie Walker.'

Wainwright hesitated, reflecting on whether the name was familiar. 'You're part of this set-up?' He inclined his head briefly towards the reception.

'Marnie's with the architect.' Stuart seemed to resent being sidelined. 'She's an interior designer.'

Wainwright ignored him. It was as if he was only able to give his full attention to one person at a time. He made another head movement. 'Are you responsible for this …' He searched for the words. '… neo-Hendonesque collation?'

'No. I'm here as a guest. I left Everett Parker to start my own practice two years ago.'

'Probably a wise move.'

Before he could continue, Wainwright noticed that Marnie's attention had shifted to a point over his left shoulder. He glanced round. A small party was approaching at a determined rate. In the vanguard was the chairman, Clive Adamson himself, flanked by Judith Gross and Philip Everett, with several minions following in their wake.

Just before the group reached them, Ian Stuart edged closer to Marnie and murmured, 'I'll catch up with you later.'

Marnie was wondering if that was a promise or a threat when the chairman's entourage engulfed them. Adamson beamed at the small group.

'I might've known I'd find you out here, avoiding the dreary speeches, probably doing multi-million pound deals behind my back. How the devil are you?'

Adamson shook hands with Stuart and Wainwright, who this time did not attempt the hug routine. The chairman was running on the adrenalin of the hour and seemed noticeably more relaxed now that the formal proceedings were concluded.

'It's only just dawned on me that I should've bought shares in Aston Martin.' Adamson twinkled a smile behind the gold rims. 'Everyone I engage on a project immediately rushes out to buy one.'

'Everyone?' Stuart asked.

'Yes. I gather Piers is the latest owner. Isn't that right?'

The artist gave a slight bow. 'You're well informed, Clive. But with your money you don't need shares. You could buy the factory. It wouldn't surprise me if you already had.'

'I think someone got in first.'

Adamson gave the slightest inclination of his head towards Judith Gross.

She picked up the signal. 'This is Marnie Walker, chairman.'

'Ah, yes.' Adamson extended his hand. 'So glad you could come.'

Philip joined in. 'Marnie used to head up our interior design team. She handed over to Faye Summers two years ago.'

'I hope you approve of your successor's work, Marnie.'

'I do. More to the point, perhaps, I hope you do.'

'Very much. Have you had a chance to look round the building?'

'I was hoping that might be possible.'

'I'm sure we can arrange it.' Another barely visible nod towards Judith Gross.

She came in on cue. 'Mr Everett has offered to give the guided tour, chairman.'

'Excellent. Who better?'

Marnie could see why some women found power an aphrodisiac. Clive Adamson had only to wish for something for it to become an immediate reality. She could also see why Barbara might have found him attractive. He was reasonably personable, but more than that he gave you his complete attention without the odour of confrontation emitted by Piers Wainwright or the self-love of Ian Stuart. Adamson focused on you with the aim of pleasing you, she thought. Few women would find that unappealing.

'Presumably, Marnie – if I can call you Marnie – you also came here in an Aston?' The smile twinkled again. 'I seem to be the only person without one these days.'

'I'm afraid not. I have a four-by-four.'

'And is it true what they say … such vehicles are only used for going to Sainsbury's and collecting the children from school?'

'I live at the bottom of a field some way from the road. Four-wheel drive's pretty essential for me, especially in the winter.'

'How interesting.'

While Adamson steered the conversation to include the others present, two further thoughts occurred to Marnie. She was now in the company of *four* men who had slept with Barbara Taverner, and she had heard Barbara talk about them all after her death. It was the strangest feeling she had ever had. Marnie felt a chill down her spine. She was virtually surrounded by men who could be involved in the murder of their ex-lover, her friend.

As rapidly as they had arrived, Adamson's posse withdrew and the host continued the rounds of meeting his guests. Marnie was relieved that both Stuart and Wainwright had become locked in conversation with other visitors. And she noticed that both of them now had a woman by his side. It came as no surprise to see that Stuart's consort was Amanda Gilbert-Reeves, the young woman from the reception desk at Bermuda Reach. Where had she been when Stuart had approached Marnie? *This is a delightful surprise …* he had said. Was it a surprise? Had he told the girl to occupy herself elsewhere while he sought out Marnie? She could imagine him … *Can you go off and powder your nose for a while, darling …*

Wainwright's companion looked as if she had stepped out of the pages of *Vogue* magazine. Marnie could guess which designer label would be found inside the well-cut suit she was wearing. Her hair was beautifully groomed, her shoes hand-made from calf leather. Apart from the colouring, she could have been Barbara's sister. That was obviously Wainwright's taste in women. Or was it? Did he just seek them out as potential clients for his paintings and then drop them once they had helped line his pockets?

Marnie had had enough of the reception. She did not want to offend Philip, but she had no desire to wait around until he came back to give her the guided tour. Who could tell when he might be free? As architect for the new building he would be sought after by many of those present, and it would be unfair to expect him to spend time with her when he might be gaining new clients in the City. She turned to lean against the terrace rail for a last look at the view before leaving. Power and domination, she thought. Wainwright had not disagreed. He had expressed these forces clearly in his painting. The power of the major institutions dominating the City and the people who lived in its shadow. That was something Barbara's men seemed to have in common. They were all dominant characters, each in his different way.

'Marnie.'

It was a quiet voice but it still made her jump. She had not noticed the man who had come up behind her.

'Mike. I didn't expect to see you here.'

Mike Brent smiled. 'Nor I you. What's your connection?'

'I came to admire Philip's achievement …' She made a gesture towards the building. 'We worked together for years and still do projects together. What about you? Are you a member of the Aston Martin Owners' Club?'

'No. Despite what Adamson was saying just now, I'm not one of the fortunate ones made rich by his dealings.'

'But you have some interest in the company?'

'You didn't listen to the chairman's speech, Marnie.'

'Er, no … not very carefully.'

'Then look down there. What do you see?'

'The river Thames?'

'Well observed. Beside it … going round the building?'

Marnie craned forward and saw for the first time a stretch of water like a tributary to the river, a docking area. On both sides were promenades, new paving and lamps in the shape of globes. Two boats were moored together. One was a river police launch, the other a floating gin palace.

'That's your connection, Mike? I thought the Thames with its by-waters came under a separate body.'

'It does, but BW has one or two interests related to it. That used to be a canal serving local industry. It's a kind of anomaly, but somehow we ended up owning it. Because there isn't anybody else to liaise with, Head Office asked the Little Venice team to keep an eye on it for this project. So it came down to me. You should've seen it. The place was a real mess before work began.'

'It looks charming now.'

'Yes. He's good, your friend Philip.'

It was a casual enough chat between two people who had known each other for a few years, but Marnie could not help thinking of Mike Brent's involvement with Barbara Taverner. She now knew five people, six including her husband, who had slept with her. She felt like a poker player with a full house. The experience was heightened by the thought that one of them, possibly one of the four she had seen that day, might also be her murderer.

Marnie excused herself from Mike Brent. He wished her a safe journey as she went off to find the exit. By chance her path crossed that of Judith Gross near the lifts. She had been escorting a VIP guest from the function and organising his transport.

'I must be off, I'm afraid.'

'Of course. Everyone has such busy lives. It's been nice to meet you, Marnie, even if only briefly.'

'Could you possibly tell Philip that I'll call him soon.'

'Certainly. It's a pity you can't have your tour of the building. Come back another time. Just give me a ring and I'll arrange it for you.'

'I'd like that, thanks.'

'Is there anything else you need before you go? They'll call you a cab from main reception downstairs. I have a taxi firm on standby.'

Marnie smiled. Judith Gross was the power behind the throne. 'Actually, there is one part of the building I'd like to visit before leaving …'

'No problem. To avoid the queue, take the lift to floor one. You'll find the Ladies just round the corner on your right as you come out. Don't go left or you'll be heading for the car park.'

As the lift doors closed, Marnie did not see one of the guests detach himself from the crowd, speak quickly to one of the staff and make a discreet exit by the door to the stairwell.

• • • • •

There was a New Modern feeling in the toilets that Marnie recognised as typical Faye Summers design. She was just reflecting that Faye would get on well with Anne, when she noticed the beginnings of a ladder in her tights. Determined to stop it spreading below her knee and becoming visible, she quickly dug in her bag and found a pot of nail varnish. The repair was simple, and she waited a short while for the dab of varnish to dry. It had been an odd trip and she realised that she now wanted nothing more than to rush back immediately to Glebe Farm and the rural haven of Knightly St John. It was not to be.

A rapid brush of the hair, and Marnie was ready to face the world and the journey home. She was just leaning towards the mirror for a final check of teeth – no mark of lipstick – and eye shadow – no smudging – when she heard a low rumble from somewhere in the vicinity. It reminded her of those buildings that have the Tube running not far down beneath them, but the Underground did not extend to this area. A noise from the lift shafts? Some kind of generator starting up? She could think of nothing in a modern building that would produce that kind of sound. Hitching the bag over her shoulder with a mental shrug, she pulled open the door and exited the Ladies. At that very moment the fire alarm began ringing.

The nearest door was beyond the lifts and led to the car park. The alarm in the lift lobby was uncomfortably loud. Marnie raced to the door and yanked it open. It was like walking into Hell.

• • • • •

Marnie was still in a state of shock while travelling north on the train. By the time she reached Euston station the rush hour was in full swing. Unable to cope with the crowds of commuters, she found a single window seat in first class and flopped down, grateful for the relative peace and extra space. She made a quick call to Anne to give her arrival time and learned that Ralph was already heading back.

She wondered if there would be a problem in upgrading when the ticket collector came along. She held out her standard class ticket. 'I'd like to pay the extra for first class, please.'

He took one look at her and bent down to speak quietly. 'Are you all right, miss?'

'Er … yes, thanks.'

'Don't mind me saying this, but you look a bit …'

'I've just witnessed a rather bad accident and … I'm not quite feeling myself at the moment. I'll be all right.'

The man looked vaguely at her ticket and handed it back. 'One minute, please.'

He walked off down the carriage, leaving Marnie wondering if there was some kind of procedure he had to follow. She really could not be bothered with any more hassle.

The images came flooding back to her. The overwhelming horror of the sight of the underground car park was etched into her mind. The fire, the heat, the smell, the noise. She had felt stunned when she opened the door by the lifts. By chance it led onto the first level, the level where she would have parked. It was mayhem. The fire seemed to be centred on a vehicle not far from the entrance. It stood tall, a four-wheel drive like her Discovery, a Range Rover perhaps or a Mercedes, engulfed in flames and black smoke. Worst of all, someone seemed to be caught up in the blaze. She hoped it was her imagination, a trick of the shadows, but her brain told her she was not deceived.

There followed some moments of indecision. What should she do? The alarm was already sounding. What *could* she do? The heat of the inferno was too intense for her to be able to get nearer to the car to investigate. Then the options were taken out of her hands. The door behind her burst open. Security officers raced in. Someone grabbed her and pulled her away. Everyone rushed to the stairwell, and Marnie found herself guided carefully but quickly down to the ground floor and out into the cool air. It took her some while before she realised that the man standing beside her, holding her arm, was Mike Brent.

'Marnie,' he was saying insistently, 'Marnie, listen to me. What were you doing in there?'

He had to repeat the question several times.

'I was going to get my car.' She was speaking hesitantly as if not understanding what she was saying.

'Was it your car that was on fire?'

'I think … no, no … What happened? Who was that in there?'

Mike look horrified. 'There was someone in there … in your car?'

'Not my car … no, another one. My car isn't there.'

'Marnie, you're not making much sense. Did you see what happened?'

She shook her head.

'Oh, thank God!'

Mike turned sharply at this new voice. Judith Gross had arrived. She looked agitated in the extreme.

'Thank *goodness* you're safe, Marnie. I've been looking *everywhere* for you.'

'You knew she'd be at the car park?' Mike said.

'No, no. Marnie didn't come by car. She changed her plans at the last minute.'

'Then why was she down there? I don't understand.'

'I sent her there to use the … the facilities. There was a queue on the twelfth floor, and she was on her way out, so …'

Mike turned his attention back to Marnie. 'How are you feeling? You look very shaken.'

'There was someone there.'

'Someone *there?*' Judith repeated.

'Did you see who it was?' Mike asked. He was gripping her arm more tightly.

'By the car … I'm not sure … just a shape … horrible … *horrible* …'

'I think we need to get you medical attention.' Judith Gross was back in charge. 'I'll take her, Mr Brent.' She was in her element, head of secretariat, the person who gets things done. 'You'll need to make sure your name is on the list of …' She almost said *survivors*. 'The list of guests evacuated from the building. This way, Marnie.'

And that was it. Marnie was presented to the paramedics who checked her over, saw that she had no physical injuries and passed her on to members of the company staff who were offering tea and biscuits. It was like a scene from the *Blitz*. After three sips of strong tea, Marnie slipped away from the crowd and minutes later she was on her way back to Euston by taxi.

She became aware of a hand touching her arm. A woman was holding a glass of water, the ticket collector hovering in the background. She had a kind West Indian face, etched with concern, and a lilting accent.

'Would you like this, my love? You've had a nasty shock, haven't you?'

Marnie took the glass with a weak smile. 'Thanks.'

'We're getting you a cup of tea.'

The kindness of strangers. Where had she heard that phrase? The train staff gave Marnie space but let her know they were there if she needed them. When the express pulled into Milton Keynes Central someone came along to make sure she was ready to get off and operate the door for her. Marnie only realised days later that the conductor had not charged her the extra fare for the upgrade to first class.

Ralph was waiting on the platform and hugged her, keeping the other passengers from jostling her on the crowded stairs. He had arrived back some minutes earlier, already alerted by Anne that something was amiss. Anne had detected the strain in Marnie's voice in her call from Euston.

Ralph drove the Discovery home. The journey passed in a blur, Marnie leaning back against the head restraint, eyes closed, with no questions asked and not a word passing between them. At Glebe Farm she took a shower on *Thyrsis* and afterwards accepted a glass of brandy. Over the lightest of suppers on *Sally Ann* Marnie told Ralph and Anne what had happened.

When she reached the end, Ralph said, 'It was on the radio news. You were correct in your impression that someone was … involved in the fire. There's been no announcement from the police about who it might have been. I don't think anyone has come forward to identify the … person.'

'I saw who it was.'

'You did?'

Marnie nodded. 'It was Ian Stuart.'

46

Tuesday morning was one of those days when it feels good to be alive. A shower of rain in the night had washed the world clean, leaving the air cool and fresh. The canal was sparkling, and to her surprise after the ordeal of the previous day, Marnie felt calm and restored. As usual Anne had gone on ahead to the office barn after breakfast while Marnie and Ralph returned to *Thyrsis*. With teeth brushed and hair combed, Marnie left the bathroom to Ralph and set off through the spinney. It was not yet eight o'clock.

If Marnie had been of a religious disposition she would have been giving thanks for her survival of the fire at Spice Quay. She was wondering how she could feel so elated after yesterday's trauma and depression, when she saw Anne coming rapidly towards her through the trees. The girl's face registered anxiety.

'We've got visitors.'

• • • • •

DCI Bartlett and DS Marriner were waiting at the door of the office barn. Bartlett managed his version of a sympathetic smile as Marnie let them in. Anne guessed correctly that this was an occasion when they would accept coffee. They even agreed to sit down.

'You probably know why we're here, Mrs Walker.'

'About what happened yesterday, no doubt, though I am a little surprised to see a senior officer like yourself, Mr Bartlett.'

'I think the reason for that will become clear very soon. And before I go on I'd like to say how sorry I am that you had such an unpleasant experience. Do you feel up to talking to us today?'

Alarm bells were ringing in Marnie's head. This kindly approach from Bartlett was worrying. 'I feel much better, thank you.'

'Then I'd like to ask you a few questions about the … incident.'

Marnie nodded. 'Fine … though I can't say I'm much good as a witness.'

'It seems the person who died had some connection with you, Mrs Walker. Is that correct?'

'You haven't yet told me the name of the person who died.'

'You don't know?'

'I have an idea, but everything was so … sudden and violent … and I was shocked.'

'The deceased was … a Mr Ian Stuart.' Bartlett watched Marnie intensely. 'I believe you knew him quite well.'

'What gave you that impression?'

'Is it true?'

'Not at all. I'd had a meeting with him once … a business meeting. That's all … apart from seeing him at the reception yesterday.'

'You wouldn't describe your relationship with him as … close.'

'I wouldn't say we had a *relationship* at all … except a business one.'

Anne brought coffee for the detectives. She looked enquiringly at Marnie who shook her head.

'How did you feel about Mr Stuart?'

'I didn't have feelings about him. He was a business contact, that's all. He seemed pleasant enough.'

'But you knew of his feelings about you.'

Marnie looked blank. 'I honestly don't know what you mean.'

Bartlett glanced quickly at Marriner and turned back to Marnie. 'I thought women were perceptive about such things.'

'I still don't follow.'

'His colleague … or perhaps I should call her his *girlfriend* … she was perceptive enough to know.'

'To know what?'

'She was jealous of you.'

Marnie could feel her face redden. 'What are you talking about?'

'How did she put it, Ted?'

Marriner referred to his notebook. 'She said … *Mr Stuart was very attracted to Marnie Walker … I was quite annoyed about it … about how much he fancied her.*'

Bartlett continued. 'Are you saying you were unaware of his feelings towards you?'

'That is exactly what I'm saying.'

'Can you think of any other reason why he would've followed you?'

'*Followed* me? Look, Mr Bartlett, I really don't understand any of this. Ian Stuart was in the car park ahead of me. He can't have been following me. Do you see?'

'Let me spell it out for you. He saw you at the reception. He went there with a woman colleague with whom he was having a relationship. Does the name Amanda Gilbert-Reeves mean anything to you?'

Marnie nodded. 'Bermuda Reach … she was on the desk there … the day of our business meeting.'

'She said he'd been *delighted* when he saw you at the reception yesterday. He told her to enjoy herself and left her to talk to you. That's why she was annoyed.'

'We did talk, but only for a minute or two … about his role in the Spice Quay development … nothing more.'

'When you left the event, Miss Gilbert-Reeves said Mr Stuart excused himself from her a second time and went after you. He followed you out. Did you speak with him again?'

'No. I've already told you. I didn't *see* him again … well, at least not until … in the car park … if that was him.' Marnie shuddered, leaned forward on the desk and put her head in her hands, her head filled with flames and smoke.

'I'm sorry if this is distressing, Mrs Walker.'

Anne went quickly to the kitchen area and appeared beside Marnie seconds later to put a glass of water down beside her. Marnie took a sip. 'Are you suspecting me of something, Mr Bartlett? I don't understand what you're driving at.'

'This was a violent and suspicious death. I don't need to tell you how terrible it was. We're just trying to establish what happened.'

'I've told you everything I know. What do *you* think happened? Silly question. You never tell me anything … always treat me like a suspect.'

'We're treating you like a witness. It's just that there seem to be inconsistencies in your account, compared with what other people say happened.'

'Tell me about it.'

Bartlett spoke to his sergeant. 'Ted?'

Marriner read from his notebook. 'Miss Gilbert-Reeves followed Mr Stuart after he left her the second time. She heard him ask a member of staff where Mrs Walker had parked. He was told the first level in the downstairs car park, floor one of the building.'

'But that's not true,' Marnie said. 'I went by train and taxi.'

'Marnie,' Anne interrupted quietly. 'You were booked to use that car park, remember? You changed plans at the last minute.'

Marnie put a hand to her mouth. 'Yes … that's right. Whoever spoke to Ian was using an old list. I only spoke to Judith Gross about the change.'

Marriner went on. 'Okay. Mr Stuart was told to take the lift to the first floor. He did so and that's where …'

Bartlett took up the questioning. 'Did he know your car, Mrs Walker?'

'I suppose he could've seen it at Bermuda Reach the day of our meeting. Come to think of it, I did mention I had a four-by-four at the reception yesterday.'

'In his hearing?'

'I'm not sure. I was talking to the chairman, Clive Adamson. Several other people were there.'

'Is that significant?' Bartlett asked.

'He might've heard me say it.'

'I meant is it significant that you said you had a four-by-four?'

'The car on fire was that sort of vehicle.' Marnie suddenly grasped the inference. 'Oh, my God … you think the burning car was meant to be mine. You think that would explain why Ian Stuart was there … looking for me.'

'It could explain all sorts of things, Mrs Walker. It doesn't explain why he was there ahead of you. It doesn't explain what you were doing on the first floor at that time, since you hadn't travelled by car. And it also doesn't explain why you were in the car park at all.'

Marnie reflected. 'I can explain that.'

'Please do.'

'If you *must* know, I went to the loo on my way out of the building. Judith Gross told me there was a Ladies on the first floor. While there I found I had a ladder in my tights and I repaired it with nail varnish. When I came out, the fire alarm was ringing. Knowing I couldn't use the lifts, I took the nearest exit door and found myself in the car park.'

Marriner was writing rapid notes.

'Do you have the tights?' said Bartlett.

'They're in the waste bin in the bathroom on *Thyrsis*.'

'I'd like to see them.'

'I can go and fetch them,' Anne offered.

Bartlett shook his head. 'Thanks, but we'll go.'

Marnie led the way through the spinney towards *Thyrsis*. 'I hope this will help tie up the loose ends, Mr Bartlett.'

'No doubt. But we've still got plenty more of those.'

'Concerning me?'

'Not really. But we don't yet know why Mr Stuart was in the vicinity of a car of a similar type to yours. We don't yet know how it caught fire so suddenly. And we don't know who caused it to ignite.'

They walked on. DS Marriner broke the silence. 'I remember my mother used to do that … repair her stockings with nail varnish.'

Marnie smiled at him. 'I learnt the trick from mine. Will you want the tights as evidence?'

Bartlett replied, 'That won't be necessary.'

'I suppose that's a good sign. It shows you can't be suspecting me of anything … or can you?'

'Not at all. Though it is strange how you keep turning up when there's trouble about.'

• • • • •

Ralph had joined the group when they went on board *Thyrsis* and now, with the damaged tights back in the waste bin, he and Marnie escorted the detectives to the courtyard. Watching the unmarked police car drive up the field track, Marnie rested her head against Ralph's shoulder.

'So that's that. Thank goodness their questioning's over and I can forget about it.'

'Mm …' Ralph seemed lost in thought.

Marnie looked up into his face. 'What's the matter? Don't you think it's over?'

'Well … I think there are other questions that haven't been answered … or even asked.'

'Such as?'

'Why was Stuart really following you?'

'Because he wanted to … talk to me?'

'In a car park? We only have the account of the Gilbert-Reeves woman that he was attracted to you. I ask myself what I would've done in his place. I see a very attractive woman at a party and I decide I want to talk to her. Would I chase after her like that? No. I'd phone her the next day if I had her number – which he did – and try to arrange a drink together or perhaps lunch.'

'Yes. That would be more his style, too. So why *was* he following me?'

'There is one answer that you wouldn't want to contemplate.'

'That he wanted to do me harm? Why would he?'

'He was on your list of possible suspects. Perhaps he had a more sinister idea in mind.'

Marnie gasped. 'To kill me?'

Ralph shrugged. 'Being brutally honest, it's got to be a possible answer.'

'But he was the one that got killed.'

'Messing about with fuel tanks must be a volatile business. Perhaps there was a blow-back or something. There was certainly a fire … and it wasn't spontaneous combustion.'

Behind them in the office a phone began ringing. A few moments after it stopped, they saw Anne in the doorway.

'Do you want the good news or the bad news?'

• • • • •

Marnie's first action on hearing the news was to phone Charles Taverner.

'I've just had a call from the boatyard. It seems they had a burglary last night. Someone broke into a few of the boats, stole some equipment. We were lucky. *Perfidia* was tied up near the office. The boatyard says we can collect her. Whoever got in, they knew where the CCTV camera was located and kept clear.'

'I don't suppose the police can do anything about it.' Charles sounded indignant.

'They responded to the alarm.'

'That's better than nothing, I suppose. I'm assuming whoever did it got away.'

'Yes.'

'Which reminds me, Marnie, did you get hold of information about alarm systems for the house?'

'I did … brochures have arrived from several companies. We can go through them next time I see you.'

'I'll ask Ellen to sort out a time. I should be free to come up in a few days.'

'Or I could come to see you, if you'd prefer. I have some commitments, but nothing that I couldn't change.'

'No, you carry on as planned, Marnie. Never thought I'd have to be thinking about security in a place like Knightly St John … amazing. Nowhere's safe these days. You'd better get quotes for trench digging and barbed wire fencing.'

The next call on the list was to Mike Brent.

'The boatyard has completed the work on *Perfidia*. I haven't inspected it yet, but if everything's okay, we can get her back to you and your purchaser.'

'That's great. Do you want me to organise a crew to bring *Perfidia* down to London? I know you're very busy.'

'That would be helpful, Mike.'

'Leave it with me. I'll fix something up.' He paused. 'How are you, Marnie … after yesterday?'

'Better than I was. Thanks for getting me out of the car park. How are you feeling?'

'I still can't believe it happened.'

'You heard who it was … at the car?'

'Ian Stuart, yes.'

'Did you know him?'

'Met him once or twice … planning meetings, you know … nice bloke … always very smart.' Mike spoke hesitantly. There was emotion in his voice.

'Mike … I don't suppose you know why Ian was in the car park?'

'Why he was … wasn't he just going down to collect his car to go home? Why else would he be there?'

'Of course. Look, I'll get over to the boatyard and confirm back to you that all's well with *Perfidia*.'

'Talk to you soon, Marnie.'

• • • • •

They closed the office for an hour at lunchtime and drove up to inspect the boat together in the Discovery with Marnie at the wheel, Ralph beside her and Anne on the back seat checking the file against the schedule of works. They arrived at the yard as the sun broke through the clouds and lit up *Perfidia* like the star of the show. She lay at her berth, paintwork shining, totally overshadowing the other boats clustered around her like members of the chorus.

The interior looked just as good. New fabrics and flooring combined to make her as good as the day she was first commissioned. Even with Anne poking into every cranny, the inspection lasted only twenty minutes. Marnie pronounced herself completely satisfied and arranged for the boat to be moved as soon as the ferrying crew could be mustered.

Back in the car, Ralph was incredulous. 'Were you serious there, Marnie?' Ferrying crew? What was all that about?'

'Mike offered to send some people to navigate her down to London. I thought it made sense. Don't you?'

'Well, I shan't be here of course, but I thought you and Anne might take a couple of days off and make the journey yourselves … unless you're too busy? I don't see any other time you'll get a break this summer.'

Marnie hesitated, eventually calling over her shoulder, 'What do you think, Anne?'

'You can guess my answer, Marnie.'

'I suppose we could …'

'Great! And there's another thing … you wouldn't want some big clod-hopping blokes putting their dirty boots on our new floor, would you?'

'Since you put it that way …'

They agreed on a plan to collect *Perfidia* from the boatyard. Ralph was flying to Washington on Thursday morning. Marnie and Anne would set off that same afternoon to make a good start. As soon as they arrived back at the office Marnie rang Mike Brent to confirm the new arrangements. He declared it was no problem and wished them a pleasant journey. Marnie rang Charles to bring him up to date and spent the rest of the day clearing the decks in the office ready for their absence. Anne dealt with filing and correspondence, but Marnie noticed she was not scribbling a list of things to do.

'No list, Anne? You can't be feeling well. Perhaps you're not fit enough for the journey.'

The printer beside Anne's desk stopped whirring and Anne pulled off the page it had produced. She waved it in triumph. 'Done! I'm fully automated now. I made this list from the last time we travelled. It's got all the things we need to take and everything that has to be done.'

Marnie shook her head wearily. A few days in the company of Anne would be just the tonic she needed.

• • • • •

When the phone rang later that afternoon, Marnie expected it would be her sister. No one in the business world made phone calls just before six.

'Marnie Walker, good afternoon.'

There was something familiar about the voice, but it took her completely by surprise. 'Marnie, hallo. I wasn't sure if I'd find you in your office at this time of day. Or am I ringing your home number? This is Clive Adamson.'

'Oh … hallo … no, this is the office. I'm usually here till about seven.'

'Me too. I hope you don't mind me calling you out of the blue like this.'

'Not at all. What can I do for you?'

'First, I wanted to say how sorry I was that you had such an awful experience here yesterday. Are you all right?'

'Much better, thanks.'

'Dreadful business … *terrible*. Poor Ian. Anyway, I'm sure you don't want to dwell on that. Marnie, I was wondering … would you like to come down for the tour of the building that you missed? Of course, I'm not expecting you to do so immediately, but perhaps … next week one day?'

Her reaction was in the nature of an automatic response. 'That's nice of you. I would like to see the building if it could be arranged. My diary's a little unclear at the moment. I'm out of the office for a few days. Should I ring Judith Gross and fix a time for her to show me round when I've got things sorted out?'

'Let me give you my direct number, Marnie. You can ring me any time that's convenient … any time. I was rather looking forward to the pleasure of conducting the tour myself. I thought perhaps we might include lunch in my private dining room here?'

'That's very kind of you.'

It had been another automatic response, and yet even as she spoke the words, Marnie began to feel a chill descend her spine. But why should she react like this? Clive Adamson was inviting her in his usual polite tone of voice, simply offering a tour of his new empire and lunch. It was all totally innocent.

Adamson continued. 'Perhaps I could give you another ring next week when your situation is clearer?'

'Fine.'

But was fine the right word? After they had disconnected, Marnie sat staring at the phone. She had been discussing social matters with a man who had been a lover of Barbara Taverner, had discarded her and was possibly on the list of suspects in her murder.

Marnie was running several job lists on Wednesday morning: one for clients' projects, one for renovations of the farmhouse, one for the journey down to Little Venice. Anne had gone out to take coffee to the builders, so that when the call came in, Marnie noticed it on the fourth ring and picked up the phone. For the second time in two days she heard a vaguely familiar voice that she could not at first identify.

'Before you ask me how I got your number, let me tell you I have friends in low places.'

Marnie froze. There was not exactly menace in the voice, but the tone was undeniably confrontational. Then it lightened up.

'Are you there, Marnie? Did I scare you?'

'Who is this?'

'You know who it is … and you were expecting me to ring. At least, that's what I was hoping.'

'If you don't tell me your –'

'Piers Wainwright.'

'Oh …'

'Was that pleasure … or disappointment?'

'Neither. Look, Mr Wainwright –'

'Piers.'

'Piers … I'm sorry, I was in the middle of … what did you mean, *friends in low places*?'

'I got your number from one of Clive Adamson's minions.'

'One of his staff gave out my private details? Why would they do that?'

'Because of my unfailing charm … and because I said you asked me to get in touch and I'd mislaid your business card.'

'So you lied.'

'Not a *serious* lie … anyway, you did express interest in my work, or at least an understanding of what I do. That's more than most people, who just see my paintings as wall decoration for the boardroom.'

'Piers, much as it's a pleasure to hear from you …' *What am I saying?* 'I do have a living to earn and I'm up to my eyeballs right now.'

'When are you coming to London again to see my work?'

'I don't know. I haven't any plans.'

'Marnie there are few people who can tell me what one of my paintings is about just after seeing it for the first time. Wouldn't you like to see more? Now, where were we?'

'You were trying to persuade me to come and see your etchings.'

It was a weak joke that barely jogged the Richter scale of humour, but it had an unexpected impact on Wainwright.

'*Etchings!* So you do know more about my work than I thought. Not many people know I do etchings. When are you coming to my studio? There's *loads* of stuff I'm *dying* to show you.'

'I'm heavily committed for a while … lots of projects on. I just don't know when I'll be free.'

'That's okay. I'll give you my number … no, it's on my web site … no, better still, I'll call you in about a week from now.'

'Don't hold your breath.'

He chuckled. 'I don't give up easily, Marnie. And you'll enjoy seeing my stuff, I promise you … everything I've got.'

When they hung up, Marnie thought, *Oh boy, how does he manage to get close enough to the canvas to paint without his ego getting in the way of the brush?*

Anne breezed in carrying an empty tray. 'Bob wants to talk to you about the services for the kitchen in the farmhouse. He says you'll need to decide very soon if you're going to install an Aga.' She went over to the kitchen area and pressed the button on the kettle. 'Are you ready for coffee, Marnie?' She fetched milk from the fridge and reached up to the shelf for two mugs. 'Marnie?'

'What? Sorry, Anne … what were you saying?'

'Who was that on the phone?'

'Piers Wainwright.'

'So that's why you've gone all thoughtful.'

'Got it in one.'

'Don't tell me … another invitation to the Bright Lights and the Big Smoke … come up and see me sometime?'

'Yes.'

'You didn't accept?'

'What do you think?'

'I think something's bothering you, Marnie.'

'Two days ago he and I were at an event during which one of the guests, a colleague and friend of his, is horribly killed in what may or may not have been an accident. I know I'll be seeing that blazing car in my dreams for months to come. Yet he didn't even mention it … not a word. That's what's bothering me.'

●　●　●　●　●

After coffee, Marnie reached for her own phone calls list and dialled the first number. Her sister was at home. Marnie explained that she and Anne were coming down to Little Venice and hoped they might get together with Beth for lunch or something.

'You cannot be *serious*! You're winding me up, right?'

Oh God, Marnie thought, *she's gone into John McEnroe mode*. 'Of course I'm being serious. Why shouldn't we come to Little Venice? We often do that, Beth. Hadn't you noticed?'

'With all the trouble going on there right now?'

'Trouble? What trouble?'

'The place is *crawling* with drug dealers having gang wars … and police trying to stop them. Didn't you hear about the sack they pulled out of the canal the other day in Regent's Park … containing a body … in pieces?'

'Ugh! No, I didn't. But what's that got to do with us?'

'Some of the people involved were boat people. Several boats have been raided … people arrested …'

'Okay, I'll be careful.'

'People you know, Marnie ...'

• • • • •

Ralph had gone into town for last-minute shopping before his trip, and Marnie did not want to worry Anne with news about gangland killings and drug wars, so she had no one to tell about the events in Little Venice. She checked the phone calls list again. Next name, Jane Rutherford. She rang as soon as Anne went off to prepare a sandwich lunch on *Sally Ann*.

'Well, yes, I suppose it is a serious business, Marnie, but you know London. Life goes on whatever happens.'

'So you aren't cowering under the table while the cops and villains have daily shoot-outs on the canal banks?'

'Not quite. No more than usual.'

'What about the police raids on boats? I heard there'd been boat people arrested.'

'One or two up the Paddington Arm. I didn't know them ... except for Belle Starkey, of course.'

'Belle Starkey ...' Marnie repeated the name. 'Wasn't she the so-called *witness*, the one who told the police she'd seen Neil Gerard come back that night?'

'That's the one. You spoke to her, didn't you, Marnie?'

'Shortly after the murder. Was she involved in drugs?'

'They took her in on suspicion. It may have been her boyfriend's supply, though some said she was dealing on the side herself.'

'Where is she now? Have they released her?'

'She was being held at Lisson Grove nick, last time I heard.'

'My sister's been trying to warn me off coming down.'

'So you thought you'd check if the coast was clear?'

'No. Actually, there are two things. First is that Charles Taverner doesn't want to change the name, *Perfidia*.'

'Fair enough. Is he superstitious? A lot of people don't like changing a boat's name.'

'He said it was Barbara's choice and he didn't want to go against her wishes.'

'Understandable.'

'I suppose so. The other thing is I'd like to invite you on board for a drink or maybe lunch when we reach Little Venice.'

'Great. Just give a shout when you get here.'

'Do you know if Mrs Jolly's around? And I was thinking of asking Roger and Marjorie Broadbent. Maybe my sister and brother-in-law, too.'

'Leave the Little Venice crowd to me, Marnie. I'll check 'em out.'

• • • • •

They sat on *Sally Ann*'s stern deck eating their sandwich lunch. Ralph's mobile rang, and he wandered along the docking area to take the call. Anne drank from her glass of designer water and looked at Marnie.

'You know I haven't seen my folks for a while?'

'That's right. But you often talk to them on the phone, don't you?'

'Oh yeah, every week. Well, I was wondering …'

'Go on.'

'D'you think we might be able to see my mum when we're going through Leighton Buzzard? Perhaps she could meet us for tea or something?'

Marnie pointed at the papers on Anne's lap. 'Put it on the list. Or do you think we should get our social secretary to make the appointment? Jane's getting good at that kind of thing. We could put her on the payroll.'

'It's okay. I'll handle it, Marnie. I'll get my people to talk to her people and get it factored into our schedules.'

Marnie blinked. 'Sounds impressive. That should do the trick.'

She was smiling as she took another bite. But the smile faded at the thought of secretaries making arrangements … of Judith Gross … of Clive Adamson's minions … and the disaster at Spice Quay.

• • • • •

After making love that night, Ralph and Marnie lay with their arms around each other in the sleeping cabin on *Thyrsis*, their heads close together on the pillow. Ralph could smell Marnie's hair and the faint perfume spray she used after showering. Down at the moorings there were no lights to penetrate the darkness and few sounds to disturb the silence of the waterway. They heard a plopping sound somewhere nearby, probably a fish jumping, then stillness returned.

'What are you thinking, Marnie?' Ralph breathed softly in her ear.

'I'm afraid it's nothing very romantic … only that I seem to be flavour of the month just now.'

'That's not bad. You are flavour of the month as far as I'm concerned … every month.'

'Good. But I was thinking about those phone calls.'

'Adamson and Wainwright?'

'Both phoning to invite me to see them.'

'It's not surprising. But something tells me you don't find it flattering. Does it worry you?'

'Not exactly …'

'But?'

'I was at that reception with all the men on Neil Gerard's list of Barbara's ex-lovers. Now, one of them is dead – in very mysterious circumstances, possibly connected in some way with me – two more have phoned wanting to see me, and I'm travelling to London to meet the other one.'

'So many men in your life.'

'No … only one.' She reached forward and kissed him.

'Yes … and he's about to abandon you.'

Marnie drove Ralph to the station on Thursday morning to catch the Gatwick airport service shortly after six. She was back in the office well before seven and made an immediate start on the paperwork, fortified by a croissant and a glass of orange juice produced by Anne. They both worked solidly until, by lunchtime, they had put in virtually a day's work.

As soon as they had packed, Anne booked them a taxi. While they waited for Rajeev the local cab-driver to pick them up, they ticked items off their lists: milk and papers cancelled till next week, answerphone message altered, spare keys to Angela Hemingway, Angela to feed Dolly and take in mail …

Marnie smiled to herself when they helped Rajeev to pack their luggage and provisions into the boot of the taxi. However much she tried to conceal it, Anne was excited again at the prospect of a boat journey.

Up at the boatyard Anne stowed their belongings while Marnie dealt briefly with the manager. In a few minutes they were ready to go. The engine started at the first touch of the button, and Anne was about to push *Perfidia* off from the bank when Marnie raised a hand as a signal to stop her. A boat had come into view on the mainline, crossing their path at rightangles a short way ahead. Another had crept up slowly on the approach to the junction and it came to a halt beside them. Nodding at Marnie, the steerer let his eyes wander along the length of her boat. He leaned forward against the hatch of his much older craft, which was showing the signs of scrapes and bumps along her topsides and hull.

While they waited for the boat up ahead to pass, he pointed at *Perfidia*'s glossy paintwork. 'You're not seriously going to drive that, are you?'

Marnie wondered if this was a sexist affront to her skill as a boater. 'Why not?'

'I'd have thought that was obvious. If you drive her on the canal she might get bumped into – scratched – by ordinary boats like mine. It'd be a crime.'

Marnie smiled. 'Nothing wrong with your boat … but that's a risk I'll have to take.'

'Sooner you than me, darlin'. Which way are you heading?'

'South.'

'That's a relief. I'm going north. No risk of scraping you in the locks. Have a good trip!'

When the other boats had passed, Marnie waved to Anne, who pushed off from the bank and stepped onto the gunwale in the bows. As they eased forward, Anne signalled all-clear, and Marnie steered the beautiful boat out from the Blisworth arm into the mainline of the Grand Union and accelerated through the bridge hole to cruising speed. Their last journey on *Perfidia* had begun. They were taking her home.

• • • • •

Marnie would have liked more sunshine, but weather that was cool, dry and overcast made for a comfortable journey. They encountered little traffic that afternoon, and only passed two other boats in Blisworth tunnel. Anxious not to cause the slightest blemish to *Perfidia*'s immaculate appearance, Marnie slowed virtually to a halt to let them pass and otherwise kept the boat in mid-channel with all lights blazing on its passage through the darkness. Reaching Stoke Bruerne, they had an easy descent of the seven locks and settled down to uninterrupted cruising for the next couple of hours.

It was shortly after six when they passed *Sally Ann* and *Thyrsis* at their home moorings and tried vainly to glimpse the buildings of Glebe Farm through the trees. The strangest feeling came when they saw Dolly curled up asleep on the hatch of *Sally Ann*. Neither wanted to call out to disturb her. Watching her there, Marnie had a premonition that she was never going to return to their home and would never see it again. She was watching her old life from the outside like a ghost whose time among the living was over. Turning back to concentrate on steering, she noticed that Anne too had an odd expression on her face.

Marnie busied herself with the cruising guide. 'If we press on for another couple of hours, we could make it to Great Linford.'

Anne checked the guide over her friend's shoulder. 'We could have supper in the pub.'

'Good thinking, Batman.'

The moment had passed.

· · · · ·

They made it to Cosgrove in less than an hour and found it curiously deserted. The lock was full, and in the still water one gate hung open. The place looked abandoned. Their passage through was quick and they had just begun the slow crawl along the line of moored boats south of the lock when Marnie's mobile began to warble. It was Jane Rutherford.

'This is your social secretary speaking. Arrangements are all sorted. Everyone's available and looking forward to seeing you again. It's been too long, Marnie.'

'You're right … I'm losing touch with you all.'

'So I don't suppose you've heard the latest news …'

'You told me about the drugs raid …' Marnie lowered her voice. '… and the body in the bag.'

'That's yesterday's news. There's more … and it'll be of *particular* interest to you.'

'Why me?'

'Your connection with the Taverners.'

Marnie stiffened. 'What's happened?'

'Remember I told you Belle Starkey – your witness – had been pulled in by the police? Well, she's been talking.'

'About Neil Gerard and Barbara?'

'She's not been very discreet, apparently … things she's said to other people being held … about the evidence she gave at the trial. Someone who was released from custody told reporters about it and they got on to the police.'

'Has she retracted her evidence or what?'

'I don't know all the ins and outs, Marnie, but on the local news they said her comments were being taken seriously.'

Marnie was pondering Jane's phone call when Anne came up from below to join her. She had disappeared inside after working the lock, and now emerged carrying a tray with two glasses of spritzer and a bowl of olives.

'Aperitif time,' Anne announced. 'We have to maintain the high standards to which *Perfidia* is accustomed.'

Marnie accepted a glass, wrenching her mind away from the thought that those high standards included the murder of the owner. They raised their glasses together as the boat crossed the Iron Trunk aqueduct towering over the river Ouse that marked the county boundary.

'Are you all right, Marnie?'

'That was Jane on the phone. She's fixed up our get-together in Little Venice.'

'Great.'

'There's more.'

Marnie recounted the developments concerning Belle Starkey. Much as it conflicted with Marnie's natural inclination to shield Anne from unpleasantness, she knew her friend would hear about this sooner or later.

'Do you think Mr Taverner knows about it?'

'Good point. I've been wondering whether to tell him.'

'Do you have any choice?'

Marnie went below to make the call, leaving Anne at the tiller. As usual Charles's answerphone cut in. Marnie spoke as invited, after the beep.

'It's Marnie, Charles. Are you there?'

She waited a few seconds and he picked up the phone. 'Hallo, Marnie. You got my message?'

'No. I'm not in the office. We're collecting *Perfidia*.'

'I need to talk to you. I'm coming up to the rectory for the weekend. Will you be at Knightly on Saturday?'

'No. We'll be long gone by then, Charles. We've already passed Glebe Farm. We're on the outskirts of Wolverton.'

'So you've actually set off for London.'

'Yes. We should arrive after the weekend. Are you wanting to talk to me about Belle Starkey?'

A pause. 'Yes.'

'I've just heard from a friend that she's been saying things … talking about her evidence …' There was no reaction. Marnie looked up at the window. Perhaps they were under a railway bridge and she had lost the signal. 'Charles … can you hear me?'

'Yes.'

'I gather she spoke to some of the other people about what she saw that night, and the story got out to the press. Is that your understanding?'

A hesitation. 'Not … quite as simple as that, Marnie.'

'Oh?'

'Not the sort of thing I'd want to talk about on the phone.'

'I see …' Marnie did not see.

'Look … let me know when you get to London. Things may well have moved on by then, but I'll still want to talk to you. Perhaps we can meet in Little Venice?'

'Of course. I'll be in touch. Was there anything else?'

'Various things I want to do at the house. I had hoped we could talk about security, for example.'

'We've got a fair number of brochures in a folder in the office barn. You could get them if you want to. Angela Hemingway has the keys.'

'Good. I'll do that.'

'Shall I ring to tell her you're coming?'

'I wanted to see Angela anyway. I'll contact her. Where will I find the brochures?'

'On one of Anne's shelves. It's easy to spot … one of our usual blue folders, clearly marked. You can't miss it.'

'Good. We'll talk when you get to London, Marnie.'

• • • • •

In the pub that evening over supper, Marnie tried to give all her attention to planning the journey. Anne had brought the cruising guide and together they mapped out their targets for each day. If the weather stayed fine and dry it would be a pleasant run through charming scenery, the best way to approach the capital. Anne seemed to have no qualms about travelling on *Perfidia* again, no thoughts of Barbara's death on board.

For Marnie every journey taken on a boat felt like a stolen season, like truanting from school. She loved that sense of freedom. Travelling on the hidden highway of the canal those few days, slipping past thousands, even millions, of people who had no inkling of the boat's presence, she felt she was living in a parallel universe concealed from the real world.

To describe the journey to London as *uneventful* would be an injustice. They endured no disasters, no unfortunate experiences with the small number of other boats they passed, had no accidents or technical problems. Uneventful, perhaps. But progressing through pastoral landscapes, operating the ancient technology of the locks, passing under bridges and occasionally over rivers and roads, all these filled their senses in a way that was wholly satisfying. Going to bed pleasantly weary each night with only the sounds of the country, a fish jumping, an owl hooting in the distance, and waking up each morning to see a heron on the bank, the early light reflected off the still water, these may not have been *events* but they combined to form a rich mixture of sensations and pleasures.

They set off early on Friday morning and passed round the northern and eastern edges of Milton Keynes. As soon as they had cleared the shallow lock at Fenny Stratford, Anne phoned home and agreed a time to meet her mother in Leighton Buzzard. *Perfidia* reached the moorings in the town centre within a few minutes of their ETA to be greeted by a wave from the bank. The three spent a convivial hour together over lunch before Jackie had to get back to work at the hairdresser's in time for her next appointment.

For a few hours *Perfidia* travelled south, surrounded on all sides by pastureland, climbing steadily towards the Chiltern Hills. The last time they had passed that way Ralph had chosen to walk the towpath between the locks that appeared at frequent intervals. Now, Marnie handed the tiller to Anne while she tramped on foot from lock to lock. For mile after mile the open countryside enhanced Marnie's theory of a parallel universe. Occasionally she caught a glimpse of a train in the distance across the fields, but otherwise she had only birdsong and the faint rumbling of *Perfidia*'s engine to accompany her walk.

At any other time Marnie would have felt refreshed and invigorated by the quiet of the countryside and the pleasure of an afternoon's walking. But that day she was glad to climb back on the boat to rejoin Anne for the approach to Marsworth Junction. The solitude of the landscape had induced in her an uncharacteristic melancholy and, although she was reluctant to admit it, she had a sense of foreboding about what lay ahead.

Watching the elegant lines of *Perfidia* as Anne guided her into the last of the Seabrook locks, Marnie realised that she was looking forward to transferring the boat to Mike Brent to sell. She hopped aboard after shutting the lock gate behind her, put an arm round Anne's shoulders and squeezed, smiling cheerfully. Deep down inside she rejoiced at the thought that once the journey was completed, she would hand Mike the keys and put *Perfidia* out of her life forever.

• • • • •

They tied up for the night in Marsworth, had supper in the pub and were in bed soundly sleeping soon after ten o'clock. A yawning early start on Saturday saw them clear the seven lock flight before nine, and they chugged through the deep cutting of the Tring Summit under a lowering sky that threatened rain.

At about the time that Anne was hunting in the boat's cupboards for wet weather gear, the phone was ringing in cottage number three at Glebe Farm.

'Good morning, Angela Hemingway.'

'Angela, this is Charles Taverner. Sorry to bother you, but I wonder if you're around this morning. One or two things I'd like to discuss about the … the old vicarage.'

'Only for a short while, I'm afraid. I've got a meeting – I chair the lay readers' group – have to get away quite soon. I'll be out for the rest of the day.'

'Oh …' Disappointment.

'Is there anything urgent? I'll be here for the next twenty minutes. Anything we can discuss on the phone?'

'Er … let me see … No, it's all right. What about tomorrow?'

'Sunday?' said Angela, the vicar.

'Of course … silly of me. There is one thing … Marnie has some papers for me. She said I could collect them from the office barn. You have the keys, I believe.'

'Er … yes, I do, but I don't know anything about –'

'I could get her to ring you, if you're in any doubt about it.'

A pause. 'No … no. I'm sure it'll be okay if you've arranged it with her.'

'Good. I'll be down straight away.'

•　•　•　•　•

The first raindrops hit the roof of *Perfidia* while Marnie was stepping off at Cowroast to work the lock. She had pulled on a yellow cagoule as a precautionary measure, hoping it was no more than a passing shower and that the run down to Berkhamsted would not be in a downpour.

Standing on the counter in a bright blue cagoule, Anne inched *Perfidia* forward, glancing back over her shoulder as the rain caught her cheeks. There were no other boats in sight, no one to share the lock. She raised a hand to Marnie who pulled on one gate, went round the balance beam and pressed the small of her back against it to walk it open.

They had begun their descent to the capital.

•　•　•　•　•

Angela Hemingway checked her papers, bag and keys and looked at the kitchen clock for the umpteenth time. It was with relief that she heard the scrunching of tyres on gravel and went to the door to find Charles emerging from his Jaguar.

'Very good of you to do this, Angela. I appreciate it.'

'A pleasure, Mr … Charles.' Try as she might, she could not get used to calling him by what she regarded as his Christian name. 'Sorry I'm in such a hurry and can't give you my full attention.'

They crossed the cobbled yard together. Angela fiddled with the bundle of keys and found the right one at the second attempt.

'I should've thought to have the office ready for you,' she muttered, pushing the door open. 'Only I'm not sure where things are in here, of course. You know where to find what you want?'

'Marnie said it was on Anne's shelf.'

Angela pointed. 'That's her desk, over there.'

Charles walked quickly across the room. Anne had left her desk very neat and tidy. He admired that. Finding the blue folder would be a doddle. He ran a hand along the wall shelf and brushed several folders all labelled in felt tip pen. None of them was blue. He checked a second time.

Angela hovered behind him. 'Everything all right?'

Charles frowned. 'Sure Marnie said a *blue* folder,' he muttered to himself and turned to examine the desktop. 'I'm damned ... er, blessed if I can see it. Marnie said there was quite a lot of bumph ... should be easy to spot.'

Angela bent forward and peered at the shelf. 'No blue folders here.'

'Is there anywhere else she might have put it?' He looked at Angela's blank expression. 'You wouldn't know, of course, any more than I would.'

Angela's eyes strayed to the wall clock and scanned the office, coming to rest on the loft ladder. 'Ah ... I wonder ...'

'Yes?'

'Did Marnie say the shelf in the office, Charles?'

He shrugged. '*Anne's shelf* ... I think ...'

'Well, her room is in the attic above us.'

Charles saw the gap in the ceiling. 'Up there?'

'It's the only other place I can think of where Anne would have a shelf.'

Charles hesitated. 'D'you think I should ...?'

On balance, Angela thought he should probably not go up to Anne's room without Anne being present or at least giving her permission, but she sensed that Charles would do whatever he wanted to do. And she knew he would touch nothing that did not concern him.

'That wall ladder's the only way up. I'll wait for you down here.'

Charles needed no prompting. He mounted the ladder with an agility that belied his age. Angela heard the click of a light switch and footsteps proceeding cautiously overhead. Another sound reached her ears. Through the open doorway she heard a phone ringing across the courtyard.

'Charles, I think that's my phone. I won't be a moment.'

There was a muffled reply from the attic, and she sped from the room. By the time she had finished the call Charles was outside closing the rear door of his car. He held out the keys.

'I've locked up.'

Angela caught a glimpse of blue on the back seat. 'Did you get what you wanted?'

'More than enough to keep me occupied by the look of it.'

Angela smiled. 'Very thorough is Marnie ... and Anne too, of course.'

'Yes, they make a good team. Hope I haven't delayed you too much.'

They shook hands and went their separate ways.

• • • • •

Intermittent showers followed them all the way down to Berkhamsted, and a light drizzle settled in for the rest of the morning. Even so, Marnie spent most of that stretch on the towpath, except between the locks that were spaced further apart. By twelve-thirty they had reached the swing bridge at Winkwell, and Marnie took a decision. They tied up for a pub lunch at the Three Horseshoes.

They were waiting for their food to be served when the mobile in Marnie's cagoule pocket began vibrating. In deference to the other patrons she took the call outside the front door.

'Hi Ralph, don't tell me about the weather you're having in DC, okay?'

'Bad as that, is it, Marnie?' He sounded cheerful. 'I won't mention that I'm having breakfast on the terrace of the hotel. Otherwise how are things?'

She told him about the drugs raids in Little Venice, about Belle Starkey being indiscreet while in the cells, and the story getting into the papers that her evidence at Neil Gerard's trial was probably unreliable.

'What action's being taken on that?' Ralph asked.

'Not sure. I spoke to Charles on the phone. He knows more about it than he was willing to say.'

'Interesting. I suppose that means he's got involved somewhere in the background.'

'How could he?'

'He's probably got his QC lobbying like mad for an appeal or a retrial. I expect you're pleased, aren't you, Marnie?'

'Of course I'll be glad if Neil's case is going to be re-examined.'

'But we'll be left with a big question.'

'Yes, if not Neil, then who did it?'

'Exactly. That's interesting … really quite intriguing.'

'Why do you say that, Ralph?'

'Well, we've said before that if it wasn't Gerard, the next most likely suspect could be Charles himself.'

Marnie tried to grapple with that idea. 'I don't think Barbara was planning to leave Charles, if that's what you're suggesting.'

'That's not really the point. I think it's about their whole relationship.'

'Yes. Thinking of the tapes … the more I heard, the more convinced I was that what she felt for Neil was probably the real thing.'

'And that's precisely what puts Charles in the frame.'

•   •   •   •   •

The clouds began to clear in the afternoon while *Perfidia* was passing through Boxmoor. Waiting for the lock chamber to empty, her thoughts wandered up the hill towards the prison where she had first met Neil Gerard, where he had later tried to hang himself. So much had happened since then, and now he might be on the brink of being released. She could hardly believe it.

They stopped to take on stores for supper that evening at the supermarket south of Hemel Hempstead. When they came out, Anne asked if she could have a spell at working the locks. Among their purchases was a newspaper and, while Marnie steered the boat, she read about the latest developments in the Little Venice Murder case. She had noticed that all the papers on the news-stand were running the *Odd Couple* story, still fascinated by the idea that the campaign for an appeal by a convicted murderer was being led by the victim's husband.

The report in the *Independent* that Marnie was reading mentioned that Charles Taverner had "gone to ground" and could not be contacted for comment, while his "cohorts" were pushing for Neil Gerard's early release pending further investigations. The editorial described it as "the most sensational legal story of the decade".

Marnie took another decision late in the afternoon. Consulting the cruising guide had convinced her that they could reach Little Venice by Sunday evening if they made a determined effort. They could certainly not make it in time for lunch.

'Cassiobury Park,' she stated, pointing at the map.

Anne was perched on the edge of the counter between locks. 'So another lock or two?'

Marnie nodded. 'Yep. That should give us somewhere peaceful to tie up for the night. I'll keep a look-out for a spot.'

The *spot* was in the middle of the park but felt remote as if far out in the country. Anne asked if she could take a shower before eating, and Marnie packed away the stores that had been left on the galley worktop.

They prepared supper together, Anne declaring that one of her favourite aspects of boating was the simple meals and the relaxed atmosphere at the end of the working day. Chatting amiably about the weather and the sights they had seen on the journey, they produced a meal that was an old favourite: herb omelette, a baguette, tomato and basil salad, a simple French red *vin de pays*, Greek yogurt with a swirl of honey.

Taking their seats, Anne stretched and arched her back with pleasure. As usual, she was almost purring with contentment. 'Marnie, this is *perfection*.'

Marnie laughed and poured the wine. 'You're very easy to please. You appreciate the simpler things in life. I must say it's really pleasant travelling with you, Anne.'

They chinked glasses and sipped the wine.

Suddenly, looking at Marnie over the rim of her glass, Anne's expression shifted. She was still smiling, but a subtle change had come over her. She spoke softly and reflectively. 'You haven't really been travelling with me, Marnie. You've been travelling with Neil Gerard ... and Barbara ... and Charles Taverner. I bet you know the newspaper story off by heart.'

• • • • •

Sunday morning did not look promising, unless the promise was for rain. Marnie decided that they did not need to hurry, but once they were up and about there seemed little point in idling when they could make steady progress on their journey. They had not long set off, with Marnie at the tiller, when the mobile trilled.

'Didn't get you out of bed, did I? Hi, Marnie. It's Jane.'

'Sure, you know what the Grand Union's like. We were out clubbing till dawn. How are things?'

'Slight change of plan at this end. Little Venice is in a state of chaos.'

'Why's that?' Marnie dreaded the reply. 'More raids?'

'Raids?' Jane sounded bewildered. 'Oh ... *raids* ... no ... well, not in the sense you mean. We had an invasion last night. A whole convoy of New Age travellers descended on us. Things here are, to say the least, very crowded.'

'Trouble?'

'Not really ... just lots of boats. Someone said they were on their way to a festival in the west country. Mike Brent's here trying to sort them out. He's not best pleased, having to come in on a Sunday.'

• • • • •

They reached Rickmansworth at eleven. The locks were spread out evenly in this sector, and after making a quick phone call, Marnie called Anne on board to discuss the change of plan over coffee while they chugged the short pounds. She explained that Mrs Jolly had insisted on them having a buffet lunch at her house. Beth and Paul could not get away but Roger and Marjorie were free. They agreed to get *Perfidia* as close to their destination as possible by the end of the day, ready for a prompt arrival on Monday morning.

Slowly descending in the next lock, Marnie phoned Mike Brent. 'I hear you've got problems, Mike.'

'You could call it that.' There was laughter in his voice. 'It's complete chaos here, but we're getting it sorted.'

'Trouble?'

'Just boats moored all over the place.'

'You sound fairly calm ... in the circumstances.'

'Yeah ... well, what can you do? They had quite a lively time in the local pubs last night, by all accounts, but they're no real bother ... just so many of them ... it's like a New Age fleet.'

'What do we do with *Perfidia?*'

'Er ... you can leave her up near the end of the line beyond the houseboats. I'll find her a mooring later ... once our *guests* have moved on.'

'I'll drop the keys in at the office.'

'Okay. Gotta go, Marnie. See you!'

Marnie disconnected and rang the office to check the answerphone. *How did people live before we had modern gadgets?* she wondered, listening to the ringing tone. One message.

'Marnie, this is Sarah. Isn't it *wonderful?* Neil's solicitor thinks there's a real chance he'll be released soon pending a review. I'm *so* grateful for all your help. We'll talk soon. Bye!'

50

On Sunday night they had stopped within easy reach of Bull's Bridge and enjoyed a dinner of baked salmon with herbs, a tossed salad and sliced fresh pineapple. The galley smelled of hot bread, a part-baked small stick finished off in the oven, as Anne unstoppered the rest of the red wine. They had left themselves a final run the next morning of around four hours to their destination, but the last of the locks was behind them, and with their customary early start they expected to be in Little Venice in good time for lunch.

Monday morning saw Marnie guide *Perfidia* under the white-painted arch of Bull's Bridge to turn left onto the Grand Union's Paddington Arm. An hour or so later she was steering a twisty course through an industrial zone before heading towards open parkland. Marnie had a private rule never to phone anyone before nine o'clock in the morning. She checked her watch. As the second hand swept to the top of the dial, she pressed buttons and dialled Charles's mobile.

He sounded tired. 'Hallo, Marnie.'

'Everything OK?'

'Yes, thank you.'

'Do you want us to meet in London today? We're about two hours from Little Venice.'

He hesitated. 'I'm not sure. There's a lot happening and I can keep in touch just as easily from up here without being pestered by journalists.'

'I understand. I've been reading about the situation in the press. Can you fill me in?'

'Well I er ... don't like to –'

'What's the problem, Charles? I don't get it. All that *can't talk on the phone* business goes back to when calls were put through by operators. No one can hear what you're saying.'

'I suppose not.' His voice was flat.

'So what *is* going on?'

'Over the past few days there've been ... developments. You know that the so-called *witness* was arrested last week in a drug operation by the police.'

Marnie was getting impatient. 'The whole country knows that, Charles. It's in all the papers.'

'While she was being held, she told one or two people that she'd "assumed" it was Gerard who returned to *Perfidia* on the night of the murder. She said she couldn't swear she'd seen him clearly.'

'But she did ... swear, I mean. She gave evidence to that effect.'

'Which is why what she said in custody was important.'

'But what she said to drug suspects wouldn't count as reliable evidence, surely?'

'It's not as simple as that, Marnie. One of the people was ... an undercover police officer. That's why I was reluctant to talk about it. It's all strictly confidential. You won't read that in the papers. Keep it to yourself.'

'Absolutely. So this undercover person reported what he'd heard?'

'She … it was a woman officer. She got Belle Starkey talking and became convinced she was telling the truth.'

'Would the police want that story made public? I thought they were certain of Neil's guilt.'

'They didn't have much choice, Marnie. The story was public anyway. Other suspects had heard her and they blabbed to the press after they were let out.'

'So where does that leave Neil Gerard?'

'My QC is pressing for an early release pending a re-examination of the facts. One fingerprint on a gas valve isn't enough to convict a man of murder when the only witness to his presence at the scene admits she could've been wrong.'

'I suppose it changes everything.'

'Of course. We're arguing it's suspicious that only Gerard's fingerprints were found on the gas system.'

'And the fact that you, Charles, are involved in seeking his release must add *huge* weight to the argument. But I bet the police won't be happy at being made to look foolish.'

'On the contrary, Marnie, it speaks volumes for the integrity of Bruere and his colleagues.'

'Will he be in trouble because of the wrongful arrest and imprisonment of Neil?'

'No, his investigation was done by the book. Gerard was right: everything was properly conducted, except the wrong person was convicted. I'm just so relieved it's turning out like this.'

Marnie had a sudden insight. 'Do you think you know who did it, Charles?'

'No. I have no idea. But I'm absolutely certain it wasn't Neil Gerard. I believe he's a man of complete honesty … at least in that regard.'

'That's very generous of you, considering …'

'I have to face the facts, Marnie. I have to accept that Barbara played her part in deceiving me. Any man might have succumbed to her beauty and charisma. I know I did.'

There was nothing Marnie could say. Having known Barbara and heard the tapes, she knew he was right.

Charles had the last word. 'I keep thinking, thank goodness we don't have capital punishment, Marnie. If we did, Gerard would have been hanged.'

• • • • •

For Marnie, Little Venice was the prettiest place on the whole canal system, or at least as much of it as she had seen. Returning to *Sally Ann*'s old base always felt like a home-coming. From gliding slowly past the first of the moored boats, to passing under the bridge and into the pool by Browning Island was always magic. But not that day.

Within sight of the first moorings Marnie brought out the binoculars and focused into the distance. Even at that range she could see a mass of boats clustered round the island. The telephoto effect made it look as if the travellers formed an impenetrable mass of vessels, and she could imagine the struggle that Mike Brent and his staff were having, trying to keep the passage clear for through traffic. She passed the binoculars to Anne, the word *chaos* in her mind, and rang Jane Rutherford to let her know they were approaching. Her next call was to the BW office, where she left a message for Mike Brent on the answerphone to tell him they had arrived.

The first craft in line was a houseboat, a converted barge, and in accordance with Mike's instructions Marnie tucked *Perfidia* in behind it. Muttering *excuse-me* to the absent owner who was at work, they stepped onto the bank, walked through his tiny garden and out by the gate into the street. Halfway to the bridge they were met by Jane beside her boat. She surprised Marnie by linking arms with her as she told them the whole story of the police drugs operation while they walked to Mrs Jolly's house.

The word in Little Venice was that the police came across the drugs ring as soon as they began investigating the dismembered body in the sack. A tattoo and DNA had led them immediately to the house of the corpse where they picked up a trail to the local drugs network. It had been a piece of inspired, opportunistic policing that had caught the underworld off-guard and led to dozens of arrests. Significantly, Marnie thought, Jane did not mention that it was an undercover police officer who heard Belle Starkey's rash utterances and reported them up the chain of command. That remained a secret.

They stopped at the bridge to look down on the pool. Where normally the only craft present were the waterbuses at their station on one side and the art gallery and other barges on the other, with the tree-covered island in the middle, today all was a shambles. Stacked three and four abreast all around the pool, the travellers' boats presented an outlandish spectacle. Most were in dire need of a lick of paint; many were piled high with logs, sacks of coal and bicycles on the roof; some were covered overall in tarpaulins in various shades of black and grey; rust was a favoured option. Of the occupants nothing was to be seen.

Anne spoke first. 'Blimey. It looks like the Harbour from Hell.'

'I thought Mike was supposed to be sorting this out,' Marnie observed in a neutral tone.

Jane was uncertain. 'There's some sort of meeting going on, I think.'

'So where is everybody?'

'Don't worry about it, Marnie. Mike'll handle it.' She tugged her arm. 'Let's go and have lunch.'

• • • • •

Predictably, the conversation at Mrs Jolly's house centred on the body in the canal, the drugs raid and the impact of Belle Starkey's recanting on the Neil Gerard campaign. There was only one part of the whole situation that interested her, and she waited patiently for the chance to raise it.

'Roger, as a lawyer, what do you think are Neil's prospects for getting an appeal or a retrial or whatever? What's likely to happen to him now?'

Roger Broadbent dabbed his mouth with a napkin. 'Any number of things are possible, Marnie. It depends what's going on behind the scenes. I imagine there'll be discussions between the judiciary, the Crown Prosecution Service, the police ...'

'Charles Taverner's got a barrister involved, a QC. Would that make a difference?'

'It can't do any harm. We'll never know the details of what they're discussing, but if the various parties agree that the case against Gerard was unsafe after all, he could be released quite soon. There are procedures.'

'And does it seem that way to you, from what you've heard?'

Roger shrugged. 'It's impossible to tell, Marnie. Why don't you ask Charles Taverner? You're still in touch with him. He'll know everything that's going on, I'm quite sure of that.'

·　·　·　·　·

It was about the time when Marnie thought they should be leaving, that she discovered her mistake. While looking in her shoulder bag for a paper tissue, she spotted *Perfidia*'s keys. *Damn!* she muttered under her breath. Anne noticed this from across the room and raised an eyebrow. Marnie lifted the keyring out of the bag. In reply, Anne's mouth formed a letter O.

Mrs Jolly noticed this exchange. 'Something wrong, Marnie?'

Marnie raised the keys higher for all to see. 'I was supposed to drop the keys into the BW office for Mike to move the boat.'

Glancing towards the window, Roger said, 'I doubt much will've happened over the past hour or two.'

'Even so … I know they want to get things sorted out as soon as they can.'

'Why not pop over there now?' Anne said. 'I promised Mrs Jolly I'd help clear up. I'll stay here, and you can give me a ring when you want me to come over.'

'Good idea,' Mrs Jolly agreed.

Marnie got up. 'I expect I'll be about fifteen, twenty minutes.'

·　·　·　·　·

Two surprises followed in quick succession. As Marnie reached the bridge she caught her first glimpse of the pool. Someone had waved a magic wand; the travellers' boats had vanished. She scanned the whole area. Not one remained. It was as if they had never been there. Then her eyes fell on an unexpected sight. Tied up on the far side of the pool, just beside the waterbus moorings lay … *Perfidia*. To reassure herself that she was not mistaken, Marnie reached into her bag and pulled out the keys attached to their familiar ring with the green cord and the cork ball. She frowned in concentration. How had *Perfidia* been moved to this new place from the far end of the moorings when Marnie held the boat's keys in her hand?

What were the possible explanations? Had she been towed down from where they had left her? Unlikely. And why would they do that? There was one way to find out. Marnie walked briskly along the footpath, over the next bridge and down to the BW office in the old toll house. It was a charming Regency cottage with iron railings round the tiny courtyard entrance. She rang the bell and pushed open the front door. A third surprise awaited her. The lobby by the reception desk was almost filled with a pram. Three women were standing round it, talking in hushed voices, and they looked at Marnie with expressions that urged her not to make a noise. The occupant of the pram was sleeping.

One of the women recognised Marnie and smiled at her, indicating that they should talk outside.

'Sorry about that, Marnie. Karen hasn't chosen a very good day to drop in on us. She used to work here. We haven't seen her since she left to have the baby.'

'You've had quite a busy time, I gather. Actually, I came to see Mike.'

'Sorry, he's not here at the moment. He popped out to see one or two people when the travellers began leaving.'

'When will he be back, do you know?'

'Not sure. He's always in and out, you know what he's like.'

'Will you tell him I called by. And thank him for moving *Perfidia*. I've just got to fetch some things from the boat before I leave.'

'That's no problem.'

Marnie walked slowly under the bridge and stood for a short while on the towpath contemplating *Perfidia*. Something was bothering her. It felt like a dream that had evaporated on waking and was impossible to recapture. She tried to concentrate hard, and was attempting to get back to the source of her concern by a process of systematic thought when she heard a voice behind her.

'Excuse me ... excuse me.'

It took Marnie a few seconds to realise the voice was addressing her. She turned to see the woman with the pram.

'Yes?'

'I'm sorry, but ... you're blocking the path. I need to get by.'

Marnie snapped back to consciousness. 'Oh, yes ... thoughtless of me.'

'I would've said it was the opposite.' The woman smiled brightly. 'You seemed to be full of thoughts.'

Marnie stepped aside to make room for the pram to pass. 'Yes, I was. But it's no excuse.'

'That's all right. I saw you in the office just then. You used to have a mooring here, didn't you? You won't remember me, but everyone knows you.'

They began walking slowly along the path. 'You're Karen,' Marnie said. 'And you used to work in the office until junior here came along.'

'That's right!' She seemed delighted. 'It's great being a mother, but somehow you become invisible. Everyone gives all their attention to the baby.'

'Do you mind that?'

'No, not at all.' She laughed quietly. 'It's just such a surprise to be reminded that I'm a person in my own right.'

'When did you leave?'

'Christmas.'

'So you had a combined leaving do and Christmas party ... a nice send-off.'

'Not really. Don't you remember? There was that dreadful flu epidemic. It was like the Great Plague of London round here. There were no parties, not even a glass of wine.'

'Of course. The office was virtually shut down. You must've been the only one left in the place.'

'More or less. At the end there was only Mike and me.'

'Mike? I thought he had a bad dose, too.'

'He did. He had the worst dose of all, apparently. I heard he went off the same day that I left, so the office had to be shut down early. I remember putting something in his in-tray – something he'd left on the photocopier – and then I just went.'

'So no memorable send-off on your last day.'

Karen looked serious. 'It was memorable, all right. I can't ever forget it.'

'You felt so lousy with the flu?'

Karen shook her head slowly and lowered her voice. 'It was the day Barbara Taverner was murdered ... the fifteenth of December.' They had come to a halt beside *Perfidia*. Karen looked at it as she continued. 'The boat was moored just round in the arm, next to Belle Starkey. It's awful to think I was coming out of the office at about the time she was ...'

They both stared at the boat. It lay at rest, a silent witness unable to tell its story.

Marnie put a hand on Karen's arm. 'You've got other things to think of now.'

They parted company on a more cheerful note, and Karen pushed the pram up the slope to the bridge. Marnie watched her go and then let herself in to the boat. Unbeknown to her, her conversation with Karen had been observed from the bridge.

Something was wrong. Marnie dumped her bag on the table in the boat's dining area and sat down while confused thoughts assailed her from all sides. She tried to untangle everything. *What's bothering you, Marnie? Make one of Anne's lists. Put your worries in order.*

She sat back. Her bag was lying on its side, and she could see the boat keys that she had just dropped in it. *The keys ...* what about the keys? All right, she thought, there's a question about the keys. Just leave it like that for now. That's item one.

Who had moved the boat to the pool from the end of the moorings? That was easy. It must have been Mike or one of his staff. But there was something else that concerned her about moving the boat. It was a memory from way back, and she only now realised it was a question that should have been asked some other time. Confusion was creeping over her again, and she decided to leave the matter of moving the boat as item two.

The greatest source of doubt was Karen. It had been a simple conversation, just a few words spoken between near strangers, but it had unsettled Marnie for reasons she could not fathom. The flu epidemic ... *It was like the Great Plague of London round here* ... What could it be that was troubling her? The fifteenth of December, the day Barbara was murdered.

Marnie added up her mental list of questions: the keys, moving the boat, the flu epidemic, the day Barbara died, Karen in the office, abandoning it because she felt too ill to struggle on. The questions flew around in her mind, racing out of control. But gradually they fell into a pattern, formed a perfect circle. Everything began to fit together. All had become clear. It all made sense, and in that moment she knew exactly what had happened.

The knock on the side door made Marnie jump. She was gathering herself to reply when the doors opened and someone came backwards down the steps. As she watched the black shoes and the dark business suit descending, their wearer turned and Marnie found herself confronted by Charles Taverner.

'*You,*' she said. 'I thought you were in Knightly St John.'

Charles remained where he stood. He looked grim. 'There were things I had to attend to here, after all.'

'I ... I was just thinking about you.' She immediately regretted saying that.

'About me?'

Marnie nodded. 'I've been thinking about what happened to Barbara. You know beyond any doubt that Neil Gerard didn't kill her, don't you?'

'Yes. What were you thinking about me, Marnie?'

'It was something you said about life ... being about women. *That's the system ... that's how it works*, you said.'

'Well, of course, I was wrong.'

'You don't believe that any more?'

'It's only part of the story ... part of the *system*, so to speak.'

'What's the rest?'

'The rest, I suppose, is children ... the most basic thing of all. Have you got children, Marnie?'

She realised how little he knew about her compared with how much she knew about him. 'No.'

'Nor me. I never had kids ... from either marriage ... not my greatest success.'

'There are all sorts of reasons why people don't have children, Charles.'

'Of course, forgive me. I wasn't thinking.'

'I wasn't talking about my own circumstances ... just people in general.'

'Yes. I didn't mean to imply anything about you, Marnie. Anyway there's still time for you to start a family ... if you want one.'

'It's none of my business, of course, but ... is that what you wanted?'

'Isn't that what most women want ... the *system*?'

'But it wasn't possible for you?' Marnie was horrified to be talking like this, but she felt drawn along by the conversation and by Charles's frankness. 'There was a biological reason?'

Charles cleared his throat. 'The medics eventually discovered that the problem lay with me.'

'Are you saying it was a problem for you and Barbara?'

Charles shrugged. 'Barbara never made a fuss about it, but ... I think she regarded it as ... an imperfection intruding into her life. I saw you speaking to the woman with the pram, Marnie. Such a simple thing for most people, but a huge failure when it doesn't work out, especially for someone with such a lust for life as Barbara had.'

A flash seemed to erupt in Marnie's head. Could Barbara have been pregnant when she died? She racked her memory for any reference to that possibility in the press reports of the trial. If it had been the case, her whole theory would be blown apart. And her supposition about who had murdered Barbara would be based on false premises.

Marnie became aware that while her mind was racing over these ideas, Charles was looking around him.

He shook his head. 'I never thought I'd stand here again,' he said quietly. 'Marnie, I have to go. I just came to make sure everything was all right. I'll leave you to do the necessary. Sorry to inflict all this on you.'

Before she could reply, he was gone, closing the doors behind him. Marnie caught sight of Charles through the window walking quickly away. She breathed out audibly and sat back in the seat, releasing the tension in her body. Her thoughts were all a jumble now. The pattern she had created seemed to lie in fragments before her.

She got up and looked through the window on the water side. The willow on Browning Island was in fresh leaf, its fronds brushing the surface of the water, almost concealing the swan's nest at the edge. Without thinking, Marnie went to a cupboard in the galley and found the bottle of Cognac. The nearest glass to hand was a heavy whisky goblet. She took it and poured herself a generous measure. Standing in the middle of the saloon, she sipped the brandy, felt its warmth in her throat and closed her eyes. It occurred to her that she was standing very close to the spot where Barbara's body had lain, but she was past caring.

She was taking another sip of Cognac when she heard movement at the far end of the boat. A key was turning in the lock near the tiller. The door was opening and there were footsteps by the engine room. Seconds later, Mike Brent came into the cabin. His face registered surprise when he saw Marnie. Pleasant surprise.

'Oh … you gave me a shock, Marnie.' He smiled. 'I didn't expect you to be here. I was just coming back to make sure the boat was locked up and secure. I didn't have time to check properly before.'

'You were preoccupied with all the travellers' boats. You had a lot on your mind.'

'You can say that again.'

'That's why you made your mistake.'

'Did I leave a door unlocked? I know I didn't check the side doors. I was certain you'd have made sure the gas and electrical systems were –'

'That isn't what I meant, Mike.'

'What did you mean? The boat looks fine to me … even more beautiful than before.'

'I've just met one of your colleagues. Karen was visiting the office … brought the baby to show everyone.'

'Nice girl … and a good colleague.'

'I could imagine she was … the dependable sort, one who'd stay to the bitter end, even if she was feeling ill.'

'Feeling ill? I don't get you, Marnie.'

'You told the police you were away with flu the evening Barbara died.'

'That's right. The staff confirmed it. We were all interviewed.'

'When were you interviewed, Mike?'

'As soon as we came back after the Christmas break … all of us … along with everyone else in Little Venice.'

'Not quite all. Karen wasn't around then, was she? She was on maternity leave.'

'I don't think they regarded Karen as a suspect, Marnie. And we could all vouch for each other's whereabouts that day. By that afternoon we'd all gone home because of the flu.'

'Who locked up the office that evening?'

Mike returned her gaze evenly. 'The cleaners … as usual.'

Marnie wavered. She had not thought of that. 'But Karen knew you were there that afternoon, Mike … the one person the police didn't question.'

'How would she know that if she went off with flu?'

'She put something in your in-tray when you'd popped out, something you'd left on the photocopier.'

Mike shook his head. 'You're forgetting that I'm the manager here, not a clerk. I don't touch the photocopier. My secretary deals with all that sort of thing.'

'Not when she's away through illness, she doesn't.'

Mike sighed. 'Marnie, I think you're muddling things up. The police did a very thorough job. They checked with us in case we'd seen anything. They were satisfied we weren't involved. You should leave them to do the detective work. They know what they're doing.'

'But they can't know everything. They couldn't know about the keys, for instance.'

Mike looked puzzled. 'What keys? What about them?'

'Another distraction, Mike. You must have the keys for so many boats at one time or another, it didn't occur to you that this was one set of keys you shouldn't have. I've got the keys from Knightly St John, the spare set that Charles kept. There were always two sets on the boat, Barbara's and the ones in the locker in case of emergency. The police kept that set, thinking they had Barbara's. But you've got hers, Mike.'

Involuntarily Mike's hand moved to the bulge in his pocket. 'The emergency set,' he muttered.

'Good boating practice,' said Marnie. 'Never risk losing your keys overboard and not having spares with you. Barbara was always well organised.'

'Yes.' He seemed far away in his thoughts.

Marnie continued. 'That's how you were able to bring the boat down here from where I left her. It's only when I started to wonder how you'd moved her, that I worked it out. But you had too much on your mind with all the chaos of the travellers' boats. You didn't have time to think of the implications of what you were doing.'

'Didn't you think, Marnie, that I might've had a spare set cut after Barbara died? I needed to take care of the boat when the police were holding the keys along with all her other personal effects.'

Marnie had to think quickly. 'So there's no chance of Barbara's DNA being on the ones you've been using, presumably … if you had a new set made?'

'I …' He closed his mouth slowly. 'They've been on the boat … they could've picked up traces … it must be possible.'

'It's no wonder you didn't think about that. You told me ages ago you'd been moving *Perfidia* around to make space all through the winter … up to Camden Lock, Lisson Grove, all over. I've only just realised the significance of that. You had keys all that time. You had Barbara's keys. The police had the other set. You automatically did what you always did with boats in your charge, moved them when you had to. Only you shouldn't have been able to do that.'

'This is all very interesting, Marnie. But one set of keys is very like another, like thousands of boat key rings used all over the waterways. Who's to know how many sets Barbara might've had cut?'

'I think it could be worked out, Mike,' Marnie said quietly. 'Barbara was very methodical about everything.'

'You think you've got it all sorted, Marnie? I don't think it adds up to very much.'

'I know you were still around on the day she died. Karen would testify to that. Leaving a piece of paper on the photocopier … such a small detail. And of course you wouldn't realise you'd done it, because you had that letter in your in-tray, where you'd expect it to be.'

Mike looked defiant. 'What about the eye witness?'

'You know you can forget Belle Starkey's story. You must've read the papers. The police will work out that it was you she saw that evening. You're about the same size as Neil Gerard … it was dark … an easy mistake.'

Mike perched on the corner of the table. 'I must say I'm really quite impressed with how you've worked things out. If it wasn't so far-fetched I'd have to agree your theory hangs together. But it just hangs by a thread, doesn't it? I mean, you couldn't prove any of this.'

'It's not my job to prove anything, Mike. That will be for the police and their experts to do. They might also be able to link you with the death of Ian Stuart.'

'What are you talking about?'

'I think you were trying to kill me that afternoon. You didn't know I hadn't gone by car and neither did he. My guess – and I grant you it is just a guess – is that you thought you were tampering with *my* car. Ian got in the way and became your victim.'

'This is nonsense!'

'Possibly. But if the police look into it and if you were involved, they'll find evidence from your clothes, no matter how tiny or invisible the traces. They can do that these days.'

'Marnie, if you go around making these wild accusations –'

'I think I've got things worked out pretty well.'

'You haven't answered the most important question of all. What reason could I possibly have for wanting to do away with Barbara Taverner? She was a client like hundreds more. Our relationship was purely professional. Anyone will tell you that.'

'Neil Gerard knows otherwise.'

Mike spluttered. 'Who's going to believe him? Come on, Marnie. Get real. You'll need more than that.'

'What if I told you I'd heard it from Barbara's own lips?'

'Well she's not around to testify, is she? Or had you overlooked that small detail?'

'Barbara made recordings on cassette tapes. They're in my possession.'

Mike's eyes widened and his mouth gaped open. '*You've* got them.'

'You knew about –?' Marnie did not finish her question. The penny dropped. 'It was *you* who burgled Neil's flat. You were looking for the tapes.'

'And you found them.' Mike's voice was hoarse, almost a whisper. 'She told me she'd made them. She taunted me that night … here in this cabin. She said she'd recorded details about everything … said I was just a one-night stand. I think she thought of me as a bit of rough.'

'You were never that, Mike. Whatever she felt about you, she didn't think of you like that.'

'What did she think of me? If you've heard the tapes, what did she say?'

'Actually, she hardly said anything … just a brief mention.' Marnie knew it was tactless as soon as she had spoken. She tried to put it right. 'There was nothing that would've incriminated you.'

Mike's shoulders sagged. He closed his eyes. 'Clever women.' It was the same hoarse tone. 'They think they can do what they like … say what they like. They think they can get away with murder.'

He had become almost comatose, and Marnie was wondering how to bring this to an end. She took a sip from the brandy in the whisky tumbler that she had been holding throughout their conversation. *Clever women*, he had said, using the plural. Was he lumping her together with Barbara? Did he see them as two of a kind? The implication was only just dawning on her, so it came as a complete surprise when the attack came.

With a groan that became a roar, Mike leapt from his casual position and flung himself across the cabin at her, his hands reaching out before him. Marnie had no time to react. She staggered back, bumped into a low chair and lost her balance. Falling backwards, she swung her arm up to defend herself, but knew it was hopeless. The pain was sudden, excruciating, but mercifully short-lived. The blackness overwhelmed her in a second and she was gone.

• • • • •

Marnie knew she had to fight back. Someone was grappling with her, trying to strangle her. She could feel hands at her throat, and tried to open her eyes, but everything was an opaque grey and the pain hit her a second time. In desperation she pushed a hand in the direction of her attacker and it met flesh. She squeezed as hard as she could.

'Ouch!' A familiar voice. 'Marnie, that hurt. Lie still. I'm trying to undo your collar so you can breathe better.'

'Anne?' she croaked.

'Of course. Just take it easy for a minute.' There was a rustling sound, a hand lifting her head, something soft pushed under her. 'There, that should make you more comfortable.'

'Where's –'

'Don't speak. Just rest. I've got to make a phone call.'

Marnie took deep breaths. There was a pain enveloping her head and neck, as if a gorilla was gripping her tight. It was still impossible to open her eyes without great discomfort. She gave in and lay there trying to recall what had happened. Anne was pressing buttons on the mobile. Three buttons.

'Oh yes,' Marnie heard her say, 'ambulance, please, and police.'

Anne waited to be connected. In the few seconds delay, she surveyed the scene in the cabin. There was blood on the new curtains and it was splattered on the new flooring. But Anne had other things on her mind than the damage to the boat's decor. Another voice came on the phone, asking her to describe which services she needed and why.

'There's been an accident.' She gave precise details about *Perfidia*'s position. 'Two people involved. One is conscious at the moment. I've tried to make her comfortable. And there's another person … a man. His condition? I think he's … I'm not sure.'

• • • • •

The hospital was just around the corner, and Marnie for all her groggy state wanted to book a minicab. Anne persuaded her she would be seen more quickly if she was delivered by ambulance. Her only worry was that she might have to share with Mike Brent. He was now making low groaning sounds, but was not attempting to get up from the floor. Once he began showing signs of life, Anne inspected him cautiously and saw a monstrous lump turning dark red on his temple and blood oozing from the top of his head. His hair was matted and sticky with it. She gently pressed some paper tissues on the wound before the paramedics arrived.

While they waited, Anne gave Marnie a few sips of water, lifting her head and supporting it from behind. There was a thick-bottomed whisky tumbler lying on the floor, but she thought it best not to touch it. The cabin smelled of brandy, and there was another odour that she thought was probably the blood. Anne had a dozen or more questions to ask, but she restrained her curiosity for later. Her main task for then was to stop Marnie trying to stand up.

She was grateful when she heard a siren in the distance and knew that an ambulance was on its way.

• • • • •

The paramedics had taken one look at the situation in the cabin and given their first attention to Mike Brent. Marnie insisted she could walk to the ambulance with help from Anne, who understood that Mike Brent's injuries were more serious. She nonetheless shot indignant glances at the kneeling figures who were making more efforts to help the attacker than his victim.

Marnie sat on the steps of the ambulance and rested her aching head on the door. 'Phone Mrs Jolly, Anne,' she murmured. 'Get her to ask Roger to come and take care of the boat, will you?'

Roger arrived breathless at the same time as the police car. No doubt mention of a serious incident on the narrowboat *Perfidia* in Little Venice had spurred the local CID into action. A young officer who identified himself as DS Langton took in the scene, raced to look into the cabin through the side doors of the boat and saw the paramedics at work. After a quick exchange he turned to Marnie and was met by the solid shape of Roger Broadbent.

'And you are, sir?'

'This lady's solicitor. We'll talk to you as soon as she's received treatment for her injuries.'

'If it's all the same – '

'Have you spoken to Chief Inspector Bruere about this?'

Langton looked wary. 'DCI Bruere?'

'I think you'll find that if you inform him Marnie Walker is one of the injured parties, he'll want to be involved.'

• • • • •

DS Langton accompanied the ambulance to the hospital and questioned Anne in the waiting area. Roger sat with them and listened intently to Anne's account of what she had seen. A nurse came out to let them know that Marnie had been sent for X-ray. An hour later another nurse came to tell them she had been admitted for an overnight stay. She was suffering from concussion and they wanted to keep her under observation.

Langton asked about Mike Brent. His injuries were more serious. X-rays had shown up a fractured skull and there was some evidence of bleeding in the brain. He was being prepared for surgery. The detective went out to phone a situation report back to base. He returned briefly to explain that he would be returning to the station.

Questioning Marnie would wait until the morning.

51

Anne awoke in a strange bed. She felt tired but was surprised to have slept at all that night. The alarm clock showed it was almost eight. Blinking up at the ceiling in Mrs Jolly's spare bedroom, she pieced together the events of the previous day and was glad it was all over. Mike Brent, if he survived surgery, would probably be tried and sent to prison for murdering Barbara. Neil Gerard would be released. The *Odd Couple* campaign would be completed, and Charles Taverner would finally have closure.

There was a sound from downstairs; Mrs Jolly was active in the kitchen. Anne called down to ask if she might take a shower before breakfast. Covering herself in suds, she went over the jobs to do, people to inform. Before anything else she would phone the hospital to check on Marnie.

Mrs Jolly stood beside her in the hall while she rang the ward sister. Yes, Marnie had had a peaceful night. Yes, she was feeling much better. Yes, they could visit her later that morning and she would probably be allowed to go home. No, they could not speak with her at that moment; she was with a police officer. Was it DCI Bruere? The nurse hesitated. Yes, she believed that was his name.

Anne left Mrs Jolly's contact number in case she was needed. Eleven o'clock seemed a long time away.

• • • • •

It was outside normal visiting hours when Anne arrived alone at the hospital, but she insisted she had only come to take a patient home and was allowed up to the ward. Marnie was sitting up in bed, wearing a hospital nightdress. Anne hugged her gently and took a seat. Marnie explained she had to wait for a doctor to see her before she could be discharged.

While they waited, Marnie told Anne everything that had happened after she left Mrs Jolly's: the chance meeting with Karen and her baby, the unexpected appearance of Charles and the confrontation with Mike Brent. She spoke softly so that no one in the ward would overhear.

'You took a big risk, Marnie. You must've known he'd attack you. Weren't you scared, being alone with someone you suspected of being a murderer?'

'I felt angry ... just couldn't stop myself. Once I'd started, I just went on and on, each time he tried to argue his way out.'

'How did you immobilise him?'

'I remember he dived at me. After that ...' Marnie shrugged and winced. She rubbed the back of her neck with one hand.

'Are you sure you're all right, Marnie?'

'I can't wait to get out of here.'

'Did the police say you could go home? They told me Mr Bruere was here earlier.'

'He had someone with him. They took down everything I said to make a statement.'

'Then what?'

'When it comes to court, I'll be called as a witness.'

'And Neil Gerard?'

'A sore point with Bruere. He was in a meeting yesterday with Charles's QC when your three nines call was picked up. He reported back afterwards, and the lawyers acted immediately. Bruere said Neil would be released very soon. The police weren't opposing the petition submitted by the defence team.'

'That's good. Do you know what happened to Mike Brent?'

'I asked Bruere. Mike's in intensive care. He was in the operating theatre for four hours. They said his condition was critical but stable.'

Anne was wide-eyed. 'Does that mean he could die?'

'He's got a reasonable chance of surviving. Bruere thinks I caught him a lucky blow on the temple with the heavy whisky glass and he hit the corner of the radiator head first.'

Anne grimaced. 'I'd call that an *unlucky* blow … for him. Lucky for you.'

They had not noticed that a doctor and nurse had arrived. Anne was asked to wait outside while they examined Marnie. Eventually a nurse came out to fetch Anne, and she returned to find Marnie dressed and ready to leave.

'You're sure you feel all right, Marnie?'

'I will be when I get out of this place. Let's go.'

But she was not all right. In the ground floor reception area, while Anne was wondering where they would find a taxi, Marnie suddenly leaned heavily against Anne and almost fell. They collided with a passing nurse, a young man with a shaved head and brilliant white teeth in a deep brown face. He led Marnie to a seat and asked about her condition. Anne did the explaining. Marnie was back on the ward less than ten minutes after leaving it.

• • • • •

Mrs Jolly was surprised but unfazed when Anne reappeared on her doorstep, and she welcomed her back with coffee and biscuits and the offer of the spare room for as long as she needed it. Anne spent the rest of the morning on the mobile. Charles Taverner was not reachable by phone, and she could guess he would be closeted with his QC and the police. For a fleeting moment she wondered if Bruere might now regard Charles as a suspect, but she dismissed the idea as absurd and continued with her calls.

As she worked through the list, she wondered if real people had vanished from the world, leaving only answering machines in their place. She left messages for Jane Rutherford (progress report on events and Marnie's injury), Roger Broadbent (ditto), Angela Hemingway (return delayed, please continue looking after Dolly). She even left a message for Ralph on the voicemail service of his hotel in Washington and included Mrs Jolly's phone number.

Half an hour later Ralph rang, fresh from the breakfast terrace in DC. He listened in silence to Anne's account, asked a few rapid questions and announced he would be on the next available flight back to Britain.

Preferring action to worrying, Anne went round to *Perfidia* after lunch to sort out the boat. In the saloon she gasped when her eyes fell upon the bloodstains on the corner of the radiator and on the floor. Leaving the area that had been the scene of one murder, one murderous attack and a collision that might yet prove fatal, she quickly packed the two kitbags, cleaned and tidied the boat and locked up. She paid a brief visit to the Little Venice office to tell the staff where she could be reached if needed.

Back at Mrs Jolly's, Anne interrogated the office answerphone and began another round of calls to keep Walker and Co up and running. At four o'clock Mrs Jolly tapped on the dining room door and came in with tea. Anne was querying a delivery date for materials, scribbling rapidly on her pad. Mrs Jolly could see it was covered in notes and numbers and she marvelled that this *slip of a girl*, as she regarded her, could be so businesslike. Anne ended the call, wrote something on the pad and looked up.

'You're a life-saver, Mrs Jolly. Thank you.'

'No, that's you, Anne. I can't imagine what Marnie would do without you … and you so young.'

'Oh well, I've –'

She was interrupted by the phone ringing. It was Marnie.

'How's the patient?' Anne asked.

'Better than I was. What about you?'

'Everything's fine here and at the office. I'm at Mrs Jolly's.'

'Did you go to the boat?'

'Yep. Locked up … checked her over …packed our bags. Everything's done. We don't have to go back any more.'

'Where are our bags?'

'They're here. Don't worry about anything. It's all under control. I'll fill you in on the details at visiting time.'

'Er … look, Anne … there's no need to come this evening.'

'Oh? What's up?' Suspicion.

'Nothing.'

'Marnie …'

'It's been a tiring day, that's all. Did you get in touch with Ralph?'

'He said he'd be coming back straight away.'

'There's no need, really.'

'Too late to stop him now. Are you sure you're all right, Marnie?'

'Of course. I'd better go. Talk to you later.'

Anne reported the conversation to Mrs Jolly who had hovered, listening to Anne's side of it. At the end she delivered her judgment.

'Well, I can only say I'm glad Marnie's being sensible. I think you must be a good influence on her, Anne.'

Anne tried not to look too incredulous. As the old lady left the room, she sat at the table softly tapping the pad with her pencil.

• • • • •

A brief announcement that the police were about to re-open the Little Venice murder enquiry made the nine o'clock news on BBC television. Until that reminder of the outside world, Anne had been feeling totally cosseted. It was like staying with granny. They had been watching Mrs Jolly's favourite sitcom, after which she left the room, returning minutes later with mugs of hot chocolate. The drink was still too hot to sip when the newsreader gave out the police statement. Anne exchanged glances with Mrs Jolly, wondering how the media got hold of information so quickly.

The round-up of regional news for the London area added no more details, and

Anne sat curled up in an armchair, holding her mug in both hands, thinking through the implications of this new development.

Someone else had also been doing some thinking. Mrs Jolly was surprised when the phone began to ring and was muttering that no one ever called her so late when she went out to the hall. Anne put her mug on the coffee table and uncurled herself. It had to be Marnie. Anne was on her feet as soon as Mrs Jolly came into the room.

'Did you see the news, Marnie?'

'Yes. This is what I want you to do …'

• • • • •

Barely twenty minutes passed before the taxi pulled up outside the hospital. The spring evening had given way to dusk, and darkness was descending. Marnie had been waiting inside and emerged looking brighter than she had been in the morning.

'I can't believe you're doing this, Marnie.' Anne pushed the kitbags out of the way and shifted over so that Marnie could climb in. 'Can you just do that, discharge yourself without the doctor's permission?'

'Of course, I was a patient not a prisoner.'

'Isn't there such a thing as doctor's orders?'

Ignoring the question, Marnie sat back as the cab pulled away. 'You've told the driver Euston station?'

'Just like you said.'

On arrival at the terminus Marnie headed straight for the first class counter and booked two tickets on the next train to Milton Keynes Central. They caught it with a minute to spare and found seats in a quiet corner of an almost empty carriage. The train had just begun moving when Marnie dug out her mobile and pressed buttons while Anne looked on.

'Hi Angela, it's Marnie. Just wanted to let you know we're on our way back. I didn't want you to get a surprise when our taxi turned up so late.'

'Anne's message said you were in hospital, Marnie. What are you doing? Nobody gets discharged at this time of night.'

'Long story. The fact is I'm fine and there was no need for them to keep me in.'

'Has this anything to do with the item on the news?'

'You mean the police reopening the Little Venice case?'

'No. I mean what I've just seen on ITN, News at Ten.'

'Something new?'

'A solicitor's issued a statement that Neil Gerard's conviction will be judged as unsafe and he's about to be released.'

'I see.'

Despite Marnie's protests, Angela insisted on meeting them at the station. The tunnels outside Euston prevented any further arguments by cutting them off.

'What do you see?' Anne asked.

Marnie outlined the latest development. 'I've done the right thing. By tomorrow morning the news media will be camping on the hospital doorstep waiting for me.'

'That's why you waited till it was dark before checking out.'

'Yes.'

'But how would the news people know you were there, Marnie?'

'God knows, but they would. They'd be queuing up to pounce on me as soon as I walked out of the door.'

'Mystery Woman Nails Little Venice Murder Suspect …' Anne suggested.

'You've almost got a future in tabloid journalism … headlines department.'

'Almost?'

'You missed out *Shock Horror*.'

Marnie could not believe how tired she had felt when they arrived back at Glebe Farm on Tuesday night. Now, in bed and still feeling exhausted the next morning, she could not believe she had set the alarm for six o'clock. Eyes closed, she groped on the shelf above her head and pressed the button to switch it off. The sound continued, and she recognised it as the intermittent ringing of the phone.

'Marnie Walker,' she croaked.

'Hallo, darling. I didn't catch you in the shower, did I?'

'Not that I noticed.'

'How are you?'

'Wonderful.'

'Seriously.'

'Don't push it.'

'Okay. Listen, I'm booked on an early flight tomorrow morning. It's the soonest I could get.'

'What day is that?'

A pause. 'Thursday. Marnie, are you sure you're okay?'

'Do you want me to fetch you from the airport?'

'I've arranged a taxi. I'll ring when I arrive at Heathrow.'

'Have a safe journey.'

After disconnecting she flopped back on the pillow. Her last thought before dozing off was that she had not thanked Ralph for phoning.

• • • • •

Anne decided to let Marnie sleep for as long as she needed before preparing breakfast. As soon as the village shop opened, she drove up in the Mini and bought a copy of every daily paper. This was becoming a habit. She piled them on the passenger seat and headed back to a pot of coffee and a solid session of reading and marking up.

It was almost eight-thirty and long after they normally started working when Anne saw Marnie emerge from *Thyrsis*, stretching both arms above her head. There was a faint mist hanging over the countryside that promised a fine day. Anne got up from the table, turned the gas on under the kettle and lit the grill for toast.

'Hi, Marnie. How are you feeling?'

'Amazingly, you're not the first person to ask that question so far today.'

'You've been talking to the mirror? Bad sign.'

'Ralph phoned.'

'From Washington. That's nice.'

'I'm going to kill him.'

Anne smiled brightly. 'Is this a new gratuitous violence streak or do you have a reason?'

'He phoned at six o'clock.'

'How kind of him.'

'That's what I thought.'

'Yes. He must've waited up till one o'clock local time especially so as not to disturb you. He knows you're an early bird.'

Marnie saw the truth in what Anne was saying. She had not thought of it like that. 'Okay. He's just been reprieved.' She sat down and drank some orange juice.

'Talking of reprieves …' Anne indicated the pile of papers on a chair.

'Are those today's?'

'Yep. They're full of the *Odd Couple* story. I've gone through the whole lot and picked out the Neil Gerard articles. You were right to get out of London last night. The paparazzi will be swarming all over the place.'

Marnie dabbed her lips with a napkin. 'It's not going to be so easy for Neil.'

• • • • •

Like Marnie, Charles Taverner had returned to Knightly St John. As far as he knew, the purchase of the vicarage had never been made public. The media had always focused on the glamour angle in the Barbara Taverner murder case, stressing the link between Little Venice and the 'luxurious Docklands residence' at Templars' Wharf. The Taverners' cottage in Sussex had been mentioned once or twice for lifestyle colour, but the *Old Rectory* had remained a secret.

At about the time that Marnie and Anne were walking through the spinney to the office barn, Charles was picking up the phone in his study a short distance away. He was surprised to hear the answerphone telling him there was no one available to take his call at Walker and Co. He left a brief message and passed to the next name on his list.

The solicitor had barely reached his office in the City of London when Charles's call was put through. After the briefest exchange of pleasantries, Charles came straight to the point.

'Listen, Guy, there are various things I want you to do as a matter of urgency. And whatever happens I want to remind you that all this is strictly confidential between us. I'm talking to you as my solicitor, not as a friend.'

'Of course.'

'You're not recording this conversation?'

'No.'

'Very well. Please bear in mind that my name is not to be mentioned in this matter at any stage. Is that understood?'

'Absolutely. It goes without saying.'

'Good. Here's what I want you to do …'

• • • • •

'No luck?' Anne was looking at Marnie across the room. Marnie had replaced the receiver.

'Line's engaged. Charles must be working through a list. If he's going to work from the vicarage he ought to think about having an extra line installed so that he doesn't block incoming calls.'

'Shall I add that to my list?'

• • • • •

Unusually for him, the solicitor dialled the number himself without involving his secretary. The operator on the prison switchboard answered immediately.

'Good morning. I'd like to speak to the governor, please. This is Guy Taplow of Sheridan Taplow Cornelius, solicitors. It concerns Mr Neil Gerard on whose behalf we are acting.'

• • • • •

Marnie admired Angela's radar system. She always seemed to arrive in the office when coffee was brewing. On that occasion she was wearing the concerned-vicar expression from her repertoire.

'To save you asking, Angela, I'm fine.'

'I'm so relieved to hear it. Is it true what they put in the papers, about you capturing the murderer?'

'It depends which paper you read. Most of them got it roughly right. One of the tabloids had me wrestling him to the ground and beating his brains out. That was slightly exaggerated ... I was unconscious at the time.'

'Thank goodness you're all right, Marnie.'

'Thanks for looking after Dolly.'

'As Anne would say, *no probs*. Oh, and I let Mr Taverner in for the burglar alarm brochures. He said he'd arranged it with you.'

'Was he able to find them?'

'Yes.'

'So what other excitement has there been in Knightly St John?'

'I've got some news.'

'Randall is going to make an honest woman of you?'

'Working on it, Marnie. Even more surprising than that ...' She beamed. 'I can move into the new vicarage whenever I want. Of course the diocese will write to you formally and pay you for the notice period.'

Marnie waved a hand. 'Don't worry about that. What are your plans?'

'The removal people are coming on Friday, and I thought I'd have a housewarming party on Saturday evening. Can you come?'

'I'll need to check the social calendar with Central Headquarters –'

'We're free,' Anne chipped in.

'That's great. Will Ralph be back?'

'He's borrowing Air Force One from the President for the journey.'

'Naturally. I've already invited Mr Taverner, by the way.'

'He's accepted?'

'Yes.'

'That's a good sign.'

• • • • •

As soon as Angela had left, Marnie tried Charles's number again. He was screening calls but picked up the receiver when he heard her voice. She reported on her confrontation with Mike Brent, and he filled her in on the remaining details from his side of the story.

'Charles, are you sure you've got enough actual evidence to make this stick?'

'More than enough, Marnie. We've got your testimony for a start.'

'But that could be regarded as my word against his. What if he says he tripped and fell into me ... an accident in a confined space?'

'No jury would believe that. And don't forget we've got Belle Starkey's change of heart.'

'Something overheard after a drugs bust?'

'Not quite.'

'I know there was an undercover policewoman there, you told me.'

'More than that, Marnie. It's still confidential but ... the conversations were recorded.'

'Bugged? Is that allowed?'

'The police routinely use bugs in their cells. It's not like telephone tapping. This is admissible evidence.'

'So what next?'

'The Home Office will make an announcement before the end of the week. Neil Gerard will be released pending a re-examination of the case.'

'And you're convinced that Mike Brent was the murderer.'

'Marnie, there isn't the slightest doubt in my mind. Neil Gerard was entirely innocent, just as he maintained all along.'

• • • • •

Guy Taplow looked down at his list of phone calls: the prison, the Home Office, the QC. All of them were ticked off. Only one item remained. It was one of the strangest things he had ever been asked to do, even by the standards of a City of London practice.

'Good morning, Linford Cruising.'

'Good morning, I wonder if you can help me. It's rather short notice, I'm afraid, but would you have a boat available for this week?'

'I'll see what we can do, sir. How many berths do you need?'

'Er ... not many.'

'We have boats that can sleep up to ten people.'

'Oh, no, just a small one would do.'

'Four berths? That's the smallest we have.'

'That would be fine.'

'For how long?'

'A month.'

'A month ... I'll just check for you. Would you mind holding on?'

The man was back in two minutes. 'Yes, we can manage that, sir. We have one of our newest boats available. We're just coming into the high season now, but we can offer you a discount for a long booking like that.'

'Thank you.'

'When would you like to pick the boat up?'

'Soon. I'll get back to you on that.'

'Certainly, sir. We'll check her over today and she'll be ready for you any time from tomorrow morning onwards.'

'That's fine.'

'Now, can I take your name and credit card details?'

• • • • •

Neil Gerard was looking more relaxed than ever, sitting at a table in the visitors' room opposite his sister. Sarah came up every other day and they had begun making plans for his freedom. The duty officer interrupted their conversation with the news that another visitor had arrived. They looked up expecting to see Guy Taplow, Marnie or Charles Taverner, but were surprised to find it was none of them. A young man in a bomber jacket and jeans was being led to the table. The brother and sister exchanged glances, each as baffled as the other. Neil stood up and shook hands, introducing Sarah. It was an odd location for such social niceties.

'I'm David Sumter. I work for Mr Taplow.'

'What can I do for you?'

The visitor spoke in a low voice. 'Shall we sit down? Less conspicuous.'

'Of course. Have a seat.'

'I'm here to make arrangements … for your release.'

'Arrangements?' said Sarah.

The young man looked at Neil. 'Is it possible to talk in private?'

Sarah looked alarmed. 'Why would he want to do that?'

'Mr Sumter, my sister has run the campaign to get me out of prison. There's nothing anyone can say that she can't hear.'

'And I'm the one making arrangements with my brother for when he's freed.'

'Are you aware how much media attention you'll receive, Mr Gerard?'

'Yes, and I'm dreading it, but it's inevitable.'

'Not necessarily.'

'I think you'd better tell me what you have in mind.'

53

On Thursday Ralph arrived home from his meetings as the evening meal was in preparation. It was like a normal day, apart from the fact that the meetings had taken place in Washington DC and he was returning by taxi from Heathrow. While he showered and changed, Marnie blended an avocado, two hard-boiled eggs, an onion and mayonnaise, an old favourite, for the first course and Anne set the table on the bank under the parasol.

It was a cheerful scene that greeted Ralph when he stepped out of *Thyrsis*, a harbinger of summer meals to come. Marnie invited him to open the bottle of sparkling wine, a Spanish Cava, and there was a satisfying pop as he performed the task without a trace of spillage. They sat down, shaking out gingham napkins, and Ralph asked if Marnie could bear to give him the latest news. With no display of emotion she described everything that had taken place.

At the end of the story Ralph poured more wine into their glasses, his expression thoughtful. Replacing the bottle in the cooler, he muttered, 'Yes.'

Marnie picked up her glass. 'Charles is convinced they've got the right person this time.'

'So are you, I should imagine, Marnie, after what he tried to do to you.'

'I am, though he was the last person I suspected, to be honest.'

'That's how I felt, but there was something that made me wonder … It was only while I was pondering all this during the flight that I realised what it was. Mike Brent knew you were working for Charles Taverner, but he *couldn't* have known you were involved in the Neil Gerard affair. Then those indistinct photos appeared in the papers. Only someone who knew you could recognise who that person was, and even then it wasn't easy at first. I think that's how he made the connection.'

'I bet he scanned every photo to try to see who the *mystery woman* was,' Anne said.

'Yes. The other ex-lovers had never seen you before, Marnie, so they had no chance of working out who you might be.'

'But they all met me later.'

'Sure, but not in any way that would help them recognise you from the photos.'

Marnie nodded slowly. 'There's something else that's been bothering me, Ralph. Have you had any thoughts about why Neil's fingerprint was on the gas valve?'

'Oh, I think that's probably fairly straightforward.'

'Elementary?' Anne suggested.

'Perhaps. Neil is knowledgeable about boats; Barbara was concerned about the safety aspect and the new regulations. It'd be natural for her to ask him to check everything was all right. So how was he going to do that … short of dismantling the interior and testing the whole system?'

'Just see that everything was securely fastened?' said Marnie.

'I think so. What else could he do? He probably gave the valve a tug, found it was firmly in place and that was that.'

'Makes sense. It's funny how the so-called *evidence* – once you've broken one part of the story – doesn't seem so convincing any more. The *witness* proves to be totally unreliable, there's a perfectly good reason for the fingerprint and Sarah's story seems credible. The whole edifice falls down and he's going to be set free.'

'When will that be, Marnie, any idea?'

'Any time now, as far as I know.'

• • • • •

Earlier that afternoon a Ford Escort had drawn up at a side door of the prison on the outskirts of Milton Keynes. Two men got out and went inside. One was carrying a holdall.

Fifteen minutes later two men exited by the same door, heaved the holdall in the boot, got in the car and drove off unhurriedly.

No one paid any attention to a man who walked out of the front door with other visitors and boarded a minicab waiting for him at the kerb.

The paparazzi were scanning all the people entering and leaving the building, but they recognised no one. Their concentration was intense, like hunters stalking a wild and dangerous prey. Some had motorcycles standing nearby ready for pursuit. Their jobs depended on results.

• • • • •

The evening was becoming cooler, and they decided to have coffee on *Sally Ann*. Anne poured Ralph a brandy and surprised them by announcing that she had been working out one of the questions.

'I know it's not very important in solving the actual crime, but I've been thinking about those dates in the diaries. They were just blinds, weren't they? Barbara got me to put them all in our calendar to make her diary look convincing.'

Marnie had made that deduction long before. She said simply, 'It convinced Charles all right. He thought she was seeing me frequently about the projects.'

'He wouldn't question any appointments with someone reliable. It would be as if you were vouching for them.'

'You're right, Anne. In that way I was being used ... without knowing it. We all were, I suppose. Barbara was good at camouflaging her tracks, and we were part of the camouflage.'

Anne picked up her coffee cup in both hands. 'I'm sorry it was Mike Brent ... never thought it would be him ... didn't know he could have such a temper.' She shuddered.

Ralph swirled the brandy in his glass. 'People can react in unexpected ways if they think they're being put down ... or if they think a woman is getting the better of them. You found that out the hard way, Marnie.'

'Certainly did.' She reached across the table and touched Anne's arm. 'I'm sorry too that it was him. You liked Mike, didn't you, Anne?'

'Yeah. It was probably just a flare-up ... now it's ruined his life ... and Barbara's, of course.'

'And Charles's too,' Marnie said quietly.

• • • • •

The phone had rung that afternoon in the study at the old vicarage, and Charles had looked up from the correspondence he was reading. He waited for the answering machine to cut in. When he heard the voice, he did not pick up the handset.

'Hallo, this is Sarah Cowan ... Neil's sister? I'm just phoning to say how grateful I am for your support ... despite everything. I never really thought you'd get involved. It was a long shot. I just did everything I could think of to try to get my brother released. And we both appreciate what you're doing so that he won't have to face the media until he's ready for all that. This whole business has taken its toll of him, as you know. Anyway, I don't know if I'll get the chance to see you in person or even speak to you on the phone. But thank you so much, from the bottom of my heart.' The voice faltered. she cleared her throat. 'He's a good man, my brother. Thank you.'

There was a click, a beep and the line went dead.

A good man, she had said. *Yes, I've known that for quite a while*, he thought.

• • • • •

At the time of Sarah Cowan's phone call the unremarkable Ford Escort drew into a visitors' parking slot at a marina on the edge of Milton Keynes. David Sumter from Sheridan Taplow Cornelius, solicitors, got out and went in to reception, leaving his passenger in the car. Five minutes later he came out accompanied by an older man wearing overalls and a windcheater bearing the logo, Linford Cruising, and signalled to his passenger. Neil Gerard climbed out, took two holdalls from the boot and followed them along the landing stage.

The older man unlocked a boat on the end of the line and showed them in. 'Will you be travelling alone, gentlemen?'

David Sumter replied. 'No, one or two friends will be joining us shortly. We're picking them up tomorrow.'

'Have you been on a narrowboat before?'

'Many times.'

'So I don't need to show you the ropes ... tell you about locks and so forth?'

'No, thanks.'

'Let me just explain the controls of this boat, then. You'll find it all very modern and simple to run.'

They were soon on their way with Neil at the tiller. The man from the hire company watched them go, saw that the boat ran straight and true and was satisfied that it was in good hands.

Sumter waited until they were out of sight of the marina and reached into a holdall. He pulled out three objects and laid them on the roof. The first was a mobile phone.

'This is for you. It's a pay-as-you-go, not registered in any name, so it's not traceable to you. It's fully charged and loaded with about sixty pounds' worth of credit. There are no numbers stored in its memory, and you should keep it that way, just in case. We know the number and can use the phone to contact you.' He pointed to a yellow note on the back of the casing. 'This is *my* number. Memorise it and throw the note away. Use it only if you have to.'

'Right.' Neil frowned. 'Is all this cloak-and-dagger stuff really necessary?'

'The press are tenacious and quick-witted. We don't think they'll be watching the canals – no one runs away at four miles an hour – but it pays not to take any chances. It's up to you, but if you spend time chatting to your friends or family, someone could pick you up. It happened to Margaret Thatcher; it can happen to anyone. Mobiles are not secure.'

'Okay, if you say so.'

Sumter took the next item. It was a baseball cap. 'Here. Put it on now and wear it all the time you're visible on deck. It's not much of a disguise but it's better than nothing, and no one will pay it any attention.'

The last item was a small pair of binoculars.

'You think I should take up bird watching as a hobby?'

Sumter took them out of their pouch. 'Use these to scan bridges in the distance before you get close. Look out for anyone loitering.'

'If it's the paparazzi won't they be looking at me with their own binoculars?'

'Possibly. So don't spend ages studying them. Any doubts, just moor the boat on the opposite side to the towpath, close the curtains in the sleeping area and lie low for an hour. That should do it.'

'And if they're as persistent as you say they are?'

Sumter shrugged. 'They'll find you, and you'll be pestered day and night. This is the best we can do. With luck, it should get you clear.'

'Why not just drive me to an airport and stick me on a plane? I could be away at four *hundred* miles an hour.'

'Think about it.'

• • • • •

Sarah finished packing Neil's cases after making her phone call to Charles Taverner. She had already been to her brother's flat some days before and collected his clothes as planned, ready for him to get away. It was only a matter of time before the media caught up with her. She loaded the luggage into the hire car and set off through London's traffic for the M1. There were no roadworks or accidents and she made reasonably good time to Luton, where she left the bags in a lock-up storage unit. When the time came, it would be handy for him to collect the bags, make the short taxi ride to the airport and take the first available flight out of Britain.

Sarah turned the car back to the motorway and headed north. She had arranged to stay with an old school friend living in the Lake District until all the fuss had died down.

• • • • •

The Linford Cruising narrowboat was travelling at a steady pace round the edge of the new city and had put a couple of miles between itself and the marina. A bridge came into view up ahead, and Neil dutifully raised the binoculars to his eyes, keeping the boat firmly on course with the tiller under his arm.

'Uh-oh … There's someone waiting on that bridge.'

Sumter took the glasses from him and focused them into the distance. 'Good.'

'Good?'

'This is where we part company.'

The countryside around them resembled moorland rather than the outskirts of a large town, and Sumter scanned the area to make sure it was deserted. Satisfied, he gave the binoculars back to Neil. 'No need to stop, just drop me on the towpath under the bridge.'

Neil slowed, pulled over and the two men shook hands. In a trice Sumter was gone, whisked away and out of sight in seconds. The boat chugged on. *Quiet waters*, Neil thought. *Not a bad way to pick up the threads of my life.*

• • • • •

At that moment, Charles was on the phone again in his study at Knightly St John. Guy Taplow was reporting back, and Charles was listening with great concentration. Every now and then he muttered, *good … good …*

'So … all okay thus far. Thank you, Guy. You've acted above and beyond the call of duty. Now, what about the media?'

'That's something I can't fix. They're swarming all over the prison entrance. On the news there were reports that some were camping on the pavement outside Gerard's flat. At least his sister has made tracks.'

'Good. Any mention of me?'

'Only that you're not available for comment. There's a small posse at Templars' Wharf and another at Bermuda Reach. Nothing in Sussex, as far as I know. When are you planning to get away, Charles?'

'Soon.' He looked down at his notes. The media were everywhere. Sooner or later … 'Look, Guy … I wonder if you should make a statement that I've already left the country. What do you think?'

'It might gain you some space.'

'Then do it.'

When he disconnected, Charles sat pondering. He could not bear to be put through the wringer again. This was a time for quick thinking and action. He checked the notepad and dialled an unfamiliar number. It rang several times before a breathless voice answered.

• • • • •

Neil was savouring every moment of freedom. The world seemed unreal. An hour ago he had been sitting in a cell while others determined his future. Now, here he was, taking control of a boat, taking back control of his life. He breathed in deeply, looking out over fields and distant woodland. A phrase came into his head… *the grand horizons.* His world had horizons again, time that he could plan, action that was entirely down to him. Never again would he allow himself to be ruled by other people's timetables and pressures. The steps he took at this moment would set the course for the rest of his days.

The boat was now approaching an area of housing, and a bridge showed up ahead. Neil searched it with the binoculars, but there was no one in sight. He settled back to thinking about his future. What would he do next? Obviously he should get away for a month, two months, possibly longer. Sarah would help with organising his finances. Everywhere in the world accepted credit cards. Plastic had taken the place of paper money. He had savings, enough to survive on if he chose an inexpensive place. Somewhere with sunshine, somewhere with space, the sea …

He would write the first draft of his account: *The Little Venice Murder* – my story, by Neil Gerard. Ian Fleming used to write the James Bond novels in two months at his retreat in Jamaica. There should be no difficulty in writing about his life with Barbara, culminating in what really happened to her that awful night. He could use the media for his own purposes if he could bide his time. It would still be newsworthy in a few months.

He would give interviews when he got back, do a deal, maybe find an agent to handle the PR angle. There would be television appearances, exclusives in the papers.

But only when he was ready and his head clear. He would not have to race to meet their deadlines, their needs. He would never do that again.

Neil could not wait to get away. He was dreaming of somewhere with grand horizons, rounding a bend, when he heard ringing. He had forgotten about the mobile and groped at it, trying to divide his attention to what lay round the corner. He fumbled and hit the phone with his fingertips, knocking it from the roof. Grabbing wildly, he trapped it mid-fall against the open door, lost his balance and only just avoided falling over the side. breathless and panting, he turned the phone over and pressed the green button.

'Yes?'

Straightening the tiller, he heard Charles Taverner announce himself. As he listened, he could not know that the call that he had almost thrown away would change the course of his life forever.

'Listen,' Charles was saying. 'Be very careful not to let yourself be seen. The media are scouring the country looking for you. I may have under-estimated their thoroughness.'

'But surely they couldn't make any connection between me and this boat?'

'Don't assume anything. You must be vigilant.'

Neil felt a moment of panic. 'It wasn't hired in my name, was it?'

'No, my solicitor's arranged everything on my instructions. You know about wearing a hat at all times, using binoculars if you spot anyone loitering suspiciously?'

'Yes, yes, I know all that.'

'I think you would be wise to pull over now, somewhere remote if you can find it, and not travel again until dusk. Go through locks early in the morning. It's only for a few days before you can take off.'

'If the worst comes to the worst, Charles, I could face the media now that I'm vindicated. I don't want to, but I know what I have to do, I've got it worked out.'

'It may come to that, but if at all possible I want to avoid it for now. Frankly, I couldn't bear the publicity thing all over again. I imagine you'll want to write your story when you're away. No doubt it'll earn you a fortune when you get back. You can sell it to a publisher then, and I can arrange to be on the other side of the world. Do this for me, please.'

'Sure. You're a mind reader. To be honest, I'm not really up to going over everything myself. I need time to get my head together and get used to being free again.'

'I know … and I'll help you in any way I can.'

'Thank you, Charles. You've already done a lot. I don't know how I'll ever –'

'Don't say a word. It's the least I can do after what you've been through.'

• • • • •

Marnie presented herself at the door and rang the bell. She had walked up to the village by herself, glad to have a breath of air on a pleasant spring evening. Charles let her in, noticing the blue folder under her arm, and showed her into the conservatory. He had opened a bottle of chilled Chablis, and they sat looking out at the garden.

'Do you do landscape design, Marnie?' He replaced the bottle in its ice-bucket.

'I'm not really qualified in that field.'

'I can't imagine you'd do anything other than brilliantly well. Cheers.'

'Cheers, Charles. Ply me with cold white Burgundy and I'll have a go at anything.'

'We'll talk about it, then. But my first priority is to get the burglar alarm system underway. I really want to get that sorted out now, so that it's installed before I go away.'

'Yes.'

'So … what do you have on your list?'

'The frieze in here and in the hall … Anne's design.'

'Good. I'm looking forward to her painting it.'

'I'll get her organised straight away. She'll probably get it done next week. Will you be around?'

'On and off, but you still have a set of keys, I think, so she can come any time. Just let me know.'

'She'll need somewhere to store her materials, brushes, paint and so on.'

'She can use the garden shed. It's empty. You've got a key to the padlock on the ring.'

They tackled the list item by item, from tie-backs in the spare bedroom to rugs in the drawing room, the few loose ends remaining. Neither mentioned *Perfidia*. In half an hour they covered everything. Marnie declined a second glass of wine and stood up, closing the folder. Much as she loved her work, there was a bitter taste to this project and she was struck by the melancholy note in Charles's voice. He walked her slowly through the hall and out onto the drive.

'Thank you for coming, Marnie.' He looked at the gate. 'There is one thing we didn't talk about. Now that Angela's moving into the new vicarage, I think we can finally have the sign put up – *The Old Rectory* – just as Barbara wanted.'

'Of course. I'll see to it at once.' Before she could stop herself, she asked, 'Will you be staying, Charles?'

'I don't know. I honestly don't know, Marnie.' His voice was barely more than a whisper. 'I'm glad Barbara's real murderer has been caught, but nothing can bring her back from the dead. I'll never hear her voice again, or …'

'I understand.'

Charles took a deep breath. 'I'm really glad that Neil is being released. I know it's weird, but I've grown to like him in a strange sort of way over these past weeks and months.'

'You've been extraordinary. Most people in your position would've just wanted to put it all behind them, but you persisted to the bitter end.'

'I had to know for sure … couldn't bear the idea of the real murderer being free and an innocent man in prison for the rest of his life.'

'You weren't really such an *odd couple*, as they made out in the papers.'

'No. It's not *odd* to want to get at the truth in something as vital as this, Marnie.'

'What will you do next?'

'Personally, I'm going to avoid the spotlight … go away for a while, probably the Far East … let everything blow over … not come back till it's old news.'

'Good idea.'

'Marnie, I want to thank you for everything you've done. Not just the work on the house and dealing with the boat … everything, including your friendship with Barbara. I don't know how I would've coped without your support.'

Marnie nodded. 'Will you be able to put it behind you now, Charles?'

'Almost. I think I'm getting there.'

Walking back to Glebe Farm, Marnie agreed. At long last he was finally near to achieving the closure that he desperately needed. For the first time, Charles had referred to his wife's lover as Neil.

54

On Friday morning Marnie got in first. She was at her desk as usual at seven-thirty and immediately made the call. The duty officer took her message and promised to pass it to DCI Bartlett or DS Marriner as soon as one of them arrived. On the other side of the office Anne looked on with surprise.

'You actually *want* to go to the police station?'

'To sign my statement. Inspector Bruere said I'd have to. Well, I'm going *there* so they don't have to come *here*. I don't want Bartlett or Marriner back, not today, not ever again. That chapter is closed. There'll be no more visits, no more jokes about them having their own parking space.'

'So you're going to pre-empt them.'

'Yep. I shall be there at nine o'clock sharp and I don't care how long I have to wait. I'm not leaving that station until it's done.'

'Mm ... I can hardly believe it.'

'Don't tell me you're going to miss them, Anne?'

'Oh no. It's just ... I suppose it's the end of an era.'

'That's what it is. I want to turn over a new leaf ... mark a new beginning. There will be no more police coming to Glebe Farm. And that's final.'

• • • • •

Anne waited until nine o'clock before making her first call of the day. Charles Taverner readily agreed to her making a start on the frieze on Monday morning. He offered to act as tea-boy, and she accepted with a smile in her voice.

She had cut stencils from her first-choice design for the frieze and she packed them in a folder as soon as the call was over. Anne loved making preparations. All her equipment was laid out on the workbench in the kitchen area. There were stencil brushes rolled in a cloth, some clean jam jars, newspapers, J-cloths and other rags, hand-wipes and dust-sheets. Marnie would be buying the paint that day after her appointment was over.

Anne packed the kit into an old sports bag. Everything was ready, and her work up at *The Old Rectory* would be helping the new era on its way. Life would be returning to normal, starting on Monday at nine o'clock sharp.

Outside, the sun was breaking through the morning clouds. Birds were singing. It was a season of new beginnings.

• • • • •

It was clear that Bartlett felt the same about Marnie as she did about him. By the time she walked into the reception area of the police station in Towcester and was ushered into Bartlett's office, the statement was on his desk, faxed up from London.

She declined coffee and read the one page document. It was fair and accurate, and she took out her pen to sign it there and then. In less than half an hour she was back on the road. Next stop, a D-I-Y supermarket on the outskirts of Northampton. Paint for the frieze from the Farrow and Ball traditional range.

Marnie was enjoying the freedom of doing ordinary things, released from the anxiety of police procedure, witnesses, mystery and evidence. She packed the tins of paint in a box in the boot and set off for the Weedon antiques centre by the canal. Her last stop of the morning was to find a housewarming present for Angela Hemingway.

Success! Angela had been worried that the furniture from the vicarage would be too big for her new semi. Marnie found what she wanted almost as soon as she entered the centre. It was a mahogany coffee table, probably Edwardian, but in a timeless style that would blend in with other pieces from any period. An assistant helped her stow it on the back seat of the Discovery.

Driving home, Marnie was sure she had made a good choice. The new table would be more suitable in scale for the living room in the modern house. A few weeks earlier, when Marnie made an offer for the refectory table in the old vicarage kitchen, Angela had accepted at once.

'Of course, Marnie. It's just right for the country kitchen in your farm house. It'll go well with an Aga.'

On the way home Marnie debated with herself whether to keep the gift a secret until Saturday night or let Angela have it to put to use straight away. The decision was taken from her as she drove into the yard. Angela was talking to Anne and Bob the foreman outside the house. Offered the choice, Angela opted not to wait for her present and was delighted when Marnie opened the door to reveal it. She thanked Marnie with a hug.

'Where shall I put it?' Marnie asked.

'In number three?' Angela suggested.

'Or we could take it to the new house and install it. I could drive it up now ... it would save unloading it twice.'

'Why not?... if you have the time, Marnie.'

They climbed in and set off up the field track. Passing the old vicarage, Angela remarked that she would arrange for the refectory table to be transferred to Marnie's area in the removals store.

'Is Mr Taverner settling in now? It must be a huge relief to know they've got the right man at last ... oh sorry, Marnie, if that's a painful subject.'

'That's fine ... not painful at all. I'm putting it all behind me. And yes, I think Charles is finally managing to do the same.'

'Is he still going ahead with the change of name ... *The Old Rectory?*'

'I plead client confidentiality.' Marnie smiled. 'My lips are sealed.'

Angela laughed. 'No need for me to turn a deaf ear, then.'

• • • • •

While the Discovery swung past on its way to the new vicarage, Charles was in his study in the old one. He could never understand why it took so long for Neil Gerard to answer the mobile.

'Hallo, Charles.'

'Where were you? It rang for ages.'

'Lying on my bunk, dozing. There isn't a lot to do here. The question that interests me most right now is not where I am, but where I'm going.'

'You're just filling in time.'

'Oh well, I've got plenty of experience at that. I'm an expert.'

'How are your provisions lasting?'

'I'll need some more pretty soon.'

'Right. I might ask Marnie to help with that. We'll get you some books and magazines as well. Let me know what you'd like. You see, you've got to stay within reach so that I can replenish your supplies.'

'I suppose so. I could do with my laptop. Any chance?'

'Too risky trying to get it. I'll let you have some writing materials.'

'Okay. Otherwise I'll die of boredom.'

'It's only for a few days.'

'What if I need to hide for longer?'

'You won't, but I've booked the boat for a month. That'll be more than enough.'

'A *month*? God, it's like being back inside. *Heron* has become like one of those prison hulks.'

'*Heron*?'

'The boat you've hired for me.'

'A *prison hulk* … yes. Not much of an improvement for you, is it?' Charles pondered for a few seconds. 'Listen, Neil, I have an idea …'

Not normally an early bird, Neil was happy to get up with the cockerel on Saturday morning. He had something to look forward to. That evening would be the first social event of his new life. In the early hours he untied the mooring ropes and steered Heron towards the lock at Cosgrove. No one else was stirring. It was cloudy and still with a cool smell rising from the water. He did not care what the weather did; all weather was good weather as far as he was concerned. Freedom!

Wearing the baseball cap, with the mobile in his pocket and binoculars hanging round his neck, he was confident that the plan was working. If the paparazzi were after him, they were paying no heed to the sleepy waterway that was his escape route, probably did not know it existed.

Clearing the lock, he cruised past the boats moored through the village, slipped under Solomon's bridge and headed out between the fields where the only onlookers were cattle grazing.

• • • • •

In Knightly St John certain residents were also awake early at the beginning of their weekend.

It was catching up time at Glebe Farm. In the office barn, Marnie was going through paperwork, reviewing designs, checking delivery schedules for materials, compiling lists of people to phone. In the attic, Anne was reading her project dissertation for college, adding new paragraphs and illustrations. In his study on *Thyrsis*, Ralph was drafting an article for *The Independent* following on from his visit to the USA.

The Reverend Angela Hemingway blinked at herself in the bathroom mirror in cottage number three … the temporary *New Vicarage*. It was her last morning as a resident of the Glebe Farm complex, and as usual she was feeling distinctly un-reverend at that hour of the day. Already her mind was coming to grips with the party that evening. Tea and toast would fuel her on her way to the shops for last-minute items. She knew it would be a struggle to concentrate at her morning's meeting with the committee from the Women's Institute.

Charles was still in bed after another disturbed night, thinking that his sleep pattern was shot to hell these days. Even the knowledge that Mike Brent was in custody and Neil Gerard safely in hiding had done nothing to improve it. He could not remember the last time he had slept for a whole night without waking. Of course he could; it had been his last night with Barbara.

Now, one side of the bed felt cold and empty. He wondered what the future held for him. It was a bleak prospect.

• • • • •

Neil recognised the place that Charles had described and pulled over. He had been travelling for an hour and a half and had begun to catch glimpses of the tower of the church at Knightly St John dead ahead. Here was the long straight run between the fields and meadows with the tall spire of another church far off to the right on the horizon. The land on that side was sloping gently away, forming the shallow valley of the river Tove, little more than a stream, invisible between hedges and clumps of trees, before the ground rose steadily into the distance.

He had passed no other boat, in fact he had seen no one at all, even when he scanned everywhere with the binoculars. In moments of paranoia he imagined photographers jumping out at any moment from hiding places along the way or lurking behind bridges. But no, his cover was safe. It had been a masterly plan. Who would believe it possible to travel undetected through the heart of England when the whole apparatus of the media was in pursuit? The secret world of the waterways had given him sanctuary.

Neil hopped ashore to tie up on the opposite side of the canal to the towpath. Up ahead, the canal began a long curve to the left, with trees and bushes lining the water's edge.

He switched off the engine and went below, pulling the door shut behind him. He closed all the curtains on the side facing the canal and towpath, made coffee and turned on the radio, Classic fm. He had a long day ahead of him and knew he had no choice but to idle it away. Standing at the landside window, mug in hand, he could see that his unofficial mooring was beside pastureland, but there were no animals using it at that time, and no farm in sight.

The cruising guide revealed a cluster of buildings after the bend before an accommodation bridge up ahead. There was a name beside the buildings, and he strained his eyes to read the tiny print: *Glebe Farm (ruins)*. That evening he would climb the hilly field to the south of Glebe Farm, keeping well clear of it in case the map was out of date, and make his way up to the road leading to the vicarage.

It would be a day of dozing and watching the hours roll by, but he was used to that. This time it was made bearable by the knowledge that there was brightness on the horizon. He could almost dare to believe in the future.

• • • • •

Anne put down her drawing pen and sat back. 'Finished,' she announced triumphantly.

Marnie came across to see. Anne had produced a pen and ink drawing with colours added in.

'That's wonderful! It looks just like Angela's new house … well, a slightly improved version. I take it the hanging baskets and trees in blossom are in your imagination?'

'Of course. I copied the general shape from the estate agents' photo. Then I sort of embellished it. Do you think it has a touch of Disney about it?'

'You mean the bluebirds fluttering around?'

'Yes. Also, there's a bit more artistic licence … the church tower isn't really visible in the background from this angle. It's more sort of symbolic, Angela being the vicar and all …'

'Doesn't matter. Are you going to frame it for her?'

'I hadn't thought of that. It's really just a good-luck-in-your-new-home card.'

'Which reminds me,' Marnie said. 'We'll need to take down the *New Vicarage* sign from cottage number three.'

'I'll do it, Marnie. I'll pop up to the new house and fix it in place this afternoon. Then everything will be ready for this evening.'

• • • • •

As the hour of the party approached, Marnie walked round the side of the farm house, stepping past paving slabs stacked against the wall ready for laying as a new pathway and terrace. She stopped at the rear, confronted by the wilderness that was soon to be tamed. It was hard to imagine it as a garden with lawn, shrubs, trees, flowers. She would plan it at the same time as she designed the garden for *The Old Rectory*.

It had been a last-minute decision not to buy flowers for Angela from a florist but to take some from Glebe Farm, and Marnie wondered for a second or two if it had been wise. But she threaded her way through the overgrown tangle and found a clump of narcissi and some wall-flowers, enough to gather into a bunch that would go well together in a vase.

Turning, Marnie looked up at the mellow limestone of the house and imagined it with curtains, table lamps shining in the living room, polished furniture, pictures on the walls. She looked back at the jungle, knowing she was looking forward to the future.

• • • • •

At the appointed time, Neil jumped from *Heron* onto the bank, careful where he trod. It had been a long time since he had had to think of his appearance and he was determined not to ruin the effect by treading in something agricultural left behind by cattle. With a glance over his shoulder, he set off up the slope.

Charles had given him precise instructions. *Walk up the hill to the field gate between two tall trees.* Neil saw them at the top and headed in that direction. When he reached the gate it was fastened shut with a chain, and he ducked behind a tree while a car went by, before clambering over. He felt very exposed, standing at the side of the road, but there was no one to pay him any attention.

Turn right at the road and immediately cross over to the other side. It's less than fifty yards to where you're going. Neil hurried on. It was strange to feel like a fugitive when he had just been set free.

The rectory is the first house, surrounded by a high hedge. Look for a doorway. It's practically invisible. It'll be unlocked. Come through and you'll be concealed from view.

Neil could hear his heart pounding but told himself to relax – he was not guilty of anything – and he found the door in the hedge just when he thought he had missed it. He turned a handle and the door swung inwards smoothly without a squeak. Shutting it behind him, he paused for breath. A path led him through a dense shrubbery to the edge of a wide lawn. On the far side stood an elegant Georgian house of pale stone under a slate roof. Three pairs of French windows backed onto the terrace.

• • • • •

'You look wonderful, darling.' Ralph smiled at Marnie, who was wearing pale green silk trousers with a matching jacket over a peacock blue top.

'Thank you, Ralph. It's meant to be cool and casual for an informal spring evening.'

'It succeeds …' He kissed her. '… admirably.'

'What's that you're holding?'

'A bottle of Champagne … a little extra for Angela to share with Randall when they have a quiet moment to themselves … their own private celebration.'

Anne came down the loft ladder from her room, also carrying a bag, also wearing trousers.

'Which car are we taking?' she asked.

'I thought we might walk,' said Marnie. 'It's a pleasant evening and we won't have anything to carry back.'

'Except ourselves,' Ralph suggested.

Anne laughed. 'We can take it in turns!'

· · · · ·

You'll see French windows at the back of the house. The ones nearest to you will be open. You can come in that way. I'll probably be in the drawing room having a whisky, and you'll probably be needing one, too.

Neil traversed the lawn at a rapid pace, even though there were no houses nearby to overlook the garden. He had tried to duck out of the evening in their last conversation, saying he was not ready to be sociable, but Charles had talked him round.

'Look, we'll go in my car, all right? It'll only take two minutes, but that way you won't have to see anyone till we get there.'

'Won't the vicar mind me turning up uninvited? I don't like the idea of gate-crashing.'

'No, she's pleased you're coming. I asked her. She said it was open house. And Marnie will be there. You'll be among friends.'

He had liked that idea. He turned the handle on the French windows and walked in. For a moment he stopped, overcome by the beauty, comfort and elegance of the room. Antique furniture, brocade curtains and Wilton carpet were a long way from the surroundings he had been enduring in prison, and he felt emotion well up inside him. He shook his head and took a deep breath. Advancing to the middle of the room, he called out.

'Charles?'

A muffled reply. 'Yes. Down in a minute … just coming.'

Neil was taking in the style of the room, wondering if it was Marnie's handiwork, when he heard footsteps on the stairs and in the hall. Charles entered the room and stopped. The men looked at each other, their expressions uncertain, both adjusting to the new circumstances, no longer prisoner and campaigner. A moment of awkwardness, as if neither knew how to greet the other.

Charles spoke first. 'I think a drink is in order, don't you?'

'Absolutely.' Neil wondered if he should put out a hand. 'A whisky would be very much in order.'

'Good man.' Charles turned towards the sideboard where a cluster of bottles stood to attention. 'I have a single malt that'll be just the job.'

'Excellent.'

'Could you perhaps shut the window, Neil?'

'Of course.'

When Neil turned back to cross the room, Charles's hand was already extended towards him. But instead of a glass of golden liquid, Charles was holding a revolver. Neil gasped.

'What on earth –'

'I heard the tapes,' Charles said simply.

'The tapes ...' Neil was aghast. 'But Marnie –'

'Nothing to do with Marnie ... well, not directly.'

'But the tapes show that I could *never* have hurt Barbara.'

'I know ... quite the opposite in fact.'

'Then why this?' He pointed at the gun. 'I don't understand.'

'Yes, you do. The tapes prove that Barbara loved you.'

'Charles, I was not her only lover.'

'Yes you were. The others meant nothing to her. You were the big love of her life ... the only one who would cause her to leave me. It's ironic that I like you because you're such a decent chap ... and that's why I have to kill you. It's the only way I can ever resolve things.'

'You're not serious about this. You're trying to frighten me.'

'I think you know I'm serious.'

'But the other people at the party, they know I'm coming and you won't be able to pass that off lightly.' Too late Neil realised the truth. 'You didn't ask her, did you?'

'Sorry, I lied about that. I don't make a habit of inviting strangers to gatecrash social events when I myself am just a guest.'

'How did you get the tapes?'

'I found them by chance ... I was looking for something else. They were in the girl's room, Anne's room. I was looking for brochures about alarm systems. That's what gave me the idea of a situation gone tragically wrong ... me thinking I had a dangerous burglar in the house.'

'But your solicitor arranged my getting away. I can't believe he'd connive in this. He'll surely have to testify against you.'

'Ever heard of legal privilege? My solicitor can say nothing about any of this.'

'But you booked the boat for me; you can be traced.'

'My solicitor booked it.'

The colour had drained from Neil's face. 'So you've thought of everything ... What about your justification for shooting me? Your solicitor isn't going to be able to help you with that.'

'You obviously don't know about the spate of violent break-ins round here. Marnie has been trying to sort out an alarm system for ages. It was the next job.'

'You don't think it will incriminate you, that you shoot the man who was condemned as your wife's killer?'

'Neil, you're forgetting something. We're the *Odd Couple*, you and I. I'll be shattered to find it's you, but it's your fault for sneaking in at the back of the house as a surprise. The press will go to town on that ... it'll be a tragedy.'

'You must have known Barbara had lovers ... sooner or later our affair would end.'

'The more I got to know you, the more I learnt about you ... and what Barbara thought about you. The others were shits, more or less. They didn't care about Barbara. You were the only one who really took her affection away from me. Having heard the tapes, I'm pretty sure she would eventually have left me for you. You're the only one of her lovers that I actually like as a person ... and the only one that I hate.'

'After all you've done for me …what are you really going to do?'

'I'm going to shoot a dangerous burglar who's got into my house, leaving footprints in the garden, and sneaked in through the French windows – which I had not yet locked before going out. In my haste and panic, I didn't realise it was you. It will be a serious criminal offence, but everyone will believe my remorse because I had just got you freed from prison and we were a famous team. I was your protector and saviour, your greatest ally and friend. There's not a jury in the country that would convict me.'

'You can't do this. What about the boat? You can't expect David Sumter to cover for you.'

'I'll phone the hire company, say we've had a change of plan, ask them to collect the boat. It won't bother them; they've been paid for a month by credit card, no trace back to you … or to me.'

'The police will check the mobile and see that I rang you.'

'What mobile? Untraceable.'

'My God,' Neil was horrified. 'You planned everything … every detail.'

'Yes.'

The noise of the gun firing in the confined space was shocking. Even Charles flinched. He fired at short range and could not miss. Neil crumpled and fell in a heap, blood flowing from his chest. Charles breathed out slowly, lowering the pistol. It was done.

Curiously deflated, Charles gazed into space and was surprised to see the image of a face floating before his eyes. Its mouth was open like the picture, The Scream, by Edvard Munch. It took him an age to realise that the face was not imagined, but recognisable. Anne was looking in at him through the window in horror. At that moment the doorbell rang and immediately afterwards a fist was hammering on the front door.

On auto-pilot, Charles walked through the hall in a daze. Ralph was at the door and rushed in as Charles stood to one side. He placed the pistol carefully on the hall table and followed Ralph back to the drawing room. Anne was standing inside the French windows, holding her face with both hands. Marnie was kneeling beside Neil, trying to find a pulse. Blood was spreading in a dark sticky puddle on the carpet. She quickly grabbed the mobile from her bag and hit three buttons.

'Why are you here?' Charles asked quietly.

Marnie handled the emergency call as calmly as she could. It was Ralph who replied. 'We thought it would be nice to take you with us, so that you didn't have to arrive alone.'

'Why was Anne …?' His voice petered out.

'She wanted to drop off the frieze materials in the garden shed.'

'I see.'

In the background they heard Marnie's voice.

'Yes, shot … I can't find a pulse … none at all, I'm afraid.'

Marnie, Ralph and Anne left the police station the next morning having given their statements. Marnie had insisted on going there at the earliest opportunity, determined that the police would not be coming to Glebe Farm.

They returned to Knightly St John in sombre mood, driving down the high street to the accompaniment of church bells calling the faithful to Sunday matins, and wondered how Angela would cope with a service so soon after a man had been gunned down in her former living room. It was a warm spring morning, and they put a table and chairs from *Sally Ann* out on the bank for coffee.

When they were settled, Ralph said, 'You seemed disappointed the police wouldn't let you speak to Charles.'

'Yes. I wanted to know what had driven him to do that.'

'It must've been the tapes,' Ralph said.

As Charles had been led away the previous evening, he had been muttering about the tapes, and Marnie had gone into his study to see them stacked on his desk beside one of her blue folders and a cassette player. Angela later confirmed that Charles had gone up to Anne's room to find the folder, and at that moment Marnie had understood.

'Of course. He must've thought that Barbara was involved with Neil in more than just an affair that would blow over in a short while. I think he may have been right, too.'

'You didn't notice the tapes were missing from the box, Anne?' Ralph asked.

'No. I tried never to think about them.'

Ralph shook his head. 'My God ... what must he have felt when he heard the recording of them making love?'

Marnie winced.

'He didn't hear that one,' Anne said.

Marnie and Ralph looked at her.

'How can you be sure?'

'I couldn't bear to have it in my room ... couldn't bear the idea that anyone else would ever hear it again. It was too private.'

'What did you do with it?' Marnie asked.

'I dropped it in the canal on the way down to London.'

They lapsed into silence until Anne spoke again. 'There are one or two things that puzzle me. Can I ask you about them?'

'Go ahead,' said Marnie.

'Those mystery visitors who came down to Glebe Farm ... the cars that arrived and immediately took off ... do we have any idea who they were?'

Ralph replied. 'I think we have to assume that was our burglar checking us out. Any sign of occupation and he was away. But if he'd found the place empty, it would be perfect ... secluded ... no neighbours to see or hear anything.'

'Yes.' Anne nodded. 'That's what I wondered.'

'Was there something else on your mind?' Marnie asked.

'That evening ... the day Barbara was killed ... what actually happened then? What was all that about the row and Belle Starkey seeing someone come back?'

'It seems pretty clear that Barbara had had what she regarded as a fling with Mike Brent,' Marnie explained. 'Her affair with Neil was quite a different matter. When they were in Little Venice Mike must've demanded to see her, so she had to engineer a way of getting Neil off the boat for a while. She instigated the row to gain that time, knowing she would make it up with Neil later.'

'You think she was just going to dump Mike ... tell him it was all over between them?'

'I'm sure of it. The trouble is, he was so infatuated, he wouldn't take no for an answer.'

'So it all got out of hand and Barbara ended up ...'

'Exactly. He seems to have used alcohol plus a sleeping pill or two to knock her out.'

'I don't get that bit,' Anne said. 'He wouldn't have gone to see her, conveniently carrying a bottle of sleeping pills.'

'No. Inspector Bartlett told me they thought he probably saw some of Neil's things on the boat – probably aftershave and such in the bathroom – and realised what was going on. He seems to have taken the pills from Barbara's own bottle in the cabinet. Once he'd drugged her, he no doubt fixed a gas pipe, assuming she'd wake up, eventually put on the cooker and be killed in the blast. That would destroy the evidence of tampering. The gas leak could be blamed on faulty workmanship or impact damage to piping. In fact, she never did wake up.'

'And Neil's fingerprint on the gas valve was the only clue,' said Ralph.

Marnie looked wistful. 'A clue that lied.'

None of them could face the news that day, even though the story had come too late to feature in the Sunday papers. They cleared the bank, untied the boat and set off to recuperate for the rest of the day on *Sally Ann*, none of them noticing *Heron* abandoned further down the cut.

A week later, Marnie drove to Northampton on a cloudy Sunday morning that threatened rain. She took a route that had become all too familiar over the past couple of years and had the usual difficulty in finding a parking space. It was a long walk, almost the whole length of the car park, before she reached the block that housed the ITU.

She rang the bell and waited at the visitors' door until a nurse appeared to admit her. Only one intensive care bed was occupied that day, and Marnie walked in to find the patient propped up on pillows.

'Good morning, Neil. Hallo, Sarah.'

Neil smiled weakly, his face pale, his pleasant features drawn. The surprise was to see the signs of strain etched in Sarah's face. More than that, she seemed agitated and disturbed. On reflection, Marnie realised it was not to be unexpected. The bullet fired by Charles had entered Neil's chest close to his heart and lodged against his spine. Only the rapid arrival and prompt action of the paramedics had saved his life, and his heart had stopped twice on the dash to hospital. The operation to remove the bullet had been successful, and there would be no permanent damage, at least not physical. Marnie had almost passed out later that night when Sarah had phoned from Intensive Care to tell her that Neil had survived.

'How are you today?' Marnie asked.

Sarah spoke first, the words spilling out in a rush. 'Marnie, you won't believe what Neil has just –'

Neil raised a hand to silence her. 'Please, Sarah …' He waved her words away and spoke quietly and calmly. 'I'm not giving evidence against Charles. I won't do it.'

Sarah sighed theatrically.

Marnie sat down on the opposite side of the bed and laid a hand on Neil's arm. 'Will you have any choice? Surely the police will have to prosecute. I mean, Charles tried to kill you. Whatever your feelings may be, Neil, I doubt if they can just let it go like that.'

'Marnie's right, Neil. I told you –'

'I don't care,' Neil interrupted his sister, breathing heavily. 'It's my decision. After all I did to him … and all he did for me …there's no way …' He paused. 'I'm going to ask for a meeting with Charles's QC to see what he says … to find out what I can do to help him.'

Marnie was beginning to understand. Sarah was staring at her, willing her to try to persuade Neil to change his mind. Marnie knew that nothing would change his mind, and she wondered what she would do in his place. She squeezed his arm gently. 'It's an odd decision, Neil, but it's your choice.'

Neil's voice was faint, his eyelids drooping. 'We're an odd couple …'

EPILOGUE

Later that Sunday afternoon, Marnie and Anne were in the office barn tidying up everything connected with Barbara, Charles and Neil. Over lunch, Marnie had explained Neil's wish not to give evidence against Charles, and Ralph had suggested that the most he could do was urge the court to show understanding of Charles's position and adopt a merciful approach to his crime. It was clearly, Ralph thought, a *crime passionnel*, and although the crime was attempted murder, even an English court would have to recognise the extreme circumstances. Marnie hoped the tapes would not be needed in evidence.

Marnie had contacted Linford Cruising and two men had duly arrived to take *Heron* back to the marina. The sale of *Perfidia* would be handled by a brokerage company to whom all the boat's papers were to be sent. The Little Venice management office, where the fateful events had started, would be liaising with the brokers and dealing with mooring matters until the purchasers came eventually to claim their boat.

Marnie began assembling the papers in a blue folder, which she marked in felt tip with the name. She looked down at the word on the cover, thinking back to all that had happened to them since the first time she had seen it in the photograph of Barbara, triumphant when winning her boat-handling award at the Canalway Cavalcade.

'What are you thinking?' Anne asked from her desk where she was tidying her own pile of documents.

'I was remembering Charles saying he had no idea why Barbara had chosen the name, *Perfidia*, for her boat. He said he wondered if it was fate.'

Anne held up a small wad of papers that she had fastened together with a clip. 'It had already been chosen … nothing to do with Barbara.'

'What do you mean?'

'These are the ownership documents – log book, insurance, registration, safety certificate, everything – all the original papers from when she was first registered as new. She was always called *Perfidia* by the first owners … never anything else.'

'As simple as that,' Marnie murmured. 'Barbara must've thought it was unlucky to change the name of a boat once it had been given. A lot of people believe that.'

'What do you believe, Marnie? Was it all bad luck or was it fate?'

Marnie shook her head, believing in neither.

For more information about other books by Leo McNeir,
see the author's website: www.leomcneir.com